Triple Cross

Also by Kit Ehrman

At Risk
Dead Man's Touch
Cold Burn

Triple Cross

to Jo,

Kit Ehrman

Poisoned Pen Press

*Poisoned
Pen
Press*

Copyright © 2006 by Kit Ehrman

First Trade Paperback Edition 2007

10 9 8 7 6 5 4 3 2 1

Library of Congress Catalog Card Number: 2006902897

ISBN 978-1-59058-478-1 Trade Paperback

Poisoned Pen Press
6962 E. First Ave., Ste. 103
Scottsdale, AZ 85251
www.poisonedpenpress.com
info@poisonedpenpress.com

Printed in the United States of America

This book is lovingly dedicated to Katherine L. Graber

Acknowledgments

I am extremely thankful for my first readers (Phil Ehrman, Susan Nickoll, Rebecca Nickoll, Vicky Kirts, and Susan Francoeur) for their valuable input and observations. For her painstaking, thoughtful editorial input, I'd like to thank Beverle Graves Myers, a fellow Poisoned Pen Press "Posse" member and author of the Baroque Mystery Series featuring Tito Amato. Also on the editorial front, many thanks to Donna Marsh and Connie Kiviniemi-Baylor. At Churchill Downs, I gratefully thank Tony Terry, Director of Publicity, for giving me the go-ahead on this project. Thanks Tony! And a special, heartfelt thanks to Julian "Buckwheat" Wheat, a.k.a. "The Mayor of Churchill," for generously answering my numerous and of-tentimes odd questions. Also on the "horsey" front, thanks to Jan Yarberry and Kathleen Adams. And as always, I am grateful and extremely indebted to all the hardworking folks at Poisoned Pen Press, especially Barbara Peters and Robert Rosenwald, for their continued support. And finally, this book would not exist without my family, who good-naturedly put up with the writing process.

Chapter One

The assignment was simple enough. Pick a random subject and learn as much as you can about him. Name, address, phone number. DOB, mortgages, and property taxes. Car description and plate number. VIN if you didn't mind being obvious. A simple assignment if I'd been in Maryland. But I was six hundred miles from home, standing within eyeshot of the famed Twin Spires of Churchill Downs. Logistics would be complicated, but nothing I couldn't overcome.

First and foremost, I needed to select a subject. But on the backside, with all the "Slims" and "Ricos" and "Willies," figuring out someone's real name was a tricky proposition at best. Track employees were supposed to keep their photo IDs displayed at all times, either dangling from straps around their necks or clipped to their shirts, but most backsiders found the practice cumbersome and ended up slipping them under T-shirts or stuffing them in back pockets. And whoever I chose needed to have at least a tenuous tie to the community. On the backside, that could be a problem, too. Of course, I could have picked a jockey or a trainer or a local celebrity, but I wanted someone who wasn't in the news. Someone ordinary. Normal.

Yet I suspected there was nothing ordinary or normal about this place or time. Not in the town of Louisville, and certainly not in the barn area at Churchill Downs. Not fifteen days before the running of the Kentucky Derby.

Even before the sky had brightened, and the lights illuminating the Twin Spires lost their brilliance to the new day, traffic on Fourth Street had increased until the whine of tires on asphalt pushed through the chain-link fence that separated the backside from the rest of the world.

Today, it seemed like that fence wasn't doing any damned good.

Owners and trainers and the press hustled to make a connection, to latch onto the next big deal that came down the pipes. And it seemed to me that anyone who could beg, borrow, or steal a pass onto racing's hallowed ground had done just that.

Gallant Storm, my father's Derby runner, edged closer as I led him down the shedrow in barn four, one of Churchill's receiving barns. He leaned against me, and I could feel the sweep of his massive shoulder as he strode over the loam and sawdust path. I nudged him off, knowing he would inch back given half the chance. He was a big rangy colt. A dapple gray with a long back and razor sharp withers that topped out just shy of seventeen hands or, in layman's terms, sixty-eight inches.

Storm had done a great deal in his short life, but nothing could have prepared him for the degree of excitement that permeated the backside. It seemed to vibrate in the air around us like a summertime mirage. And it jacked up the day's tempo and resonated in the voices that carried between barns.

Like any horse, he focused on his handler's emotions in an effort to gauge his surroundings. So I kept my shoulders relaxed, my grip on the leather shank firm but elastic, giving to the rhythmic sway of his head as if I were grasping a set of reins instead of his lead. I needed to keep him calm and under control. A bump or bruise today could ruin his chances on the first Saturday in May. A catastrophic injury could end his career. Or his life. And then, there was the inconsequential fact of the horse's worth.

The buzz floating round the backside was that Mr. Utley, the horse's new owner, had forked out a little over twenty mil when he'd decided at the last minute that he had to have a Derby contender. I don't know how Utley had come to secure my father's services as trainer, but I had every intention of keeping the horse safe, even if his owner was a condescending prick.

Up ahead, Jay Foiley, Kessler's groom, stepped out of a stall. "Yo, Steve," he said to me. "Hold up next time round."

I nodded, and as we walked past, Storm cocked an ear toward Jay and ground his teeth on the brass chain that ran through his mouth like a bit.

As we rounded the corner and entered the short aisle, the track office across the lot came into view. Storm pricked his ears and lifted his head as his gaze shifted beyond a group of men talking outside the office and focused on a stocky chestnut quarter horse who stood dozing in front of the long narrow pony barn. The gelding flexed a hind leg, and the flank cinch on his heavy western saddle brushed his belly.

"See how relaxed he is?" I said. "You need to follow his lead."

Storm extended his neck, and an ear-splitting whinny erupted from his throat.

I chuckled. "Guess not," I said under my breath.

We continued to our side of the barn where a security guard leaned against the concrete block wall with his knee bent and his heel wedged into a mortared groove.

Jay was waiting for us. He bowed his head and squinted as he studied the horse's gait. "That him hollering over there?" he asked as we drew closer.

"Yeah. Thought he saw somebody he knew."

Jay set a tub of Uptite poultice by Storm's hoof. As he squatted, he tucked a leg wrap, bandage, and roll of plastic wrap between his thigh and belly to keep them off the ground where they'd pick up debris that might irritate the horse's skin. He scooped out a handful of poultice and coated Storm's foreleg from knee to hoof. The chalky white clay oozed between Jay's black fingers. His movements were quick and precise and gentle. He covered the poultice with plastic, smoothed the leg wrap around the horse's cannon bone, then wound the bandage around the works. Ten minutes later, all four of Storm's legs were encased in bulky standing bandages that protected his sleek bones and tendons.

"Put 'im up," Jay said. "I gotta find some Bowie mud to pack his feet with."

I turned Storm toward his stall, and the feel of the bandages caused him to snatch up his hind legs as he stepped forward.

"Think he'd be used to that," Jay said as I led the colt through the doorway.

It was eight o'clock on a Friday morning. We were temporarily stalled in Churchill's receiving barn, and most of the horses' attendants had completed their chores. A wiry Hispanic groom had stretched out on some bales farther down the shedrow, and a stooped old man cleaned tack near the entrance. Two girls were finishing up on the other side of the barn. Their voices filtered through the row of back-to-back stalls as they debated the outcome of some reality show.

The fact that I was here at all was a fluke. I'd worked for Kessler last summer, so when one of his employees was injured at the last minute, he had offered me a two-week, all-expense-paid "vacation." I would have been crazy to have turned him down.

I tossed the lead onto a bale and noticed that Jay's backpack had tipped over. His CDs had fanned across the ground. I righted the pack, and as I scooped up the CDs, movement at the edge of my field of vision caught my attention. I turned my head as a woman entered the barn.

She paused in the aisle and chewed on her lower lip as her gaze flitted between a sheet of paper gripped between her fingers and the bay colt that stood in the stall next to Storm's. She shot me a cursory glance, then canted her head and peered at the horse's legs.

She'd tied her sandy blond hair in a simple ponytail at the base of her neck, and she looked neat and professional in a pair of creased chinos and sky blue polo shirt tucked at the waist.

I blew the sawdust off Jay's CDs, and as I slipped them into his backpack, I noticed that he'd come better prepared for the job than I had. Besides his CD player, he'd brought bottled water and protein bars, beef jerky and animal crackers. A Ziploc bag was stuffed with candy. I lifted it out of his backpack and held it at eye level. Hershey's chocolate, Butterfingers, Nestlé Crunch Bars. Man. Jay was a regular Boy Scout. As I replaced the bag, I sensed the woman watching me.

When I looked at her, she scrunched the sheet of paper into her front pocket and moved toward me, away from the bay colt.

Her gaze flicked over a strip of masking tape that stretched across the upper portion of the Dutch door. Someone had scrawled "Gallant Storm" on the tape with a black felt marker. "Are you his groom?"

"No, ma'am. I'm just helping out."

Her mouth twitched at my use of *ma'am*. She held out her hand. "My name's Nicole."

"Nicole." I gripped her hand. "Steve Cline."

Her palm was smooth and damp, and color had risen to her cheeks. She was short, maybe five-three, and petite. Her age was difficult to judge. From behind, I could have mistaken her for a sixteen-year-old, yet the fine lines that radiated from the corners of her mouth and eyes skewed that assessment. I put her in her late twenties, early thirties, knowing I could have been off either way.

She indicated Ruskie, Kessler's other runner, with a nod of her head. "Is he yours, too?"

"Yes. He's a four-year-old. Entered in the Churchill Downs Handicap next Saturday. You work for Churchill?" I said, noting the signature logo embroidered on her shirt and the brass name-plate pinned below her collar. *Nicole Austin* was etched into the metallic finish.

She folded her arms under her breasts, looked at Storm, and nodded slowly. "Marketing. This time of year, I do tours."

"Hmm." I could see why they'd chosen her for the job. Attractive, fit. Good for PR. "You like it?"

"Uh-huh."

Storm quit picking at the haynet that hung outside his door and stretched his head toward Nicole. She smiled and cupped her hands under his chin, then smoothed the pad of her thumb over the fine hair edging the corner of his mouth.

A group of men and women walked past the barn, their voices and laughter carrying under the eaves. The women wore tailored dresses and elegant wide-brimmed hats that shaded their faces. Across the alley in Barn 5, two backsiders followed the women with their eyes while one of the guys in the group checked out Nicole's ass. I turned back toward her as she pressed her face alongside the bridge of Storm's nose and took a deep breath. Her eyes were pale, the color of a washed-out sky.

"Most of the time, I like it," she said, referring to her job.

I jerked my head toward Storm. "You miss working with them?"

Nicole cocked an eyebrow. "How'd you guess?"

"Not a guess," I said. "Familiarity. Most people unaccustomed to horses would be counting their fingers right about now."

She smiled as she gave Storm a final pat and placed her hands on her hips. "What's his breeding?"

"He's by El Prado out of Ladyruin, by Storm Cat."

"Hmm. Impressive. Who trains him?"

"Chris Kessler," I said, naming my father, a man whose name I did not share. I had met him for the first time last June, after the man I'd believed to be my father for twenty-two years of my life had been killed in a car accident. I'd worked for Kessler on and off since then and had grown to like him a great deal.

"Kessler," she said slowly. "He's not based in Kentucky, is he?"

I shook my head. "Maryland."

"Thought so." She smiled. "You have this...accent."

I raised my eyebrows in surprise. Guessed accent was relative, because if anyone around here had an accent, she did with her Southern drawl that in my opinion sounded exceedingly feminine.

Footsteps scrunched on the packed ground near the barn's entrance. I glanced over Nicole's shoulder and recognized both men as she turned toward the sound. While Bill Gannon and his groom strolled toward us, the muscles in Nicole's arms tensed as she clenched her hands.

Like any trainer, Gannon's suspicions were heightened at the sight of someone standing near his horse's stall. He looked prepared to chase her off until recognition lit up his face. "Nicole." He hustled over and clasped her hand. "My God, it's good to see you. I had no idea you were working here. Why didn't you tell me?"

"It's good to see you, too, Bill." She withdrew her hand and smoothed her palms down the front of her chinos. Her fingers brushed against something that crinkled, and I looked down in time to see her tuck the corner of her notepaper deep into her pocket. She cleared her throat and crossed her arms. "Congratulations on your Derby runner."

Gannon smiled. "Something else, isn't it? Making the cut after all these years? Here, come see him." He placed his hand on her shoulder and guided her to the bay colt's stall. The same colt she'd studied earlier.

Farther down the shedrow, Snoopy Sanchez, Bill Gannon's groom, drifted over to the clothesline that stretched between roof supports. An assortment of leg wraps and bandages hung from the line. He crimped one of the bandages to test its dryness before his gaze slid back to his boss and Nicole.

Gannon's arm rested across Nicole's shoulders in a partial embrace, and it wasn't a stretch to imagine him pulling her close. He was a handsome man in an outdoorsy kind of way, with deeply tanned skin that clashed with his blue eyes and head full of shocking white hair. And he was certainly fit, but the guy was old enough to be her father.

I watched Nicole fidget with her hands as Jay paused alongside me with a tub of Bowie mud wedged against the crook of his elbow. He followed my gaze and clucked his tongue approvingly.

"You ever want to get back with the horses," Gannon was saying, "I'm always looking for good help." He smoothed his palm down the back of her arm as he lowered his hand.

Good help, my ass.

Nicole worried her lower lip with her teeth and nodded thoughtfully as her gaze returned to the bay colt. "Thanks, Bill. I'll keep it in mind."

Gannon stared at the back of her head, and for the briefest second, his expression seemed choked with a strong emotion I couldn't place.

I turned to Jay. "What can I do to help?"

"Grab that white bucket and fill it a quarter full with hot water."

I scooped up a bucket that used to contain sheetrock joint compound about a million years ago. The green and red logo had faded beyond recognition, and the plastic sleeve over the wire handle was brittle and cracked.

When I straightened and glanced over my shoulder, Nicole and Bill Gannon looked toward the track. A group of men had strolled around the far end of Barn 5 and were heading our way.

One voice in particular stood out. "I told Ripa, I didn't know what he was thinking, buying that colt. Shit. *I* could run faster than that colt." Edward Utley. Kessler's new client.

I groaned.

Beside me, Jay turned and squinted against the bright morning sunlight.

Men and women of the press followed Utley, listening to his nonstop commentary while Kessler walked silently beside him with his hands shoved in his pockets. I pivoted on my heel and headed for the faucets at the end of the barn.

"Coward," Jay said under his breath.

I grinned and held the bucket out as if to say I was just following orders.

I was halfway down the shedrow when Nicole jarred my arm as she jogged past. Two strides farther down the aisle, she glanced over her shoulder and almost tripped. I had expected her to say something, but instead, her gaze cut toward Utley and his entourage. She spun back around and stumbled out of the barn as if her knees had turned to Jell-O. The old man had switched from polishing bits to smoothing a cloth across an exercise saddle. His weathered hand stilled as he watched Nicole squeeze between the barn and a wooden barricade draped with a row of saddles.

I stepped outside.

"What was that about?" he said.

I shrugged and moved beyond the wall. Nicole strode down the lane, skirted the grass apron at the end of Barn 3, and disappeared around the corner. From there she could have been headed to Barn 1 or 2 or the track kitchen or just about anywhere.

I filled the bucket as instructed and returned to the shedrow.

The members of the press had split up, some choosing to interview Utley and Kessler while the others zeroed in on Bill Gannon and a pale young man who had just entered the barn. As I approached the group, I felt my facial muscles contract in a grim stare.

Because of Kessler, I had toyed with the idea of getting into racing fulltime but had yet to convince myself that being a trainer was a life I wanted. And Utley's arrogance pretty much confirmed that my misgivings were dead on. Kessler was forced to put up with his bullshit, and I supposed he had the temperament for it, largely because he stayed focused on the horses. He'd grown up in the industry, and it was an industry filled with contrasts. Wealthy owners dropped a million bucks without giving it a second thought while the men and women who tended their horses often couldn't afford basic human necessities.

"He's got super pedigree top and bottom. You can't…" Utley continued in a voice that boomed under the rafters.

Edward Utley was a big man with broad shoulders and a barrel chest, but his muscling had given way to a doughy softness, and both his gut and hairline had gone south a long time ago. Kessler once told me that Utley had made his fortune in the computer industry back when outsourcing was a glimmer in some programmer's eye. A diamond flashed on his pinky ring, and I had no doubt that his blazer, trousers, and leather shoes cost more than every scrap of clothing I'd brought on this trip. Hell, the shoes alone would have done it. The cut looked European, Gucci or Prada. What he'd dished out for the pair would have put me behind a month's rent.

As I set the bucket on the ground, Utley flicked his wrist and motioned to someone in Storm's stall.

Jay.

"Come on, boy. Bring him out here where we can get a look at him."

My teeth clenched, and heat rose to my cheeks.

"Eddie, that's not a good idea," Kessler said softly. "He's not used to being taken out this time of day, especially with all these people in the shedrow."

"Oh, he'll be fine. Come on, boy. Bring him out." When Jay didn't move, Utley said, "Chris, what's wrong with your help? They deaf?" He chuckled. "Or maybe they're just dumb."

The shedrow became very quiet. The man who had been interviewing Bill Gannon lowered his notepad, and the reporter standing next to Kessler looked like something greasy had slid down the back of her throat.

"Eddie, leave the horse—"

"You." Utley pointed at me. "You understand English, or are you a foreigner, too?"

Kessler eased between us.

"Come on, Chris," Utley said. "What good's the horse if I can't show him off?"

Kessler turned from his client, leveled his gaze on me, and said, "How was he when you cooled him out?"

I unclenched my teeth. "Tense, but not bad."

Kessler nodded. "Bring him out."

I unlatched the stall guard and moved out of the way as Jay led Storm into the aisle. When the horse stepped through the doorway and snatched up his hind leg, Kessler didn't react, but Utley flattened himself against the wall.

I bit down on a smile and was turning away when the red-headed man who had been standing alongside Bill Gannon caught my expression. His eyes glimmered with amusement, and I realized he had noticed my reaction to Utley.

"Walk him up and down a couple times," Kessler said to Jay, "then bring him back."

Utley clapped Kessler's shoulder and ushered everyone outside. I crossed my arms and leaned against the wall while the group watched the big gray horse stride up and down the alley. Every time Jay turned him in a new direction, he skittered around like a kite buffeted by the wind. The fact that the tractors conditioning the track were visible in the gap between barns didn't help matters any. Not that the colt had never seen a tractor. Hell, he'd probably watched them every day of his life. But high-strung horses often looked for a reason to act up. A trigger.

After two circuits, Jay led Storm into the barn, and the show was over.

I swiveled around and leaned against the doorjamb. Jay had removed the chain shank and was smoothing his big black hand down the horse's muscled shoulder.

"That man's an asshole. Hardly seems worth putting up with," I said, thinking of Kessler's need to do just that.

"He worth it all right, 'cause this big boy here's gonna win." Jay palmed a chunk of carrot in his hand and fed the colt before slipping out of the stall.

"Yeah, well, since Utley's convinced that everyone who works in the barn is a foreigner, just make sure he forks over your groom's bonus in dollars."

"My luck, Mr. Uppity don't tip."

Chapter Two

By ten-thirty, I had hopped a TARC bus downtown. When I got off at Fourth and Jefferson, the bus blasted the pavement with fumes and heat as it accelerated into the flow of traffic. It had been months since I'd been in a city the size of Louisville, since I'd ridden a bus. Since I'd been surrounded by so much…noise.

The air around me hummed with it. Tires thumped over storm drains while a horn blared in the next block, and it seemed as if an invisible membrane stretched above the tall buildings and kept all that noise from escaping into space.

I walked to the Hall of Justice at Sixth and Jefferson. As the glass doors eased shut, voices and the clacking of dress shoes on marble tile replaced the street noise. Sunlight streamed through skylights and puddled on the floor. When the deputy cleared me through security, I considered the assignment as I crossed over to a bank of payphones. It amounted to nothing more than a simple exercise for the noncredit investigations course I'd signed up for two months earlier. A move that hadn't set well with my girlfriend.

I pictured Rachel as she pulled the comforter tight to her chin and sat up in my bed. "You're doing what?"

"Taking that private investigations course they're offering at Howard County."

She blew out an exasperated breath that lifted her bangs; then she rolled her eyes and flopped back on the bed. "Why did I have to fall for a guy who craves excitement?"

My fingers paused over the buttons on my flannel shirt. We'd stayed up late the evening before, and she had decided to spend the night, even though she suspected that I'd be at work before she woke in the morning. I glanced at the alarm clock. Five-fifty.

I shucked my shirt and slipped between the sheets.

"Hey." Rachel's eyes grew wide.

"You didn't seem to mind my need for excitement last night."

She slid farther under the comforter like a diver slipping beneath a wave. "*That* was different."

"Damn straight it was." I smoothed her black hair off her shoulder and kissed her throat. "This assignment is pushing paper. Nothing exciting about it. You'll see."

"Uh-huh."

I moved my hand beneath the oversized sweatshirt she wore, my sweatshirt as it happened, and she drew in a breath.

Behind me, footsteps scuffed the tile floor, and the woman who had stepped up to the phone next to mine glanced at me and frowned.

I jerked out of the memory and opened my phonebook. There was one backsider whose name I did know. Donald Geffen. I flipped to the G's and ran my finger down the column. D, D A, D K, Dana, Daniel, David, Dillon, E J, E K....

Shit. No Donald. And I had no way of knowing if he used an initial instead of his first name, though most of the time, initials were used by women living alone.

I drummed my fingers on the page, and the woman next to me snuck another look in my direction.

All right. I didn't plan on wasting my two weeks in town fooling around with this.

I thought back to the morning in the receiving barn and the cute blonde who worked for Churchill. I flipped to the A's and found her name on page fifteen, column one. Nicole A. Austin, 127 Everett Avenue.

Piece of cake.

I opened my notepad and wrote down her name and address; then I flipped to the front of the phonebook and looked up her zip code. So far, so good.

Using my class notes as a guide, I spent the rest of the afternoon being directed and misdirected between offices. I waited in line, asked questions, searched records, and crammed a sheet of paper with a great deal of notations on what I *couldn't* find on my subject, all the while collecting dirty looks from gray-haired women who were most likely annoyed by the idea of a guy dressed in sub-par jeans, nondescript T-shirt, and worn denim jacket uncovering everything there was to learn about a young woman.

By the end of the day, I had verified that Nicole Anne Austin wasn't involved in any legal proceedings and didn't have a criminal history in Jefferson County. Nothing that had progressed as far as the judicial system, anyway. I supposed I could have checked the Louisville PD and Sheriff's Office for incident reports that hadn't made it to court, but she didn't have that feel about her. I'd do it later if something came up.

As far as I could determine, she had never married and therefore had no divorce, alimony, or child support entanglements. She hadn't changed her name. She owned no deeds, did not have a mortgage, and had never been late paying property taxes since she wasn't a landowner. No liens had been levied against her, and she didn't have a will on file.

I glanced at my watch as I moved away from the counter. It was almost five. There were a gazillion professional license records I could investigate, but I'd run out of time. I decided to stop at the Assessor's Office before they closed, then call it quits.

The woman who helped me in the Fiscal Court Building was quick and efficient and friendly as she showed me how to access the database. She clicked through some pages on a website. "What was the number again?"

"One twenty-seven Everett Avenue."

She keyed in the address. The screen flickered, and a column of numbers and names scrolled down the page. "You know, you can access this from any computer. Just run a search on Jefferson County PVA and type in the address."

"Okay."

"Here it is. Parcel number 092D13344401, owned by Eunice D. and Ralph L. Grand." She read off the lot's legal description. I jotted it down as she clicked on the parcel number, and the screen changed. "The property's assessed value is $245,000."

I wrote that down, as well. "Thank you."

She clicked back to the homepage. "You're welcome."

Doubling back to Main, I looked for a place to eat and decided on the Bristol Bar & Grille, where the waitress suggested Green Chili Won-tons and something called a Hot Brown. The restaurant had an interesting play of opposites going for it. Warm coffee-colored walls and a cherrywood bar offset the black lacquered tabletops and partitions of wavy glass. Odd-looking glass sculptures hung from the ceiling, and appropriately enough, I'd been seated next to an oil painting of graceful horses.

I had drained my second Hoegaarden by the time the meal arrived. Although my waitress had described the Hot Brown—thinly sliced turkey breast, bacon, tomato slices, and bread smothered in Mornay sauce—I frowned when she set the dish on the table with an oven mitt.

"Be careful," she said. "The plate's very hot."

I nodded. "Thank you."

The "sandwich" was served in a shallow bowl and was visible only as a lump under thick sauce. But it was delicious, nonetheless. I ordered a third beer and rounded out the meal with a Nutty Irishman—a concoction of Baileys, coffee, and whipped cream—and a slice of Derby Pie. Hell, when in Louisville....

Even though the restaurant was packed, and a line snaked onto the sidewalk, I took my time over dessert. I intended to check out Nicole's house but didn't particularly want to do it while it was still light.

After I'd squeezed the remaining crumbs between the fork's tines and scraped the last pecan off the plate, I pulled the TARC map out of my back pocket and smiled. Transit Authority of

River City sounded so...I don't know...pretentious for a bus system. I unfolded the map and spread it across the table. It took me a moment, flipping back and forth from one side to the other, before I pinpointed the bus route I'd have to take to get to Everett Avenue.

All in all, I had learned more than I'd expected about Nicole Anne Austin despite the fact that I'd had to navigate the various offices and their archaic procedures and protocols. But the process had been tedious and boring as hell. Maybe I wasn't cut out for this. Then again, a licensed investigator would have bypassed much of what I'd done today by using one of the Internet services available to professionals. Hell, he could have done it from his desk in half an hour. Even so, I wasn't quite ready to leave the horse world. I'd had it in the back of my mind to combine the two somehow, horses and investigation, but the logistics remained to be seen.

I paid the check and stepped outside. A tourist snapped a photo of a glitzy statue of a horse that stood prominently at the restaurant's entrance. I'd seen others around town but liked this one best. A mosaic of blue and gold glass and mirror chips covered the horse from nose to tail, creating a vibrant splash of color that contrasted with the washed-out buildings across the street. I walked to the end of the block, headed north toward the river, then crossed under I-64 as tires thumped and hummed overhead.

The *Belle of Louisville* and her sister ship were moored bow to stern in their berths as the muddy waters of the Ohio slid past. Seconds earlier, the bottom tip of the sun had slipped beneath the edge of the world, turning the Ohio into a wide ribbon of molten lava. The bridges that spanned the river glowed orange, and their steel trusses resembled brittle papier-mâché skeletons that, given another second or two, would dissolve into the shimmering water. In the east, a full moon hung over the river, its face a pink disc against an azure sky.

I stood there and listened to the sound of a distant speedboat. The engine's high-pitched whine toyed with the drone of traffic on I-64. I walked south to Jefferson, caught the number seventeen bus, and headed east. Half an hour later, when I found Nicole's house in a quiet residential area, the sky had darkened to an indigo blue, and the moon glowed brilliantly in the sky.

The class project didn't necessitate my tracking down Nicole's residence, but it was the only way I would be able to get her vehicle information since those records are restricted to licensed investigators. I slipped my hands in my pockets and smiled as I recounted our instructor's request that we avoid tailing our subjects. The last thing he wanted was to field a bunch of phone calls from the cops when we got ourselves in trouble. However, I had no intention of being seen by Nicole, and with a little luck, I would finish up tomorrow afternoon, type out the report, and be done with it.

The homes in Nicole's neighborhood were massive three-story structures with wide front porches and oversized dormers in the attics. Most of the lots were cramped and narrow, their side yards wide enough to accommodate the requisite foundation shrubs and little else.

As I paused in front of 127 Everett, I noticed a Churchill parking sticker on the windshield of a black Maxima parked by the curb and suspected I'd found Nicole's ride. I wrote down the tag number, then turned and studied the house. Decorative mailboxes lined the wall to the right of the front door. I'd been wondering how she could afford living in this neighborhood, and now it made sense. The house had been converted into apartments.

The rooms to the right of the entrance were dark. On the left, a strip of light angled through a gap between heavy drapes. A television's blue light flickered in the attic. The window was cracked, and canned laughter drifted into the night. I glanced around, then started toward the porch. The branches of a fat-trunked maple spanned most of the front yard. Grass grew in patches, and the sidewalk buckled where roots cut beneath the slabs like iron cables. My boots pressed into grit and dried twigs that littered the ground.

I climbed the steps.

The idea of Nicole discovering me on her front porch was not a pleasant one. I had no easy explanation. I stepped softly to the door and read the names on the boxes. An uppercase "B" followed by *Austin* was printed in raised white letters across a strip of red plastic on the second mailbox. I tried the front door and was surprised when the doorknob turned under my fingers. I eased the door open and peered inside.

The home's original layout was immediately obvious, but its elegance had been butchered with the renovation. A wide staircase stretched to the second floor, and the central hall it had once dominated had been walled in and felt claustrophobic. Apartment A was on the left. Nicole's apartment was on the right. I closed the door and moved to the edge of the bay window fronting her apartment.

Although she'd left the apartment dark, light from the house next door slanted through a side window's lace curtain. It reflected off the polished curve of what appeared to be a French Provincial sofa and dappled the carpet where it pooled in the center of the room. A built-in bookcase spanned most of the back wall, except where a paneled door accessed a back room.

Nice apartment. Nice neighborhood.

I retreated to the street as two skateboarders whizzed past. The peculiar hollow sound of plastic wheels on rough pavement and vibrations echoing between the fiberglass and ground set the neighborhood dogs barking.

I jammed my hands in my pockets and strolled past Nicole's car. Couldn't see much of the interior without being obvious since the nearest streetlamp was a block away. I stepped off the curb and looped around the back bumper. Light glinted off something metallic lying in the street beneath the running board on the driver's side, and when I realized what it was, a shiver of apprehension threaded along my spine.

A set of keys lay on the ground. I scanned the street, then picked them up. The metal felt cool and was coated with a film of dew. They'd probably lain there for some time. I slid the key into the door lock to verify that it did, in fact, belong to this car. The mechanism turned under light pressure. I tried the handle and realized I'd just locked the car. I unlocked it. So, where the hell was she?

I glanced down the empty street. Okay, there were probably a half dozen innocent scenarios. She could have stopped to visit a neighbor and hadn't discovered that her keys were missing. A friend could have met her on the street, and they could have driven off together. Hell, for all I knew, she was taking a walk. But none of that explained why she hadn't heard them hit the ground in the first place.

I jiggled the keys in my palm, then slipped my fingers under the door handle. The seal broke as the Maxima's door popped open. The dome light switched on, and a shaft of light telescoped across the pavement. I leaned into the car and placed the keys on the vinyl mat near the base of the seat where they weren't easily visible. Better than leaving them in the open.

A car moved down the street as I walked back to Patterson. Somewhere in the next block, a dog yapped. Voices drifted through an open doorway, and the barely audible hum of traffic on a distant thoroughfare created a backdrop to the night.

When I reached Patterson, I glanced down Nicole's street one last time and hoped that the concern I felt was due to nothing more than an overactive imagination.

Chapter Three

Four o'clock Saturday morning, I left the motel and walked along Central Avenue toward Churchill. The roadway arched above a knot of train tracks and a strip of parking lot that jutted from Cardinal Stadium. As I crested the hill, far off in the distance, I caught a glimpse of the Twin Spires nestled between the blocks of new grandstand. In the west, the full moon slipped toward the horizon with its light frosting the grandstand's slate-colored shingles.

Traffic was sporadic as I cut across Fourth Street. Beyond the chain-link fence, most of the barns were dark except for an odd light left burning in a shedrow or tack room and the scattered pole lamps that shone on barn roofs and cast the eaves into deep shadow. As I approached Gate 5, two vehicles eased into the employee parking lot across the street. I slipped my ID out of my back pocket and clipped it to my jacket.

One of the guards waved me through. Out on the road, grit crunched under tires as a third car slowed before turning into the lot. A light switched on in Barn 1. The backside emerging from its slumber.

Before I left work yesterday afternoon, an official from the track office had informed Jay that the stalls we'd been waiting for in the Derby Barn would become available before nightfall, and sure enough, the receiving barn was empty. I turned left at the end of 5 and followed the lane that parallels the track.

There were a dozen paths that would take me to Barn 41, but this one seemed the most straightforward and least intrusive for the horses not yet rousted by their grooms. To my right, the clockers' platform stood vigil over a silent track. In an hour or so, the men who timed the morning workouts would be keen on their task, binoculars in one hand as they manipulated multiple stopwatches, timing the horses set to work near racing speed.

One of 41's security guards stood outside the entrance. After he checked my ID against a list attached to his clipboard, I stepped into the aisle and took in the layout. Gallant Storm was housed in the third stall on my left. He turned his big gray head in my direction, pricked his ears, and nickered, a deep rumble in his throat.

Russian Roulette, a.k.a. Ruskie, my favorite horse in Kessler's string, stepped into his doorway, pressed his muscled chest against the lower portion of the Dutch door, and locked his gaze on me. In the aisle between their stalls, a bulky shape shifted in the deeper shadows, and I realized Jay had set up a cot. A blanket slipped off his shoulders as he lifted his head.

"It's just me," I whispered as I approached him.

He swiveled around and sat up, readjusted the blanket across his broad back. "What you doing here so early?"

"It's not early," I said. "It's already four."

Jay ran a meaty hand over his shaved head before propping his elbows on his knees.

Storm stretched his neck and touched my shoulder; then he eased his nose down my jacket front. When he felt my badge, he flapped his lips and tried to suck the plastic into his mouth. Leaning back, I cupped my hands on either side of his muzzle. "Hey now. You can't eat that."

"Colt tries to mouth everything," Jay mumbled.

"Why'd you set up here?" I said, indicating the cot. "You're gonna wear yourself out doing this. Plus, it's freezing." Jay shrugged, and I shook my head. "You've got it bad."

"What?"

"Derby fever."

Jay grunted. "He got restless 'round midnight. Don't like the traffic noise none."

I nodded. Barn 41 parallels Longfield Avenue. Even with the hundred-foot-wide grassy verge that separates the back wall from the perimeter fence, when a truck rumbles down the road, it sounds like the grille is going to crash through the wooden stall planks.

Working at Churchill felt odd compared to working on a horse farm in a rural setting. The city presses in on every side with its inherent noise and energy and smells, though I'm sure the locals have a thing or two to say about the odors wafting from the backside. Even Maryland's Washington Park felt rural because of the scrubland and woods surrounding its borders.

I slouched on a straw bale and leaned against the wall, wishing I'd worn another layer of clothing. At the far end of the shedrow, a doorknob rattled. Light flashed down the aisle as a tack room door swung inward on squeaky hinges. Two Hispanic men shuffled through the doorway, one of them pulling a sweatshirt over his head. I recognized him from yesterday morning. Snoopy Sanchez, Gone Wild's groom. When the horses had been moved out of the receiving barn, they'd been installed in this one in the exact same order.

Both men acknowledged the guard stationed at that end of the shedrow before cutting around Barn 43. The backside was still quiet, but in half an hour, most of the grooms and hotwalkers and foremen would be straggling into the barns.

I rested my head against the rough planks and rubbed my face. "Why don't you take a break before it gets busy?"

Jay nodded and stood. He bent to fold up the cot. "I'll do that."

He straightened and yawned, jerked his head toward one of the tack rooms on our end of the barn. "Goes in there against the back wall. But leave it for now. Guys in there haven't woke up yet."

"You know," I said. "We can switch off at the Hilton. That's what Kessler got the room for."

"Maybe later, when Storm settles in."

I shook my head. Kessler was paying a premium for that room, and Jay was sleeping on a cot. Though I didn't blame him. Not with Storm running in the race of his career. There were three hundred tack rooms at Churchill and just over a hundred dorm rooms, and men were still doubling up, trying to find a place with a roof over their heads where they could spread out a sleeping bag or blanket.

After Jay's break, we got busy prepping the horses, and by six o'clock, the sky had lightened, and building edges and rooflines that had been obscured moments earlier slowly emerged from the shadows. Noise filled the barn. Gruff, sleepy voices, the raspy swish of a scrub brush against a plastic water bucket, a chain rattling. Even though it was Saturday, the sounds of the city had intensified as well.

Ruskie lifted his head and concentrated on a horse being led out of Barn 43 by a female groom. His liquid blue-brown eyes tracked their progress into the alley, and after they disappeared around the corner, his gaze never wavered. Every fiber of his being was caught up in the act of watching and waiting. Waiting for his turn on the track.

Unlike Storm, Ruskie ignored the traffic and the press and the crowds. All he wanted to do was run, and it was a damn shame that the beginning of his career had been wasted with a trainer less skilled than Kessler. Otherwise, I suspected he would have been a formidable Derby contender in his third year. But that opportunity had been squandered by bad luck and timing.

Jay rapped a brush against the wall in the stall next to ours and coughed.

"What are these two scheduled for this morning?" I said.

Jay grunted, and I imagined his beefy shoulders shrugging under the worn flannel shirt he wore. "Storm's gonna put in a work. Don't know about Ruskie."

The colt nickered, and when I looked up, Kessler had moved into the doorway. He held a Styrofoam cup in his right hand, and the pungent aroma of freshly brewed coffee wafted into the stall and set my mouth watering.

"Morning," I said.

"Unfortunately," Kessler mumbled.

I smiled. Kessler's skin resembled lumpy dough, and his puffy eyelids sagged above bloodshot eyes. He looked like he'd slept on his belly with his face smashed into a pillow, if he'd slept at all. "Rough night?"

"Party," he said as if that explained everything, and I supposed it did. "He's not hooked up," Kessler said, indicating Ruskie.

"He likes to look out. Doesn't want to miss anything."

Kessler peered at Ruskie, then scratched the colt between his massive jawbones. "Good for him." He yawned as he lowered his hand, and I heard his vertebrae pop when he rolled his shoulders. "When Garcia gets here, help Jay tack up Storm and lead him over to the gap. We don't want any mishaps."

"All right."

Kessler yawned again. "How's the hotel?"

"Fine." I'd heard that Kessler was Mr. Utley's guest at a bed-and-breakfast downtown, and I wondered if he wouldn't have been happier on his own. "I've been trying to talk Jay into using the room, but he's not interested."

Kessler looked toward Storm's stall.

"You brought me here to help," I said, "and I don't feel like I'm doing anything."

"You are. Security's good, but I want one of you with them at all times. Anyway, take advantage of the lighter workload while it lasts. I have a feeling we'll all be dealing with a lot more pressure a week from now. As for Jay, he may never have another Derby runner, so I don't expect he'll ease up until it's over."

I nodded.

Beyond the corner of Barn 43, Juan Garcia strolled into view in his peculiar bow-legged gait. A small saddle draped his forearm, and his lips were pursed as if he were whistling. A Buick Park Avenue and slick-looking Cadillac STS eased up behind Garcia. As soon as the jockey turned into the alley, both vehicles parked on the shoulder. A spray of blackish mud marred the Caddy's platinum finish and caked the wheel wells.

I gathered my gear and unclipped Ruskie's lead as a penetrating voice that could only belong to Mr. Edward Utley caused the colt to flick his ears. Kessler's jaw clenched momentarily before he arranged his features into a neutral countenance, and I reflected that I could learn a lot more than animal husbandry from my father. I glanced to my right as I exited the stall and saw Utley scowling at the guard.

"But I'm the owner. Certainly, I don't have to sign in."

The guard, a black man with a thin goatee and a lot of hard muscle under a crisp uniform, stated quietly, "Everyone signs in, sir."

Kessler walked over to see if he could help as Bill Gannon, Gone Wild's trainer, and the young man who'd accompanied him yesterday paused in the entrance. Gannon waited in front of the tack room door while his companion watched Utley with an amused expression crinkling the skin round his eyes. I wondered how he was connected to Gannon. On some level, he appeared to have the demeanor of an owner; yet, he couldn't have been much older than I.

Kessler said something to the guard, but Utley ignored him. "If you knew your job," Utley continued, "you'd know who I am, and I wouldn't have to waste my time with this nonsense."

"I know who you are, sir," the guard said, and I smiled.

Gannon's friend had reached up to rub the back of his neck, and as he rotated his head sideways, he caught my expression. His grin broadened as Gannon glanced at both of us and frowned. Utley acquiesced, scribbled his name in the log, and started down the aisle.

"How's my boy this morning?" Utley said.

I tuned him out and went to help Jay tack up. I held Storm while Jay tied down the horse's tongue and tightened the saddle's overgirth and double-checked the bridle's fit. He slotted the loose ends into keepers, then signaled to me. "Tell the boss we're ready."

I ducked under the stall guard and stepped into the aisle as Kessler explained to Mr. Utley that Storm was going to work five furlongs.

Utley stood to the right of the doorway with his back to me. "I think you should wait until tomorrow at the earliest," he said to Kessler. "He just got off the plane a little over forty-eight hours ago."

"He shipped fine, and the work will help settle him. Plus, it's going to rain tomorrow. Hard."

"Oh, shit, Chris. They couldn't predict the weather if they were looking out a window."

"You hired me because you had faith in my ability," Kessler said softly. "So trust me now." He stepped in the doorway and said to Jay, "You ready?"

Jay nodded.

"Bring him out."

I hooked a lead to Storm's off side, then we led him out of the barn.

"Chris, you better not screw this up," I heard Utley tell Kessler.

"I'm not."

Storm pranced between us, his neck curled against our hold, his eyes wide with a touch of white showing round the edges. As we strode down the alley toward the track, I looked up, and a chill that had nothing to do with the cold feathered down my spine. The buildings on our left and the line of barns to our right framed the Twin Spires on the distant horizon. I had spent the last couple of days admiring them from different vantage points, but there was something about the trip from one of the Derby barns that raised goose bumps on my skin. I sensed a hitch in Jay's stride and suspected he'd had a similar reaction.

Storm gawked at all the people loitering along the path, and his steps grew tentative until he noticed the horses working on the track. His gaze locked on them and that stretch of dirt and white rail that gleamed in the pale morning light. He snorted, and an exasperated squeak escaped from his throat as he tried to muscle against me with his heavy shoulder. When we neared the track, Kessler and Garcia matched their pace with Storm, and Kessler legged Garcia onto Storm's back. The jockey slipped his feet into the stirrups and gathered the reins.

At the gap, Jay handed the colt off to a man employed to pony Kessler's horses, and Storm and the dun gelding broke into a collected jog. Garcia eased into a standing position and pressed his hands into the colt's black mane.

Oftentimes, the help doesn't get to see the horses work, but with only two horses to care for, Jay and I drifted farther down the rail to watch Garcia put the big gray through his paces.

A member of the press and one of the camera crews that had drifted onto the backside before daybreak gathered around Utley and Kessler. Bill Gannon had joined them at the rail, and like Kessler, his attention was fixed on Gallant Storm.

Utley puffed out his chest and posed with his back to the track. "As you well know, it's not easy locating a Derby contender this late in the season, but after considerable persuasion on my part, I was able to...."

I turned away, leaned my forearms on the chain-link fence, and concentrated on watching Storm. They trotted clockwise, near the outside rail. Eventually, the pair circled, and as they eased toward the inside rail, Storm slipped into a collected canter. His pace steadily increased until the two horses separated. With each stride, Storm lengthened the gap between them. Garcia was crouched low over the horse's withers now, his body motionless as the horse rocked beneath him.

There's a weightless quality to a horse galloping full out. Sure, with the sound of hooves pounding the ground, your senses tell you this is not so. But sight and sound are at odds with one another, and it seems that gravity's hold is tenuous at best.

The jockey eased Storm up after five furlongs, and the show was over.

The man who had accompanied Bill Gannon both mornings paused alongside me and held out his hand. "Rudi Sturgill," he said. "I own Gone Wild."

I pushed off the fence and shook his hand. "Steve."

He smiled. "We aren't all like that." He noted my quizzical expression and jerked his head toward Utley, who was still at it, chatting up the press and generally being his obnoxious self. "Wealth doesn't necessarily equate with snobbery and prejudice or god-awful manners. I gotta tell you, guys like Eddie over there give entrepreneurship a bad name."

I smiled.

Sturgill inclined his head in Storm's direction as the colt jogged on the far side of the track. "Talented horse you've got there. It ought to shape up into an interesting race, wouldn't you say?" He leaned on the fence.

"Yeah," I said and wondered why this guy was even talking to me. "It ought to."

"I hear you're Chris Kessler's son," he said, and that explained part of it.

"That's right."

"This your first time in Louisville?" he said, and I thought how so many natives butchered the pronunciation of their home-town. He'd run the vowels together and had practically swallowed the word. Of course, Baltimoreans were no exception.

"Yeah." I shrugged. "Well, I was here once when I was a kid, but whether I have any recollection of that visit or just think I do is debatable."

Sturgill nodded. "Hey, you know about Thunder, right? Kicks off the Derby festivities?"

"Hard not to," I said. Talk of the air show and fireworks that routinely kick off two weeks of Derby festivities had saturated the media.

He fished out his wallet and handed me a card. "I'm throwing a party in the National City Tower this afternoon. You can't miss the building. A big black monolith on the corner of Fifth and Main, two blocks from the river. My father rents some office space, all of the thirty-ninth floor as a matter of fact. Up there, you're so high, you practically look down on the planes. I swear, we've got the best damned seats in the whole town. Why don't you drop by? Bring a friend. Music, great food. Open bar…."

I fingered the card. "Thanks."

Sturgill picked up on my hesitation. "Casual dress. Nothing fancy." He gestured to the card. "Just show that to security, and they'll buzz you up."

"Great."

He clapped my shoulder. "First time in Louisville, you shouldn't miss it."

"Sounds good." I tucked the card in my back pocket, nodded to Sturgill, and started toward the gap.

Gallant Storm's head bobbed in rhythm with his walk as he approached the opening in the rail. He looked so relaxed, I had a feeling he would have brushed his nose in the dirt if Garcia had let him. His dappled gray coat had darkened to black and glistened with sweat, and his cannon bones and bandages were caked with dirt.

After we returned to Barn 41 and untacked Storm, I held him in the alley while Jay bathed him. The colt canted his head and fiddled with the chain on the lead, sucking the brass links into his mouth. He ground his teeth on the metal, then flipped his head in annoyance, like it was someone else's fault that he'd gotten them in there in the first place.

Jay slopped a sponge full of Vetrolin brace across Storm's back, and a lacy curtain of sudsy water flowed down the colt's barrel and streamed off his midline. The mixed aromas, a stirring blend of mint and horse, filled my head. There was nothing glamorous about working on the backside, but being around these magnificent animals was certainly in my blood. I couldn't imagine trading these sights and smells and the physical labor for the flicker of a computer screen, the acrid odor of a photocopier's toner, and an ergonomic chair. Not for one minute, even if it meant living near the poverty line for a while longer.

I didn't know what Rachel would think of that. Well, hell. I guessed I did. She was taking courses at night to further her career. One of these days, she'd expect me to get serious. Serious about her, I supposed, and serious about a job that provided more than a pittance.

I cooled out Storm, then did the same for Ruskie after his work, and by eight-fifteen, when the track reopened after being conditioned, we had already finished the morning's work.

"Why don't you hit the hotel?" I said to Jay. "Get something to eat, use the shower. Hell, take a nap."

"Horses gotta eat at ten-thirty."

I sighed. "Tell me what you give them, and I swear to God, I'll measure it out grain by grain. And if they leave one tiny oat in their feed tubs, I'll call you."

Jay hooked his hands on his hips and stared at the ground.

"Look." I showed him my watch. "I'll even set the alarm. See?" I thought I discerned a flicker of movement at the corner of his mouth. "You'll do a better job if you're well fed and rested," I said.

He nodded. "I'll be back by one."

"Take all the time you want."

He ignored me. "You think something's up, give me a call."

"Not a problem."

At half-past twelve, I was slouched on a bale with my back pressed against Ruskie's stall. My eyelids were weighted, and my breathing had slowed and deepened. A motorcycle roared down Longfield Avenue. I sat up and rubbed my face. Only a few track employees milled around the barns, and the steady drone of traffic and lack of activity dulled the senses.

I yawned and turned my head. The guard who was seated in a folding chair by the entrance nodded, and I lifted my hand. I had just closed my eyes and was thinking that at least I would have been busy if I'd been working my regular job, when a horse to my right grunted and stomped the ground. When he did it a second time, I got up and paused in Storm's doorway. He stood along the back wall with his head lowered, eyes half closed. I continued on to the next stall. Gone Wild, Rudi Sturgill's Derby horse, swished his tail as he thumped his belly with a hind hoof. My first thought was that he was colicking until he swung his head around and flicked his tail, and a fly buzzed out of his stall.

The guard stepped to my side. "He okay?"

"Yeah. Just a fly."

The guard nodded, and as he returned to his post, I pictured Nicole looking in on this colt yesterday morning and wondered if she'd gotten into her apartment. Or were her keys still lying on the Maxima's floorboard? I had called her number before going to bed. Not that I had intended to speak to her, but I'd been curious and had found it disconcerting when she hadn't picked up.

Chapter Four

Jay relieved me at one, and by five o'clock Saturday afternoon, I had showered and shaved. I worked some gel into my hair, then pulled on a pair of oyster-colored slacks. I topped them off with a pale blue gingham shirt and was knotting a yellow silk tie at my throat when the phone rang.

I snatched up the receiver. "Cline."

Kessler chuckled. "You sound so damned serious. Most people answer with a 'hello,' you know?"

I smiled. "What's up?"

"The Thoroughbred Racing Association is throwing a party at the Galt House this evening. I'll be attending with Mr. Utley and wondered if you'd like to join us."

I pictured spending the evening in Edward Utley's presence, listening to his pompous bullshit. "I've been invited somewhere else. But thanks."

"When I'm satisfied that Storm's come out of his work okay, I'll be heading out for a day or two to check on the rest of the string."

"I thought you might."

"I know you and Jay will do a good job, but Abby might come out for a bit. It's hard to say, now that Gordi's out of action," Kessler said, referring to one of his top employees.

"It'll be good to see her," I said and pictured my sister as I'd seen her last, standing in the shedrow, hands braced on her hips, issuing orders as she capably orchestrated the care of a dozen or so horses. "But if you need me helping out at Washington Park instead, let me know."

"No. This is your vacation." Kessler paused. "Well, when you're not in the barn, it is. Speaking of which, you don't need to baby Foiley," he said, referring to Jay.

"I'm not."

"When was the last time you took a vacation anyway? I know you've missed a lot of work in the past year, but a real vacation?"

I thought back to the week I'd spent in Cancun at the end of my sophomore year at Georgetown when I was still living in my parents' house. "Almost three years."

"Christ. You're as bad as any racetracker."

"Not so," I said. "Jay's no doubt sitting in the barn right now."

"True. But where it really counts, Storm's more his than Utley's."

"Maybe so, just don't let Mr. Utley hear you say that."

Kessler chuckled, then disconnected.

I called Rachel only to be transferred to voicemail. I left a message, pulled on a blazer, and caught a bus downtown. The ones I'd ridden thus far had been lightly patronized, but today they were packed. Riders funneled up the steps at each stop, and before long, I gave my seat to a woman and little boy. He clutched a drool-smeared plastic ring in his fist as he clambered into his mother's lap.

He snuggled against her as they swayed to the motion of the bus, and even though the weather was mild, she tugged a blanket across his back. I watched his eyelids drift shut and tried to picture my mother holding me like that when I was his age but couldn't. She had delegated mothering to a succession of nannies and housekeepers. Socials and charity work had consumed her, but now that my father was dead, I wondered if they were enough.

I wondered if she regretted the choices she'd made as much as I did mine.

I jerked out of my thoughts as we neared the Ohio, got off, and joined the flow of foot traffic heading north. In the distance, the pumpkin-colored steel lattice of Fourth Street Live angled sharply above the roadway. The glass roof it supported sheltered an entertainment district that encompassed a city block.

When a Stealth bomber glided across the sky behind Fifth Third Bank, the prospect of an evening spent somewhere other than a horse barn or hotel room suddenly seemed exhilarating. I slipped Sturgill's card out of my pocket and read the embossed lettering: *Rudolph Sturgill, Wellspring Farm, 1497 Spring Station Road, Midway.* The text was printed across a muted but tasteful photograph of what I assumed was the farm's entrance. Broad fieldstone gateposts and intricate wrought iron gates framed the requisite tree-lined drive. The address was followed by phone, fax, and e-mail, and a suggestion to visit the website for additional information.

Midway, as I recalled, was just outside Lexington, the purported "Thoroughbred Capital of the World." I wondered what his father did that necessitated renting the entire thirty-ninth floor of some majorly prime Louisville real estate and figured I'd find out soon enough.

A sudden outburst of laughter drifted through the open doors of Sully's Saloon. Although the block was closed to vehicular traffic, it hummed with a blend of music, voices, and laughter.

Someone knocked into my shoulder as the crowd maneuvered around me. I started walking, and as I emerged from the tunnel of steel and glass, two F-18s blasted across the sky.

Once again, I wondered why Sturgill had invited me. Since Kessler had a Derby runner, he was automatically afforded a certain standing in the community, but being his son meant nothing.

I paused in the National City Tower's forecourt, and as I looked up at the sheer wall of black glass, the reflection of a C-130 transport slipped silently across the surface while the drone of her engines overrode the distant whine of traffic on I-64. I pushed through a revolving door.

A line of visitors snaked toward the lobby desk on my right where three security guards checked IDs. I observed the check-in procedure as I waited in line, and in the brief time that I stood there, a couple of hundred people must have streamed down the sidewalk. When my turn came, I produced my license and Sturgill's business card, got a vinyl band fastened around my left wrist, and crowded into the next available elevator.

The last couple got off on twenty-one, and I rode solo for eighteen floors until the car eased to a stop.

The doors slid open with a gentle hiss of air that was drowned out by the throb of Nickelback's latest release, a blend of gritty, no-holds-barred vocals and percussion. I stepped out of the car onto black granite polished to a high sheen, and what struck me most about the thirty-ninth floor was the breathtaking view and an overriding sense that you could step out into space if so inclined. The elevator bay was essentially an island in a vast open area, or an anchor, depending on your perspective.

Natural light streamed down the corridor from the windows to my right. As I exited the bay, my eye was drawn to a dramatic black sculpture cut into the shape of a flickering flame. Its outline was mirrored in a gold logo embossed on the pedestal's rim, followed by the words ACS INDUSTRIES, INC. *innovation, exploration, foresight.*

My gaze shifted beyond the sculpture. Louisville stretched toward the horizon, and the Ohio looked like a silver ribbon curling back onto itself.

"Great piece, isn't it?" My host, Rudi Sturgill, paused alongside my shoulder and gestured toward the sculpture with a nod of his head. "You're looking at the largest piece of sculpted obsidian in the world."

"Impressive. What's the flame represent?"

"Energy." He took a sip, and when he waved his glass toward the lettering, the acerbic odor of bourbon whiskey drifted past my nostrils. "ACS Industries is the largest fully integrated oil and gas production company east of the Mississippi. We've got hundreds of natural gas wells throughout the Appalachian region and lease blocks in the Gulf as well as onshore in Louisiana." Sturgill grunted when his gaze drifted over the gold lettering. "Innovation, exploration, foresight. My father's creed."

Shadows fluttered across the windows like strobe lights in reverse as two Apache helicopters turned south.

Sturgill extended his finger, and the ice cubes shifted in his glass. "This specimen formed during a lava flow in Glass Buttes, Oregon, nineteen million years ago, which is about as old as obsidian gets since it's unstable." He paused when I frowned, then added, "From a geologic perspective, that is."

"Rock that isn't stable?"

He drained the glass, then smoothed his knuckle along the lower edge of his mustache. He kept his hair short and spiked on top. The color was closer to brown than red, but his facial hair was a brilliant orange that clashed with his ruddy complexion. "Nothing in this world's stable when you think about it, but technically, obsidian isn't rock. It's congealed liquid that forms when lava cools quickly. Although it's got some microscopic mineral crystals, they don't have time to grow, so its properties are more like glass. Volcanic glass, you might say. But after so many millions of years, it gradually changes back into rock."

"I knew that," I said, and Rudi chuckled. My gaze shifted over his shoulder. A tall blonde wearing a slinky black dress scanned the crowd as she walked through the lounge. She spied Sturgill and headed in our direction with a fluid grace derived from strength and poise and athleticism.

"Native Americans loved this stuff for arrowheads and blades," he was saying, but my focus was on the blonde.

She paused alongside Sturgill but looked at me.

"Since it's like glass," he continued, "it fractures in smooth conchoidal shapes, and the intersections of those fractures form edges sharper than any razor."

The woman's gaze left my face and lingered on the sculpture where the thickness of the glass—or rock, or whatever the hell it was—thinned to a centimeter or less and seemed to trap the sunlight that cut through the window.

"Amazing that something so beautiful was commonly used as an instrument of death," she said.

Sturgill nodded. "Almost all the obsidian deposits in the country were discovered prehistorically."

She slid her arm around Sturgill's back and rested her hand on his shoulder in an oddly masculine gesture. "What's truly fascinating," she said, "is that each deposit has a unique assemblage of trace elements, so we can identify the original source locality for any obsidian artifact. This particular specimen owes its jet-black color to magnetite, hornblende, pyroxene, plagioclase, and biotite. Trace element analyses would tell us exactly where it formed if we didn't already know."

Sturgill glanced at his empty glass and frowned. "Hey, if I ever own a black racehorse, I think I'll name it Obsidian. That would be a clever name, don't you think?"

The woman rolled her eyes before her gaze locked on my face. "Rudi, you haven't introduced me to your friend."

"Oh, sorry." He waved his glass between us. "Paige, this is Steve Kessler. Steve, my sister, Paige Sturgill."

I held out my hand. "Cline. My last name's Cline, not Kessler."

Rudi frowned as Paige shook my hand. Her grip was cool and firm and gelled nicely with the assurance that shone from her blue eyes. "What department do you work for?"

I glanced at Sturgill. "I, ah…I work at the track."

"Oh?"

"I thought you were Chris Kessler's son," Sturgill said.

"I am," I said as Paige tilted her head and looked at her brother.

"Who's that?" Paige asked.

"Chris Kessler trains Gallant Storm," Rudi said. "He's running in the Derby."

She raised an eyebrow and nodded slowly, and the movement cast the black spheres that hung from her earlobes in a slow spin. "Interesting."

Her gaze traveled down my body, then flicked toward her brother, and I privately wondered if her comment referred to the fact that I didn't share Kessler's name or that I worked for the competition.

"Well, enough of this geophysical mumbo-jumbo," Rudi said as he directed us away from the sculpture. "Where are our manners? Let's get you something to drink."

Paige spun around. Her dress was backless, the cut tapering in a V that showed off the taut muscling along her spine, and the way she moved under that slinky fabric caught more than one guy's attention in the room.

"Come on." Rudi jerked his head for me to follow. "We're in the boardroom."

We entered the lounge, where the granite floor gave way to thick carpeting. Intimate groupings of leather armchairs and sofas were accented with graceful potted plants and pools of soft light. Nearly half the guests stood by the windows, sipping drinks and waiting for the next flyby. Except for the space occupied by the elevator bay, the open area spanned the building from its northern, western, and southern boundaries. Only the eastern portion of the floor was walled in, and that's where Paige led us, down a central hallway with numerous pebbled glass doors spaced at regular intervals. Legal, Marketing, Financial. Nothing pertaining to oil production as far as I could determine. But what did I know?

The corridor terminated with a double set of mahogany doors inlaid with polished stone. My mother would have thought them garish, but they suited the feel of this place. Paige paused at the threshold as a group maneuvered through the doorway carrying drinks and plates piled with food. The men were dissecting potential U of L basketball prospects while the women talked about some Barnstable-Brown event that sounded even more upscale than this.

When Paige turned suddenly and called to one of the women, Rudi almost bumped into her. A dark-skinned man, possibly of Middle-Eastern descent, got caught in the bottleneck. As he waited for the crowd to exit the room, his gaze lingered on Paige, and there was something wholly licentious and condescending in his expression that made my skin crawl.

"ZZ Top's going to be there," Paige yelled with delight. "Can you believe that?"

"God, no," the older woman said. "I can't believe they're still *alive* much less touring."

"I saw a picture," Paige said. "They still look the same."

"Hard to say with all that hair."

Paige's teeth gleamed as she laughed. She had a great smile, totally unselfconscious and vital. When she spun around and strode into the room, the dark-skinned man quickly averted his eyes and walked past with his gaze on the floor.

The boardroom featured an expansive mahogany table whose polished surface reflected the outside world as accurately as a mirror. Leather chairs were generously spaced around its circumference, but today, instead of neatly distributed reports and Cross pens, the table held a hundred flickering tea lights and bouquets of red roses and baby's breath. In the center of it all stood a lighted ice sculpture carved in the shape of a racehorse.

A bar had been set up on a raised platform where a podium might have stood, and banquet tables lined the wall to my left. The boardroom's layout was similar to the lobby's, offering an unobstructed three-way view of the city and southern Indiana.

Rudi placed his hand on my shoulder and guided me toward the food. "Get something to eat, then join us. We're sitting over there." He pointed to some empty seats along the table's far side as his trainer, Bill Gannon, paused alongside us. Rudi introduced me. "Bill, this is Steve Kes— I mean, Cline."

Gannon held out his hand. "Steve." He raised an eyebrow. "Don't you work for Kessler?"

"Yes, sir."

Gannon flicked a speculative look in Rudi's direction.

"Steve is Chris Kessler's son," Rudi said, and I had a feeling I could have been Willie Shoemaker's son and it wouldn't have made any damn difference. After all, I represented the competition.

"Is that so? Been in Louisville long?"

"Arrived Thursday night," I said, and Gannon frowned.

"But you've worked at Churchill before?"

"No, sir."

Gannon drifted away without saying another word.

Rudi tapped my arm. "See you over there."

I nodded and watched him greet people as he returned to his chair. He seemed equally at home hosting a high-end party or hanging out with Bill Gannon's crew in the barn.

I loaded my plate with a slab of roast beef, country ham, and finger sandwiches; then I joined Rudi as a waitress replenished his drink.

"And what can I get for you, sir?" she said as I set my plate on the table.

"An Old Fashioned, please."

I glanced over my shoulder as Paige Sturgill moved past the window behind us. She held a champagne glass to her lips and took a sip of pale gold liquid as she listened to a petite brunette.

They paused, and when the woman finished describing some kind of sample, Paige nodded. "That's right. The first was taken near an active intermittent stream at 3 to 10 BGL intervals, but the soils were saturated with water, so we needed to retest at 2 BGL."

"Atmospheric washing," the brunette said thoughtfully.

The waitress returned with my drink as two Black Hawks hovered over the river with sunlight pulsing off their rotors and the water churning to a brown froth beneath their skids.

I swallowed a mouthful and only half-listened to Paige.

"...diluted by soil gases diffusing to the atmospheric sink, but even with the sampling irregularity, DF-27's total hydrocarbon value was still well within the 300 microgram per liter contour interval."

"I agree."

"And in a very short time," Paige said as the two women continued their stroll around the room, "atmospheric washing will be of little consequence."

Rudi leaned toward me. "Fascinating stuff, isn't it?"

"Riveting."

He chuckled, then swirled his drink and lifted the glass to his lips. "Give me a thoroughbred any goddamn day of the week."

"Well," I looked around, "if you've gotta work in an office, this isn't half bad."

He swallowed hard and coughed, then touched a napkin to his lips. "These offices are mostly for show. Now, don't get me wrong, actual work does take place, but the heart of the operation lies some sixty miles east of here, in Versailles. In an unpretentious office complex and at the refinery itself, amid a labyrinth of pipes and valves and pumps. A dreadful, smelly place." He looked around the room. "This is the public side of the company that efficiently puts the first-impression phenomenon to good use. Potential investors typically start their tour here before heading to Versailles."

I bit into a sandwich filled with a pale green paste.

Rudi leaned back in his chair. "My father's a marketing genius, really. He can sweet talk millions out of potential investors before they've finished their first Don Carlos stogie. I've seen it countless times."

"Is he here?"

Rudi shook his head. "He usually treats our investors to a long weekend in Louisville during Thunder. Puts them up at the Brown Hotel, chauffeurs them around." Rudi waved his hand. "This party tonight, tours of the refinery and the farm, other miscellaneous functions, but he's on a business trip." Rudi frowned at his drink. "In New York, I believe."

"So…you work in Versailles?"

His gaze slid to my face, and his eyes glimmered with amusement. "Nah."

Paige stepped behind him, gripped his shoulders, and bent forward until her cheek brushed his ear. The maneuver puckered her dress's silky fabric and afforded me a titillating view of her breasts. I could see all the way to her navel, and it didn't take much effort on my part to imagine how she'd look if she shed that dress.

I shifted in my seat.

"My baby brother work? Hardly." She reached forward and clasped her arms around his neck.

Rudi tilted his head back and smiled as he smoothed his palm over her forearm, and I was struck by the similarities between the two. Both had pale skin and eyes the same shade of blue, and the underlying bone structure was the same as well.

"Unfortunately," Paige said, "porosity, permeability, and stratigraphy aren't in your vocabulary, are they?"

"Only if you're talking about brewing coffee."

Paige giggled, then spoke to me. "Send Rudi here to check on one of our lease blocks in the Gulf, and he's likely to get sidetracked fishing or parasailing or God knows what."

"Awh, come on. That's not true. I did okay with that kind of assignment. It's all those scientific analyses that cause my eyes to glaze over."

Chapter Five

When twilight gave way to night, a white haze bled into the eastern sky as a full moon inched above the curve of the earth. Its light cut a shimmering path down the Ohio. I crossed over to the south-facing wall. Louisville stretched out before me, an array of twinkling lights that terminated abruptly where earth met sky. We were on the thirty-ninth floor, so I figured that put us, at a minimum, around 450 feet. If I'd thought about it earlier, when it was still light, I probably could have seen Churchill's grandstand or, at the very least, Six Flag's steel coasters.

I wandered past the only wall in the room that wasn't constructed of glass. A large grid map of the coast of Louisiana hung above the dessert table. Whiskey Island caught my eye, and I wondered how it had come by its name. South of Whiskey Island, in the coastal waters of the Gulf, numbered markers were scattered across two areas labeled *Ship Shoal* and *South Timbalier.*

Beyond the map, portraits of company directors and photographs of onshore rigs and oil platforms were arranged in groupings. I regarded the multiple views of the oil platforms with a peculiar blend of interest and sick fascination. Large hulking monsters of steel on coarse legs rose from the seabed with nothing on the horizon except an endless expanse of choppy waves. They'd been photographed at midday and when the sun lay beneath the horizon, and the sea had turned to pewter. And they had been photographed after dark when their shimmering lights stood out against an emptiness that seemed eternal. I couldn't imagine working on that tiny speck of artificial land for a day let alone months on end.

I stepped up to the bar and ordered another Old Fashioned. While the bartender splashed equal portions of Buffalo Trace and club soda into the glass, I let my gaze drift around the room.

Paige had long since abandoned her brother for some rough-looking guy wearing baggy jeans and a blazing white T-shirt that could have been mistaken for an undershirt except for its weight. He appeared to be working on his sullen act as she threaded her fingers together around his neck and draped across him with her pelvis pressed firmly against his thigh. When she stood on tip-toe to whisper in his ear, that black dress of hers hiked up a notch as her lean muscles flexed under silky skin.

Man, I would've been all over that. Feeling the press of her crotch against my leg and the swell of her breasts brushing my arm. But Doofus kept up the "too cool for you" persona, and I found myself disliking him even more. He finally rewarded her with his attention, listened briefly, then lifted his eyes and panned my end of the room. His gaze abruptly shifted a degree or two, and our eyes met.

"Your drink, sir."

I took the glass and turned away with an uncomfortable feeling that Paige's date had correctly read my thoughts. Had my expression been that obvious? I didn't think so.

Rudi had gone off somewhere, but he returned now, accompanied by the Middle Easterner. "Yeah, yeah, yeah. I know," Rudi was saying as he paused and handed me a second drink even though I'd obviously just refilled mine. "There's always something cataclysmic on her radar, but it would be silly not to stay now that you're here."

"Radar?" the guy repeated.

"Something critical." Rudi frowned, then shrugged. "Important."

"Ah." Rudi's friend nodded. "I see."

"So," Rudi said, "watch the fireworks. Enjoy yourself."

"I do not know. I have change that must be implemented tomorrow."

Rudi rolled his eyes. "What idiot scheduled a change the day after Thunder?" When the guy shot a glance in Paige's direction, Rudi rocked back on his heels and laughed. "Of course. What was I thinking?" Rudi turned to me. "Steve, Mr. Yaseen Haddad. He works in Paige's department."

Yaseen bowed ever so slightly. "Senior Software Engineer."

"Good to meet you."

"Yaseen's thinking about heading out," Rudi said, "but I'm trying to convince him otherwise."

Yaseen nodded. "The traffic will be light if I depart now."

"True, but hang around long enough after the show, and it won't matter."

Yaseen snuck a look at Paige, and I wondered if my earlier assessment had been overly harsh. First impressions are often based on the physical, and Yaseen's bone structure and coloring had likely had a subliminal effect on my response. He wasn't tall, but his long nose and droopy eyelids created the illusion that he viewed the world and the people in it with disdain, while his dark complexion and deep-set eyes lent him a sinister appearance. And there was his cultural upbringing to consider. He probably felt uncomfortable around a woman like Paige, and I'd possibly mistaken his unease for contempt.

Yaseen squinted at his watch. "I am sorry for my difficulty, but I feel I must leave." He bowed his head. "Thank you for inviting me."

"Anytime."

Yaseen turned to me. "It was pleasurable meeting you."

"The same to you."

When Yaseen started for the door, his hesitant gaze fastened on Paige as if drawn by a magnet.

Rudi gestured toward the drink he'd just handed me. "Have you tried a Mint Julep?"

"Can't say that I have."

"Well, now's your chance. You can't come to Louisville for Derby without trying one."

I slid my index finger across the top of the glass, braced an ungainly mint sprig that had been jammed into a bed of crushed ice, and reflected that Rudi wasn't the first person I'd run across who'd dropped the "the" before Derby. Louisvillians referenced the race as if it were a holiday. For Christmas. For Easter. For Derby. Interesting.

I swallowed a mouthful and blinked. Resisted the urge to crinkle my nose.

"Different, isn't it?" Rudi said.

"Uh…yeah."

"After the second or third one, you won't notice."

I couldn't imagine getting through the first.

The music switched off, and the voices that had been drowned out a second earlier seemed overly loud. The room grew quiet as the lights dimmed, then went out altogether, and we were left standing with the tea lights flickering at our backs and a thousand streetlights glittering beneath us. A patriotic piece replaced the earlier rock 'n' roll as a helicopter pulled an American flag across the sky. We were picking up on a live feed from the show.

During the next half hour, we watched the fireworks that Yaseen had forgone, and I doubted he understood what he had given up. I could feel the resultant percussions beneath the soles of my shoes, and a subtle vibration pulsed through the glass and set the multicolored lights reflected there wobbling in miniature arcs. As Rudi had predicted, the view was spectacular. I turned to comment on it and was surprised to find that he'd moved.

Most of the guests lined the windows, and except for the bartender and several wait staff, the center of the room was empty. I scanned the darkened room as a new series of shells exploded at my back. When the white strobe light blasted into the room, I caught sight of a knot of people by the door. Rudi, Paige, and the boyfriend. He slouched against the doorjamb, working on his look, while Paige spoke to her brother. The silver bracelets on her wrist caught the light as she jabbed the air with her index finger, and I had an overwhelming impression that she was not simply arguing a point but demanding something.

Rudi's reply seemed to infuriate her. She stepped closer. As light from the last shell faded, I could no longer read their expressions. When the room again flooded with light and color, Rudi seemed to be staring directly into my face until I realized he just as easily could have been looking past me at the pyrotechnics.

Paige had gripped his arm. As he turned back toward her, she glanced in my direction before continuing their discussion unhindered.

On a whim that only the wealthy are capable of indulging in, and with a hint of boredom regarding the status quo, Rudi decided to move the party to Fourth Street Live. In short order, we were seated at tables in Sully's Saloon. A dozen people had followed us. A larger group dispersed into any number of bars and clubs that Fourth Street had to offer, and I'd been surprised to note that a significant number of guests had remained behind.

"How long will that party go on?" I said as we took our seats. "The one in the office."

"All night, if the past is any indication."

Before we had gone down in the elevator, and after I called Jay to verify that all was quiet at the track, I had watched Rudi consult with a slender, unobtrusive man dressed in a suit and tie. He would have blended into the décor if not for his shocking yellow hair which he thankfully had the good sense to keep short.

"But you left someone in charge," I said.

"Observant, aren't you?"

I shrugged.

Rudi looked up as Bill Gannon draped his jacket over his forearm and squeezed between tables. "My God, Bill. I've never known you to stay this late."

Gannon shrugged. "Wife's not home, so she won't be wondering where the hell I'm at."

Rudi lifted an eyebrow, and I had a feeling he was working hard at modulating his expression. He watched Gannon claim a seat next to his sister. "Wondering who you're with is more like it," he mumbled to himself.

"What?"

Rudi dispelled my question with a flap of his hand as our waitress chose that moment to consult with him. He waved his arm, and a discreet ceiling light winked on his wedding band, but there'd been no Mrs. Sturgill in attendance the entire evening.

I slipped off my blazer and draped it over the back of my chair. The bar's doors stood open, and even though the night air that eddied in from the street was cool, the room's interior felt warm.

Fourth Street consisted of a unique blend of bars and clubs, but what surprised me most was the level of security. Everyone who entered the block was carded and tagged. I now sported a second vinyl band around my wrist.

And the place was loud.

Sully's featured a large-screen T.V. over the bar. The sports announcer's commentary competed with music piped in from hidden speakers, but overriding all that noise was the blast of a rock group performing on a stage set up in the middle of the street. The Velcro Pygmies, if I remembered correctly.

"These four tables," Rudi was saying to the waitress. "Just get a tab rolling. Anything they want." He handed her a credit card and ordered our drinks and a round of appetizers.

I had almost declined the offer of continued partying but remained curious. Curious about Rudi and his family's dynamics. Curious about the life he lived, for its opulence was very much what I had given up when I'd left my father's house. At times like this, when my future seemed uncertain, the pull to return to that life was formidable. So, here I was, an outsider by choice, observing a world that could have been mine. That still could.

But most of all, I'd been curious as to why Rudi would initiate a relationship with a hotwalker. I'd caught snatches of a good many conversations throughout the evening, both in the boardroom and lobby, and none had concerned horseracing, except for the superficial observations and speculations that dominated even fleeting exchanges this time of year. As far as I could determine, Gannon and I had been the only racetrackers in attendance.

And I realized with a touch of amusement that I'd been waiting for the answer the entire evening. Waiting for him to get around to asking me about Gallant Storm. Waiting for him to offer me a bribe. Waiting for *something*.

So, I flat out asked him why.

He smiled, but there was little humor in his eyes. "Have you ever noticed? Most of the stable hands on the backside have this air of diffidence about them. Subtle, but it shows up in little ways. In their posture. Their expressions. Their avoidance of eye contact. This time of year, that gulf between the help and powers-that-be seems magnified by all the pre-Derby bluster. Then I run across a guy like you, and you're blasting my long-held observations to smithereens." Rudi chuckled. "God, I thought you were going to knock Eddie on his fat ass yesterday morning. So, I asked around, and when I learned that you're Kessler's son, I suspected we had much in common."

"But now, you're not so sure?"

"Oh, I think we do." He scanned the room before his gaze returned to my face. "You live in your father's world," he said softly, "without truly engaging in it. I mean, you're working as his hotwalker, for God's sake."

I waited for him to go on, feeling surprise and embarrassment tighten the skin around my eyes.

"So, I wondered how you dealt with that or even if it bothered you. You see? I was given every opportunity to excel in the company and have still managed to disappoint my father. But, I'm curious. Why don't you share your father's name?"

Our waitress stepped between us and distributed our drinks before stretching across the table and gathering the crumpled napkins and balled up straw wrappers left by the table's previous customers. She wore a killer outfit: short black skirt, black nylons and heels, a low-cut sweater with a strip of lacy bra showing at the edge.

I swallowed a mouthful of my drink and ran my tongue around my teeth. As I watched her spin around and expertly navigate the crowd on her way back to the bar, I considered how much I wanted to tell Rudi.

"Although Chris Kessler's my father," I said calmly, "I've known him for less than a year."

"I don't understand," Rudi said.

I took another drink. "My mother was not exactly steadfast in her marriage. When my fa—" I paused, then cleared my throat. "When the man who raised me was killed in an automobile accident last summer, I learned about Kessler. So I sought him out."

Rudi remained quiet, and for some reason, I felt compelled to fill the silence. "I was hurt and angry, but curious as well."

I rotated my glass, and its beveled base dragged a film of condensation across the polished wood. You're still angry, I thought as I watched people descend from the upper level on an escalator whose underpinnings were totally exposed, a mass of gears and belts and pulleys illuminated with softly glowing blue and green lights. Different. Like the entire complex. I glanced down our row of tables. Paige had her arm draped around her boyfriend's neck, and for a change, he was paying attention to her. Gannon sat alongside her, but he'd hunched forward and cupped his hands over both ears in an effort to hear someone on his cell phone.

"Having two fathers must be weird," Rudi said. "But look on the bright side. You still *have* a father."

"At a huge cost," I said bitterly and wished I hadn't. I grew up believing there was something seriously wrong with me, that I was unworthy somehow because my father couldn't stand the sight of me.

Couldn't love me.

We rarely spoke in the two years before his death. Not ten goddamn words. And what haunted my sleep and shadowed my waking hours was the fact that he'd tried to reconcile, and I had made the worst mistake of my life.

I'd turned my back on him.

I drained my glass in a single gulp and caught Rudi staring. When he glanced at something over my shoulder and did a double take, I swiveled around in my chair.

Four men had entered the bar and paused at the hostess' podium. All four were dressed identically in black, head to toe. And that's where normal ended and bizarre began. Three of them wore black harnesses with glowing power packs slung across their lower backs. Each harness supported a bracket that suspended a flat screen computer monitor above the wearer's head.

"I don't believe it," Rudi said. "Portable commercials."

"Only in Louisville," I mumbled.

"Yeah, but what are they advertising?"

I shrugged. The fourth man appeared to be their handler. He told them where to stand, and the guys wearing the harnesses did as instructed and stared straight ahead as if they weren't human.

Rudi chuckled. "Takes balls to do that, wouldn't you say?"

"Uh-huh. Looks like Woodford Reserve Bourbon's hooked up with thoroughbred ownership."

"Oh, yeah. They're pushing that hard."

We watched the portable commercials for a while, and what struck me most was the lack of reaction from the crowd. After they cleared out, I excused myself and headed toward the back of the bar.

I glanced at my watch as I pushed open the door to the men's room and was startled to see that it was almost midnight. Before I went in search of a bus, I had planned on getting something to eat to take the edge off the booze, but it was too late. As it was, getting up in the morning was going to be a bitch.

The men who followed me into the restroom didn't look like trouble.

The first one headed for the stalls, but the Hispanic, a young guy with a shaved head and nose stud that flashed under the fluorescent lights, moved in front of the paper towel dispenser as I splashed water on my face. A stall door banged open, then another. I cupped my hands under the faucet and checked the Hispanic's reflection in the mirror. He faced the row of sinks, feet spread, arms folded across his chest. When his gaze cut to the white guy as he stepped in behind me, I let the water drain between my fingers.

Chapter Six

My scalp tingled as I gripped the faucet left-handed and cranked it closed, hoping like hell the delay before I turned to face them would buy me a couple of seconds to formulate a plan.

Two against one, with a crowd of revelers in the bar at the end of a short hallway, didn't seem insurmountable. But that crowd might as well have been on Mars as far as I was concerned. The jumble of voices and laughter and the throb of a bass guitar ensured that no one would hear us. And worse, the alcohol I'd drunk left me feeling flatfooted and sluggish.

I lifted my eyes and caught a glimpse of the guy standing behind me as I curled my fingers around the pocketknife I carried. He wore a Yankees ball cap low on his forehead, and as he adjusted his stance, our eyes locked.

My time was up.

I pivoted, but he'd already begun to move. He delivered a roundhouse kick that buried the toe of his boot deep into my thigh. Electric pain shot from my toes to my spine, and my leg buckled. I hit the counter on the way down, grabbed the edge. My fingers slipped across a film of water, and I landed hard on the floor with my right arm pinned beneath me.

My knife clattered under the pipes and came to rest alongside the baseboard.

The Hispanic latched onto my hair and jerked my head so that my cheek pressed into the gritty tile. Rolling me onto my stomach, he grunted as he knelt on my head.

Jesus.

Blood pounded against my skull, and I had absolutely zero leverage.

New York upped the ante when he clamped down on my left arm, bent my thumb back, and rotated my wrist outward until my palm faced the wall and every joint in my arm locked up. Then he planted his boot on my triceps.

I'd managed to free my right hand and landed a blow, but New York tightened his hold. He rotated my arm like he was working a corkscrew, until my wrist felt like it would explode; then he yanked upward against my locked elbow.

Pain jolted up my arm, and a wave of nausea rolled through my stomach and flooded my mouth with saliva.

"Where's the tape?" New York said, and I thought I'd heard wrong.

When I didn't respond, he increased the leverage, and I could hear the bones creaking against each other.

I expelled a lungful of air. "Tape? What tape?"

"The tape that bitch gave you. Where is it?"

I swallowed. "I don't know what you're talking about."

"Another inch or two, asshole, and your arm's gonna snap like a goddamn matchstick. Where's the fucking tape?"

"I, eh…" I groaned. "I don't know about any tape." I gagged on bile that clogged the back of my throat. "I swear."

"*Pienso que él habla la verdad.*"

"Maybe." New York dug the heel of his boot deeper into my flesh. "But let's make sure."

He put his back into it, and the bones grating against each other sounded like a string of firecrackers popping on wet pavement. My groan rose into a cry that echoed against the walls.

"I swear," I gulped, "I don't know about any tape."

New York lifted his foot off my arm, and when the pressure eased, my shoulders slumped onto the cool tile. "Check his pockets."

While his partner patted me down, my chest heaved in an effort to drag more oxygen into my lungs.

"Got anything?"

"Nada."

New York slammed my arm against the floor with such force, the impact shuddered across my clavicle like vibrations pulsing across a guy wire. A piece of plastic spun past my face and wobbled to a stop under the sink. Boots scuffed the tile. I lifted my head, and as I looked toward the door, New York pivoted around and kicked my leg in the exact same spot he'd hammered before.

I closed my eyes and gritted my teeth as the door swung open. A mix of rock 'n' roll, sports commentary, and voices blasted into the room, followed by the heavy aroma of fried food that turned my stomach. I shifted as the door eased shut, and in the brief second before it settled against the frame, someone hurried to catch up with the two men as they headed toward the bar.

"Hey!" I yelled. "In here." I blinked the sweat from my eyes and waited. After a minute, I twisted around until I was sitting upright. The overhead lights dimmed. I rolled back over and vomited.

Wonderful. Just wonderful.

I dragged the back of my hand across my mouth as white specks of light flickered along my optic nerve. This was not the first time I'd run afoul of some nasty men in a public restroom, and if it happened again, I'd probably avoid them for the rest of my life.

When the queasiness in my stomach backed off, I clambered to my feet, an odd maneuver since my right leg seemed incapable of supporting weight. The blows had been well placed, effectively scrambling nerve impulses and transforming my leg into a leaden mass of useless bone and muscle. I cradled my left arm, hopped over to the sink, and turned on the faucet. I rinsed out my mouth, then splashed my face one-handed before leaning against the counter to wait for the wiring in my leg to sort itself out.

Just what the hell had happened, anyway?

A straightforward robbery wouldn't have been surprising with the crowds and the partying and me stupidly setting myself up as an easy mark by drinking too much. But they'd wanted a tape and had seemed damned confident that I would know what they were talking about.

They must have confused me with someone else. After all, I'd been in Louisville less than forty-eight hours. I'd met a handful of people and crossed paths with a dozen more, so why would someone think I had a goddamn tape?

The door to the hallway swung inward.

I jerked my head up as Rudi Sturgill stepped into the room. He glanced at the mess on the floor, then studied me with his eyes narrowing in concern. "What happened?"

"Good question."

I told him as he walked over to the counter, giving the crud on the floor a wide berth.

"Do you need to go to the hospital?" His gaze took in my awkward stance. "And can you walk?"

"Hmm." I straightened my leg, and an electric jolt fizzed along my nerves when my foot bore weight. I took one step, then another. "I'll be okay."

Rudi used his cell phone and called the cops, then insisted on keeping me company.

We had been allowed the use of the bar's office, where it was relatively quiet and where I discovered I no longer had my wallet.

I closed my eyes and listened to one of the cops key his mike and repeat the descriptions I'd just given him. They'd been quick taking my statement, but if the assholes who jumped me had already left Fourth Street, no one was going to catch them.

Rudi had been in and out of the office during the report-taking, but he was back now, leaning against the manager's desk and flipping open his cell. He made a call while I signed an incident report. After the cops left, the manager's assistant apologetically handed us gift cards. I nodded my thanks and privately wondered if I'd come back.

"I'll give you a ride home," Rudi said.

My initial inclination was to decline his offer, but I was limping badly, and the ache in my arm had spread from my fingertips to my jaw. "Thank you."

We exited the short hallway and threaded our way through the crush of people lined three deep at the bar. I looked across the room and saw that some of Rudi's friends still sat at the tables, but Paige and her boyfriend and Gannon had left.

I caught up with Rudi at the podium and yelled over the music. "What about your guests?"

He waved his hand. "They can take care of themselves." A decidedly lopsided grin crinkled the skin around his eyes when he noted my surprise. "They've got my tab going, don't forget."

The hostess, I saw, had collected my jacket and handed it to me with a shy smile.

I thanked her, then limped after Rudi, losing sight of him once as we wound our way through the crowd massed in front of the stage. He cut into a side corridor, and we emerged on Fifth Street. Rudi scanned the block, and I was thinking he couldn't have had so much to drink that he'd forgotten the way, when an engine revved, and a silver Mercedes convertible accelerated down the street and slid smoothly to a stop at the curb with its 360 V8 engine purring under the hood. Although you could scarcely feel it, a thin mist rode the wind currents and was visible in the air that swirled past the headlights.

The driver opened his door, and when he exited the vehicle, I was mildly surprised because I knew him. The yellow-haired gentleman in the dark suit and tie. Rudi crossed in front of the hood and nodded his thanks as he folded himself behind the wheel. I opened the passenger door, slid less gracefully onto the bucket seat, and clicked the door shut.

My head sagged against the headrest, and I watched Rudi's man stand motionless on the sidewalk as we accelerated away from the curb with the rain-spattered glass refracting the ambient light and the tires hissing on wet pavement.

"Where are you staying?"

"The Hilton Garden Inn," I said. "You know it?"

"Off Crittenden? By the fairgrounds?"

"That's it."

Rudi navigated a maze of one-way surface streets, then rocketed the Mercedes up a ramp and onto I-65. He glanced at me. "Do you have any pain medication? And antiseptic for your face?"

I touched the abrasion on my cheek. "I've got some ibuprofen." Not to mention a surplus of alcohol coursing through my veins.

"If the hotel doesn't have a decent sundries selection, they'll be able to tell me who's open, and I'll pick something up."

"Thank you, but you've already done enough."

"Well, I hate to burst your bubble, but a bathroom's not the most sanitary place to get thumped on, and your skin's raw, if you haven't noticed."

"Hmm."

"Curious, though, wouldn't you say? Them wanting a tape you don't have."

"It's curious, all right, getting mixed up in something and having absolutely no fucking idea why." I relaxed against the bucket seat and sighed as I imagined my girlfriend's reaction when I told her what happened. If I told her. Rachel simply would not believe that I hadn't done *something* to get myself in trouble. But the only thing I'd done even remotely out of the ordinary had been that assignment which had nothing to do with a tape. And for the most part, I'd maneuvered through the bureaucratic process anonymously, in offices that dealt with thousands of inquiries a day.

Rudi pulled me out of my musings. "I wonder what kind of tape they were looking for?"

I shrugged.

He eased the Mercedes under the hotel's portico and switched off the engine.

"They must have mistaken me for someone else," I said.

Rudi nodded thoughtfully. "How many people do you know at the track? Maybe the tape is linked to one of them."

"That can't be it. I don't know anyone in this town, except for Kessler and his groom. And now you and Paige."

"What about Eddie?" Rudi said, referring to Edward Utley.

"I've known *of* him ever since he moved Storm to Kessler's stable, but Friday morning was the first time I've actually laid eyes on him." I shook my head. "No. It can't be related to the track because that would mean I was followed, which I wasn't."

Rudi's gaze shifted to the front doors. "Well, let's see if they can fix you up."

The mist had increased to a steady drizzle that coated the white azaleas blanketing the ground on either side of the entrance. Cradling my left arm against my waist, I clumsily levered myself out of the car and limped through the lobby to the front desk.

The night clerk, a young black man with an easygoing manner that masked his intelligence if you weren't paying attention, stepped out of the office and asked what he could do for us.

"Uh...I've lost my key."

He glanced at the damage on my face and the way I held my arm, which I suspected looked awkward, then said, "Name?"

"Cline. But the room's registered under Kessler. Room 333."

His gaze lingered on my face before he fiddled with a computer positioned out of sight beneath the countertop, and I was fairly certain he remembered me from when he'd checked me in Thursday night. He keyed a new card and handed it to me. In the meantime, Rudi had been scanning the shelves to the left of the front desk, selecting an assortment of medicinal items from among the gum, breath mints, and laundry soap.

He purchased them without comment while I stood there feeling foolish. After the clerk bagged the items, Rudi handed them to me along with some folded bills.

"What's this?"

"Take it. Pay me later if you must," he added when I opened my mouth to object, "but take it. You were my guest, and now you've got no money."

"Thank you."

I watched Rudi stroll down the foyer, then step into the night as raindrops slanted beneath the scattered lights in the parking lot and cut under the portico. He hurried around the car's low-slug hood. I was thinking that Kessler had been wise to work Storm when he did when Rudi opened the Mercedes' door and paused. He lifted his head and looked straight at me. The lobby's automatic doors slid shut, blocking out the traffic noise on Crittenden. After the car revved to life and zipped silently out of the lot, I went up to my room.

Five minutes later, I had downed some ibuprofen and was loosening my tie when I caught sight of my reflection in the full-length mirror on the closet door. Whether my trousers would be salvageable was questionable, which was a damn shame. The shirt and tie, I threw in the trash. I brushed my teeth and showered, then cranked the hot water as high as I could stand it and stood under the spray until the tension drained from my muscles.

After I'd toweled off, I sorted through Rudi's purchases with amusement. Triple antibiotic ointment, medium-sized adhesive gauze pads—sterile, a packet of Band-Aids in assorted sizes, a bottle of Simply Sleep. I swallowed two of those and climbed under the covers, feeling cold and feverish at the same time. If I hadn't known better, I would have suspected I was getting sick, but the unease that lingered in the back of my mind was, pure and simple, a byproduct of the attack.

Being rendered powerless, when you have no idea how far your tormentors are willing to go, is a predicament I'd just as soon avoid in the future. And those two had known what they were doing. Especially the white guy, who'd been well versed in pressure points and leverage and pain-inducing holds.

I stared at the ceiling as my eyes slowly adjusted to the darkened room. In three short hours, I had to report to work at the track. Calling in sick wasn't an option, not with Jay being the only other employee. I should have left the damned party earlier; then none of this would have happened. I shifted under the blankets and rubbed my elbow, wondering just how useful I'd be.

Chapter Seven

An obnoxious buzzing jarred me out of a deep sleep. I opened my eyes to a pitch dark room, to a smoke detector's red light shining near the ceiling where it shouldn't have been. To an unfamiliar pillow flattened under my head and a stiff bedspread weighted across my chest. Then I remembered why I wasn't in the loft, in my own bed. I rolled onto my side, and as I reached for the alarm clock, the stiffness in my arm brought back the memory of last night like a toggle switch being flipped.

I hit the snooze button, but as I let my weight rock me onto my back, the noise started up again, and I realized the ringing hadn't been the clock, after all. I dragged the phone across the nightstand, lifted the receiver an inch above the cradle, and let it clatter back into place. I sank into the mattress and closed my eyes.

The phone rang a minute later. I squinted at the alarm clock's readout and bolted upright. Snatched the receiver.

"Where you at?" Jay said, and I thought it obvious. "Boss gonna be here any minute."

I groaned. "Do you have to talk so loud?"

Silence on the line, then a faint chuckle. "You hung-over?"

"What the hell gave you that idea?"

"Um, um, um. Gonna be a long morning."

I ignored him. "I'll be there in fifteen."

"Hope you got a poncho, 'cause the rain's coming down like a bitch."

After I got dressed, I patted down my clothing. No wallet, a handful of change. I strapped on my watch. The glass was missing, but it still worked. I slid the room key and Churchill ID across the polished desk, pocketed them, and checked the slacks I'd worn the night before. Located Rudi's cash and transferred it to my jeans, then took it out again. As I fanned the bills, I felt my mouth open. I had assumed that he'd handed me a couple of fives or tens with maybe a twenty thrown in. I thumbed through the hundreds, all six of them.

I yanked off my poncho as I slopped into Barn 41 Sunday morning with my jeans plastered to my shins and water oozing between my boots' stitching. Getting unquestionably sloshed never bodes well for the morning after. The buzz that I'd had going last night was just now downgrading to a pile-driver of a headache, and my mouth felt like I'd swallowed a bagful of cotton balls.

Jay sat sideways on a hay bale positioned against the wall between Ruskie and Storm's stalls. I paused in front of Ruskie's doorway, and the big chestnut colt nudged my chest.

"Hey there, boy. How you doing this morning?" I said softly. "Better than me, I hope."

For answer, the colt lifted his head and sniffed my damp hair; then he curled his upper lip away from his teeth, a common studdish behavior that allowed him to process unusual smells more thoroughly. He bobbed his head, and if I'd been in the habit of attributing human emotions to a horse's actions, I would have sworn he was annoyed.

I smoothed my hand down the colt's face as I glanced at Jay. "Is Kessler here, yet?"

"He's around and weren't too pleased that you late." Jay stood. "Let's get started with Storm."

The rain hadn't let up, so we did all the prep work in the stall. I slipped a chain shank through the rings on Storm's halter and held him while Jay sponged the poultice off the colt's legs.

Storm shifted his weight at every opportunity, and his ears flicked around like radar antennas on speed, listening to and categorizing every sound. A gravelly voice in the next stall. Rain pelting the roof high above the hayloft. The soft metallic clink of blanket surcingles brushing against each other as a bay colt walked past the doorway.

Kessler's stalls were located near one of the barn's entrances where metal gutters spanned the eaves. They caught the rain sluicing down the shingles and channeled it into the alley. But farther along the shedrow, the gutters ended, and the rain poured off the eaves in a solid curtain of water that pulsed into the barn when the wind shifted.

As Jay finished up, I considered the prospect of walking a hopped-up, thousand-pound animal when I wasn't at my best. A Derby runner, no less.

I watched Jay squat lower in the straw and take extra care drying the back of Storm's pastern. When he straightened, his knees popped, and the sound triggered a vivid memory of last night. I flexed my elbow. "I think we've got a problem."

Jay narrowed his eyes but said nothing.

"He's getting cold walked, right?"

Jay nodded. "Soon as Mr. K checks his legs."

"Uh…well. Listen, Jay. My left arm's not one-hundred per-cent this morning, and I don't like the idea of walking him when I'm not on my game."

"This got anything to do with that case of rug burn you got?"

I touched my cheek. "Sort of."

Jay nodded. "You muck out. I'll walk."

"Thanks."

We prepped Ruskie next, then waited for Kessler. Jay grabbed an old camper's stool from a tack room at the end of the aisle and sat down while I leaned against the stall front and watched the horses walk past. By my estimation, three horses were being walked in the shedrow. A fourth had gone to the track to work in the rain and the dark. Compared to my previous two days on the grounds, the backside felt isolated. The weather had pushed everyone inside, and the press was holed up somewhere, either in their vehicles or the Rec building.

Snoopy Sanchez, Bill Gannon's groom, looked similarly idle as he slouched on a hay bale with his head resting against the stall front. As late as Gannon had stayed out, I suspected Snoopy would be waiting a while longer.

Headlights slashed through the dark as a car moved slowly down the access road with its wipers on high.

I pushed off the wall. "Kessler's here."

He parked and hurried into the barn with the sports section of *The Courier-Journal* tented over his head. As he folded the sodden paper and brushed rainwater off his collar, I was once again struck by the similarities between us. We both shared the same dirty blond hair and brown eyes. The same straight eyebrows, narrow nose, square jaw. I'd had no difficulty believing that he was my father when I'd met him for the first time last summer at Washington Park, in a shedrow much like this one. The threat he'd faced then had taken a toll, etching lines of worry across his forehead and tightening his mouth, and the same telltale signs of stress were back in force.

We gathered in front of Storm's stall, and I noticed with amusement that Ruskie had moved to his doorway to watch. Horses intuitively know their ranking in the herd, whether that herd is equine or human, and he'd been number one in Kessler's barn until Gallant Storm joined the string.

Kessler nodded at Jay, then turned to me. "I need you here at four-thirty, not—" He narrowed his eyes. "What happened to your face?"

I glanced at Jay and felt my cheeks flush. "Last night, I got robbed..." I said, and Kessler's expression hardened as if his muscles had turned to stone. "Sort of."

Kessler looked me up and down, and his instincts were dead on as his eyes automatically focused on the way I had subconsciously braced my arm against my side. "Are you okay? What's wrong with your arm?"

"My elbow's a little out of whack," I said and felt Kessler's penetrating gaze bore right through me. I straightened my arm. "If it's all right with you, Jay and I are going to switch off this morning, with Jay walking the horses and me mucking out."

He waved his hand. "Fine. When did this happen, and what do you mean by 'sort of'?"

"Last night, at Fourth Street Live. You know? That—"

"Yeah, I know it."

"I think they mistook me for someone else because they thought I had a tape."

Kessler frowned. "What tape?"

"Good question. The way it went down, the robbery seemed more an afterthought than anything," I said as Kessler shook his head. "For some reason, they were convinced that I had a tape of theirs, and when they didn't get it back, they took my wallet."

"Jesus." Kessler peered at me. "You sure have an uncanny talent for digging up trouble."

I shrugged. Kessler slid two fingers into his wallet, and as he held out a couple of twenties, I said, "I'm good for cash, but I need to talk to you about that, too. Later. When you have a minute."

Kessler nodded. "Did the police get the guys who did it?"

"No, and I doubt they will."

On that note, we got busy. Kessler examined Storm's legs for swelling; then Jay did him up with polo bandages, fastened a lightweight blanket over the colt's back, and took him into the shedrow. I mucked out the stall in quick order, piling the soiled bedding in the center of a canvas tarp. Not a technique I was accustomed to, but mucking out was mucking out. I pulled on my poncho, folded the ends of the tarp together, and hefted the bundle onto my back.

The sky had finally lightened to a dreary gray. Cold rain stung my face as I crossed to the manure pit. A black horse stood farther down the alley with his head lowered and ears canted against the downpour while his groom slopped hot sudsy water across his muscled neck. Water vapor rose from the bucket's rim and rolled off the horse's glossy coat, a shimmering aberration in the shifting rain.

◇◇◇

By eight o'clock, Jay had gone off in search of something to eat, and I was sitting on a bale with my left forearm braced across my waist and the chill air seeping into my damp clothes.

A platinum-colored Cadillac swept into an open spot on the access road. The passenger got out and ran through the downpour with his body bowed over an exercise saddle that he'd tucked under his jacket's flaps. The driver cracked his door and popped open an umbrella before climbing out. Bill Gannon.

He walked unhurriedly into the barn and joined his employee outside Gone Wild's stall. "Should have worked him yesterday," he grumbled. "How bad's the track?"

"Greasy. Like peanut butter," Gannon's exercise rider said in heavily accented English.

I picked up the strands of baling twine that I'd tossed out of the stall earlier and wound them around my hand.

Gannon leaned on the doorjamb and scowled at something or someone in the horse's stall while his rider handed his saddle over the stall guard. "After you've warmed him up, do a mile and a half at an easy gallop," he said as he lifted his cap off his head and slicked back his thick white hair. "If he feels the least bit backed off by the footing, jog him."

His rider acknowledged the instructions with a barely perceptible nod of his head.

Gannon turned away from the stall and frowned when he noticed me. I stood and moved into Storm's doorway as a sudden gust of wind sent a spray of rainwater swirling under the eaves. Out in the alley, the sound of hooves scrunching through water echoed between barns.

Kessler appeared out of nowhere and paused at my side. "So," he said, "what did you want to talk about?"

I glanced over his shoulder as Sanchez led Gone Wild out of his stall. Gannon legged his rider onto the horse's back, then watched them step into the rain. He waited until they'd moved off before bending forward and working the catch on his umbrella. The black nylon mushroomed open with a soft click and hiss of air.

Kessler followed my gaze, first by watching Gannon stride toward the access road, then Sanchez as he strolled into an office at the end of the barn.

"Something's up with Rudi Sturgill, the guy who owns Gone Wild," I said.

"What do you mean?"

"He invited me to a party last night. That was the first thing that didn't feel right. He qualified it with some bullshit story about my being your son and not knowing my way around."

"And…."

"Well, if most of the people on his guest list were employed in the horse industry, the invitation might have made sense, but it was nothing like that. As far as I could tell, except for Bill Gannon, everyone worked for his father's oil company."

"Interesting."

I leaned against the wall, crossed my arms over my chest, and scanned the aisle. Making sure no one was close enough to hear our conversation, I said, "Not only did he invite me, he encouraged me to tag along with him the entire evening. There had to have been a hundred, hundred fifty people there easy, and he chooses to spend his time with me?"

Kessler shrugged. "Nothing wrong in that. I suspect the two of you have more in common than you realize. Similar backgrounds, horses…."

"He has no idea I'm from old money. Hell, I've almost forgotten what *that* feels like," I said and glimpsed amusement in Kessler's eyes.

"A friend of mine's been known to say, 'Money smells money,' and I think that's accurate. You might not be living the high life now, but the components are still in place. Your demeanor, tastes, vocabulary, they're all colored by your upbringing."

"I don't see that being a factor," I said as I looked out at the dismal morning. At the rain streaming off the eaves and pounding the alley in a relentless assault. A red Buick Park Avenue eased into the spot behind Kessler's rental. "Last night, I kept waiting for Sturgill to work the conversation around to Storm. Maybe learn something he could use to advantage. But he barely spoke about the race. Not directly, anyway. So I wondered if he was trying to gauge me, to evaluate whether or not I was likely to accept a bribe in exchange for information. Or worse."

Kessler shook his head. "You said he knows you're my son. You wouldn't be a good choice. Jay would be better."

"Jay's not exactly…approachable," I said, and Kessler smiled. "Inviting me was a stretch. Asking Jay would have been ludicrous. No. He saw me working as your hotwalker where tradition suggests I should be acting in a higher capacity. So he figured there must be some underlying animosity between us. Of course, he had no way of knowing that I didn't grow up in the business and am just filling in. At one point, I even wondered if he was trying to get me out of the way, or at least keep track of me. So I called Jay to check up, but the barn was secure and looked to be staying that way. And why didn't Rudi go to that Racing Association banquet you attended?"

The Buick's driver tapped the horn. A woman sat in the passenger's seat, her face a pale oval behind the rain-spattered glass.

"And listen to speeches all evening?" Kessler stepped away from the center of the aisle as a bay colt pranced down the shed-row. His groom pressed his elbow into the bay's shoulder and struggled to contain the horse's pent-up energy. "I only went because I had to. Maybe his reason for the invite was genuine." Kessler paused. "Or maybe he's gay."

I pictured Rudi sprawled in his chair in Sully's Saloon, legs spread with his right arm hooked over the back of his chair. I remembered his expression as he watched our waitress bend over the table, a tray of drinks balanced in one hand as she laid napkins on the scarred walnut.

"He isn't." The Buick's high beams flared in the downpour. I nodded toward the access road. "Is that for you?"

Kessler looked over his shoulder, paused, then raised his arm, signaling that he knew the car was there. "Yeah. Mr. Utley wants to show me some yearlings he bought at Fasig-Tipton."

"Before you head out…." I made sure we weren't being watched before I slipped the bills Rudi had given me out of my pocket. Kessler frowned as I unfolded the hundreds and fanned them between my fingers. "After the robbery, Sturgill gave me a ride back to the hotel. He left his guests without a backward glance when he just as easily could have asked the hostess to call me a cab. When he dropped me off, he gave me these."

"What did he say?"

"Something like, I was his guest, and now I'm out of money."

Kessler rubbed the back of his neck. "Well, Steve. A guy like that," he gestured toward the bills, "six hundred bucks is probably chump change. Don't worry about it. He hasn't done anything wrong…yet. If he invites you to some other event, though, go for it. If he's got something planned, I want him approaching you."

I nodded.

Utley tapped the horn a little louder.

"You okay?" Kessler said as he unbuttoned his coat. He'd come to work wearing dress slacks and a long fawn-colored trench coat treated with an efficient water repellent. A pinstripe dress shirt with a Windsor collar and a silk tie finished out his look. Not exactly backside attire.

"Yeah. I'm fine."

He nodded, then headed down the aisle. When he reached the exit, he lifted the coat over his head and hurried to the waiting car.

Bill Gannon returned to the barn in a darker mood than when he'd set out, and I figured the footing had been worse than advertised. Gone Wild returned five minutes later with a film of watery mud coating his legs and chest.

Horses went to the track and came back to hot baths and clean, sweet-smelling stalls and a lot of extra work on everyone's part, and all of it was done in relative quiet and with little enthusiasm. By ten o'clock, the aisles had been raked smooth. By ten-thirty, most of the horses' attendants had streamed out of the barns, heading for the track kitchen or Wagner's Pharmacy.

I was standing in Barn 41's doorway when a silver Mercedes convertible eased into the alley between barns. The rain had slackened from downpour to drizzle, and I could hear the wipers track across the windshield and the sound of raindrops drumming on the car's soft top. Rudi Sturgill squinted through the driver's side window and scanned the shedrow. He had a cell phone pressed to his ear and said something before closing the phone and climbing from behind the wheel. He left the car running.

Rudi strolled into the barn with a white paper bag dangling from his hand. He nodded to the guard and asked if Gannon was around.

"No, sir."

Rudi lifted a Styrofoam cup out of the bag and handed it to me. "Coffee?"

"Thanks."

"I thought I'd catch Bill."

"He left about an hour ago."

Rudi glanced around and said, "Where's that big black guy you work with?"

"Eating, washing up. Something like that."

"He uses the motel, too?"

"Hardly. He's somewhere around here. He doesn't like straying too far from the horses."

"Roughing it, huh?" Rudi propped the bag on the ledge beneath the clothesline and peeled the triangle out of his plastic lid. "Now me, I couldn't get the hell up this morning." He grinned over the rim of his cup. "Didn't think I'd see you here, either. After last night."

"I'm stiff, is all," I lied. In truth, my shoulder and elbow ached like a bitch. The only improvement I'd managed was walking out of the limp I'd started the day with.

I swallowed a mouthful of hot coffee. It was strong and black and went a long way toward improving my mood.

"Anything come to mind about last night," Rudi said, "now that you've had time to rethink it?"

I shook my head. "What's to rethink? It was just a weird, random event." I hoped.

Rudi nodded, glanced at his watch, then looked past the roof overhang. White clumps of broken cloud scuttled beneath a leaden cloud base that had clamped down on the city like a woolen blanket. "Guess my horse didn't do anything useful this morning with this god-awful rain."

I kept my mouth shut. What his horse did or didn't do was none of my business.

Rudi looked around as if he'd just then realized how deserted the backside truly was. "How long do you have to stay here?"

"Couple more hours, probably."

"It's quiet," Rudi said as he leaned against the doorframe. "I didn't realize it ever got this quiet."

I scanned the grounds. Across the access road, a guy strolled out of Barn 48, cut around the corner, and shook the rainwater off an ancient single-speed bike with a twisted mudguard over the rear wheel. He jammed his boot on the pedal and shoved off, putting his back into moving the old fat tires across the ground. Not much else going on.

"This is your trainer's home base, right?" I said.

Rudi nodded.

"Well, does he keep horses in other barns and Gone Wild here since he's running in the Derby?"

"Oh…I misunderstood. No. He doesn't have permanent stalls at Churchill, if that's what you mean. He prefers to run them off the farm. It's only forty minutes out, and he's got an excellent training track with a starting gate. Everything he needs, really. I'm sure he saves a great deal of money on stall rentals alone, though he hauls them in for the occasional morning workout to get them acclimated. But we decided that Wildman, here," Rudi jerked his head toward Gone Wild, "would benefit from some extra time on the grounds, give him a chance to get used to all the activity. You think it's busy now, next week will be worse. Saturday will be unbelievable."

"Makes sense," I said, and Rudi smiled.

"Perfect sense, but being on site's good for publicity, too. It gets both the horse and Bill's name out there, and that brings in more business."

Rudi hung around for another ten minutes, drinking coffee and otherwise looking like he didn't know what to do with himself. Eventually, he drove off in search of his trainer, and I was left alone for another two hours. When Jay relieved me at one, I walked back to the hotel, intent on changing into dry clothes before I went out to eat.

I swiped my room key in the security lock, levered the door open, and stepped over the threshold. As the door swung closed, a prickling sensation slid up my spine. The maid had been in my room. She'd made the bed and drawn back the curtains like she did every morning, but I seriously doubted that she'd dumped the contents of my duffel on the floor. Or shifted the mattresses. Or yanked open all the dresser drawers.

I was standing in the narrow foyer with the closet on my left, bathroom on my right. I could see most of the bedroom and bath, but there were blind spots. I lowered my poncho to the floor, pulled out my knife, and opened the blade. I scanned the slice of bathroom visible beyond the open door. No one was crouched in the space beneath the sink, and a brief glance told me that whoever had tossed my room hadn't bothered with the bath. The countertop had been wiped down. Fresh toiletries had been laid out, and clean towels were stacked on the wall rack.

I eased forward until I could see through the crack between the door's hinges. The maid had tidied up the shower curtain by gathering it into a foot-and-a-half wide strip that centered on the tub. Not enough cover for someone to hide behind.

When I'd gone out last night, I had left the closet sliders stacked one in front of the other, and that hadn't changed. I stepped over a bottle of Deer Park water that must have rolled into the foyer when my visitor dumped my gear. I checked the closet. Wooden hangers, my blazer, an empty laundry bag. I drew in a slow breath and strode into the room. Pivoted to face anyone who might have been waiting for me around the corner.

Nothing there but a blank wall.

I checked the rest of the room, then called security.

Chapter Eight

Precisely ten minutes after I made the call, someone rapped on my door.

I had spent two of those ten minutes sifting through my gear. Nothing was missing, which wasn't a surprise since I hadn't brought anything of value on this trip. And I had spent the remaining eight minutes suspecting that the search for the mysterious tape had risen to a new level.

And how the hell had they known where to find me?

"Security," a female voice said as I opened the door.

I supposed I held some preconceived notions about hotel security. I imagined that the department would be staffed with older men who wore their grizzled hair cropped short out of habit and whose muscles were softening with age and inactivity. Ex-military or law enforcement, close to retirement and bored with a job that paid the bills but paled when compared to earlier exploits. And I supposed my presumptions were evident in my expression, because the woman who stood before me squared her shoulders, and a challenging glint shone in her eyes as she held out a business card.

"Fortman. Director of Security."

"Steve Cline." I backed out of the way. As she stepped through the doorway, I reflected that she'd smoothly bypassed any question of a handshake by offering her business card in its place.

She pivoted and scanned the room, then bent to unclasp a buckle on the leather satchel that swung from her shoulder. When she lifted the flap and reached inside, the cuff of her blazer caught on the edge, causing the sleeve to ride up her forearm. Fine tendons and ropy muscles flexed beneath her smooth brown skin.

She withdrew a notebook. "When did you leave your room this morning?"

"Around five-fifteen." I glanced at my watch. Eight hours and ten minutes earlier, give or take. I had missed breakfast altogether, and outside of swallowing ibuprofen like it was candy, I'd had nothing to eat except for a couple of Jay's candy bars. I'd drunk some soda and Rudi's coffee, but if I didn't get something substantial in my stomach soon, no amount of caffeine was going to keep me on my feet.

"And you returned when?"

"Right before I called the front desk."

"Did you enter your room anytime between five-fifteen and one-twenty-five?"

"No."

"When you called downstairs, you said nothing was missing. Are you certain, now that you've had time to look around?"

I nodded.

She walked toward the bathroom. "Have you noticed any damage to the room itself?"

"No."

Her heels clicked on the tiles as she swung the door away from the tub, glanced at the walls and plumbing fixtures. "Does anyone else have a key to your room?" she said as she returned to the foyer.

"Yeah, I have a roommate, but he hardly ever comes here."

She lifted an eyebrow.

"He uses the facilities at the track," I added. "And besides, he wouldn't have messed with my stuff."

"Any chance someone could have got hold of his key?"

"I suppose there's always a chance." I flipped open my cell phone and keyed in Jay's number. When his voice finally came through the earpiece, it sounded overly loud and gravelly, like a wet log rolling over a sack full of marbles. "Hey. Did I wake you?"

"Yeah…."

"Sorry. Look, did you use the hotel room today?"

"Huh?"

"Did you come over here to shower?"

"No, man. I would've got wetter on the walk."

"True." I watched the security director wander back into the room and scan my belongings, which I had left as I'd found them, scattered across the carpet. "Make sure you still have your room key, okay?"

"It's in my backpack."

"The room's been broken into, and security wants to know if somebody snatched your key, so just look."

He grunted; then I heard the distinctive sound of a nylon zipper being yanked. He came back on the line. "I got it."

"Okay, thanks." I closed my phone. "No one's had access to his key."

She nodded slowly, and I found the idea of an attractive woman looking through my gear a bit disconcerting. "What do you think they were looking for?"

"It depends. Have you had a lot of break-ins lately?" I asked, though I seriously doubted she'd admit it if they had. I was hoping for a change in her body language or nuance in her voice that would tell me what I needed to know.

"No. We haven't," she said without hesitation. She withdrew a black device that resembled a bulky PDA out of her bag. A keypad covered the lower portion, although the casing fanned out at the top to accommodate a narrow screen. "So, what does 'it' depend on?"

"Well, I was hoping this was random. You know, someone looking for valuables or drugs? Part of an ongoing problem, but since it isn't…." I briefly outlined what had happened the night before.

The director of security frowned as she listened to my story. When I finished, she said, "I think you should move to another room. I'll check with the front desk and see if they can arrange it."

"Thank you."

"Now," she said as she brushed past me and propped open the door to the hallway, "let's see who's been in your room." She pulled a cardkey out of her bag. A thin data cable trailed after it. She clipped the free end into the PDA and inserted the cardkey into the lock. The device beeped as she powered it up and worked through a menu.

"What can that tell you?" I asked.

"Pretty much everything. There's a minicomputer behind this plate." She tapped the lock's brass housing. "It stores the date, time, name, and type of key used for the past five hundred entries, including mechanical overrides."

"Overrides?"

She nodded. "Systems fail. Guests get sick and can't open their door for themselves. We had a bunch of kids here a while back. They'd mixed alcohol and drugs and were unresponsive. We bypassed the lock, but they'd thrown the fliplock, so we still couldn't get in. We had to cut through the drywall that time."

"Hmm. You mentioned names?"

"Yep. Guest keys are encoded with the user's name, same as the staff keys."

"So there's a record of who goes where and does what?"

She nodded. "Within the building? Yes." The skin crinkled between her eyebrows as she studied the readout. "You entered the room at one-thirty-seven this morning with a newly issued key."

"Yeah. The original got snatched with my wallet."

"Okay." She pressed a button. "Housekeeping was in at nine-forty-five, then someone made three attempts with your disabled key at ten-fifty-one. I'm assuming that wasn't you."

"You assume correctly."

Her frown deepened. "At eleven-oh-two, you accessed your room with a duplicate of the newly issued key."

"Wasn't me."

"No. I need to talk to the front desk." She packed up her gear. "I'll get back with you." She turned and strode toward the elevator bay, and I figured my tagging along was not on her agenda.

I went back inside, straightened up, then took a shower. I was getting ready to leave when Fortman called.

"Someone claiming to be you said he left his key in his room by mistake. He gave your name and," she said, sounding disgusted, "one of the staff gave him a duplicate without asking for identification. I'm sorry. I've talked to the manager, and he's willing to give you a discount on your stay here." I was thinking that Kessler might appreciate that when she added, "And we'll be happy to move you to another room if you wish, or you may prefer that we just change the lock and issue you a new set of keys."

"Thank you. Changing the lock should suffice."

"Okay, I'll have someone deliver new cardkeys to your room."

"I'm going out," I said. "I can pick them up."

"Fine."

"Wait. Ask what he looked like."

"All right." Dead air filled the line, and I realized she'd put me on hold. Very discreet, our Ms. Fortman. A moment later, she came back on. "White. Average-looking. That's all the clerk remembers. Certainly nothing stood out about him."

When I described New York, the clerk couldn't confirm or deny his involvement. "What about the police?" I said.

She hesitated. "Nothing was taken."

"I'd like to know who was in my room."

"I don't mean to diminish this, but the call would be low priority for them."

"I suppose you're right. Thank you." I hung up, wondering if I'd accidentally stuck the cardkey envelope in my wallet. The hotel used the small envelopes, practically the same size as the cardkey itself, so maybe I had. Then the guys who jumped me would have known a great deal more than my name. They would have known what hotel I was staying in *and* my room number. I didn't believe I'd kept the envelope, but I couldn't remember throwing it away or leaving it on the bureau.

Outside, the cloud cover had lightened, and a wedge of blue sky had seeped into the western horizon. I stopped at the track and gave Jay the new room key before riding a bus downtown. I ate fish and chips at The Pub, an imitation English restaurant in Fourth Street Live, then caught the seventeen bus.

As soon as I turned the corner onto Everett, I saw Nicole's Maxima parked exactly where she'd left it Friday afternoon and knew with certainty that I would find her keys on the floorboard. I clicked open the door and verified that they were resting on the vinyl mat.

What the hell was going on? I meet this woman purely by chance. Choose her as my subject, a decision that was also random, and work up a preliminary report—a report that, as far as I could determine, no one knew existed. Now, it looked like she'd disappeared, and someone was convinced I had a tape. A tape given to me by a woman.

A jogger looped the end of the block and headed back as I crossed Nicole's front lawn and climbed the porch steps. I gave up on subtlety as I knocked on Nicole's door, but no scrape of furniture or thud of footfalls vibrated through the floorboards. Somewhere upstairs, the hyped-up cadence of a television commercial seeped through the walls.

She could have left for the weekend. A friend could have picked her up as soon as she parked, but I didn't believe it.

Besides, I've never believed much in coincidence.

I left the building and cut through a narrow alley between Nicole's house and her neighbor's. A musty odor of damp earth and rotting vegetation hung in the air, and the flagstone path was slick with moss. As I neared the corner, the exterior wall gave way to a back porch. The walkway emptied into a tiny backyard bordered by a privacy fence and a two-story carriage house at the far end. I took the back steps two at a time.

To my left, a porch swing hung motionless. The windows behind it were uninformative with sheer curtains drawn behind the glass. The pair of windows to the right of the back door fronted a kitchen. Blue, green, and amber bottles lined the sill and sash.

I started toward the door. With each step, the door's thin panes of wavy glass reflected the backyard in a moving kaleidoscope—cool greens of the yard replaced by rusty browns of the distant carriage house that glowed orange in the day's last light. The image played across all the panes but one.

I froze.

The square directly above a clunky brass doorknob gaped open, and a ruffled curtain moved against the sash, shifted by a thin breeze.

The glass was missing.

When I stepped closer, I saw that the door wasn't latched but rested against the jamb. I pressed my knuckles against the wood, and the hinges creaked as the door swung inward.

"Hello? Anyone home?"

Except for the sound of water dripping into the kitchen sink, the apartment was eerily still.

"Nicole?" I nudged the door, and more of the room came into view.

Someone had torn through the place. Half the cabinet doors stood open. Canned goods and cereal boxes and paper plates and a bag of red plastic cups had been pulled down from the shelves. Pots and pans spilled onto the floor from the cabinet alongside the stove, and an open box of Cheerios lay on the kitchen table with the contents sprayed across the polished walnut.

I slipped my hand under my T-shirt, squatted, and curled my index finger around the door down near the sill. I pulled the door back against the jamb. The cops would be looking for fingerprints but not there.

I moved back to the window alongside the swing and shifted until I found an angle that cut the glare and allowed me to see through the sheer curtains. Nicole's bedroom. Someone had ransacked it, but nothing about the scene indicated that she'd been present. I returned to the front porch and saw that they'd tossed the living room as well.

I stood on the sidewalk in front of 127 Everett and considered my options. Simply going over the basics with a patrol officer would take an hour, easy. If I wanted to connect all the dots, I'd need to speak to a detective, and I could imagine his skepticism and mounting suspicion as I tried to explain my actions—running a record's check on Nicole, a woman I had briefly met and certainly did not know, going to her neighborhood, calling her house. If I wasn't careful, I'd become his number one and possibly only suspect.

To complicate matters, I'd had three and a half hours sleep last night, and now that the adrenaline had worn off, I was crashing. Swore I could actually sense the brain synapses shutting down. Not an ideal situation if I were to come under scrutiny. I fucking didn't want to step in front of *that* train.

I found a payphone on Bardstown Road and dialed 911, told the dispatcher they had a B&E and possible missing person's case at 127 Everett, and disconnected. If Nicole didn't turn up in the next couple of days, I'd go to the cops.

A metallic click dragged me from the depths of a dreamless sleep.

I had no memory of falling asleep. Couldn't, in fact, remember slipping between the sheets. I was lying on my back with an inadequate pillow flattened beneath my head. My skin felt cool, and I realized I'd flung off the bedspread sometime during the night.

Another click. The sound hadn't come from the air-conditioning unit as I'd first thought, or the thermostat on the wall directly to my left. It sounded like it had come from the other side of my door.

I held my breath and listened. Had I flipped the…what had Fortman called it? The fliplock? I couldn't remember.

Another softer click was followed by a subtle shift in the room's air pressure and a definite change in the background noise. A yellow shaft of light telescoped across the ceiling, then collapsed back onto itself and disappeared as the door to the hallway opened, then closed.

Someone had stepped into my room. One person, judging from the length of time the door had been open.

I could hear his breathing as I eased my arms from beneath the sheet. The top corner of the bedspread lay curled over like a wave rolling onto a beach. My jeans were buried somewhere beneath it, and the only weapon I owned was tucked inside the front right pocket. I slipped my arm between the folds, and my fingertips brushed cool denim.

The guy at the door hadn't moved. He'd stepped from a brightly lit hall into a pitch black room. I pictured the layout as it must have appeared to him. Thanks to the crack under the door, he would have a good bit of light around his shoes, but I doubted it stretched beyond the foyer. I'd drawn the drapes, and the token nightlight incorporated into the hairdryer holder in the bathroom had burned out. The faint green glow from the clock's digital readout and an occasional flash of red from the smoke detector wouldn't help him much.

I'd found my jeans' waistband. I inched the material through my fingers until I felt the snap. Curled my fingers around the knife's casing. Withdrawing the knife, I struggled to control my breathing. My only chance of getting the upper hand was to convince him that I was asleep.

The sound of a shoe pressing into carpet reached my ears.

I unfolded the blade.

Chapter Nine

For no particular reason, I had picked the bed closest to the door, and I'd awoken on the side nearest the bathroom. I shifted closer to the edge of the bed and eased my feet off the mattress, freeing them from the sheets.

He stepped into view, a huge bulky form barely visible against a darker background. His head moved in a slow reptilian arc as his gaze shifted from one bed to the other. He stilled as his attention settled on the bed I was lying on.

Blood pounded in my ears, and even though I was trying to breathe quietly, I was certain he could hear each breath I took. I tightened my grip on the knife.

He cleared his throat before stepping into the gap between the bed and wall.

I held my breath and waited for him to move closer.

Clothing rustled as he took another step and leaned forward.

He squawked when I sprang off the mattress and latched onto his jacket. My momentum sent him crashing into the wall, and a bundle that he was holding tumbled to the floor. I jammed my blade alongside his Adam's apple.

His hands came up. "Whoa, whoa, whoa."

"Oh, Jesus Christ." I lowered the knife, and Jay's hands strayed to his throat. I glared at him. "What the hell are you doing, sneaking in here in the middle of the goddamn night?"

He coughed.

I squeezed around him, crossed over to the desk, and switched on the light. Sweat glistened on his forehead.

"What the fuck, man?" Jay rubbed his throat. "What the fuck's wrong wid you?" He eased his bulk onto the foot of the bed.

"Sorry. I thought the guys who'd tossed my room had come back."

He rubbed his throat some more.

"You cut?"

He scowled at me.

"Sorry, Jay. I really am. Why didn't you call? Shit." I gestured to the door. "Why didn't you turn on the fucking lights?"

"I hit the switch," Jay said. "You must've turned it off at the lamp, and I did call. Twice. You never picked up."

"Oh."

Jay lowered his hand and looked at his fingers.

"You bleeding?"

"Ain't nothing."

I switched on another light and checked for myself. He was right. It was nothing. A scratch. I looked in the narrow path between the bed and wall and saw what had landed at my feet. He'd dropped his backpack. I picked it up and placed it on a chair. "So, what's up?"

"I need you to go to the track. I feel like shit. Must have caught the bug going 'round."

I smiled. "Hell of an introduction to the upscale accommodations, huh?"

He shrugged.

I picked up my denim jacket. "How many people know we have a room here?"

"Sanchez knows, so probably half the barn do. Said he saw you get off a bus in front of the Cardinal Hall of Fame joint and cut across the parking lot. Wanted to know why I was the one got stuck with the grunt work."

I paused with the jacket sleeve pulled halfway up my arm. "What did you say?"

"That it weren't no fucking business of his, but since he asked, come post time Derby day, his jock better got Velcro stuck to his ass 'cause he gonna get caught in a slipstream when Storm leaves the gate. That big boy gonna leave Gone Wild in the next county, ain't no doubt about it." Jay scowled and looked around the room. "I shouldn't fucking be here."

I chuckled. "You need anything? Some medicine? I've got a bottle of ibuprofen in the bathroom, and the front desk has all kinds of shit. You want me to pick something up for you before I leave?"

"No. Just get to the track."

I left five minutes later.

Cloud cover hung low in the sky, glowing with an eerie fluorescence as the moisture-laden air refracted the available light and cast halos around lamp poles and headlights. The backside lay beneath a hazy fog, a quiet dark place ripe with the rich earthy smells of damp straw and horse.

I stretched out on the cot Jay had left in the shedrow and fell asleep immediately, that is until the morning stable routine lurched into motion precisely at four-thirty, as unfailing as the turning of the Earth. I fed and watered the horses and groomed them. I unwound the bulky standing bandages from their legs and massaged their tendons with a cooling brace; then I waited for Kessler.

A half hour later, he trudged into the barn with a Styrofoam cup in his hand and paused when he saw me sitting on a bale with the horses' bridles arranged neatly beside me. He cut his eyes to the horses—both had their heads attentively poked through their doorways—and correctly concluded that Jay was not in one of their stalls.

"Where's Jay?"

I stood and brushed straw off my jeans. "At the hotel, sick."

"Damn. I'm scheduled to fly back to Baltimore for a couple of days."

I shrugged. "I doubt he'll be down long," I said and paused. "I know the horses' routines, what they eat and when they eat it. I assume you've already scheduled their works."

"Yeah. Jacinto Dominga will be taking over from Juan. You'll meet him this morning."

I thought over the routine start to finish. "The only difficulty I foresee is that I'll need someone to hold them for their baths until Jay gets back on his feet. The rest of the chores can be done solo. Tacking up's not a problem, and I can always muck out while the horses are on the track."

Kessler frowned. "What about your arm?"

"It's still sore," I said. "But it'll hold up."

"You know where Jay keeps everything?"

I nodded.

"Hmm." Kessler glanced at his watch. "Let's get the leg checks over with while I think about it."

I picked up a chain shank and held Ruskie while Kessler palpated the colt's legs. When he finished, he straightened and jerked his head. "Your turn. Tell me what you find."

I smiled softly. Kessler was more worried about leaving the horses in my charge than he might admit, but his misgivings were unfounded. I'd medicated, palpated, injected, and otherwise been solely responsible for the medical needs and oddities of two hundred-plus horses for the better part of three years. If I couldn't take care of two racehorses for a couple of days, I might as well go home.

After tying Ruskie to the ring bolted to the wall, I started with the front left leg as Kessler had done. I worked my way around the horse, palpating knees, tendons, and ligaments, smoothing my fingertips along shin bones, fetlocks, and pasterns. I checked the digital pulse. In the front legs, especially, a pounding pulse indicated inflammation farther down the limb. I cupped my hand over Ruskie's hooves, feeling for heat and finding none.

I straightened, gazed at the horse's legs, and summed up my findings. "He's got a medial splint on the left fore that's set up. It's hard and cold to the touch and doesn't involve the knee or surrounding tendons. There's a minor amount of filling around the superficial flexor just above the fetlock in the same leg, but he's not tender, and there's no heat. In his left hind, there's some minor distension along the long planter ligament, but my guess is, it's old. He's probably had it since he went into training as a fresh two-year-old."

When my evaluation met a wall of silence, I looked up and caught Kessler studying me.

"Why the hell aren't you in this business fulltime?" he asked.

I exhaled and decided I might as well tell him. "I've been toying with the idea of working as an investigator, either in law enforcement or the private sector."

Kessler all but rolled his eyes before his good humor brightened his face and crinkled the skin at the corners of his mouth. "This," he gestured toward the door and the general direction of the track and grandstand, "isn't exciting enough for you?"

I forced a smile.

How could I tell him what I truly felt without sounding sanctimonious? Most of the time, I loved this industry. I loved these animals more than I thought possible. I enjoyed being around them on a daily basis, and more than anything, I would miss that connection if I left. My difficulties were of the two-legged variety—the ubiquitous greed that permeated every level of the industry, the prevailing attitude that these animals were disposable. Throwaways. Hell, although it was never stated openly, the human component, the hotwalkers, grooms, and exercise riders, were frequently viewed in the same vein. For whatever reason, I couldn't seem to set aside my annoyance with the Utleys of this world and just focus on the horses. My half-sister, Abby, had once pointed out that these animals would be here whether she was or not, and her efforts and hard work and caring made their lives more tolerable. I liked her attitude, but for the life of me, I seemed incapable of adopting it.

"I have a difficult time with the routine," I said, answering Kessler's question, truthfully in fact.

He nodded, and I suspected he was more disappointed than he let on.

"On the surface," I said, "your job appears glamorous, with the social commitments and the press and flying around the country to search for new prospects, and you sure as hell have earned every bit of recognition that's come your way. But I know how hard you've worked to achieve it. That you rarely take a day off or spend time with your family, and I don't know if I want that, either."

"That's fair, but what a waste. You know how long it would take?" he said with frustration casting an edge to his words, "how many *years* it would take for me to find someone who can read a horse's legs the way you do?"

"Any vet—"

"You know that's not what I mean."

"Okay," I said. "I do."

"Well…will you keep my offer in mind if the avenues you're exploring don't pan out or are less than you'd hoped for?"

I smiled. "Definitely."

"Okay." Kessler nodded and hooked his thumbs in his pockets. "There's one other thing you need to convince me you're capable of before I feel comfortable leaving you here by yourself, in charge of eighteen million dollars' worth of horseflesh."

"Huh. I thought Utley shelled out twenty mil for Storm."

"Close enough, wouldn't you say?"

"I guess."

Kessler told me to gather together some cotton sheeting, rundown pads, and rolls of Coflex; then we went into Storm's stall, and he demonstrated how to apply a rundown bandage. After he finished, he watched me wrap the colt's right hind leg.

"What did you think of the racing prospects you looked at yesterday?" I said as I carefully looped the bandage under Storm's fetlock in a manner that would offer support and protection.

"Mr. Utley's got some nice horseflesh, I'll give him that."

"Where's he stable them?" I said because I didn't picture a man like Utley living in the country.

"Millcroft Farm, in the southeast corner of Jefferson County, which is surprising. I didn't think there was any open land that close to Louisville."

I finished off the bandage with tape and straightened. "His farm?"

"No. He boards them so he can move them when and where he wants." Kessler frowned as he smoothed his hand over the wrap I'd just applied. "Jesus."

"I passed, then?"

"That's damn good."

"I've wrapped a lot of legs in my time," I said, and Kessler shook his head.

By the time Jacinto showed up at six-thirty Monday morning, Kessler had made arrangements for one of Bill Gannon's hotwalkers to hold the horses while I bathed them, which I did under the scrutiny of two television crews, cameras whirring in the background. The clouds had dispersed, and as soon as there was enough light to film by, the press had arrived in force. Otherwise, the morning routine unfolded without a hitch, and by nine o'clock, I'd run out of things to do. Kessler had driven off after watching both horses work, but presently he returned with two Styrofoam cups and a white paper bag balanced in his hands.

The sun had cleared the rooftops, and its light glinted off the car's hood and the scattered puddles that dotted the roadway. I stood and watched Kessler nudge the car door shut, then start across the alley.

All around us, the workday unfolded, the usual backside routine colored by the nearness of the first Saturday in May. A Hispanic man whizzed past Kessler's rental on a kid's bike with a groom's towel flapping from his back pocket. Like most stable hands working the backside today, his jeans were dirty and damp from the knees down. He cut past Barn 43 as a group of men wearing business suits and polished loafers rounded the corner, their voices edged with excitement. The wind had kicked up, and it lifted their hair and caught their ties while the leaves in a nearby tree shuddered against a brilliant sky.

Kessler paused at the entrance and talked to the guard, who nodded as he wrote something in his clipboard; then he joined me outside Storm's stall. He handed me a coffee before setting the bag on the tack trunk. "I didn't think you'd had a chance to eat, so there are some eggs and hash browns and pastries in there."

"Thanks."

Snoopy Sanchez, Bill Gannon's groom, walked past. His gaze lighted on Kessler's back then lingered on me before he continued down the shedrow.

"I meant to ask," Kessler said. "Have you learned anything about the robbery or the motive behind it?"

I shook my head as I hooked my fingertips under the cup's lid.

"Anything else I need to know about before I leave?"

Thinking of Nicole, I paused with the lid peeled halfway off. "No."

Kessler narrowed his eyes and waited.

"Really," I said. "Um, are you taking your laptop with you?"

"Not on this trip. Why?"

"I have to finish a project I'm working on, and the business office at the Hilton only has two computers. Catching one open is a crap shoot. If Jay's on the job before you get back, I'd like to wrap it up."

"Sure. You know where I'm staying?"

I shook my head.

Kessler gave me directions. "The room's mine until we all pack up and go home. I'll arrange for a key to be left for you." He cleared his throat. "You've convinced me that you're fully capable of taking care of the horses, but I'm flying another one of the crew out this afternoon." Kessler held up his hand when I opened my mouth to protest. "For security. You can't be here every second of the day. I don't expect that, but I also don't want the horses left unattended."

"How will I know him?"

Kessler smiled softly. "You'll know."

I frowned. "What?"

Ignoring my question, Kessler glanced at his watch before withdrawing an envelope from his coat pocket and handing it to me. "I'm running behind schedule. My flight leaves in less than two hours, and I still have some unfinished business to attend to, so I need you to drop this off frontside when you have a chance. Doesn't have to be today. Tomorrow's fine."

"Okay."

He held out his hand, and there was a brief awkward moment when more could have been said, but wasn't. We shook.

"Call me if you have any questions or problems, right?"

I hooked my thumbs in my jeans, and as I did so, it dawned on me that it was something I'd often seen Kessler do. "Right."

I watched him drive off, then turned the envelope over. *Bookkeeping Office* was printed in Kessler's scrawled hand.

Chapter Ten

By eleven o'clock Monday, the backside was as deserted as it ever gets. Kessler's horses were stalled on the north side of Barn 41, and the air was chillier inside than out. The guard at my end of the shedrow had risen to stretch his legs and was now standing in the sunlight, a cell phone pressed to his ear. His voice was slow and melodic, and I had a feeling he was talking to his girlfriend.

After eating the breakfast Kessler had brought, I'd snatched a folding chair from one of the tackrooms. My feet were propped on a straw bale, my spine slid low in the nylon webbing. My eyelids closed of their own accord, and I was conscious of my breathing and the background hum of traffic on Longfield Avenue. A train's whistle sounded in the distance, but the skies were quiet. The winds must have forced the jets onto a different approach, because they weren't roaring overhead every couple of minutes like they had during the past three days.

Three days. It felt longer. But drinking and losing sleep to partying and work had a way of doing that. Three days since I'd researched Nicole Anne Austin. Since she'd dropped her keys in the street.

I dragged out my cell phone and called Information. Got the number for Churchill Downs and thumbed the keys, then asked for Marketing. I rested my head against the chair's tubular frame and listened to dead air followed by a series of clicks, and eventually a husky female voice came on the line.

"May I speak to Nicole Austin, please?"

The woman paused before responding. "She hasn't come in."

"Did she call?"

"Hold on." Cloth rustled against the phone's mouthpiece. "No. She hasn't."

"Well, was she scheduled to be off?"

"No. Who is this?"

"An acquaintance. Look, is this unusual, the fact that she hasn't called or shown up?"

"I've never known her to do it in the past."

"Thank you." I hung up and keyed in Nicole's home number. When her answering machine kicked in, I closed the phone.

Fuck.

I sat up straighter, tossed the cell on the bale, and pulled out the notepad I kept in my back pocket. I listed the facts as I knew them.

Thursday: arrived in Louisville.

Nowhere to go with that. I had gone through the usual airport routine, checked into the Hilton, and gone to bed.

Friday: first morning at the track.

Actually, my first time ever on Churchill's grounds. Well, the backside, anyway. I may have been frontside for the races when my family visited Louisville, but I didn't remember it. I'd made it to the receiving barn by five a.m. and had met Nicole Anne Austin approximately three hours later. I wrote down her name.

I wondered why she had gone into the barn in the first place. She did mention that she gave tours, so maybe she needed to collect information for the narrative she delivered. The more I thought about it, the more likely it seemed. Part of the backside tour would include a summary of each horse running in the Derby. Even though the tram didn't come close to the Derby barns, she probably identified the horses as they went to the track. That would explain her studying Gone Wild's legs, looking for markings or characteristics that would help her pick him out of the crowd. She'd even brought along a sheet of loose leaf.

An image of her tucking it into her front pocket came to mind. And what else had she done? She talked to me about Storm.

I turned my head and looked in at the horse. He stood along the back wall, neck muscles relaxed, eyes half-closed, lower lip drooping, about as asleep as a horse can get and still be on his feet. Why hadn't she written down anything about him? Maybe because he was the only gray in the race.

I dragged my thumb across the edge of my notepad, riffling the pages as if they were a deck of cards. My initial impression of Nicole had been that she was competent, efficient. But beneath that competence, I had sensed an underlying tension, and that impression had intensified when Bill Gannon and Snoopy Sanchez entered the barn. I printed their names below hers and underlined them. Then she'd practically bolted out of the barn, but I'd turned my back and was heading down the shedrow on Jay's errand, so I hadn't seen anything that might have triggered a reaction like that. I thought back to what I had seen.

She hadn't paid Sanchez much attention. In fact, she'd hardly looked his way, but he'd had his eyes on her. And I didn't think she saw Jay until she turned to leave. What else had gone on that morning?

A crowd had entered the barn from the east. I listed their names: *Kessler, Edward Utley, Rudi Sturgill,* and assorted members of the press. Since her job was in Marketing, it was conceivable that she knew someone in that group. I hadn't looked beyond them, but I supposed she might have seen someone or something that had upset her, though I couldn't imagine what.

Friday afternoon, I spent downtown, searching for data on Nicole Anne Austin. Unless an employee in one of those bureaucratic departments knew Nicole and had alerted her, working on the project had been the most obscure thing I'd done since arriving in Louisville.

Saturday: Rudi Sturgill.

Although I'd seen Sturgill in the shedrow Friday, I didn't actually speak to him until he invited me to his Thunder party. There, I'd been introduced to his sister, Paige, and the Middle-

Eastern guy, Yaseen. Tapping the pencil on my teeth, I remembered his liking for titles and smiled as I wrote *Haddad, Senior Software Engineer.* I'd been half tempted to introduce myself as Steve Cline, temporary hotwalker, but knew that would have screwed with his grasp of English, not to mention his sense of humor. Who else? Gannon, and…how could I forget? I added *boyfriend* to my list as I pictured Paige fawning over Mr. Doofus all night.

Sunday:

I underlined the word three times. Sunday had begun with a close-up view of a grimy restroom floor and a lesson in pain. And it ended with the realization that the search for the mystery tape was very much alive and ongoing and had expanded to the trashing of both my hotel room and Nicole's apartment.

Monday: Where is Nicole?

I sighed and leaned back in the chair. How were these events connected? I had no idea. I went at it from the opposite direction. How were the people that I'd come in contact with connected? I listed two columns.

PARTY	CHURCHILL
Rudi Sturgill	*Nicole*
Paige Sturgill	*Bill Gannon*
Yaseen Haddad,	*Snoopy Sanchez*
Senior Software Engineer	*Rudi Sturgill*
boyfriend	*Edward Utley*
Bill Gannon	*Kessler*
	the press

I circled Rudi and Gannon's names since they appeared on both lists, but that didn't get me anywhere. Most of the people involved in racing knew one another. Right now, the person I needed to focus on was Nicole; she was the key. If I could just talk to her, I was certain I would be able to figure out what was going on.

I looked up as Snoopy Sanchez strolled down the aisle with his arms full of damp bandages and quilted leg wraps and at least one plaid cooler. He hadn't gathered the cooler's nylon surcingles, so they swung free and tangled with his legs every couple of strides. As he passed the fourth stall on the left, with his attention focused on the clothesline strung between roof supports, one of the wraps rolled off the pile. He didn't notice but continued down the shedrow. I looked over my shoulder as he braced the front of his body against the barn's waist-high exterior wall, effectively pinning the bundle of laundry against the rough concrete blocks. I stood and stretched, watched him untangle a red polo bandage before flipping it over the line. I scooped the wrap off the ground, shook it out, and glanced in at Kessler's horses before I joined Sanchez.

I draped the quilted wrap over the line and crimped it to keep it from blowing off before Sanchez had a chance to stick on a clothespin.

He looked at me and raised an eyebrow.

"You dropped it."

He nodded and went back to work, shaking a fleece bandage loose from the tangled mass.

I rested my hip against the wall and crossed my arms. "You know Nicole Austin, right?"

"Who?" Sanchez said with his attention focused on finding the free end of a particularly vile-looking cotton wrap stained with what I recognized to be old blotches of nitrofurazone ointment and bloody serum.

"The woman your boss was talking to Friday. She works in Marketing and gives tours."

"What about her?"

"Well, for starters, what do you think of her?"

"Besides being hot?"

I smiled. "Yeah, besides that."

"She use to work in the barns, so she's one of a few frontsiders who knows the score. Knows this ain't no easy job and that we ain't bums doing it."

"Did she work for Gannon?"

Sanchez grunted.

"What did she do for him?"

He flicked me a look. "Walked hots. Rubbed a couple horses."

"Anything else?" I said, and he caught my drift.

"With Gannon, ain't no telling what she did for *him*."

"He's married, isn't he?"

"Yeah, but he needs reminding."

"When did she stop working for him?"

"The hell I know?" Sanchez was down to the cooler, in this case, a red-and-beige plaid terrycloth that was cut to fit the horse's contours. Sort of like an equine version of a bathrobe. He bent to untangle the surcingles. "What's it to you, anyhow?"

"Just curious."

Sanchez tossed the cooler over an empty section of clothesline.

"Do you know why she quit?"

"None of my business."

"Do you know if she worked for any other trainers besides Gannon?"

He shrugged and moved down the line, shifting clothespins off the rope and clamping them over the bandages.

"How do you like working for Gannon?"

"You thinking 'bout working for him, you won't like it. He don't serve breakfast, and he sure as hell don't put nobody up in no goddamn motel." Sanchez turned and strolled out of the barn, heading in the general direction of the exit.

Okay. That went well. You learned a whole lot with that nice bit of questioning.

I strolled back to my station, jammed my hands in my pockets, and leaned against the wall. Thinking that I might catch Rachel on her lunch break, I flipped open my cell and keyed in her number.

"Hey, it's me," I said when she picked up.

"Hey, yourself." She swallowed, and something crinkled by the phone. A napkin, I guessed. "I was beginning to wonder if you were going to wait 'til you got back to call."

"Sorry. Didn't you get my message?"

"Uh-huh. I just thought I'd hear from you more often."

"Sorry…. You might get a chance to see me. Some camera crews filmed Storm getting his bath this morning."

"Really?"

"Yep." I explained how I'd filled in for Jay; then I described what Churchill was like and how odd it was to have an audience on the backside.

"It must be bizarre."

"Yeah. Normally the backside's one of the most isolated places I can think of."

"What's Louisville like? Is everyone as hyped as they make it seem on T.V.?"

I chuckled. "Pretty much. I think what they say is true, that it's evolved into a two-week party. Louisville's version of Mardi Gras. People even decorate for it."

"You're kidding?"

"Nope. They put out flags and lawn ornaments and all kinds of stuff." I told her about the air show and fireworks but avoided the rest. Getting into that discussion on the phone would not be my first choice.

Rachel talked about work and her night classes, and when we eventually said goodbye, I pulled Ruskie's wool cooler out of the tack trunk, draped it over the chair, and settled in for a long afternoon of doing absolutely nothing. The spring meet didn't start until Saturday. Then the pace would pick up, but for now, only a few stable hands milled around the barns in the afternoons.

Somewhere in the distance, the low throb of a diesel engine echoed off a barn wall. Snatches of conversation drifted from the other side of the barn, but the topic of discussion had moved beyond my rudimentary Spanish. I tuned them out and scanned the notes I'd made on Nicole.

◇◇◇

The engine noise grew louder, penetrating then becoming part of a nonsensical dream I'd been having. Somewhere in the jumble of distorted images, I heard a voice. The voice repeated itself, and I realized I hadn't dreamt it after all.

"Must be nice, getting paid to sleep."

I smiled as I opened my eyes.

Corey Claremont stood over me with her arms crossed under her breasts, her soft smile crinkling the skin around her eyes.

As I lowered my feet off the bale and stood, I realized I was grinning like an idiot. I cleared my throat. "Jesus. No wonder Kessler didn't tell me who he was sending out."

Corey's eyes lit up. "Didn't want you getting too excited, huh?"

I chuckled.

She looked past me as Ruskie popped his head over the stall guard. "Oh," she cooed. "You cutie pie. How's my favorite horse?" She stepped around me, and when she rose on tip-toe and slipped her slender arms around Ruskie's neck, the big chestnut colt responded by lowering his head and curling his neck around her. He nuzzled the back of her thigh.

I'd known Corey for a long time. Three years, actually. But it wasn't until a couple of months ago, when her brother had gone missing, that our relationship had moved beyond superficial. And in unguarded moments, the answer to Bruce's disappearance still shone ragged and raw in her expression and the stoop of her shoulders.

The smell of food drifted past my nose. I scanned the aisle and noticed a drink carrier and Arby's bag sitting on the tack trunk.

Corey glanced over her shoulder and followed my gaze. "Mr. Kessler said you might not have had a chance to eat, so I picked something up."

"Thanks. Here," I said as I fished out some folded bills. "How much do I owe you?"

Corey's pale blond hair flipped across her cheek as she shook her head. "Your dad's covering my expenses." She gave Ruskie a pat before she moved down the aisle to Storm's stall.

"I'm surprised you're here already," I said before stuffing some fries in my mouth.

"I flew out of BWI at ten-oh-three, landed at two-fifty-five, checked in at the Hilton, and caught a cab. The driver was amused by the Arby's detour. Guess he isn't often asked to go in a drive-thru."

I glanced past Corey as Snoopy Sanchez strolled toward us in his arrogant don't-fuck-with-me swagger. "Guess not," I mumbled in response to her comment, but my attention was locked on Sanchez. He slowed as his gaze lingered on Corey's slight frame. He looked from Corey to me and smirked, and when he cut behind my chair to reach Gone Wild's stall, he groaned—a low animal sound in the back of his throat that I hoped Corey hadn't heard.

She brushed off the tack trunk and sat on the lid. As she wriggled backward, she said, "If I'd known the track was this close, I would've walked."

Sanchez was talking to Gone Wild, his soft rhythmic Spanish muffled behind the stall wall. "Just as well you didn't," I said. "My food would've got cold."

Corey had leaned against the stall front and drawn up her legs so that she was sitting Indian-style. She rolled her eyes and blew out a breath that lifted her bangs. "Food. Is that all you guys think about?"

I smiled as I took a bite of my sandwich.

"I saw that, Cline," she said, then stretched forward and levered her soda out of the carrier.

Cline? She'd never called me Cline before. I wondered what was up with that as I watched her tap a straw out of its paper tube and jam it through the slit in her cup's lid. She was keyed up, a little nervous, and I didn't know why. But I guessed being around me was dredging up all kinds of unwanted feelings. As much as I hated to admit it, I suspected she'd never be able to look at me without being reminded of her brother.

I finished my sandwich, scooped out a couple of fries that were lying in the bottom of the bag; then I grained the horses.

Since Corey seemed perfectly happy where she was, I reclaimed the chair.

"What's this?" Corey nudged my notepad around so she could read what was printed on the top page.

"You wouldn't believe me if I told you."

She bent forward with her elbows planted on her knees, wrists crossed over her shins, and studied me with those clear blue eyes of hers. "Try me."

So I told her. I told her about Nicole and the attack and how both our places had been tossed. I told her about everyone I'd come in contact with and how there were too many pieces of the puzzle missing for me to begin to figure out what was going on. She listened without comment, and when I finished, I realized I hadn't noticed Sanchez leaving or that several track employees had drifted back to the barn to feed and water their horses. Two of them hung around a tack room at the far end of the shedrow, and someone had turned on a radio on the south side of the barn. Matchbox 20's bass pulsed under the eaves.

Corey closed the notepad, stretched forward, and held it out to me. "So, what are you going to do?"

When I jammed the pad into my back pocket, the wire binding caught on something that crinkled. "Oh, shit." I pulled Kessler's envelope out of my pocket and glanced at my watch.

"What's wrong?"

I explained that I was supposed to deliver some paperwork for Kessler, and Corey said she'd watch the horses while I went frontside.

I had imagined walking into the bowels of the huge grandstand and finding it deserted but quickly discovered my preconceived notions had been wildly inaccurate. Teams of painters and maintenance crews crossed my path, pushing wheeled carts and carrying ladders and moving scaffolding. The pari-mutuel windows to my right were locked down, silent and dark, but lights blazed within the Churchill Downs store where the staff opened cardboard boxes and stocked shelves while another crew squeegeed the windows fronting the store.

I had no idea where the bookkeeping office was, so I asked some guys working on a service elevator and was directed to a low building behind the paddock.

"And Marketing?"

They both paused, and the older of the two straightened and pulled a greasy rag out of his back pocket. He wiped his hands, then gestured in the direction I'd been heading. "Over that way. A green door to the left of them glass doors."

I nodded my thanks and passed another bank of pari-mutuel windows and an ATM machine before being let through a set of gates that barricaded the paddock runway. So far, everyone I'd seen working frontside wore large ID badges with VISA printed across the bottom. I had an ID badge, too, but it wasn't going to get me where I wanted to go, and when I found the door that accessed the administrative offices, I saw I had another problem. A cardkey slot was built into the doorframe. As I stood there, a janitor walked around the corner, inserted his key, and went through the doorway.

I continued past as the door eased shut and thought about tactics. Attitude was everything, and acting like I belonged would go a long way toward gaining entry. I didn't really need to see Nicole's workplace, but any scrap of information I could gather might help me figure out what was going on. Once I reached the entrance to the Derby Museum, I turned around and headed back.

The guy manning the runway gates was a problem. He was the only person paying attention to his surroundings. I didn't look directly at him but sensed him tracking my progress across the open courtyard that would be crammed with thousands of people come Derby day.

Two girls dressed in navy overalls rounded a pillar and walked purposefully toward the door accessing the administrative offices. Timing my approach so that I would catch up to them as they reached the door, I withdrew Kessler's envelope and pretended to study it as I stepped in behind them. The first girl slotted her cardkey in the lock. They were talking about some guy and paid me little attention as I followed them into a long utilitarian hallway.

I found the Marketing office on the second floor. Its door stood open and accessed a medium-sized, windowless office crammed with four cubicles hugging the walls on either side of a narrow central aisle. A receptionist's desk faced the door. In the corner to my left, a television and VCR sat on a rolling cart alongside a row of file cabinets. I paused just inside the room. Although I could hear voices, they were muffled, and I was fairly certain that the office itself was deserted. I stepped past the receptionist's desk. There was an interior door at the end of the narrow aisle. It was closed, and that's where the voices originated. One voice now, a male's, explained something I couldn't discern. I glanced at my watch. Four-twenty. A Monday afternoon staff meeting.

The first cubicle on my right didn't have a nameplate, but the canvas partitions were pinned with family pictures—three teenaged boys, two dogs, a balding husband. I moved on to the next one. The desk was a mess. Yellow sticky notes all over the place, a pile of open binders, dried coffee cup rings on the few cleared surfaces. Not Nicole's style. The last cubicle across the aisle served as a common area with racks of phone books and binders. I backtracked to the first desk on the left and immediately suspected it belonged to Nicole.

A horse calendar was displayed prominently on the wall. I scanned the desktop, then glanced at the closed door at the end of the aisle before picking up a call slip centered on the blotter. Nicole's name was scrawled across the top margin. The message simply read *Your mother called.* From the lack of messages on her desk, I suspected her phone was set up with voicemail.

I glanced around the rest of her workspace. Pencils and pens stood upright in a mug depicting Sunday Silence, winner of the 115th Kentucky Derby. Her computer monitor was dark, but a red light pulsed on the tower, and a faint electronic hum competed with the buzz of fluorescent lights overhead. I pulled out my cell phone, depressed the END button, and cradled it against my waist while it powered down. I doubted anyone would hear the chime, but I didn't want to risk it. I lifted Nicole's phone out of its cradle, dialed my cell, and waited for it to ring through so I could capture her number, then I hung up.

A woman had taken over the meeting in the adjoining room. Although softer, her voice was more animated. I looked through Nicole's desk but found nothing out of the ordinary. Just the usual office paraphernalia. A bookshelf behind her chair held phonebooks, binders, and a row of composition books, the black-and-white kind similar to the ones I'd used in Chem. lab. Interesting. I'd seen a stack just like them on the coffee table in her apartment.

I withdrew one and fanned the pages. It contained notes from various meetings held earlier that year. Nicole had methodically dated each page in the upper right-hand corner. Another book held notes on advertising contacts. A third contained lengthy notes on QuarkXPress. As I slipped it back into place, one of the composition books farther down the row caught my eye.

The black binding had faded to gray, and when I inched it toward the edge of the shelf, I saw that the cover was mottled with brown stains. I opened it. The pages were dated four years earlier, but time alone wouldn't have discolored the book so thoroughly. As I leafed through pages containing notes on the day-to-day operation of a horse farm, I realized Nicole had carried it with her. It had probably been left baking in the sun on some farm truck's dash or, closer to hand, on a straw bale in a dusty barn.

The conference room door clicked open. Voices and laughter rolled into the outer office.

"When's the next meeting?" someone called as I jammed the notebook back into position. A heavyset woman had paused in the doorway with her focus directed back into the conference room. She flattened her palm on the doorframe. "Wednesday. Same time, same place."

I was in the main corridor before she had a chance to turn around.

Chapter Eleven

Corey had commandeered the chair in my absence. She slumped against the nylon webbing with the wool cooler wrapped around her shoulders. The thick fabric bunched up her silvery blond hair in a silken bob except for a few strands that floated above the rest, charged with static electricity. She'd propped her feet on the tack trunk, ankles crossed, a posture that might have appeared relaxed except for the fact that the girl could not keep still. She jounced her head and bumped her feet together, and as I drew closer, I heard her humming under her breath.

I smiled as I gripped the chair's backrest and leaned forward until my mouth was alongside her ear. "What are you doing?"

She twisted to face me. "How can you stand this?" she said, and a butterscotchy aroma wafted past my nose. "I'm going nuts here."

I straightened, stepped over to Storm's stall, and lifted a lightweight stable blanket off the tack trunk. "You have a CD player with you?" I asked as I ducked under the stall guard. "A paperback novel?"

"No." Corey rested her chin on her shoulder as she watched me unfold the blanket across Storm's back.

As I did up the surcingles, I said, "Don't you have a lot of down time when you're eventing? You know, between cross-country and dressage or whatever?"

Corey rolled her eyes at my ignorance. "Not as much as you'd think with the grooming and bathing and schooling. And don't forget the requisite wardrobe changes." She lifted her chin and gazed over the waist-high wall. The barns that surrounded 41 were largely deserted. "Unlike here," she said, "the barn area's crawling with people, and we all know each other, and now that most everyone hauls their campers to the shows these days, it's one big party after-hours. Card games, drinking, gossiping."

"The mornings are busy," I said as I checked Storm's water bucket and glanced at his haynet. I did the same for Ruskie before settling on a straw bale alongside Corey. I pulled out my notepad and cell and flipped it open.

She raised her eyebrows. "I thought you were heading out."

I hit the CALLS MISSED softkey. "While I was over there, I got a look at Nicole's desk."

"Impressive."

"Not really. The staff was in a meeting with no one left guarding the fort."

"Silly them."

I studied Corey. She looked cold even though her breeches and long-sleeved shirt were made of Polartec. Her purple knit vest was the same one she'd worn last February. She'd been cold then, too.

She planted her elbows on her knees and cradled her chin on her palms. "So, what are you going to do next?"

"If you're ready to work a shift," I said, "I'll head over to the hotel for a while."

She nodded. "Any instructions?"

"No. I'll be back for their night check at nine."

"That early?"

"Jay would have my hide if I didn't see to it myself." I planted my hands on my knees. "Do you need a break before I head out?"

"Nope. I'm good."

I let the notepad cover ease shut. Having extra barn help was well and good, but frankly, I was disappointed with Kessler's solution. Corey was capable enough, but I sure as hell wasn't going to leave her alone in the barn. Not at night. And exchanging places was problematic. Knowing her, she wouldn't think twice about walking, and the trip over the new Central Avenue Bridge was a desolate one. But if she caught on that I was trying to protect her, I suspected she'd be insulted.

As far as learning more about Nicole, I decided to go back to the hotel and shower, then make do with a couple of hours work before I relieved Corey. Convincing her to take a cab would be the hard part.

I stood, and as she tilted her head and looked into my eyes, I was all too aware of her beauty. Her pale skin was remarkably clear, with a hint of blush coloring her cheeks, and she had the most incredible blue-gray eyes. "Are you warm enough?" I asked, and somehow the question sounded way too intimate.

"Sure. I just didn't expect the end of April to be so chilly."

"It was thirty-one this morning."

"Brrr."

I scribbled my cell number on a blank sheet of notepaper and handed it to her. "In case you need anything."

She nodded. "Did you turn in that envelope while you were in the grandstand?"

"Yep."

"Well, you go ahead. The horses will be fine."

I smiled. "I know."

Fifteen minutes later, I strolled past the Hilton's front desk on my way to the elevator bay. I glanced in the business center as I passed and was surprised to find it empty. I backtracked, pushed open the glass door, and stepped into a room roughly the size of a walk-in closet. Two workstations occupied an L-shaped countertop, both up and running. An outdated printer sat on a stand to my right. The shower would have to wait.

I flipped open my notepad. Okay. Start with the basics.

I pulled the Greater Louisville phonebook off the shelf and nudged the mouse to bring up the desktop. I ran a general search on Nicole and came up empty. Trying a different approach, I keyed in "Nicole Austin" + "horse" and got nowhere. I linked her name with various equestrian terms with the same result. It seemed I had uncovered everything on the Internet that I was going to with my unofficial status and limited resources. If I wanted to learn more, I would have to find her or interview more of her acquaintances. So far, that hadn't gone well, either.

I redirected my focus to her ex-employer, racehorse trainer Bill Gannon. The search results listed page after page of news accounts covering his Derby campaign with Gone Wild. This was Gannon's sixth bid for the Derby, and Gone Wild was a heavy favorite.

Not surprisingly, Rudi Sturgill's name came up as I skimmed a dozen or so articles. I clicked on William Gannon Racing Stables' homepage. Like most trainers, he followed the racetrack circuit, but his base of operations, a farm on Dry Ridge Road in Routt, Kentucky, offered related services: breeding, sales prep, and lay-ups for horses needing a break from racing. I jotted down the phone number and address before leafing through the phonebook. Gannon's residential listing shared the same address. I copied down his home number.

I found nothing on his employee, Eduardo "Snoopy" Sanchez, though I would have been surprised if I had. Like most racetrackers, he lived a nomadic life, following the horses from track to track.

Since I'd lost Sturgill's business card along with my wallet, I pulled up Wellspring Farm's website and copied down the farm's contact information; then I clicked through the navigation links. The farm looked like every other topnotch thoroughbred breeding facility in Kentucky—extravagant barns, rolling pastureland crisscrossed with pristine four-board fencing, a perfectly harrowed training track—all of it reflecting a lifestyle steeped in tradition and funded by old money. And I thought *my* family was wealthy.

Next, I typed in Rudolph Sturgill and hit enter. The screen flickered and came back with over 9,000 hits. I examined several pages of search results. Many of the capsule summaries covered his bid for the Derby, but nearly half referenced his family's oil company.

Out of curiosity, I opened the most recent news articles on ACS Industries and learned that the company had been generating industry headlines for the past decade. Apparently their decision to upgrade to 4-D seismic imaging had profoundly strengthened their exploration capabilities, especially in the Gulf.

4-D? Did that mean what I thought? I skimmed the article and learned that 4-D seismic imaging combines seismic readings of a specific area over time. Then the data sequence is amalgamated to create time-lapse imagery that shows changes in fluid flow, viscosity, temperature, and saturation deep beneath the Earth's surface.

O-k-a-y.

The terminology reminded me of Paige's conversation at the Thunder party. What had she said? Something about an intermittent stream at the BGL interval and gases diffusing to the atmospheric sink. What the hell was an atmospheric sink, anyway? I leaned back in my chair and pictured her strolling down the length of the boardroom with the city's lights reflected in the glass behind her. She'd also said that something would be of no consequence in a very short time, but I couldn't now remember what. I jotted down *intermittent stream, BGL interval,* and *atmospheric sink* and felt damned silly doing it.

As I let my chair rock back onto all fours, a reference to ACS Industries on *OilOnline* caught my attention. Rumors and speculation abounded that ACS Industries' Exploration Technologies Department had made a significant breakthrough. Although details were vague to nonexistent, the hype seemed to be fueled by the following announcement.

On March 10th, ACS Industries entered into an agreement with a private company to acquire oil and natural gas properties in southeast Louisiana for $120 million in cash. The transaction includes a three-year exploration partnership covering over a million acres...

The door behind me opened. I glanced over my shoulder, and when I caught sight of Corey leaning into the room with her hand on the doorknob, I sprang to my feet. My chair spun across the tile.

I stepped toward her. "What's wrong?"

"Nothing. Sorry." She stepped inside and brushed her hand across her mouth as if she were hiding a fleeting smile. Her gaze flitted around the tiny workspace. "I didn't mean to startle you. Jay relieved me, and when I was walking down the corridor just now, I saw you in here."

"Hmm. What kind of shape's he in?"

"Good, I guess. With him, it's hard to tell." She moved closer, and the faint scent of horse barn trailed after her, displacing the metallic odor of warm electronic circuits. She glanced at the open workstation. "Can I help?"

The image of her looking up at me in the shedrow flashed in my mind. I'd been attracted to her, no question, but that didn't mean we couldn't work together. "Sure." I reeled in my chair and watched her get settled. She wiggled her mouse as I placed my notepad on the counter between us. "If you don't mind, bring up Yahoo's People Search, then go through these pages and look up every name and business that I've listed. Write down anything I don't have and anything that differs from the information I've already compiled, okay?"

Corey nodded, and as she waited for her screen to build, she looked at my monitor and scrunched her eyebrows. "Why are you reading about oil production?"

"Remember I told you Nicole seemed nervous that morning in the receiving barn?"

"Uh-huh."

"Well, until I figure out who's so desperate to get their hands on the mystery tape, and why, I might as well learn as much as I can about everyone who was in the shedrow that morning. Of course, her being nervous might not have anything to do with them or the fact that she disappeared later in the day, but it's all

I've got right now. Anyway, Sturgill was there. Plus, he's piqued my curiosity in other ways."

"How so? Because he invited you to the fireworks party?"

"That's certainly a factor, but there's something else about him that just doesn't feel right." I looked at my monitor. "I don't know. The guy's a paradox. He's smart and insightful, and with his family's backing, he could literally do anything he wanted, *be* anything he wanted, but he's content to just...." I leaned back in my chair. "I don't know, Corey. He doesn't seem to do much of anything."

"Except be a playboy."

"He doesn't even do that well."

Corey glanced over her shoulder and noticed that her screen was waiting for input. She keyed in Yahoo People Search and turned back around. "How old's this guy?"

"Hmm. I'd guess about ten years older than me. So, around thirty-three. Why?"

"That could be your answer right there. Guys are slower to mature," she said, and I felt myself smiling at her frankness. "A rich guy who doesn't have a reason to grow up, he doesn't need to be ambitious." She swiveled back around. "Where do you want me to write this stuff down?"

"In the notepad. Just pick up where I left off." I watched her for a moment, wondering what she thought of me.

I found ACS Industries homepage and clicked through the navigation links until I came to the directors and officers page. I read the biographical summary on Matthew Sturgill, Jr., Chairman of the Board and Chief Executive Officer. Rudi's father. Though factual and dryly written, his accomplishments were remarkable. After forty years of innovative leadership, Matthew Sturgill, Jr. appeared a tough act to follow. I could certainly appreciate how Rudi must feel, growing up in that family when he didn't have the desire or, according to his sister, aptitude to continue in his father's footsteps.

Rudi's older brother, however, seemed up to the challenge. After obtaining bachelor's degrees in accounting and finance and a master's in business administration, Matthew Sturgill the III had risen quickly through the ranks to the position of Senior Vice President.

I discovered a write-up on Paige under the Exploration Technologies Department. She'd gone to the University of Wyoming, where she'd earned bachelor's degrees in geochemistry and remote sensing and a master's in geophysics. At thirty-seven, she was senior scientist in charge of the department. No doubt about it, the girl was impressive.

As I recalled, Yaseen Haddad worked in her department, but not surprisingly, he wasn't listed on the site. I ran an independent search on his name and drew a blank. I switched to Google and keyed in "Haddad" + "Middle East" and found two links directing me to the same site which contained a list of email addresses. Four men had the same surname, but Yaseen was not among them. The directory was prominently linked to Assyria Online, so I clicked on the link and discovered that Assyria was not a recognized country but an area incorporating parts of Syria, Turkey, Iran, and Iraq.

"Hey, look at this," Corey said.

I swiveled around in my chair.

"When you click on this More-Information link in People Search, you get shuttled over to something called Intelius. Besides the current address, it tells you where they lived last." Corey tapped the screen. "See? Edward J. Utley used to live in Georgetown, and for a mere $49.95, you can get a background check that includes criminal history, sex offender check, bankruptcies, tax liens, legal judgments. You can even find his family members and neighbors and any aliases he might have used." She sat back in her chair. "This is scary."

I chuckled. "Where's he live now?"

"Five-twelve Poplar Hill Woods. Louisville."

"Where'd Nicole used to live?"

"I don't know. Let's see." Corey bent forward and placed her fingers on the keyboard. The screen flickered. "Midway."

Midway. I frowned. Rudi Sturgill lived in Midway. "Could you check everyone's past residence?"

"Sure. Oh, and I couldn't find anything on this Snoopy person."

"Try Eduardo Sanchez," I said.

"E-d-u-a-r-d-o?"

"You got it."

I turned back to my screen, ran a search on Utley, and found his company: Computer Management Services, headquartered in Lexington. I paused when I noticed the Storage and Data link. I'd assumed that the missing tape was either an audiocassette or video tape, but what if it contained electronic data? I ran a new search on "data tape" and viewed the latest in data storage. LTO Ultrium headed the list with a 200GB capacity. I slid my chair back, ducked down to read the label on the *hp* computer I was using, and confirmed what I'd already suspected. One tape could capture everything on a personal computer without the need for compression.

Corey turned to see what I was doing. "What's wrong?"

I told her what I'd found.

"Where would she get her hands on a computer tape?"

"I don't know." I scooted my chair closer to the counter and stared at the monitor. "What I can't figure is why those guys are convinced that I have anything to do with this."

I reached past Corey, picked up the notepad, and printed *Yaseen* and *Utley* since they were both involved with computers. I drew a circle around their names before sliding the pad back to Corey. The clock on the wall read seven-fifty.

I leaned back in my chair and rubbed my neck. "Utley lives in Louisville, right?"

Corey flipped over a page. "Yep. Poplar Hill Woods."

"Where does Yaseen live?"

"Clifton Road in Versailles."

I clicked back to Utley's computer company website and found the address: 692 Iron Works Way, Lexington. "Okay," I said, thinking out loud. "Yaseen lives in Versailles. Utley's company is based in Lexington. Nicole used to live in Midway. Rudi lives there now. All three towns form a tight little triangle, but I don't see how their paths would have crossed. Unless...."

I sat forward and keyed in Millcroft Farm, the name of the facility where Utley boarded his horses. Kessler told me the farm was located in Jefferson County, but some operations had satellite farms, and if they had a division in the East....

I clicked open the website, then scrolled toward the bottom and found the address: Millcroft Farm, 2957 Dry Ridge Road, Routt, Kentucky. Not what I'd expected, but interesting nonetheless.

Corey peered over my shoulder. "What?"

"Read off the address for Gannon Racing Stables."

She flipped through the notepad. "2700 Dry Ridge Road."

"One thing I know for certain, Nicole worked for Bill Gannon at the track. If she also worked at his farm on Dry Ridge Road, there's a damn good chance she knows Edward J. Utley."

Chapter Twelve

Tuesday morning, the alley between barns flooded with light as the sun cleared the horizon and cast a pink hue on the concrete block walls. I tossed a straw bale into Ruskie's empty stall and slid a cursory glance over Storm as he poked his head into the aisle. His attention focused on a camera crew as they hoisted equipment onto their shoulders and prepared to film a Derby horse being bathed in the alley. Water vapor, tinted pink in the early morning light, rose from the colt's top line as a groom slopped a minty brace over the bay's sweat-soaked skin.

You bring home a win eleven days from now, I thought as my gaze slid past Storm and settled on Corey, you had better get used to all that attention. Rudi Sturgill stood beside her as he studied his horse and speculated on their chances come the first Saturday in May. Both Gone Wild and Gallant Storm had gone to the track in the dark, when the new day was just a whisper on the eastern horizon, and Rudi had hung around to catch an interview or two and to watch his horse cool out. And, for all I knew, to watch Corey.

Farther down the shedrow, Bill Gannon and Snoopy Sanchez emerged from one of the tack rooms. They paused in the aisle while Sanchez spoke rapidly. Gannon had his hands shoved deep in his trouser pockets. When Sanchez paused for breath, Gannon appeared to question him, because the Hispanic nodded in the affirmative.

I stepped into Ruskie's stall, unfolded my knife, and popped off the baling twine. As luck would have it, I had spent the night in the barn, although I could not swear to the fact that I had actually slept. Jay had called around nine-thirty, shortly after I'd finished a late meal in the hotel's restaurant. Not surprisingly, his overambitious return to work had triggered a relapse.

I thought about the progress I'd made with the Internet searches as I shook out the flakes of sweet-smelling straw. Lack of progress might have been a more apt description, but at least I hadn't hit a wall. Not yet. I still had a few avenues to explore if Nicole didn't show, but in all honesty, I wouldn't have been surprised to catch a glimpse of her leading a tour through the backside. For all I knew, she could have steered clear of whatever trouble she might have gotten herself into, or made amends with whoever was after the tape.

Sometime around two in the morning, I had considered the fact that the Maxima I'd seen parked at the curb didn't necessarily have to belong to Nicole. I had assumed it did, and that assumption was most likely correct, but I hadn't looked at the registration. The idea that the car did not belong to Nicole triggered all kinds of possibilities.

What if she had a boyfriend who worked at Churchill? The Maxima could be his. Either way, when she discovered that her apartment had been trashed, she might have gone to stay with him. As I bent to pick up the few remaining flakes, a subtle shift in the level of light and sound filtering through the doorway caused the hair on the back of my neck to tingle. I straightened and looked over my shoulder as Bill Gannon stepped into the stall. His face was flushed, and an ugly, distended vein throbbed over his temple.

He moved toward me and unclenched his teeth. "I want to know why you've been asking questions about my personal life."

I didn't say anything.

He stepped closer, and my eyes cut to the pitchfork that I'd left propped by the door.

"Who the hell do you think you are, questioning my help and stirring up trouble?" His breath smelled foul, a combination of stale coffee and poor dental hygiene.

"Seems like Sanchez is the one who's trying to cause trouble."

Gannon narrowed his eyes. "You keep your nose out of my business, understand? If I hear that you've so much as uttered a word to anyone, about me or my horses or my personal life, I will ruin you. And your father, too." He spun around.

"Where's Nicole?"

Gannon's shoulders tensed under his nylon jacket. He turned to face me. "I have no idea what Nicole told you," he whispered, his voice husky with emotion. "But know this. I wield a great deal of power in this town, and you and your father will wish you'd never set foot on these grounds if you cross me."

He spun around and charged out of the stall, and the unexpected movement startled a horse being led down the shedrow. The colt threw up his head and lunged forward, precipitating an annoyed string of oaths from his handler. Oaths, I assumed, by tone only.

I stepped to the doorway and watched the colt prance down the shedrow with his handler leaning against the horse's shoulder as he struggled to contain their forward momentum. I looked to the right and caught a glimpse of Gannon exiting the barn. Corey and Rudi stared openly at me, undoubtedly wondering what the hell was going on.

Ignoring them, I slipped back out of sight and grabbed my pitchfork. I worked the tines through the bedding, fluffing the straw and banking it against the walls. I was shaking out the last flake when I heard them move into the doorway.

"What?" I said. When they didn't answer, I turned around. They stood shoulder to shoulder, framed by the thick doorposts. "What?"

"You tell us," Rudi said.

"You'll have to ask him. I'm not supposed to talk about it."

"The hell...?"

I shrugged. "You want to know what Gannon's problem is, you're going to have to speak to him."

Rudi narrowed his eyes. "This is bullshit."

I looked past them, at the constant stream of people and horses. Ruskie would be back in a couple of minutes, and I hadn't set up for his bath. I stepped to the doorway and waited for them to move.

"Steve?"

I sighed. "Don't worry about it, Rudi. Now, if you'll excuse me...." I slipped past them.

Corey glanced at Rudi, then silently watched me splash Vetrolin into two wash buckets. She trailed after me when I went to fill them with hot water.

"What's going on?" she whispered once we'd reached the faucets.

I cranked open the hot water spigot. "Word got back to Gannon that I've been asking questions about his relationship with Nicole."

She pursed her lips. "Oh. Think he knows more than he should?"

"Hard to tell." I switched out buckets and watched the water swirl through the green liniment. "He'd overreact if he had anything to do with Nicole's disappearance, but if he's been fooling around with her, anyone asking questions about the two of them would freak him out." I shrugged. "It cuts both ways."

"Hmm. I see what you mean." She crossed her arms and chewed on her lower lip as she stared pensively into the foaming water. She looked up and caught me smiling at her. "What?"

"Nothing." I twisted the spigot closed and asked her to go back inside and get a lead out of the tack trunk.

The morning routine wound down without further incident, and by ten-thirty Tuesday morning, I was standing on the sidewalk across from Nicole's house. The Maxima looked as undisturbed as it had the last time I'd been in the neighborhood. Moisture from the branches jutting over the pavement had pocked the powdery grit that coated the roof and hood.

I glanced around, then casually worked the cuff of my sweatshirt over my hand as I crossed the street. I made sure the fabric covered my fingertips before I tried the door handle. Someone had locked the car.

I rapped on Nicole's front door, then circled around back when no one answered. The glass pane was still missing, but someone had locked up. Hoping like hell that that someone had been Nicole, I squatted and shifted the curtain out of the gap. A glass shard tumbled from the sash.

The room appeared exactly as it had Sunday afternoon.

Goddamn it.

Nicole hadn't been home as I'd hoped, which meant the police, or possibly her landlord, had secured the apartment. The police. I'd need to do something about them, sooner than later. And I sure as shit was not looking forward to *that*. Talking to a detective had seemed daunting Sunday evening, when I'd been exhausted. Today was no better, and possibly worse. In hindsight, I realized that the anonymous call and delay in reporting what I knew had been a huge mistake on several levels. My behavior would appear more suspicious, not less. And had I jeopardized Nicole's safety by not acting? I hoped not.

Finding her keys in the street Friday evening hadn't spurred me to call the cops, and if it had, so what? Her apartment hadn't been disturbed at that point, and even if the call had made it past Dispatch, no cop in his right mind would have acted on those circumstances alone. Of course, that had changed by Sunday afternoon.

A door hinge creaked and a faint vibration traveled through the wooden planks beneath my feet. I turned as a heavyset woman stepped onto the porch with a watering can in her hand. She had come out of the neighboring apartment and was turning to close her screen door when she caught sight of me. She froze, then eased the door wide, giving herself a clear path back into her kitchen.

I straightened and nodded, kept my hands visible, my arms loose at my side. "Morning. I'm looking for Nicole Austin."

The woman studied me for a moment. "She isn't home."

"I see that," I said as I turned my head and briefly glanced at Nicole's kitchen table through the panes of wavy glass. "It appears her apartment's been broken into."

"It has."

"I work at Churchill. We're worried because she hasn't come in this week, or called. Do you have any idea where she is?"

My apparent insider's knowledge, combined with the reference to Churchill, seemed to reassure her because she eased the screen door back against the frame.

"No. The last time I saw her was around seven Wednesday evening." She nodded as if reviewing the scene in her mind. "I remembered the time because I'd just stepped outside to catch a smoke after the news, and Nicole was coming up those steps with a grocery sack in her arms. She always uses the back entrance when she's been shopping. It's easier that way with only one door to contend with."

"You said 'remembered.' You've spoken to someone already?"

She nodded, then crossed over to Nicole's side of the porch and tipped the watering can above a cracked plastic flowerpot containing a wilted plant. "The police were here Sunday, around suppertime, interviewing everyone in the building."

Sunday. After I'd called in the B&E. "Did a detective come out?"

"Not that I know of. Two patrol cops were here though."

"What kind of questions did they ask? Do they know where she is?"

"I don't think so. They wanted to know if anybody saw or heard anything to do with the break-in, and they wanted to know when we saw Nicole last. Stuff like that."

"Do they know when the break-in occurred?"

"Uh-uh. From what I hear, nobody in the building knew about it."

"You didn't notice this glass being out?" I said, surprised.

She lowered the watering can, and water dribbled onto the wooden planks as she turned and studied Nicole's door. "No, honey. When it comes to the weekends, I wouldn't have noticed an elephant sitting on this porch. I work the dayshift at Baptist, seven to seven Friday through Sunday. Critical Care."

"Did you talk to Nicole when you saw her Wednesday?"

"Sure. About Derby…and Thunder. I don't really follow the races, but she does."

"So, as far as you know, she might have been away Thursday and Friday."

"Oh, no. She was home both days, at least in the mornings. I heard her television switch on, the one she keeps on the kitchen counter. I hear it every morning when she's getting ready for work."

"You didn't see her Friday, after work?"

She shook her head.

"Have you seen anyone out of the ordinary hanging around here in the past couple weeks? Anything unusual?"

"Can't say that I have…except for you."

I smiled. "What kind of mood was she in Wednesday? Did she seem nervous? Preoccupied?"

"Now that you mention it, she did seem kind of anxious, but I thought she just needed to get into her apartment so she could put down her groceries."

"What did she say about the Derby and Thunder?"

"Nothing much. She talked about some of the horses—her favorites—and she asked if I was going to Thunder, but I never do. It's too crowded."

"Which horses did she mention?"

She shrugged. "Like I said, I don't follow the races."

"Does she have a boyfriend?"

"You ask the same questions the cops did. I don't think she's been seeing anyone since winter, when she broke up with the fella she was dating."

"Do you know his name?"

"No. I don't see any of my neighbors that much, including Nicole. Most of them work during the week and are off on the weekends, which is exactly opposite my schedule."

"Can you describe him?"

"Um…well no. Not really. I don't think I ever saw him in the daylight. Wintertime, it gets dark so early, and the lighting isn't the best this end of the block. I'd see him out on the street, coming to pick her up or drop her off. He didn't often come in, though."

"Did he walk her to the door?"

"Sometimes. Sometimes not. I'll tell you this, he's well-to-do. Wore expensive-looking suits. Nicole always dressed up when they went out, which she doesn't do, otherwise. Oh, and he drives a sporty car, like a BMW or Porsche."

BMW or Porsche? How could she not know the difference? "Do you recall anything else about him? His height? Hair color? Anything like that?"

"He was clean-cut. Kept his hair real short."

"What color?"

"Blond. Light brown. I'm not sure."

I described Bill Gannon and asked if she'd ever seen a guy like that stop by to see Nicole.

"White hair?"

I nodded.

"No. He doesn't sound familiar."

I thanked her for her time and was heading down the steps when I remembered what had brought me back to Nicole's neighborhood in the first place. I paused midway down the flight and pivoted around. She hadn't turned back to her apartment but was standing there watching me as she absentmindedly tapped the watering can against her thigh. Water droplets darkened the front of her jeans.

"Is that Nicole's car out front?" I said. "The black Maxima with the Churchill sticker on the windshield?"

"Well, I didn't think of that, but it sure is." She frowned. "So how'd she get to wherever she was headed?"

"Good question."

I cut between houses and was approaching the end of the block when a black sedan cornered the turn off Patterson. The Ford accelerated down Nicole's street with dappled sunlight flashing across the windshield and shimmering off a pair of antennas that sprouted from the trunk. I glanced at the fat tires and their economy hubcaps. A cop car. The driver remained focused on the road, but when the woman riding shotgun leaned forward to check me out, I caught her movement and looked straight ahead, feigning disinterest. If I were a cop working Nicole's disappearance, I'd be curious about anyone I saw in her neighborhood.

The whine of the heavy engine throttled back a notch, and it was all I could do to keep from looking over my shoulder. When I reached the corner, I crossed Everett at a leisurely pace. I did not glance down the block but kept my gaze focused straight ahead. Once I was no longer in their line of sight, I cut across Patterson and picked up my pace. In two blocks, I would reach the bus stop on Bardstown Road.

When I talked to the cops, I wanted the interview set on my terms. Getting stopped on the street and questioned was something I'd just as soon avoid. As I approached Bardstown, a TARC bus motored past, heading outbound. Once I reached the corner, I scanned the traffic traveling into the city. Cars, pickups, a UPS truck. No bus. No cop car circling the block, either.

I turned right with the intention of walking to the next stop. The more distance I could put between those two detectives and myself, the better. If Nicole's busybody neighbor intercepted them, I had no doubt that she'd mention my visit, and if the cops thought there was a chance in hell that I was still in the vicinity, they'd come looking for me. I crossed Grinstead, watched the traffic, checked my back.

The street hummed with a shifting kaleidoscope of movement and noise: the stream of traffic and resultant Doppler effect pulsing off storefronts, an occasional shout, music playing on a radio, and beneath it all, the low throb of a diesel engine sounded from a delivery truck idling by the curb, stalling traffic and adding to the congestion.

I scanned the outbound vehicles funneling onto Bardstown from Baxter Avenue. I'd catch an eastbound bus if I had to, then figure out a transfer that would get me close to the track, but heading downtown was my first choice. When I was half a block from the next stop, I glanced over my shoulder. A TARC bus heading in my direction had caught the light at Grinstead.

Great. I'd be on my way in no time. I watched the cross traffic thump over a patch of rough pavement near the curb and stream past the bus' grillwork. A silver Tahoe eased toward the intersection, but what caught my attention and sent a sickening sense of dread coiling through my gut was the sight of the front panel of a familiar black sedan impatiently riding the Tahoe's bumper. The right turn signal flared, and as the car slipped farther into view, I spun around.

Don't panic. Think.

I ducked into an alcove carved out of a storefront. When I yanked open the door and practically launched myself into a plain-looking restaurant, an elderly Asian gentleman, with his hands full of silverware bundled in paper napkins, looked up from setting a table.

The glass door swung shut, dampening the street noise as I headed for a counter situated along the back wall. A casual look through the storefront windows was all it would take for them to see me. I slipped off my denim jacket and tucked it under my arm. The burgundy sweatshirt that I wore beneath it was not what they'd be looking for.

"Would you like to be seated?" the old man said as I strode past.

I paused and turned my head in his direction. "Do you have carryout?"

He nodded slowly and gestured toward the back of the room. "Yes, yes…." But I'd already moved past him.

The two women seated at a table midway down the room exchanged a surreptitious look, and I could feel their gaze boring into my back as I rested my hand on the countertop. Paper menus with *Lemongrass Café Take-Out* printed across the top lay stacked alongside the cash register. A beautiful Asian girl, half-hidden by the laminate counter, rose to her feet.

"May I help you?"

Stalling for time, I peeled off the top menu and was surprised when the thin paper did not vibrate in my grip. My hands were steady despite a rapid spike in my respiration rate. My forehead felt damp, and I could gauge my heart rate by the surge of blood pulsing along my spine. "What do you recommend?"

"Everything is good," she said in heavily accented English before launching into a well-rehearsed spiel.

I half listened as I formulated a plan. The next bus heading in either direction wouldn't come by for another ten to fifteen minutes, possibly longer, and I had no intention of spending that time on the street.

I shouldn't have felt so panicked. I'd done nothing wrong. But once I'd committed to eluding those two detectives, the unwelcome physiological response of fight or flight had dumped a shitload of adrenaline into my bloodstream, a state that did not support an innocent demeanor. As I drew in a ragged breath, I realized the young woman was waiting for a response.

I scanned the menu. "I'd like two orders of E17 to go."

She scribbled a notation on her pad. "Anything else?"

"No. How long will it take?"

She looked past me when the door to the street opened. Shoes scraped across the metal sill before the carpet swallowed the sound of footsteps. "Ten to fifteen minute," she said, but her gaze remained focused past my shoulder.

The door thudded closed as I strained to hear what was going on behind me. Why hadn't the old man asked about a table?

My muscles tensed.

A man and woman stepped up to the counter on my left. Not the cops.

I exhaled air that had snagged in my lungs and swallowed hard. "Could you put a rush on that please, and where's your restroom?"

"Through there," she said as she lifted a graceful arm and pointed to a door set in the back wall. "On your right."

"Thank you."

As I maneuvered behind the couple, I casually swept my gaze around the room, taking in the layout and glancing through the windows fronting the sidewalk. General traffic on the street. No black Ford trolling the boulevard. The women seated beneath a cheesy oriental print watched me openly now. I pushed through the swinging door and took a deep breath laced with the mingled aromas of exotic spices and fried food. A head-high stack of plastic pallets flanked the entrance to a narrow corridor that ran the length of the building. At the far end, a battered metal door had been propped open, admitting a brilliant shaft of sunlight and a refreshing breeze. The restroom was off to my right.

I slipped inside, locked the door, and stood in front of a stained porcelain sink with a corroded faucet. A cracked mirror hung on the wall. As I stared at my reflection, I was surprised to see that I looked perfectly normal despite the buzz of energy sizzling through my veins and tensing my muscles. I cranked on the hot water and splashed my face. Watched the water trickle down my nose and drip off my chin.

What the fuck was wrong with me? I grabbed some paper towels off a metal shelf and dried my face. How in the hell could a simple class assignment have snowballed into this? I now saw that whenever I chose to contact the police—whether last Sunday afternoon, this morning, or next week—I would automatically become a suspect. Guilt by association, no question.

I wadded up the towels and shot them into the trash.

Chapter Thirteen

Corey bit her lip as she wrestled a stubborn piece of shrimp out of the cardboard carton with a pair of ungainly chopsticks. Her hair slipped forward as she bent over the carton and frowned.

Now that the temperature had crept into the upper fifties, she had shed the bulky jacket that she'd worn earlier, although I wasn't surprised to find her still wearing the purple fleece vest. The sun felt warm, but the concrete walls held a chilly dampness that seeped into clothing and stiffened sore muscles. Corey had switched out yesterday's Polartec breeches for a pair of snug denim jodhpurs. Like most barn employees, she wore leather work boots, but the fluorescent green socks that bunched around her calves were not exactly standard fare.

She gave up on correct form and used the chopsticks to shovel a piece of shrimp along the carton flap and into her mouth. "A person could starve eating with these things," she said around a mouthful of food.

I chuckled as I flipped open my cell phone.

She slid her gaze my way; then she leaned sideways and looked pointedly at the Lemongrass Café bag that bulged with empty soda cans, balled-up napkins, and my food carton. "Of course, you cheated and used a fork."

"Practical."

Corey rolled her eyes and sighed as she leaned against the stall front and lowered the take-out box to her lap. "I didn't know you were going to stop somewhere."

"Neither did I."

She looked at me quizzically from her perch on the tack trunk.

Once I had left the restroom at the Lemongrass, I had walked down the narrow corridor past the kitchen and stood in the doorway that accesses a dingy, litter-strewn alley. The next cross street, Highland I believed it was, cuts across the mouth of the alley a short distance to the left. While I stood there watching the traffic, the sounds of the city competed with the hectic work taking place at my back. A constant hiss of steam and sporadic clang of metal pots amid voices spoken in a language I did not understand merged with the rhythmic, rapid-fire tapping of a knife's blade against wood as one of cooks worked at a cutting board.

I was thinking that I had stood there long enough, when the black Crown Vic cruised northeast on Highland, heading away from Bardstown. Sunlight flooded through the passenger side window, and I got a good look at the woman. A petite brunette with short hair, a slight frame, and excellent carriage. She might have seen me if she'd twisted hard in her seat and looked over her shoulder, but she had scanned the length of the alley before shifting her attention to the cluster of buildings and parking bays coming up on her right.

I had backed into the shadowy corridor and watched until the car slipped from view. Worrying about getting out of the neighborhood unseen, I had collected my order ten minutes later. But in the end, when the next bus lumbered down the street, inbound as I'd hoped, I had stepped outside, signaled to the driver, and boarded without incident.

Sitting in the relative quiet of the shedrow, I relaxed into my chair and watched Corey probe the aromatic mix of rice and tender vegetables while I considered the extent of police involvement in Nicole's disappearance. I had to admit, I was surprised that a missing person's case, minus substantive evidence that she'd come to harm, had warranted the involvement of two detectives. When Corey's brother had gone missing under mysterious circumstances, the cops had taken a report and asked a few questions, and that was about it. Maybe the Louisville cops did things differently, but their presence had an ominous feel to it. At the same time, judging by their interest in me, I doubted they had many leads.

Corey unearthed another chunk of shrimp.

"You don't like rice?" I said.

"Umm…umm." She wiggled her chopsticks at me while she chewed and swallowed. She took a sip of Diet Coke, then dragged the back of her hand across her mouth. "This is heavenly. Hot and spicy and sweet at the same time, but I try not to eat too many carbs."

"Oh, sure," I said, and she arched an eyebrow and looked at me funny.

"What do you mean by that?"

"Oh, just that it seems everyone's doing that these days."

She allowed her gaze to settle on my body. "Not everyone. Some of us are lucky."

I grinned, and when I stood and stretched, she averted her eyes and bent to her meal. She nudged a string bean and pineapple chunk aside before swirling the chopsticks through the rice.

I glanced at the horses as I strolled down the shedrow, wanting to put a little space between us. I hoped to catch Detective James Ralston at his desk and preferred that Corey not be constantly reminded of her brother if I could help it. Not that Ralston had assisted in that case. He hadn't, but my line of questioning might dredge up all kinds of memories.

I keyed in his number, checked my watch. Tuesday afternoon, twelve-twenty.

"C.I.U., Ralston."

At the sound of his voice, I pictured Ralston as I'd seen him last, his haggard expression at odds with the sharply creased suit he wore as he stood at the foot of my hospital bed after I had been shot for the second time in my life. The events of that miserably hot July had severed any vestige of innocence that I'd managed to hold onto.

"Hi, this is Steve."

"Steve…what's going on?" he said with caution resonating in his voice.

"I have some procedural questions for you."

"Hypothetical, I hope."

"For the most part."

"What the hell's that supposed to mean?"

"Well, I'm not involved in anything, not officially. Not yet. But I'd like to understand the typical response to the following scenario."

"You're talking police response, there *is* no typical."

"I know," I said, and I did. Tax base and budgetary considerations came into play more often than I would have guessed.

"What's your scenario, then, and I'm using that term loosely, you understand?"

I grinned. "A department gets an anonymous 911 call reporting—"

"What size department?"

"Louisville."

"What are you doing in Kentucky?"

"It's a long story. Anyway, they get a call reporting—"

"From you…?"

"Okay. From me."

"Let's just drop the hypothetical bullshit, then, shall we?"

I sighed. "Okay. I reported a B&E and possible missing person's case. When patrol arrived, they discovered that the apartment had been broken into and tossed, and—"

"Tell me you didn't do that…."

"No. I didn't. I just discovered it," I said. "After a little legwork, the responding officers figured out who the tenant is—a young woman—and they discovered her car parked out front with the keys lying in the foot well. My question is, what would happen after that? Would they put out some kind of an alert, like a BOLO? Would they process the apartment?"

"I assume they didn't find anyone when they cleared the rooms?"

"I don't think so."

"Were there signs of a struggle? Blood? Furniture tipped over?"

"Not that I saw."

"And by 'tossed,' describe what you mean."

"Kitchen cabinets rummaged through, books pulled off shelves, sofa cushions out of place."

"Not a typical B&E, then. Unless they were searching for drugs."

"Not drugs. They were looking for something else."

Ralston didn't speak for a moment. "What," he said slowly, "were they looking for?"

"A tape of some sort."

"A tape?" he said with dread. "And how do you know that?"

I recounted the events of the last five days, how my project had led me to finding Nicole's keys in the street, the attack at Sully's, my hotel room being tossed, then Nicole's apartment. How no one had seen her since Friday.

Except for the sound of a ringing phone that drifted over the line, my summary was met with silence. "Are you there?"

"Do you know who's running the case?" Ralston said with a tight voice.

"No."

"You do realize, with the project you've been working on, when they get around to talking to you—and they will get around to it—you'll have prime suspect stamped on your forehead?"

"It's crossed my mind."

"Shit, they'll be licking their chops, and if they can find just one witness to place you in the neighborhood the evening she disappeared, they just might terminate any other line of investigation they've got going because you look so damned good for it."

"That's what I was afraid of."

"I'll call them and track down the lead detective. In the meantime, I want you to sit tight. Do *not* go anywhere near her apartment or place of employment."

"She works at Churchill."

"Jesus. In the barns?"

"No. Frontside."

He sighed heavily. "Keep a low profile until I get back to you. At that point, you'll need to go in and talk to them."

The sound of a diesel engine grew louder until the vibrations throbbed off Barn 38's concrete block wall.

"Getting back to your original question, patrol's response when they arrived at the scene would have been complicated if they couldn't find someone to state that the woman was, in fact, missing and that the entry was unauthorized. At this point, you have a little more knowledge than they do, but think about it. All you really have are guesses."

"True."

"There are all kinds of oddball reasons for the apartment to have been left in disarray and for the resident's car to be sitting unlocked at the curb. As long as there's no evidence of violence, and no immediate reason for the responding officers to believe she was missing against her will, or endangered, the apartment wouldn't be processed."

"Really?"

"If the case turns out to be a kidnap or homicide, and they've processed the scene blind like that, without leads and a warrant, the suspect could turn out to be someone like an ex-boyfriend with clothes still in her closet. A judge might see those circum-stances as involving an expectation of privacy on the part of the suspect, and they'd lose all evidence from the apartment. If and when they develop evidence that the victim is missing non-vol-untarily, they'd get a warrant to cover themselves."

"I hadn't thought about it like that." I leaned against the wall and watched a trash truck coast down the access road while a ground crew spread out to collect the drums left between barns. "Okay, by the time Monday rolled around, they would have discovered that she'd missed work. She didn't take off ahead of time, and she didn't call in, all of which is unusual for her."

"Assuming the follow-up investigation included checking her place of employment, new information like that would likely trigger another round of questioning. But that still wouldn't be enough to kick the case into high gear unless they heard that she was afraid of someone or that she had a protective order on file, or her boss acted like he had something to hide. Anything like that would be enough to change the complexion of the case, but her missing work would not, even combined with the B&E."

"Protective order? That would be on file at the courthouse, right?"

"Her name would be in the civil files with a DV case number that you'd have to look up in family court."

"DV?"

"Domestic violence."

"I've checked both courts, criminal and civil. There's nothing on her."

"What about her neighbors? Do you know what information they had to offer?"

"Nothing, as far as I can tell."

"With what you've given me then, I'd predict a moderate investigation at best, until new information becomes available. New information, like you snooping around the apartment building asking questions, then eluding the cops."

"They can't prove I was eluding them," I said. "They didn't circle back until they spoke to Nicole's neighbor, and they certainly didn't see me duck into the restaurant."

"They won't need to prove anything. They already have enough to pique their curiosity."

"Hmm."

"Look, I'm due back in court and probably won't speak with them until tomorrow." Ralston reminded me to stay as far away from the case as possible until I heard back; then he disconnected.

I closed my cell. The trash truck had moved to another section of the backside, and the music it had obscured earlier drifted between barns. A Latino band. Across the alley in Barn 43, a groom rolled dried bandages into compact little bundles and stacked them on the sill while a blacksmith's truck pulled into the alley alongside 36. I pivoted around. A narrow slice of sunlight angled past the roof overhang and spilled over the waist-high wall, sketching a shimmering line down the length of the shedrow. Most of the stall doorways were empty, the horses presumably dozing in their stalls.

Corey sat on the tack trunk with her knees pulled up to her chest and her arms folded around her shins. Her take-out carton lay discarded beside her with the chopsticks poking out of the bed of rice like rabbit ears.

She looked so tiny; it amazed me that she handled the horses as well as she did. Not only did she gallop for a couple of trainers, including Kessler, she evented her own horse, a sport that demanded a high degree of skill and courage from both horse and rider. The jumps consisted of massive solid structures, some incorporating huge drops down earthen banks and tricky water obstacles, all taken at a gallop.

She rested her cheek on her knee and watched me walk toward her with an expression I could not read. As I drew closer, she released her legs and crossed them. Her cell phone rested beside the Lemongrass carton. It hadn't been there earlier.

"Mr. Kessler called," Corey said when I reached her. "He was just checking in. Said he'd call you later."

I nodded as I picked up her carton. I raised an eyebrow. "Are you done with this?"

"Yep."

I collected our trash, retrieved the fortune cookie packets, and handed them to Corey.

"Are you heading out, then?" she said.

I shook my head. "I need to be here at four to grain the horses. It hardly seems worthwhile going back to the hotel. Why don't you take a break and come back later this evening?"

Corey laid the packets on the trunk lid, gathered her phone and coat, and slipped to the ground. Her fingers brushed my hand as she took the trash bag then turned and headed toward the exit. "I'll be back at four," she said over her shoulder. "Then you can take a break for as long as you like."

I glanced at my hand, then stood immobile in the center of the aisle, feeling like a damned fool while the guard hustled to his feet and beamed at Corey when she nodded in his direction. We both watched her cut over to the access road.

Get a grip, Cline. She's just a friend, and that's all there is to it. She probably thinks of you as a brother which is not a bad thing, considering.

I swung the folding chair into position in front of Storm's stall, took out my notepad and cell, and sat down. Okay, I was supposed to lay low, and I couldn't think of a more out-of-the-way place than Churchill's backside, mid-afternoon, before the start of the spring meet. However, staying away from Nicole's neighborhood did not mean I was without options.

Besides being a Churchill employee, Nicole had worked on the backside for Bill Gannon Racing Stables, but knowing her entire work history would be advantageous and an avenue I had yet to explore. My instructor could access that kind of information with a few keystrokes, but I seriously doubted he would willingly supply me with it. But I knew someone who would. I ran through my stored numbers and called Kenneth Newlin.

We had met during fifth period Physics class in tenth grade. I'd seen him a couple of times since graduation, but our lives had followed wildly divergent courses, and the last I'd heard, he was working for the National Security Agency a couple of miles east of Laurel.

My call got snagged by his voicemail and an invitation to leave a message.

"Hey, Kenneth. This is Steve Cline. Call me when you get a chance." I left my number, then disconnected and moved to plan B.

I flipped through my notepad until I found the number for Rudi Sturgill's Wellspring Farm in Midway. I keyed *67 to block their caller ID, then dialed the farm's office. A woman came on the line and asked if she could help me.

"Yes, please. This is Greg Hogan calling from Limekiln Racing Stables in Conyers, Georgia. I'm running an employment check on Nicole Anne Austin. She listed you as a reference, and I'm trying to verify her dates of employment and ascertain her work habits."

"I'm sorry, but you'll have to speak to the office manager. She's currently on vacation and won't be back until Monday, the second."

"Thank you."

Not unexpectedly, I hit a dead end when I tried to run a similar ploy past ACS Industries. Their Human Resources Department suggested I send a request on company letterhead with a signed release. Edward Utley's Computer Management Services required the same formality. Nicole working for either company would have been surprising. On the other hand, Millcroft Farm, where Utley currently boarded his young stock, was a plausible choice. I called them only to learn that Nicole had never worked there.

Rudi Sturgill, Edward Utley, Bill Gannon. Three men who had been in the barn Friday morning. Three men I needed to confirm or eliminate as potential suspects in Nicole's disappearance. As far as her work history went, that left me with Bill Gannon. Nicole had worked for him at the track, but what really piqued my curiosity was whether or not she had worked at his farm, away from the public eye. Sanchez either hadn't known or didn't want to tell me, but if Gannon was as lascivious as his groom made him out to be, having her close to hand would have been more accommodating than a racetrack atmosphere.

I flipped through my notepad until I found the number for Gannon Racing Stables, 2700 Dry Ridge Road. I repeated my spiel.

"Austin, did you say?" -

"Yes, ma'am. Nicole Anne."

"One moment, please." One moment lengthened to five, then seven before she came back on the line. "She worked here from June, 2002, to July, 2003."

"In what capacity?"

"She filled in where needed. Prepping for sales, backing horses for the first time, and she may have worked the foal shift, though I'm not positive." Paper rustled in the background. "Yes, here it is. Her hours indicate that she foaled out for half a season."

Shit, what else would I ask if this call were legit? "How would you describe her work ethic?"

"I never heard any complaints, but you'll want to speak to the foreman." She gave me his name and number.

"Thank you."

Closing the phone, I scribbled the foreman's contact information in my notepad, though I had no intention of calling him. Slipping a bit of subterfuge past a receptionist whose days were consumed by the paperwork end of the business was one thing, speaking to Nicole's ex-boss was something else altogether.

I moved Bill Gannon's name to the top of my suspect list, followed closely by Snoopy Sanchez and Edward Utley. Sanchez because of his association with both Nicole and Gannon, and Utley because there was a damned good chance he'd crossed paths with Nicole. Gannon and Utley's horses practically hung their heads over a common fence, the farms were that close.

I printed *Gannon Racing Stables (June '02 to July '03)* and underlined it. June of '02, I'd just graduated from the BLS, otherwise known as Boys' Latin School of Maryland. Thirteen years of starchy academics and stringent discipline as well as camaraderie. Kenneth had gone on to NSA, and I'd gone on to…muck stalls. I smiled. I had no doubt royally fucked with their statistics.

I drew a circle around '03. Nicole's composition notebook, the one in her office that had appeared so out of place tucked among the crisp black-and-white marbled editions, had been dated 2003.

Chapter Fourteen

Not for the first time, I questioned whether I'd done the right thing by offering to be Corey's escort for what she expected would be her last night in Louisville.

Jay had returned to work shortly after two o'clock, looking well rested and healthy, a development that precipitated our having the rest of Tuesday off. I had followed a few more investigative threads with minimal success, had crashed for a couple of hours in the hotel, and was stepping out of the shower when she called my room.

"Hi," she said. "I didn't wake you, did I?"

I smiled. The girl obviously knew racetrackers because that question would not have occurred to most people making a phone call at six in the evening. "No. I was up."

"Oh, good," she said as I draped the towel around my neck and sat on the bed. "Listen, do you think Jay will still be on the job in the morning?"

"Yeah. He looked pretty fit."

"That's what I thought. I saw him in that cute little pharmacy you told me about—Wagner's?—and it was apparent his appetite was up to speed, if nothing else."

I chuckled.

"That being the case, I expect I'll be flying home sometime tomorrow."

"Kessler told you that?"

"No. I haven't spoken to him yet, but it won't be a bad idea for me to head home if you boys can make do."

Boys?

"As much as I hate to admit it, I need to get back to my *real* job. And since this will probably be my last opportunity, I'm going to head downtown and look around. I stopped at the front desk to see what attractions they recommend, but the clerks were swamped registering a bunch of photojournalism students. It seems they'll be at the track most of the week for a workshop or competition or something."

I smiled. "Just what we need."

"Oh, sure. What's another dozen photographers when you've got hundreds? Anyway, I wondered if you had any suggestions."

"You haven't been downtown at all?"

"Nope."

I had suggested Fourth Street Live and the Main Street Trolley and Waterfront Park, but sending her out on her own felt awkward, and I had offered to accompany her.

So, here we were, stepping off the trolley Tuesday evening with me questioning my motives. At the time, it had seemed the honorable thing to do. Now, it just felt selfish.

"What should we do next?" Corey said as she pivoted on her heel and gazed upward, taking in the sweep of buildings blocking out the sky.

She'd chosen a pair of low-slung, faded jeans with an intricate mesh belt decorated with beads and a fuzzy sky blue sweater that brought out the blue in her eyes. Definitely not track attire, and so far this evening, I'd had to work at keeping my eyes off her. I cleared my throat and casually directed my attention down Fourth.

What we should do next was find a place to eat, but Corey didn't appear ready to settle down anytime soon. Like a pair of goofy teenagers, we had already cut through the Brown Hotel's incomparable lobby where, rumor states, the bell captain caught a fish from the second floor balcony during the Great Flood of

'37. Farther down the block, we had stared wide-eyed at a long row of limousines idling at the Seelbach's curb before setting off to explore Fourth Street Live as bona fide tourists.

I pointed toward the drive that bisects the Galt House towers. "If you want to check out Waterfront Park, we can cut through there."

"Isn't there a highway between us and the river?"

"Uh-huh. I-64. We have to go down some steps and cross River Road and a parking lot that stretches beneath the overpass before we get to the wharf. Or, if you want, there's a plaza behind the Kentucky Center that has a panoramic view of the river."

"Let's go there."

At Fifth Street, we turned right and followed a classy prom-enade that opens onto an expansive terrace spanning I-64. The pole lamps buzzed on as we descended a flight of steps and crossed over to the railing. I hung back and watched Corey lean forward and rest her forearms on the galvanized metal. She peered over the edge and studied the riverbank, which lay some fifty feet below.

The sun had slipped beneath the horizon minutes earlier, and the expanse of earth and trees and buildings across the river melded into a hazy iron-gray ribbon sandwiched between a melon sky and the luminous waters of the Ohio. I clasped my hands behind my back, pivoted around, and took in Louisville's skyline. The Humana Building's slick façade glowed like a smol-dering gold brick, and the delicate lattice dome of the Aegon Building had mellowed from white to pink. The day ended as it had begun, an endless palette of shifting color and light.

When I didn't move alongside her, Corey glanced at me and smiled. "You don't mind heights, do you?"

"Of course not," I lied. "I just got caught up in the view," I said and only considered how that might have come across after the words left my mouth.

She turned back around, and I strongly suspected she'd done so to shield her expression. After a moment, she pushed off the railing, and we strolled to the east side of the plaza and followed a flight of steps to a lower level. Water cascaded down a terraced wall on our right and filled a reflecting pool dotted with steppingstones.

"Hey," Corey said, and the sound of her voice was snatched from the air by the thunderous pummeling of water on stone. "Check it out," she yelled.

She toed the first stone to make sure it was well seated; then she gracefully lifted her arms and started across with the water rushing past her right shoulder. I stepped after her with a great deal less theatrics, feeling the slick stones beneath my sneakers' tread and a cold spray coating my face. Midway down the path, the pounding roar grew louder, and the pungent odor of wet granite filled my head. I stretched my arm toward the waterfall and extended my fingers. As the mist dampened the sleeve of my jacket and formed miniature globes of water on the fine hair covering the back of my hand, a sudden temporal shift caused me to catch my breath. For a brief second, a hot summer sun beat down on my bare arm as a peal of laughter echoed in my ears.

I closed my eyes as a long-forgotten memory flashed in my mind—the feel of my father's strong grip as he snatched me under my arms and swooped me off my feet, a vision of my Keds swinging in a blazing red arc beneath a crystalline sky, the brilliant white laces suspended at the apex. A moment frozen in time. I remembered his clear baritone voice teasing me as I threw back my head and laughed.

I swallowed.

Thinking back, I must have been four or five, which put my brother at twelve. Maybe thirteen. He'd sprinted across the stones while Sherry watched from the sidelines. Eager to imitate him, I followed. But when I hesitated halfway across, my father snuck up behind me and lifted me in a spinning arc above his head. Then he swung me back around and trapped my legs against his thigh as he lowered my head toward the shimmering pool. I had squealed in delight and kicked my feet and dive-bombed my hands into the sparkling water to snatch coins from the slimy bottom.

When I felt him gather me up, I flailed my arms as he hoisted me onto his hip with a grunt.

"You're getting too big for this, Stevie."

"No, I'm not."

He had smiled down at me, and in my mind, I saw his face as clearly as if he were standing before me now. Eyes sparkling with intelligence and humor, white teeth gleaming in the sun. Even then, his thick black hair had been threaded with silver. Frown lines creased his forehead, a byproduct of years performing open-heart surgery, squinting through plastic goggles beneath bright halogen lamps that duplicated a cloudless noontime day. When he eventually set me down, I had marched across the stones with confidence, knowing he was close behind.

The memory faded, and the fact that memories were all I would ever have slammed into me with an overwhelming finality.

As I raised my eyes toward the west tower of the Galt House, I was convinced that we had stayed there some twenty years ago. Her bold outline rose against a darkening sky, the warm brick growing dull in the failing light while the glass planes caught the last hint of crimson lingering on the western horizon.

Corey was waiting for me on the other side, and when I turned back around, her smile faltered. She crossed her arms, stepped sideways out of my path, and watched while I caught up with her.

Her eyes looked huge in the fading light. "What's wrong, Steve?" she said, and I could barely hear her voice over the pounding waterfall.

I placed my hand on her shoulder and leaned closer.

"Did you realize something about the case?"

I shook my head.

I'd held her before, when fear and uncertainty had threatened to tear her world apart, and I desperately wanted to hold her now. I smoothed a lock of her hair between my fingers, then lowered my hand. "Let's get something to eat. I'm starving."

She fell in step beside me but remained silent with her gaze lowered as we climbed a short flight of steps and turned onto the promenade. When we reached Main Street, she wrapped her arms tightly around her waist. "Where should we go?"

"Anywhere you want." I slipped off my jacket and draped it over her shoulders.

"Thanks." She gathered the flaps together. "You pick. You know the town."

"Okay. Something uniquely Louisvillian for your last night." I slowly nodded. The Bristol Bar & Grille came to mind. Great food, excellent wine and beer selection, but I didn't know if the Bristol was unique to Louisville. "And I've got just the place," I said as the crosswalk light flashed on. "A place you won't find anywhere else in the world."

We backtracked to Fourth Street Live as the city's lights twinkled in a glittering array above our heads.

Relaxing into my chair, I shifted my plate aside and watched the overhead lights wink off Corey's fork as she teased a chunk of meat from her crab cake. I had finished a plateful of mashed potatoes and grilled onions and pork chops smothered in a molasses bourbon glaze while Corey was just hitting her stride, if you could call it that. She had picked at her spinach salad and was still working on her first crab cake, with the second lying untouched. As I drained my Old Fashioned, our waiter appeared at my side.

"Would you like to try those bourbon flights, now?"

"Which do you recommend?" I said.

"With your meal, the Wheated Flight. Old Fitzgerald, Maker's Mark, and Pappy Van Winkle's Family Reserve 20 Year will make a nice follow-up. To complement the lady's Thai seafood, the Style Flight is an excellent choice. Maker's, Knob Creek, and Four Roses Single Barrel. Both flights are presented in exquisite Riedel crystal."

I shifted my gaze to Corey and had to smother a laugh. Her fork was poised in midair as she studied our waiter with pursed lips and a frown wrinkling her forehead. "Corey?"

"Hmm. I don't know." Her fork clinked on her plate as she set it down and straightened in her seat. "Mine sounds like I'm going to shoot a bunch of roses with a shotgun after I ford a creek. Now, yours…." She rested her elbows on the table, folded one hand atop the other, and propped her chin on her knuckles. "Yours sounds rather kinky, wouldn't you say? With Old Fritz and Pappy Van Winkle?"

"That's Fitz, ma'am."

Corey's eyebrows shot up as she swiveled her attention back to our waiter. "Ma'am?"

"Yes, ma'am."

Corey looked back at me and rolled her eyes.

I cleared my throat. "We'll go with your recommendations," I said, and he nodded and went away.

She leaned across the table. "Can you believe that guy, calling me 'ma'am'?"

"It happens."

"S-t-e-v-e."

"Hey, what can I say? I guess you should be thankful they carded you. Keep up your youthful image."

"Huh." She eased back against her chair, folded her arms at her waist, and crossed her legs. She scanned the room and nodded ever so slightly. "This is nice."

I glanced wistfully at Corey's discarded crab cake before following her gaze. Maker's Mark had strived for extraordinary when they designed their flagship lounge, and they'd achieved it. The hard lines of cold marble tabletops and massive columns finished with gleaming crimson tiles were softened by a dramatic blend of warm blond wood and black leather and fluid walls of sheer curtains, all of it muted by soft recessed lighting. But the bar and glass shelving behind it were what caught the eye. Both were ingeniously lit so that the rows of amber-colored bottles displayed there, and seemingly dripping with the signature red wax of Maker's Mark, glowed from within.

"Yeah," I said, responding to her statement. "Not bad."

She smiled as she turned her focus back to our table and the plate before her. "Do you like crab? I'm not going to be able to finish this."

"Sure," I said, and when she asked for my knife, I handed it over and watched her slide the patty onto my plate. "Thanks."

She nodded and picked up her fork, fiddled with a sliver of carrot before spearing some spinach leaves and touching them to an orange sauce that coated her plate. I sliced through the crabmeat and took a bite as she said, "What happened at the fountain?"

Surprised, I looked up and found her sitting very still. I swallowed. "What?"

"You know? What were you thinking when you...you know?" She made an odd nervous gesture with her hand. "Went away?"

"Hmm." I sat back in my chair. "I was thinking about my father. Not Kessler," I added before she jumped to the obvious conclusion.

"Mr. Kessler's your step dad, right?"

"No. He's my father. I—"

Our waiter paused at my shoulder and presented our bourbon flights in the—what had he called it? *Exquisite Riedel crystal.* I half listened as he placed them on the marble tabletop while briefly describing their subtle nuances. He looked at each of us in turn and frowned at our apparent lack of interest. He drew in a breath.

"Thank you," I said and watched him turn wordlessly toward the bar. "The man I'd always believed to be my father died last June 25th. I met Kessler five days later." I picked up one of the crystal tumblers and breathed in the smoky aroma, took a swallow, and felt the warmth spread down my throat.

"When you helped me find out what happened to Bruce, you never let on...." Her voice trailed off.

"No reason to, I suppose."

Corey shook her head, and a strand of blond hair caught on her pale eyelashes. "We're both hurting. Maybe that's why I've sensed this connection between us." She tucked her hair behind her ear. "You should have told me."

"If I had, I don't think you would have accepted my help, and helping you back then was what I needed."

"Hmm. I guess I understand that."

I drained my first glass and ran my tongue around my teeth, noticing the subtle ginger and wood flavors. As I set the glass down, I considered the fact that I had become rather expert at avoidance. Get involved in someone else's troubles, and you don't have to deal with your own. I nudged the tumbler next in line, smoothed my fingertips down the cool glass. Numb yourself with alcohol, and you won't feel anything at all.

"Rudi Sturgill made the observation that it must be weird having two fathers, and he's right. I'm just now getting used to the idea of Kessler being my father, though on many accounts, he's still a stranger."

Corey rotated one of her glasses.

Wondering if she was even aware that she was doing it, I said, "When we were at the fountain, I was practically blindsided by a memory of my father that came out of nowhere, a memory so overpowering and vivid, it was like he was standing there beside me. I swear, I even smelled the cologne he used to wear."

"What do you think caused it?"

"Who knows? I've been here before. Louisville, I mean. But I suspect a combination of things triggered that particular memory. The sound and smell of the water, duplicating the physical act of crossing the steppingstones like I'd done so many years ago, that kind of thing."

"And stress."

"Stress? What do you mean?"

"The question of what happened to Nicole," she said, and I thought how that was just part of it, because my becoming a suspect in her disappearance was a distinct possibility. "Stress puts all kinds of weird demands on our psyche."

"Okay, Ms. Freud. What else can you tell me?"

"Maybe your subconscious is trying to tell you something."

"Like...go home?"

Corey smiled. "That would work."

I shook my head. "It's too late for that. A police detective I know is talking to the Louisville PD, hopefully smoothing a path for me."

"What do you mean?"

"I need to tell them what I know, but I'm afraid that when I do, they'll latch onto me, so he's talking to them first."

Corey sipped one of her bourbons and crinkled her nose. "Here, you can have mine."

"Cut it with water if it's too strong."

She made a shooing motion with her hand. "Nah. You like this stuff. It's yours."

I lined up the five remaining bourbons and smiled. "You weren't thinking of getting me drunk when you ordered these, now, were you?"

"God, no. I need you functional enough to get me back to the hotel."

"On a bus?"

"Well, y-e-a-h." Canting her head, she watched me pick up one of her samples and examine its color. When I sniffed it, she rolled her eyes. "You don't really know what you're doing, do you?"

"No, but I look like I do, don't I?"

She blew out a breath. "So, did you learn anything useful this afternoon? Jay said you went downtown."

I tasted the second bourbon from Corey's flight. Knob Creek—a hot biting spirit with overtones of burnt caramel and charred wood. I sucked my teeth and exhaled as I placed the tumbler back on the table. "I accomplished a couple of things. My original workup on Nicole confirmed that she didn't have a criminal history in Jefferson County, not that I expected her to, but I never did check for any police involvement that was either a.) outstanding or b.) didn't progress as far as the court system. So, I checked for incident reports or complaints that hadn't made it to court and found absolutely nothing, which was disappointing."

"How so?"

"If she'd recently filed a protective order, that would have been a huge lead."

"Weren't you afraid you'd be spotted by the police?"

I smiled. "My face isn't plastered on wanted posters across the county…yet."

"Even so."

"Well, you're right, I was a little nervous, but I'll bet the detectives assigned to Nicole's case work out of her district, not downtown, and that's where I went to finish up my research."

"So, what did you learn?"

"At the courthouse, I checked for criminal records on everyone on my list except Snoopy Sanchez. I've never been able to find any data on him, and you need a date of birth to access criminal records. I was curious whether I'd find anything on Edward Utley, but he was clean. Not even a speeding ticket. But I did find records on one person." I waited for her to take the bait. Instead, she asked a question.

"Are these records for the entire state?"

"No. Since I don't have an investigator's license that would allow me to access one of the online services, I would actually have to go to every single county to be thorough. That's how the records are distributed. If I want to check out Rudi Sturgill, for instance, I'd need to go to Woodford County, or Fayette."

"What about those searches you pay for online?"

"They're notoriously inaccurate, and I don't want to spend the money if I don't have to."

"Okay." She grinned, and her teeth flashed in the muted light. "Who's been bad?"

"Bill Gannon, Nicole's ex-boss."

She formed her lips into a silent "o" and widened her eyes.

"If his criminal record is any indication, his marriage is shaky. He's been arrested four times. An old charge for assault, one for DUI and, more recently, for disorderly conduct and criminal damage. Both charges were the end result of two separate domestic disturbance calls."

"Sounds like he's got an anger management problem."

"True, and it also appears that Snoopy Sanchez knows whereof he speaks. His boss can't keep his hands off the help, and my guess is, his wife knows it."

By five-thirty Wednesday afternoon, I had shaved and showered and changed into a salmon-colored polo shirt and a pair of jeans that I had yet to wear in a horse barn.

Except for a slight hangover that I undoubtedly deserved, the morning's work had unfolded without a hitch. Jay had been his usual efficient, hard-assed self, both horses had breezed and returned to their stalls without mishap, and much to my relief, Edward Utley had stayed home. On the downside, Corey had strolled into the barn with a backpack slung over her shoulder in preparation for her flight out.

Rudi had been there, too. He had joined Bill Gannon trackside to watch Gone Wild put in a one-mile jog around the oval. When he returned to the barn, he had invited Corey and me to a Derby party at his farm. Judging by Corey's reaction, she very well might have extended her stay in Louisville if he'd mentioned the party a day earlier.

When she declined the invite, I had half expected to be "disinvited," but I'd sorely misjudged Rudi's generosity. Not only that, when I told him I wouldn't be able to attend because of transportation problems, he had insisted on sending a car to pick me up.

Corey had caught a cab by nine, and the backside had seemed a lonely place without her.

I sat on the bed and glanced at my cell phone, noticed I'd missed a call from Ralston. I hit the softkey and rang through to voicemail.

"Hey, Steve. Detective Ralston here. It's almost five o'clock, Wednesday. I talked to the detective working the Austin case this morning. Her name's…." Paper rustled in the background. Ralston pronounced her name, then spelled it. "Jeanne Bonikowski. She's out of the office today but wants you to come in tomorrow. I explained that you would probably have to work in the morning, and she said the afternoon was fine." He gave me her phone number and address on Douglass Boulevard. "They're interested," he said with caution edging his voice, "but I think you'll be okay."

I closed the phone thoughtfully.

Detective Bonikowski.

I'd seen her this afternoon, pulling up to Gate 1 as I left the administrative offices. I glanced at Nicole's composition notebook where I'd left it on the bedspread. Getting into her office had been as uncomplicated today as it had been Monday, and I'd "borrowed" her book, the one that had seemed so out of place. If I'd had any idea the cops were on their way, I would have left it.

But I had it now. I picked it up and headed downstairs, paused in the hallway outside the Hilton's Business Office and tapped it against my thigh. A man and woman occupied the workstations, and neither looked like they'd be leaving anytime soon.

I decided to go to the bed-and-breakfast and was walking through the Hilton's lobby when I spotted Cortney, the clerk who'd originally checked me in. He stood behind the desk with his palms planted authoritatively on the shiny countertop. He nodded.

"Hey." I paused in front of him. "What're you doing here in the middle of the afternoon?"

"Working a double. Sixteen hours."

"Shit."

"That's what I say, but it's sweet when the time comes to cash my paycheck."

"No doubt." I rested my elbows on the desk. "Hey, look. Has anyone been asking for me?"

He checked the computer screen, then scanned a shelf below the counter and shrugged apologetically. "I got nothing for you."

"Okay. Thanks," I said, reassured that the cops hadn't decided to snatch me before the appointment.

Chapter Fifteen

I caught the number two bus outside the Cardinal Hall of Fame and opened Nicole's notebook as the bus rocked away from the curb.

Okay, Nicole. Let's find out why you left this particular notebook at work.

I realized I had thought of the notebook as simply that, a notebook. The ones in her office had certainly served that purpose, but it immediately became clear that she had used this one as a journal or, more accurately, a diary.

I frowned when I read the date for the first entry: September 5th, 2003. Wait a minute. I dug out my notepad and flipped through the pages until I found the dates Nicole had worked for Gannon Racing Stables. June of '02 to July of '03. Damn. I had counted on these notes describing her experience when she worked for Bill Gannon. Apparently, I wouldn't be getting off that easy. So, who *was* she working for?

The first entries described at length the process involved in introducing yearlings to work under saddle. Nicole was assigned to manage four fillies, and she chronicled every milestone or setback in their development. On September 7th, she wrote:

> *Sukie hates being lunged. Today marks her third week working in the round pen, and she still will not put in a decent work. I'm confident she knows exactly what I want from her, but when I feed out the lunge line, she hunches her*

back and squeals and carries on. Once I get her working on the perimeter, she flips her head and pops her shoulder and goes around the circle bent in the wrong direction, totally ignoring me while she takes in the sights. I say totally, but I can see her looking at me from the corner of her eye as if she's making sure I'm still there to annoy. Tomorrow, I'll ask Ryan if I can add elastic side reins to keep her more....

When someone tweaked the bell cord above my head, I realized I'd missed my stop. I got off at Breckinridge, walked a block west to Third, and found the Rocking Horse Manor at 1022 Third Street. I had expected some sprawling wood frame house, but the Rocking Horse Manor more accurately resembled a castle and elegantly blended chiseled stone, rich wood, and flawless landscaping. I climbed the steps and rang the doorbell. One of the owners let me in, and it was clear that Kessler had arranged for me to use his room. I was given a key and escorted to the third floor, then left alone.

Kessler's room faced the street and was a bit frilly for my taste—lots of white on white with ivy accents, white wicker furniture, ruffles—but it had a desk and spacious sitting area and a television. I swung the bathroom door open. An authentic claw-foot bathtub dominated the space. I switched on the T.V., plugged in Kessler's laptop, and powered it up.

I opened Nicole's composition notebook and started with page one. Her workspace had been organized within a hair's breadth of obsessive compulsive, and I had a feeling her apartment would have been similarly tidy if it hadn't been broken into. The very fact that she had removed this particular notebook from the pile in her apartment and tucked it among the set she kept at work suggested that it was significant in some way. But how?

There was one thing I was damned well sure of: this notebook being out of place had not been an accident.

I had intended to run a search on every proper name I uncovered but hit a brick wall almost immediately. Nicole referenced her coworkers by first names only and the horses by their barn names. *Sukie*, for instance, was undoubtedly a nickname. Many long yearlings, thoroughbreds that were roughly eighteen-months old, don't have their registered names, so the staff most likely made up names for them, a derivative or reference to their dam's breeding. Referencing them by the sire's name wouldn't work since a stallion might have forty progeny each year while a mare had one.

With growing disappointment, I skimmed more of the same—detailed notes on clipping bridle paths, introducing the bit, accommodating a nervous horse's quirks. Halfway through the notebook, my prospects improved. The day after Christmas, 2003, Nicole was taken off day work and assigned to foal watch. I bookmarked the spot with my finger and flipped through the following pages. The later entries verified that Nicole had remained as detail-oriented as ever, jotting down sire and dam information for every foal she delivered in the year 2004. The woman who'd trained me to foal out had been just as meticulous.

With some effort on my part and a little imagination, I would be able to figure out where she had been working. All I had to do was identify some of the horses she delivered and look up the breeder of record.

I returned to the place I'd bookmarked, leafed through a couple more entries, and paused. A page had been torn out. Its ragged edge jutted from the book's spine.

A sudden surge of adrenaline snagged the air in my lungs. Nicole hadn't been carrying just any piece of paper that Friday morning when she'd stood outside Gone Wild's stall. I hadn't picked up on it then, but the paper's dimensions had been all wrong for a common piece of looseleaf. No, Nicole had been glancing between Gone Wild and notes she'd written on a piece of paper torn from the book I now held in my hands.

I left the notebook in Kessler's room for safekeeping and caught a bus back to the Hilton. At one minute past seven Wednesday evening, I hustled downstairs and crossed the lobby as a Lincoln Town Car slid to a stop under the portico. The brake lights flared as Rudi's driver shifted the car into park and opened his door. He adjusted his tie, then smoothed the flaps of his sport coat together before walking around the Lincoln's immaculate chrome grille.

The lobby's automatic doors slid open, and as I stepped into the warm, fragrant evening, it was difficult to believe that ice had coated the scattered puddles between barns two days earlier. Sunday's cold rain had preceded a warm front, and the temperature had risen steadily until it finally felt like spring on this last Wednesday of April. For sure, Corey would have appreciated the change.

Corey....

I was sorry to see her go, but relieved as well since I had enjoyed her company more than I cared to admit. And that revelation had stirred all kinds of unwelcome feelings—guilt and a gnawing doubt in my ability to remain faithful to Rachel. And fear. Fear that I was incapable of staying committed to a long-term relationship. I loved Rachel, so what the hell was wrong with me? And what was up with her?

I flipped open my cell phone and checked the screen as Rudi's driver moved past the quarter panel. Nothing. I had left three messages on her voicemail, and she had chosen to ignore them all.

Rudi's driver raised an eyebrow. "Front or back, sir?"

"Front, if that's okay with you."

He bowed his head.

"And my name's Steve."

He smiled softly and clicked open the front passenger door. "Henrik Andersson, at your service."

"Henrik. Good to meet you," I said before settling onto the bucket seat. The cabin reeked of polish and some kind of cleaner.

Henrik paused before closing the door. "Sorry for the smell. I just had the carpet shampooed."

While he retraced his steps, I considered my lack of progress with Nicole's composition notebook. I had been tempted to skip the party and spend the rest of the evening working through her notes, but Rudi's last-minute invitation was a potentially useful opportunity that I was reluctant to pass up. The notebook could wait.

Henrik slid behind the wheel and pointed the Lincoln's nose toward I-65. We talked about the weather and the Derby and horses, of which he knew very little, and I eventually worked the conversation around to his job.

"You like working for Mr. Sturgill?"

"Very much. I get paid handsomely for a job I enjoy."

"Do you maintain the vehicles as well?"

"I oversee their maintenance. At present, Mr. Sturgill owns fifteen vehicles." Henrik glanced in my direction and noted my surprise. "Some, of course, are farm trucks."

"Of course." Fifteen. My God. "But you do more than drive?"

"I do anything that is required."

I turned in my seat and looked at him. "Are you a bodyguard as well?"

A slow smile touched his lips. "Of a sort."

"And do you work for Mrs. Sturgill?"

Henrik's grip tightened on the steering wheel. "No. I see to her cars, but she has her own driver."

"I see. How long have you worked for Rudi?"

"For a time."

"Hmm." Many of the Louisvillians I'd met, including Nicole, spoke with a noticeable Southern accent. Henrik had very little accent, but what I could discern sounded European. I considered his name and said, "Are you Dutch?"

"No." He smiled. "Swedish. Born and raised in Jönköping."

"What brought you here?"

He shrugged. "Just looking for a change."

After we cleared Jefferson County, Henrik eased the Lincoln into the fast lane and opened her up. We covered the miles at a deceptively sedate pace, and in no time at all, we left the interstate behind.

I straightened in my seat when he nosed the Lincoln between an elegant set of wrought iron gates. A sign to our right stated a speed limit of 15 mph, and I was amused to see that Henrik actually obeyed that limit. The paved drive wound through rolling pastureland. Raised beds of exotic-looking plants and grasses dotted the roadside and marked intersections where the drive split to access God knows what.

Henrik turned left at a fork in the road.

A training track spread across the valley, its white rail gleaming in the dusky light. We cruised past an elegant glass structure.

"What's that?" I said.

"A conservatory the Sturgills had built last summer....Mrs. Sturgill," he added as if wanting to make the distinction. "Some mornings, they take their breakfast on the patio out back and watch the horses work. Mrs. Sturgill has a fulltime horticulturist working for her. She's the one responsible for the gardens you saw on the way in. Within the conservatory itself, there are unique specimens from Africa and South America. The collection is the only one of its kind, or so I'm told."

Yeah, right. I had always thought of my family as wealthy, upper echelon, built on a century's worth of spice trading, but obviously a great deal more money could be had in the oil industry. "How many barns are on the grounds?"

"Twelve, plus the stallion barn. You'll most likely get the tour, but I'll point them out as we go." Henrik swung the Lincoln around and continued uphill past a big sweeping convoluted affair—a brick multistoried mansion with a terraced forecourt the size of a lacrosse field.

He gestured toward the mansion. "This is the main house, however, I expect Mr. Sturgill is in the marquee."

I craned my neck as the car skirted a separate drive that broke off and swept around to the mansion's lower level and a row of garage doors. "You said 'main house'?"

"Yes. They just constructed a guest house over this rise. It's a duplex, really, as you'll see."

We cruised past. Lights blazed from arched windows in the growing dusk. A white van sat in the drive.

"Painters," Henrik said. "They're making good progress." He pointed to two barns on a rise to our left. "Barns 6 and 7."

The drive wound along a terraced slope landscaped with shrubs and flowers that glowed in the failing light. Two buildings came up in quick succession before we arrived at the marquee.

Henrik gestured toward the buildings we'd just passed. "Stallion barn and the farm office."

I nodded.

He braked under a portico stretched across the drive. I climbed out before he had a chance to unlatch his seatbelt.

I leaned back into the car. "Thanks for the ride."

"Anytime."

The marquee was a spectacular sight, trimmed with garland entwined with red roses and baby's breath and twinkling white lights. Voices drifted on the evening air, and one of Vivaldi's seasons played in the background. I glanced at the guests seated at tables surrounding the marquee, and when I didn't see anyone I knew, I went inside.

The indoor/outdoor carpet felt slick as I stepped over the threshold and paused under a ceiling strung with thousands and thousands of tiny white lights. The space was crowded, but not overly so. Candles flickered on tables draped in white satin, and red roses were everywhere. Spectacular arrangements cascaded above tiered buffet tables. I wondered if Mrs. Sturgill's horticulturalist had had a say in the evening's production. And a production it was. A six-piece chamber ensemble hop scotched through Vivaldi's *Spring Concerto in E Major*. Thanks to my sister's musical pursuits, that particular piece, as well as countless others, had seeped through my bedroom wall most school day afternoons.

I scanned the room as I wandered over to a buffet table and drifted around its circumference until I found a stack of plates and bundles of silverware. Most of the guests were formally dressed, but not all. Paige's boyfriend, for instance. I had spotted him lounging in a chair across the room with his legs spread, one arm draped over the back of his chair as he sucked on a Beck's longneck. Must have been tough coming up with a tough-guy pose that didn't involve a doorframe.

Yaseen was seated at a table on the perimeter, eating something wrapped in thin pastry that sprinkled confetti-like flakes on his sport coat every time he took a bite. He nodded while his neighbor leaned forward and spoke in his ear. A man dressed in an unremarkable suit and tie stood a pace behind them, hands clasped behind his back, seemingly doing nothing.

As far as I could determine, Rudi was not in attendance, but I caught a glimpse of Paige that took my breath away. She wore a strapless, satin gown the color of a rich merlot. A slit ran up the side, revealing a flash of creamy skin and muscular thigh. Paige had gathered her platinum hair into a tight silken wave at the back of her head and pinned it with red rosebuds and baby's breath. Maybe *she'd* been in charge of the production.

I filled my plate and stood in line at the bar, listening to the music and watching Paige raise a champagne glass to her lips. She was engaged in a lively conversation with an elderly couple. The woman did most of the talking while her companion tweaked his collar and smoothed his broad, calloused hands down his jacket's lapels, looking stiff and ill at ease in suit and tie. I studied the rest of the crowd and concluded that the guests consisted of two groups, those involved in the horse industry and, if Yaseen was any indication, a group from ACS Industries.

When the couple in line before me was served, I asked for an Old Fashioned and stood sideways at the bar, watching the guests mill around. Watching Paige. She had beautifully sculpted shoulders and muscular arms unadorned by jewelry that, on her, would have been a distraction. The skin around her eyes crinkled whenever she laughed, and it occurred to me that she was considerably more dynamic than her brother. As she raised a drink to her lips, something caught her attention, and the animation drained from her face. I followed her gaze and was aware of a soft murmur rippling through the crowd. A good third of the people in the room interrupted their conversations as they turned toward the door.

Rudi Sturgill stepped beneath the arched doorway accompanied by a striking brunette and two men I recognized from my Internet research. Rudi's father and older brother.

Rudi and the brunette headed in one direction while Matthew Sturgill, Jr., Chairman of the Board and CEO of ACS Industries, and his eldest son approached Paige. She knocked back the last of her drink and watched their approach.

Her father said something, clearly expecting a response, but she said nothing.

"Your drink, sir."

I thanked the bartender and, turning back around, drink in hand, came face to face with Matthew Sturgill and his son. The son looked smug, but it appeared that the only thing that had kept the father from throttling his beautiful daughter on the spot was a healthy dose of decorum. I sidestepped them in time to catch Paige flinging a look of pure hatred over her shoulder before she spun around and headed back to her boyfriend.

I sat at a table along the perimeter that offered a clear view of the room, made small talk with my tablemates, then dug into my meal thinking that excessive wealth often wielded a double-edged sword. My parents may never have been capable of making their relationship work, but money had only widened the gulf between them, enabling them to live separate lives with ease. I bit into a crab mini-quiche. The first girl I had ever loved dumped me faster than I could say "rich and famous" since I apparently was no longer destined to be so.

I set my drink down as Yaseen and Paige walked toward the bar. In heels, she was considerably taller than the Middle Easterner.

"Jesus," Paige said. "Lectron's going to be here in a fucking week. I don't want to hear that you're having trouble, do you understand me?" Her voice rose, and the women seated at my table exchanged appalled looks.

Yaseen wrung his hands. "It is difficult."

"Goddamn it. I know it's difficult. Just do it, or I swear—" Paige glanced at my table. She turned back to Yaseen and spoke in his ear.

After he bowed and headed for the door, Paige smiled sweetly. "Ladies." She slid her gaze across the table. "Steve."

I nodded, then watched her drift back to her boyfriend.

As far as I could tell, she pretty much ignored her father and brother, who spent the next half hour making rounds, working the meet-and-greet like seasoned politicians. Rudi and the brunette hadn't moved far from the entrance. They'd been snagged by guests at the first table.

I pushed my plate aside and stood to get another drink when Rudi paused at my elbow. "Hey, glad you could make it, Steve."

"Thanks for the invite," I said. "And the ride."

"Not a problem." He glanced at my plate and empty glass. "Are you headed for the bar?"

I nodded, and he signaled to one of the wait staff. Once she took our order, Rudi yanked a chair around and sat sideways so he could watch the room. I reclaimed my seat while Rudi leaned back in his and sighed. We had the table to ourselves since the two couples had left to tour the barns on a tram of some sort. I hadn't seen it, but I'd heard a tractor earlier.

Another of the staff came over to clear the table.

"Bring us a platter, would you?" Rudi said once she'd gathered up the clutter.

"Yes, sir."

He watched her leave through a back exit, watched her ass sway beneath the hem of her jacket. Very tight pants. Exceptionally nice ass.

The wait staff, male or female, wore the same outfit: black trousers and white shirts, waist-length tuxedo jackets accented with red silk cummerbunds, bow ties, and pocket squares.

"God, it's nice to just sit back and relax." Rudi rested his forearm on the table and caught my quizzical expression. "I've been at the refinery and ACS headquarters most of the day. Required presence," he said with a healthy dose of sarcasm deepening his voice. "Trailing after my father and Matt. Son of a bitch will be President and CEO this time next month."

"Really?"

"Really."

I had a feeling Rudi would have said more, but our server returned with the drinks. When she left, I said, "Your father will remain Chairman of the Board?"

Rudi looked at me funny, and I realized that my knowing his father's current position was more than a little unusual. "Yeah. Needs to keep his hand in."

I swallowed some of my drink, savoring the sweet tang and generous quantity of bourbon whiskey while Rudi tossed back half of his bourbon and water in one gulp.

"Paige didn't go?" I said and thought Rudi would choke.

He bent forward and coughed and wheezed. Blinked back tears. Drawing in a ragged breath, he coughed again before wiping his mouth with the back of his hand. "Fuck no," he said, and his voice cracked.

A woman at the table opposite the bar stared openly at Rudi with annoyance pinching her narrow face.

"She's so pissed, I'm surprised that red dress of hers isn't hot to the touch."

It occurred to me that that dress might be hot for a very different reason.

"The fact that Matt's moving up isn't a surprise. Hell, we all knew that would happen." Rudi smoothed his fingertips down the side of his glass. "Paige knew it the day she set her sights on the scientific track and turned her back on the whole management regime. She closed that door, but good, while Matt has been racing toward it for as long as I can remember. But to announce it now…." Rudi drained his glass. "After all she's done for the company. He can be a mean-spirited bastard, I'll say that for him."

"Matt?"

Rudi shook his head. "My father. He and Paige have always been at odds. She's a genius, really. A freak. She's so goddamn smart, it's scary." He looked me straight in the eye. "You have no idea what that girl is capable of, but she's got her share of quirks, too, and she knows how to use them. She knows exactly what hot buttons to push. Always has." Rudi crooked a finger at the girl who'd delivered our drinks and signaled he wanted refills. "So he times the announcement of Matt's promotion just when Paige's department has achieved a revolutionary innovation that's going to turn the industry on its ear and catapult us to the top." Rudi cleared his throat. "And who the hell do you think will be basking in the limelight?"

"Not Paige."

"You got it."

"I heard something on the news the other day," I said, "about ACS Industries being poised to—"

Rudi laughed. "You haven't heard shit. My God. What they've done...what *Paige* has done. Let's put it this way, I won't have to worry about creditors once the company puts the new CAEX into operation."

"CAEX?"

"Computer-assisted exploration. Last year, we switched from an outmoded supercomputer to a Linux environment and will be deploying thousands of upgraded exploration packages into the field. You know what 4-D seismic imaging is?"

"Uh, a kind of movie?"

"Exactly. Images of underground formations and geologic features taken over time that create a virtual movie of what's happening beneath the surface. But shit, everyone's using that. Paige had this brilliant idea...." Rudi paused.

For a brief moment, I suspected he'd decided he'd told me too much, but he was simply organizing his thoughts.

"There's this device called a gas sieve. You stick it in the ground, and it analyzes the gases seeping from the layers below. Certain indicators reflect the presence of oil and gas deposits.

We've improved the design significantly. Paige has. The new version, aptly named the ACS-series gas sieve, collects a larger sample with considerably less noise degrading the data. The samples are collected and fed through a gas chromatographer."

"This have anything to do with atmospheric washing?" Rudi's eyebrows shot up.

"Paige was talking about it at the Thunder party."

"Oh, yeah. The new sieve is so precise, it doesn't matter that the sample's been diluted. The new design's phenomenal, but what's really exciting is that Paige had this bright idea to combine both technologies into one integrated system. We've coupled the gas sieve input with the 4-D seismic imaging program thanks to improvements in the CAEX. These portable units combine both technologies and are easily deployed...."

The girl with the nice ass returned with a hotplate loaded with the buffet's offerings that had apparently come straight from the kitchen. She set down the platter and distributed plates and utensils bundled in red cloth napkins. She smiled at Rudi. "Anything else?"

"See what Carolyn wants."

"Yes, sir."

I watched her walk over and stand alongside the brunette as the other server delivered more drinks. I hadn't finished my first. "Who's Carolyn?"

"My wife," Rudi said distractedly, which prompted me to reevaluate my take on him. This was supposedly his party—a party celebrating the Derby and racing, or so I had assumed—but Carolyn was the one playing the role of hostess while Rudi was...slumming. With me.

"So, this integrated process, it's going to have an impact?" I said.

Rudi swallowed a mouthful of drink and smoothed his finger along the edge of his mustache. "It's gonna knock the industry on its ear."

He slid his plate across the tablecloth and selected hors d'oeuvres from the platter while I relaxed into my chair. At my left, the bartenders continued a brisk business while, behind them, the ensemble had switched to one of Haydn's Prussian quartets, one of my favorites and the composer's rather unusual nod to Mozart.

Across the room, Paige and her boyfriend stood, and she entwined her fingers in his. Her father and brother had joined some guests at a table not far from where they had been seated. Paige led the way, threading between candlelit tables on an indirect path toward the bar. Her gown shimmered in the diffuse light. Compared to her, the boyfriend looked ridiculous dressed in baggy jeans and a T-shirt. Turning her head, she stopped abruptly, causing Doofus to bump into her. He didn't back up but pressed his crotch against her ass. While she talked in his ear, his hand strayed to the slit in her dress.

Rudi laid a pair of long-handled tongs between the stuffed mushrooms and poached lobster and turned toward me saying, "You want some—" He frowned at my expression, then followed my gaze as Paige plucked her boyfriend's hand off her thigh.

Rudi leaned back in his chair, closed his eyes, and blew out a breath. His sister sent Doofus to get drinks while she moved behind Rudi.

Paige leaned forward until her face was alongside his. She squeezed his shoulders. "The air quality's growing more noxious by the minute down at our end, so I thought we'd join the two of you."

"Your ears must have been burning, girl," Rudi said as she slid onto the chair next to his.

"Ah." Crossing her legs and leaning forward with her fingers laced together over her knee, she looked from Rudi to me. "Talking about me, were you?" she said without taking her eyes off me.

"Talking about how smart you are," Rudi said.

Paige made a noise in her throat, dipped her head down and looked sideways at her brother. "Not smart enough to see this coming." She swallowed. "Does he hate me that much?"

Rudi didn't answer, just looked into his sister's eyes. He reached across and squeezed her hand. "You'll come out on top. You always do."

She sat up straight and blinked away a tear. The boyfriend strolled back and handed her a drink. He lifted his beer toward Rudi in mock salute; then he nodded to me. When he raised the bottle to his lips, I noticed a jagged cut on the pad of flesh below his little finger. The cut itself had scabbed over, but the flesh around it was inflamed and painful looking.

"We're going to The Phoenix," Paige said and held up her drink. "Soon as I finish this."

"Not K2?"

"I'm tired of that place, and no offense, Rudi, but listening to this," she inclined her head in the direction of the bar and the chamber ensemble stationed beyond it and rolled her eyes, "I need something to wake me up."

Rudi grinned. "You know Carolyn. Wellspring has a certain image to uphold."

Paige expelled a breath through her nose. "She should have kept you locked away then."

Rudi chuckled. He bit into a cheese puff and waved a finger at her. Spoke with his mouth full. "You aren't going dressed like that?"

"No. I'll swing by the apartment and change into something a bit less decorous."

"Trashy, you mean?"

She grinned wickedly. "Why, Rudi?" She slid her palm across the satin tablecloth and clasped Rudi's hand. "So, what are you going to do tonight?"

"Hang around a bit longer, then I might head downtown."

"Fourth Street?"

Rudi nodded. "This is nice, but after Thunder, it's a letdown." He looked at me and smiled. "Well, I suppose not all of us have the same fond memories."

I shrugged. "That wasn't your fault."

Paige swirled a swizzle stick through her drink before placing it on a napkin. "Hard to compete with North America's largest pyrotechnic display, Rudi."

"Hmm." His gaze drifted around the marquee. "This is chump change compared to what I have in store for next year."

Paige raised her eyebrows. "You're already banking on the project?"

"Sure. Why not?"

Paige leaned back in her chair and stared into space. "Why not? Everyone benefits, don't they?"

"I didn't mean it like that. I just figured…."

She nodded. "You're right. The ETD's hard work and mine will benefit us all."

"Come on, Paige. You know you don't do it for the money."

"Well," she set her glass on the table and stood, "maybe it's time for a change." Paige bent down and kissed Rudi on the cheek. "Goodnight, little brother."

Rudi's drink and food sat untouched as he watched them leave.

"ETD?" I said.

"Exploration Technologies. Her department." Rudi nudged my arm. "Come on, I'll give you a tour."

We left by the staff's entrance, where a Bobcat ATV sat on the grass. The evening had grown dark, although spotlights shone from a two-story brick building behind the marquee.

Rudi waved toward it as he climbed in and cranked the diesel. "Farm office and breeding shed." He nodded toward the barn closest to the marquee. "Stallion barn. We'll end there. I'll show you some of the other barns first."

He pulled onto the asphalt and motored down a side road. We stopped at three barns altogether. Barns like nothing I'd seen before. Cobblestone circular drives swept past manicured hedges and ornate fountains. Arched doorways accessed wide central aisles paved with rubber bricks that provided traction for the horses and were easier on their joints. The stalls themselves were large and roomy, with ornate grillwork and lacquered wood, and the horses that inhabited them were beautifully cared for with dappled, glossy coats indicative of a perfectly balanced diet.

We drove past the house and conservatory and around a hill, heading back toward the stallion barn. For the most part, Wellspring Farm was situated on high ground with the surrounding countryside spreading out in all directions, and I was amazed at how desolate the area felt. A few lights illuminated farmyards or shone in obscure windows so that the sight of the marquee and the thousands of lights strung in tree branches across the lawn seemed wildly out of place.

When Rudi pulled up to the last barn, he cut the engine. The air smelled faintly of horse and strongly of sweet-smelling alfalfa. A security camera was suspended from the rafter near the doorway. Another one hung at the far end of the barn. The other barns I'd seen had been similarly equipped.

Rudi stopped at the first stall on the left. "This is Good as Gone, Gone Wild's sire. He's by Gone West, a stud who has eighty-one stakes winners to his name and $61 million in progeny earnings so far."

"Impressive," I said as the stallion moved to the front of his stall, boldly confident, and regarded us with a beautifully intelligent eye. "Isn't Elusive Quality one of his?" I said, referring to Gone West.

"Yes."

"I foaled one of his offspring a couple months ago." When Rudi raised an eyebrow, I added, "I was working at a farm in Virginia. Temporarily." Temporarily, I thought, because I'd been looking for Corey's brother, and his fate reminded me of my purpose tonight. Information gathering, of which I'd done very little. "I'm surprised Mr. Gannon isn't here this evening."

"Here and gone before you arrived. You know how trainers are, always worried about how late it is." Rudi moved to the next stall and paused. He folded his arms and considered me. "So just what did you say to Bill that got him wound so tight?"

"There's this girl," I said. "She's missing, and I know she used to work for Gannon, so I asked him if he knew where she was."

Rudi frowned. "What girl?"

"She works at Churchill now. Nicole Austin."

Rudi had been attentive, but his eyes widened briefly at the mention of her name. "How do you know her?"

"She was in the receiving barn Friday morning, looking at a sheet of paper. Seems like she took notes about everything. When Gannon came in, she got nervous, so I asked around."

"Aren't you a little old to be playing Dick Tracy?"

"I'd be happy not to, but I think her being missing is related to those two thugs in the restroom."

Rudi frowned. "That's ridiculous."

I shrugged.

"Anyway, why do you think she's missing?" Rudi said.

"She hasn't been to work since Friday afternoon, and her apartment was broken into."

"I wonder what happened." Rudi dismissed the topic by continuing with the tour. He ran through the pedigree of the remaining stallions, and afterwards, we returned to the party.

An hour later, he drifted back to my table. "Henrik can take you home whenever you're ready to go, but I'm heading back to Louisville now and would be happy to drop you off."

It was already ten-thirty, and Rudi seemed sober enough, so I thanked him, and five minutes later, we were speeding west toward Louisville.

Rudi seemed subdued on the drive, and the combination of long hours and alcohol had me relaxing into the seat. Once we passed Frankfort, he switched on the radio and tuned in a late-night talk show. Before I knew it, the dull commentary and soft drone of the Mercedes' high-precision engine put me to sleep.

I woke up when the engine's pitch changed as we picked up the feeder ramp onto I-65 South. The windshield wipers flicked across the glass as I straightened in my seat. In the distance, yellow hazard lights flashed out of sync while floodlights lit a work zone. A plume of hazy steam billowed off the roadbed and drifted across all six lanes. On the radio, a replay of the day's news had taken over from the talk show.

Rudi passed a pickup and was moving back into the slow lane when the mention of Churchill on the radio caught my attention. "...was found dead this morning."

A sickening chill tightened my gut.

"Thirty-three-year-old Nicole Austin worked in the Marketing Department, and her death has cast a pall over the...."

Rudi gasped, and I jerked my gaze away from the radio as something thumped into the front bumper.

A highway barrel spun over the hood in an orange blur. I ducked as the flashing warning light scraped the windshield then disappeared when the barrel cannoned over the roof, but what caught the breath in my throat was the terrifyingly clear image of the barricade affixed to the back of a highway truck. Its diagonal stripes mushroomed across the windshield.

Chapter Sixteen

The remaining second or two spooled out like a film running in slow motion. The directional arrow scrolled across the board high above the truck, its amber light swirling through rainwater beaded on the windshield. Rudi yanked hard on the steering wheel.

My head slammed into the side window while tires screamed on wet pavement. I opened my eyes as the edge of the tailgate flashed past, a streaming river of yellow and black. The Mercedes' back end had begun to fishtail. I braced my arm against the door panel. Somehow, our bumper cleared the truck, but the maneuver that saved us from one danger sent us hydroplaning diagonally across the pavement.

We punched a hole through the mist.

The concrete median loomed in front of us.

I glanced at Rudi. He'd managed to get his foot on the brake. He hauled the steering wheel to the right, but time and space were against us.

We were going to hit.

I jammed my feet against the floorboard and watched the Mercedes' sleek black nose rush toward the barrier.

The sound of the impact was immediate, shocking, a physical assault unlike anything I had ever experienced.

My ass came off the seat. I slammed against something as white light exploded in my face. I was thrown sideways as we began to spin. Felt like we were spinning forever.

I prayed we wouldn't flip. Wouldn't flip in a goddamn convertible.

My side of the car smacked against the barrier. Needles stung my ear and neck, and I was tossed against the door while the screech of tearing metal rang in my ears.

We were still moving, still spinning, but slowing.

My eyes focused in the direction of a hissing sound, and I noticed the air bag. Powdery gas escaped into the cabin as the nylon sagged against the dash. I swallowed, and an acrid foul taste coated the back of my throat.

I looked over as Rudi straightened in his seat and groaned.

"Rudi. Put your foot on the brake."

He jolted forward, grabbed the steering wheel with both hands, and slammed on the brakes.

Listing slightly, the car thudded to a halt with the nose angled toward the guardrail bordering the slow lane. We'd spun almost 360 degrees. Using my left hand, I pushed the gearshift forward and slipped it into park.

Cold mist floated through the open window.

I shivered, thinking we'd been damn lucky. Damn lucky traffic had been so light. Damn lucky we hadn't flipped.

"Oh, God," Rudi mumbled.

I turned toward him. "You okay?"

Rudi's eyes tracked slowly around to my face. Blood streamed through his sideburn and dripped off his chin. He lifted his hand and stared at it as if the gears in his thought process were slipping, a definite lag between intake and articulation. "I think I broke a finger," he said sleepily.

Shit. He was going into shock. I looked over my shoulder. Pinpricks stung my neck as I watched people run toward us. The highway crew backlit by the work zone's powerful flood lamps that turned night to day.

I ran my index finger under my collar, and bits and pieces of something trickled down the inside of my shirt. I looked around. Saw glittering glass chips sprayed across my lap, in the seat, scattered across the carpet. In my clothes. My hair.

I reached to release my seatbelt and remembered something I'd noticed earlier. There was a mini console on the frame above the rearview mirror, and nestled among air vents and reading lights was a button with SOS printed in red below the graphic of a phone. I fumbled with it, and the cover flipped down, revealing a flashing red button. I stretched my fingers and pressed it as a light shone through the windshield, illuminating my hand.

Not a flashlight as I'd guessed, but a car. It backed down the shoulder toward us. The brakes came on as the driver put the vehicle in park. Henrik climbed from behind the wheel and jogged toward us with a cell phone pressed to his ear, his sport coat flapping under his elbows.

What the hell?

"Yo, Dude. You okay in there?" One of the highway workers bent to my window and started to grip the frame until he noticed a lacy curtain of glass. "Oh, man. You bleedin'."

I touched my hair, and glass shards dribbled into my sleeve.

A tinny voice floated from a hidden speaker. "Mercedes Benz Response Center. This is Samantha. How may I help you?"

The highway worker and I exchanged a glance. "Yeah," I said, feeling slightly foolish. "We've had an accident and need an ambulance."

"I just need a moment to determine your location."

Another guy in a hardhat joined the first while Henrik leaned into the car on Rudi's side and spoke in his ear while he looked at me.

The woman from Mercedes clicked back on with her spiel, which I ignored.

"No," Rudi replied to Henrik's soft-spoken inquiry.

Henrik continued, his tone more urgent.

Rudi's murmured answer was less distinct. "…be all right… drink…late for that."

The first siren sounded in the distance while I wondered what they were talking about and why the hell had Henrik been following us?

The next half hour proceeded in an unsettling blur of noise and light, prodding hands, and endless questions. The paramedics did the whole number—backboard, neck brace, straps—and I grew clammy and claustrophobic, finding the process more threatening than reassuring.

I was released at two-thirty Thursday morning.

I shuffled out of my cubicle with the requisite paperwork rolled in my hand and one Vicodin in my pocket to hold me over until I had a chance to get the prescription filled.

Rudi had been wheeled into a cubicle past the nurses' station. I was wondering if he was still there, and whether or not I should stop by to let him know I was leaving, when I heard his voice rise in an anguished plea.

"I don't know what happened—"

"How in the hell could you not?" Paige's voice, high-pitched and quavering. She choked on a sob. "Oh, my God, Rudi. You have no idea what you've done."

A nurse bustled into Rudi's cubicle.

I began to turn away when the curtains billowed and Paige stepped through the gap. She glanced at me without recognition and walked by so quickly, a ripple of cool air swirled past my face. I pivoted on my heel and watched her cut a hurried path through the chaotic activity that unfolded around us.

Activity that defined the ER.

People shouting orders, phones ringing, machines beeping. Something metallic clattered to the floor in a cubicle on my left, and a man's high-pitched wail rose to a screeching crescendo that cut off in a choking gurgle.

An orderly ran past.

Yep. Couldn't wait to get out. Couldn't wait to be rid of the smell, either. A nauseating mix of disinfectant and bodily fluids.

I gave Rudi a minute to recover before I stepped into his cubicle. He had a fresh bandage on his head and dark circles under his eyes, and in the stark light, his skin looked lifeless, like rubber stretched too tightly across a metal frame. His left arm was done up in a light cast covered with a bandage that looked like the Vetwrap we used on the horses. A nurse injected something into his IV line as I stepped around the foot of his bed and into his line of sight.

His eyes focused on my face. "Hey." He cleared his throat. "You still here?"

"On my way out," I said.

He licked his lips. They were chapped, and his lower lip was split and caked with dried blood. "You don't look too bad."

"Just banged up a little," I said, though I was hard pressed to identify a square millimeter that was not aching, stinging, or just plain stiff. "Some bruising. A couple stitches in my scalp."

Rudi closed his eyes. "Ask Henrik for a ride." A shaky smile tugged his mouth. "If you can trust any of us."

I frowned. "You okay?"

He opened his eyes but took his time before he looked at my face. "Get some rest," he said. He swallowed and looked away.

"Okay. Take care of yourself," I said and wasn't sure he'd heard.

His nurse passed me as I turned and walked toward the exit. A commotion erupted on the other side of the nurses' station. An attractive woman, wearing a red sequined dress that barely covered her ass, burst from a cubicle. An IV pole crashed to the floor.

"My old man's gonna spit in my food," she screeched as she jerked the line out of her vein. "He's gonna spit in my food! He's gonna—"

A security guard ran toward her as an orderly lifted her off her feet. She kicked her heels into the guard's chest and straightened her back, writhing and bucking and screaming at the top of her lungs.

What a goddamn zoo.

The waiting room was quieter, the air fresher. I scanned the rows of chairs as I crossed to the payphones. Didn't see Henrik, so I fished some coins out of my pocket and dribbled them onto the stainless steel shelf. I squinted into the phonebook slot. No book. None in the neighboring booth either.

Henrik appeared from out of nowhere and stood at my side. "Mr. Cline."

I smiled softly. "Mr. Andersson."

"Would you like a ride?"

"I sure the hell would." I looked sideways at him. "You always follow Rudi?"

"Loose tail? Yes."

"Always?"

"When I'm on duty."

I scooped up my change, and we headed down a short corridor toward a set of glass doors. Paige Sturgill stepped out of a restroom and strode down the hallway toward us. Henrik paused when he saw her, and I watched appreciatively as she changed course to intercept us. What had Rudi called her planned wardrobe change? Oh, yeah. Trashy. Well, from where I stood, trashy looked pretty damn interesting. She'd pulled on a leather jacket as a barrier against the night air, but she hadn't bothered with the zipper, so there was still plenty to look at. A slinky gold mesh halter top dipped to her navel, and she'd changed into lace-up, low-rise jeans that she'd left untied. On purpose, I assumed. The palm of my hand could have spanned the distance between her crotch and waistband.

Henrik stirred beside me.

Paige glanced at me then stepped in front of Henrik. "Stay here with Rudi. I'll give Steve a ride back to his hotel."

"Yes, ma'am."

Locking her big blue-eyed gaze on my face, she said, "That okay with you?" In her heels, she was taller than me.

"Yes, ma'am," I said, and Henrik laughed openly.

"Be outside in five minutes." Paige spun around, and I started after her at a much slower pace.

I waited under a portico outside the emergency room, watching a thin drizzle swirl beneath the lights that shone down on the pavement. Three police cars were parked side by side to my right, and beyond them, a helicopter loomed out of the mist, a silvery, quiet ghost. Three o'clock in the morning, and the city was eerily silent. A sleek two-seater convertible, smaller than Rudi's, turned off the main drag.

Paige.

I folded myself onto the seat, and as soon as I got my door closed, she accelerated away from the curb and spun the little car in a tight U-turn that pressed me against the doorframe.

As I drew the seatbelt across my lap and fumbled with the latch, an iron fist constricted my chest in some kind of freakish delayed reaction. My fingers trembled, and the belt's metal latchplate clattered against the buckle. Paige braked at the stop sign at the end of the drive and reached across the space between us. Without speaking, she guided my hand with her slender, cool fingers, and the latch snicked home. She stared into my eyes for a brief moment before she shifted into first and eased the clutch out.

Her aggressive driving did not surprise me in the least, but once we left the lot, she kept the little car's speed well within the limit. I wondered if the fact that I'd just been in a crash had anything to do with it.

"How's Rudi," I asked. "He didn't look so hot."

"Hmm. Distal fracture of both the radius and ulna that will require surgery to place pins, and lower back strain. He must have been turning the wheel when the air bag deployed."

"How long will he be in the hospital?"

"Oh, they'll release him tomorrow, probably. They don't like keeping you if they don't have to."

I settled into the bucket seat and watched her shift gears and work the clutch, a fluid, coordinated effort. She'd taken off her shoes, stowed them somewhere in the car. I guessed driving in the heels she'd been wearing would have been next to impossible.

Her eyes cut to the rearview mirror. She licked her lips and glanced at me. "I was allowed to speak with Rudi, but only for a moment. What happened?"

"He got distracted, I guess. Misjudged. I wasn't paying attention."

"He's a good driver. That's not like him."

I shrugged. "We were approaching a work zone. Something came on the radio about Churchill. Maybe that was it."

"About that woman being found dead?"

I looked at her, surprised. Her shoulders were relaxed, but her grip on the steering wheel seemed tense. She took her eyes off the road and stared at my face longer than was prudent. I reflexively checked the road. "Did you know her?" I said.

"No. How would I? We heard it on the drive."

"We?"

"Brent and I."

"Your boyfriend?" I said.

She glanced at me. "Yes. Of course."

"Is he at the hospital?"

"No." Paige checked the time. "Asleep by now, I should think. We lease a suite at the Galt House year-round. My father does," she corrected herself, and the bitterness she'd expressed earlier in the evening momentarily crept back into her tone. She exhaled slowly through her mouth. "Rudi and I use it whenever we want to stay in town. He does that a lot when his horses are running. It's too damn hard getting up at three in the morning to drive all the way down here for their workouts, and he likes watching them work. Maybe more than watching them race."

Less stress, I thought, and maybe he appreciated that time of day more than she realized. There's something about being on the backside of a racetrack just before dawn that is truly magical—standing along the rail when the light's just coming up, watching the horses move fluidly across the damp earth, their dark shapes silhouetted against a rainbow sky. You stand there, breathing in the clean air, listening to the steady primal rhythm of a galloping horse, and the rest of the world simply does not exist.

Paige stopped at the light at Crittenden. She had kept to the surface streets, paralleling I-65 for a brief period before crossing beneath it.

"Thanks for the ride," I said before we reached the hotel.

"Anytime."

She zipped across all four lanes and turned into the Hilton's lot, dropped me off at the door without a word, and sped off.

Cortney, the night clerk who apparently lived at the Hilton, eyed me speculatively as I crossed the foyer's elegant marble tiles. I wasn't exactly limping, but I wasn't walking normally, either. I had stitches in my scalp, smears of Betadine ointment dotted my neck and ear, and my face was blotched with rug burns, compliments of the air bag. The funny thing was, I couldn't remember hitting it. An abundant collection of bruises were hidden beneath my clothing, and my ribs, shoulder, and lower back ached like a bitch.

Cortney grinned and rolled his head from side to side. "Hmm, hmm, hmm. Whatju get into this time?"

"Car accident," I mumbled as I turned toward the corridor.

"Don't you wanna know if somebody's been looking for you?"

I paused and pivoted slowly around. "Who?"

"Cops."

I considered the possibilities. "Think they were following up on the accident?"

Cortney shook his head again, slowly, like he was having a little too much fun because *something* was happening on his fucking shift. "These guys were heavy, man."

"Shit."

"Uh-huh. That kind of heavy."

"What did they say?"

"Asked if you were still registered and whether you were in your room or not and whether you had a roommate."

"How'd they know I was here in the first place?" I said more to myself than Cortney. I hadn't told Ralston where I was staying.

"Your room was broke into, right?"

"Yeah."

"Well, all that stuff gets put in a weekly report that goes to the cops. If they enter it into the database the way they enter their field contact reports, your name would pop up."

I lifted an eyebrow and smiled when Cortney held up his hands.

"Hey, my sister works for the LMPD as a file clerk."

"Hmm. They wouldn't even need that. They got all my information when I was robbed. Hell, the detective even did a follow-up phone interview. I just didn't realize everything was so neatly integrated."

"All the criminals we got 'round here, it's gotta be."

I patted the counter and turned to leave. "Thanks."

"They wanted me to call if you showed up."

"Oh," I said and could hear the resignation in my voice. "Give me the name and number, would you?"

Cortney scribbled the information on a slip of paper and spun it around on the counter. I squinted at the name: Larry Ashcroft.

"Hey, let me see that, would you?" He handed over the business card, and I found what I was looking for, what I had expected. *Homicide Division.* "Great." I drew in a deep breath that set my ribs aching. I fingered the card. "Mind if I keep this and you take the paper?"

"Don't matter to me."

I held up the card in thanks, rode the elevator to my floor, and took a shower, gradually increasing the temperature until some of the tension eased from my muscles. I emerged from my room a half hour later wearing a clean set of barn clothes and fully intending to get through the morning doing as little physical labor as possible.

At ten o'clock Thursday morning, Jay returned to Barn 41 with a large paper bag gripped between his meaty fingers. He'd gone off to the dorm to shower and change and had come back minus his ratty flannel shirt. He was wearing a navy T-shirt with BLAME THE DOG printed across his pecs. His muscles rippled beneath the stretched cotton as he raised an arm and smoothed his palm over his shaved head and down the back of his neck. He exchanged a few words with the guard, few being the operative word. He didn't have much use for conversation, but if he liked you, you could not find a better person to be on your side, and I needed him now.

He nodded, then strolled down the shedrow with his thick arms swinging at his side. He held the bag in front of my face.

I sat up straighter and rested my head against the stall front, closed my eyes for a moment and savored the mouth-watering aromas: coffee, bacon and eggs, fresh biscuits, and something greasy. Probably hash browns.

"God, that smells good." I opened my eyes and watched Jay remove two Styrofoam coffee cups, handing one to me and placing the other on the tack trunk.

He pulled out a sandwich wrapped in greasy paper, then tossed the bag in my lap. "Last supper," he said, gesturing with his sandwich, "thought I'd get you something worth remembering."

I paused with the little plastic triangle peeled halfway off my coffee cup. "You joke, but if you don't hear from me by, I don't know...."

"Sundown?"

I grinned. "Yeah. Sundown. You don't hear from me by then, call Kessler."

Jay nodded.

"And take this for safekeeping." I handed him a wad of papers, which he turned over in his hand. "Copies of my notes. I go in there, I don't want to start over if they're set on pinning her death on me."

Jay zipped the papers into one of his backpack's numerous compartments while I fished out my sandwich. "Nicole? She the one you were drooling over your first day here?"

I tested my coffee. "Yep."

Jay shook his head disapprovingly. "She came back to the barn later the same day, you know?"

I was stretching over to set my cup down and nearly missed the edge of the trunk. "You're shitting? Was she alone?"

"Yep. Acted like she was looking for someone though."

I yanked my notepad and pencil out of my back pocket. "What time was this?"

"I was getting ready to grain the horses."

"Four o'clock, then." I jotted down the time as Jay withdrew a creased white bag and crumpled bills from his back pocket and handed them to me. "Hey." I held up the bag containing my prescription meds. "Thanks."

We finished eating in amiable silence while the crews all around us wrapped up their morning chores and slowly dispersed. Although I had been tempted to call Detective Ashcroft the minute I got his number from Cortney, I hadn't, and I realized I had been banking on Cortney not calling either. Maybe he had. Maybe he hadn't. In either case, the cops hadn't swooped down on the barn to haul my ass away in a very public manner, a fact I was grateful for.

I gathered my trash together, left it sitting on the tack trunk, and walked over to Ruskie's stall. He poked his head over the stall guard before curling his neck around to nuzzle my waist. I hooked my arm across his neck and smoothed my hand down his face. Resting my forehead against his mane, I breathed deeply, inhaling the indescribable blended odors: his skin, his sleek chestnut coat, the sweet smell of his breath, all combined with the mix of straw and hay, and I was reminded of the generations of horses who had passed through this barn. Derby runners, most of them.

Ruskie was uncharacteristically still, and I wondered if he sensed the tension fizzing in my nerves and pressing against my skull like a bad headache.

I had no guarantee I'd be here tomorrow. None at all.

He lipped the thin belt keeper at my waist, then smoothed his muscular lips along my belt. Knowing that a nip was likely next on his agenda, I straightened.

I stopped at Storm's stall and patted him, told him to be a good boy, and when I turned around, Jay said, "What? No hug for me?"

I grinned and told him to wish me luck.

Chapter Seventeen

A sour odor permeated the walls in the interview room on the second floor of police headquarters. The combination of adrenaline, testosterone, and sweat made for a potent unforgettable smell, but the fourth component—fear—stirred dormant instincts best left repressed. Instincts I could do without if I wanted to appear calm and relaxed. And innocent.

Except for the smell, the room was unremarkable. Square, drab, with a metal table and four chairs. Black scuff marks on the tile. A cigarette butt lying against the vinyl baseboard. A video camera encased in Plexiglas hung from the ceiling in a corner where dampness had darkened the acoustic tiles.

I'd had plenty of time to take in the details. Forty minutes by my watch. Since I'd blown off my scheduled appointment with Detective Bonikowski and had come unannounced, figuring that meeting with a Homicide detective took precedence, I wasn't surprised to be kept waiting. In fact, I was grateful for it. The Vicodin pills I'd swallowed before catching a cab downtown had taken the edge off the pain, but they left me feeling drowsy. I rubbed my face and stretched my legs under the table, listened to a distant phone ringing, unhurried footsteps passing by the closed door, muffled voices. Wondering if those voices were coming from the adjacent room, I glanced at the one-way glass to my right and considered the fact that I was being watched.

A soft thud traveled through the walls, and a few seconds later, the doorknob rattled as two people stepped into the room. I stood as a tall angular man held out his hand and introduced himself as Detective Ashcroft.

We shook. "Steve Cline."

"Thanks for coming in, Steve." He gestured toward the brunette who I had seen riding shotgun in Nicole's neighborhood with her partner and, later, pulling up to Churchill's main gate. "This is Detective Bonikowski."

So, they'd teamed up. Probably because she'd caught the original missing person's case.

She nodded to me as she closed the door with her hip. A slender, petite woman, her hands were full of briefcase and audio gear and a coiled extension cord. She got busy setting up while Ashcroft slid a chair away from the table and sat at an angle so he could easily see both of us. I reclaimed my seat thinking his was an effective strategy and one I was familiar with thanks to the class that had set this nightmare in motion.

Interrogators supposedly appear less threatening sitting at a forty-five degree angle, and his distance from the table assured him a clear view of my body language. Also interesting was the fact that their positioning meant that I would have to turn my head to talk to either one of them, freeing the other detective to observe me without being obvious.

I jacked my chair closer to the table and rested my forearms on the cool metal. Before I'd walked in here, I had reminded myself to avoid fidgeting, to keep my arms and shoulders relaxed, to avoid bouncing my legs. As it turned out, the Vicodin was coming in handy in that regard, but if I wasn't careful, I could easily lose my focus.

Ashcroft settled a yellow legal pad on his thigh and withdrew a ballpoint pen from his jacket's breast pocket. He casually watched Bonikowski fiddle with a microphone, then stretch behind the table to plug in the recorder. He wore no tie, but his white dress shirt looked reasonably fresh considering the fact that he'd most likely been up all night.

He turned to me. "With your permission, Steve, we'd like to record and videotape this interview so we can refer to it if necessary."

"Sure."

He set up the opening dialogue, stating who was in the room, the location, date, and time; then he got some identification issues out of the way. I explained about not having my license because of being robbed and showed them my track ID, which seemed sufficient.

After Ashcroft had me state that I was there of my own free will and that I understood I was free to leave at any time, Bonikowski leaned forward in her chair. "You said you were robbed. When and where did this happen?"

I gave her the details.

She jotted notes in a steno pad, purple. "You looked stiff getting out of the chair just now. Is that because of Saturday's robbery? And what about the abrasions on your face? They look fresh."

"No. Both injuries are from an accident I was involved in last night."

She glanced at Ashcroft and licked her lips. She was an attractive woman, though she downplayed her looks by styling her wavy brown hair extremely short. She'd chosen a shade of lipstick that complimented her coloring, but she wore no jewelry except for a plain watch with a black leather strap. "MVA?" she said.

"Yes."

"Were you driving?"

"No, I don't have a car here."

"Now," she said, "tell us why you're in Louisville and how you knew Nicole Austin."

I took out my notepad, laid it on the table, and relaxed against the seatback. "I didn't know Nicole Austin."

I recounted how I had been asked to help with the horses at the last minute. I explained the class assignment and described how I had met Nicole briefly in the shedrow, an encounter that lasted approximately five minutes. I went through everything that happened since I flew into Louisville on Thursday, a week ago today. Both of them took notes but not necessarily about the same things. They asked questions when they needed clarification, and despite having everything laid out in my notepad, it took me over an hour.

Ashcroft had made a soda run midway through the interview. I drained the last of my Coke and was still thirsty. I yawned.

"You look awfully tired, Mr. Cline." Bonikowski fixed me with her brown eyes. "Why's that?"

"I was up all night, Detective Bonikowski." I glanced at Ashcroft. "I guess that's something you're all used to around here, but I took two Vicodin pills before I came in, and I'm wishing now that I hadn't."

They exchanged looks.

"Mr. Cline." Detective Bonikowski sat back in her chair and crossed her legs. Slipped her purple steno pad into her lap. She was wearing a business suit, matching navy jacket and straight skirt with a cream-colored silk blouse. "Have you visited Louisville before?"

"Not since I was a child."

"And how old were you then?"

"Four. Five. Something like that."

She tapped her pen against her teeth. "Have you visited any horse farms in the state of Kentucky, either now or in the past?"

"Just Wellspring Farm last night."

"So...you aren't familiar with the horse farms, say, within the surrounding counties?"

I yawned. "No."

"But you know about..." she flipped through her notes, "the two farms on Dry Ridge Road. Gannon Racing Stables and Millcroft Farm."

"Only because I looked them up on the Internet."

"You've not been on either farm in person?"

"No."

"You said you don't have a car. Is that correct?"

"Yes."

"Then how do you get around?"

"By bus, or I walk. This morning, I caught a cab to get here."

She glanced at her notes and raised an eyebrow. "Last night, you walked all the way to Wellspring Farm in Midway?"

"I got a ride."

"From who?"

"I told you. Henrik Andersson."

"And he works for…?"

"Rudi Sturgill."

"You accepted a ride and went to a farm that you've never been to before, asked by a person you barely know and believe may be responsible for Nicole Austin's death?"

"I don't believe Rudi's responsible."

"He's on your list."

"Because he was in the shedrow Friday morning when Nicole was there, and because his behavior seems off since he invited me *anywhere*."

"So, you just went?"

"Yes."

"You said you don't have a car, but do you have one at your disposal?"

"No. I don't."

Bonikowski cracked open her briefcase and angled it so I couldn't see what was inside. She sifted through the contents before settling back into her chair. "What bus routes have you used?"

"Seventeen to get to Nicole's neighborhood, four to go downtown from Churchill, and two to go back and forth from the hotel."

"Hotel to where?"

"Downtown."

"You seem to have a good handle on the bus system. Lots of Louisvillians don't know it as well as you."

I shrugged.

"Are you familiar with River Road?" She asked the question casually, maybe too casually. Clamping down on the accusatorial tone that otherwise crept into her voice.

"Yes."

"In what way?"

"Well, it parallels the river," I said, fully aware of the sarcasm creeping into *my* voice.

"Yes, it most certainly does. What portion or portions of River Road are you familiar with?"

God, this woman spoke like a damn lawyer. "The portion that runs along Waterfront Park and past the Galt House and the *Belle of Louisville.*"

"Have you ridden bus 59?"

"Fifty-nine? No."

"Are you familiar with its route?"

"No."

"Have you driven on River Road?"

"No. I told you. I don't have a car."

She went back and forth for another half hour, sometimes aggressively and always mixing it up in an effort to catch me in a lie. An interesting technique that might have worked if I'd had something to hide. I glanced at my watch. One o'clock.

"Why are your fingerprints on Ms. Austin's Maxima?"

"Like I said, when I found her keys in the street and her car unlocked, I put them in the foot well."

"Did you drive her vehicle?"

"No."

"Why didn't you call the police when your hotel room was broken into?"

"The director of security, Ms. Fortman, talked me out of it." A decision I was regretting now.

"Have you ever been on Indian Hills Trail?"

"Is that a road?"

"Yes."

"No, I haven't."

"Why did you return to Nicole Austin's neighborhood on Sunday?"

I glanced at Detective Ashcroft. As a member of the Homicide Squad, I assumed he was the lead in this case, but so far, he had contented himself with letting Detective Bonikowski manage the interview's direction and tenor. Frameless glasses lightly outlined his sleepy gray eyes, and at first glance, he appeared detached, almost disinterested as he relaxed against the chair's hard plastic. But I'd come to realize his demeanor was a cleverly executed sham.

When he thought I wasn't looking, I had become aware of his focused attention, certain he was gauging every nuance in my speech, noticing each gesture or absence of one. His deceptively light-handed approach gelled with his choice of clothing and physical appearance, which could only be described as colorless. He wore a light gray nondescript suit and white shirt. His sandy brown hair was short and minimally styled, and his glasses were almost invisible.

I refocused on Detective Bonikowski's question. "I went back to Nicole's neighborhood on Sunday to see if anything had changed with her apartment and to see if her car was still parked in the same place."

"And was everything the same as it had been on Friday?"

"No. Her car hadn't moved, but her apartment had been searched. And no, I didn't search it, and yes, I called the cops anonymously from a payphone on Bardstown."

Her eyelids fluttered as she fastened her gaze on my face. A muscle twitched at the corner of her mouth. Her taking the hard line was not how I would have run this interview. I would have had Ashcroft play the bad cop while she took my side and turned on the charm. If she had any.

"Why anonymously?"

"Like I said, I stayed up late for the Thunder party Saturday night, and thanks to getting robbed, I only got a couple of hours sleep before I went to the track. By the time I got off work and rode a bus out to Nicole's neighborhood, I was sore and tired and in no mood to answer a bunch of questions."

She raised her eyebrows. "And you're in better shape today?"

"No, I am not. But the way my visit to Louisville has played out so far, I figured I'd better come in while I was still physically capable of doing so."

"On Sunday afternoon, when you noticed that her apartment had been searched, did you go inside?"

"No. I did not."

"You didn't notice whether or not the apartment had been searched Friday evening?"

"It looked okay then."

"How do you know? Did you go inside then, too?"

I strangled a sigh and stated matter-of-factly, "No. As I've already said, I have never been in Nicole's apartment. On Friday, I looked in the bay window by the front door. The room looked neat. It didn't when I returned Sunday."

Someone rapped on the door, then opened it. I turned in my seat.

The black detective, who I assumed was Bonikowski's partner, poked his head in the room. He looked at me from behind a pair of sunglasses before his gaze flicked to Ashcroft, then settled on his partner. "Talk to you for a sec?"

She got up without speaking and left the room.

Ashcroft shifted in his seat and rummaged through his trouser pocket. He kept his weapon strapped in a shoulder harness, and the heavy automatic looked much the same as the one I'd glimpsed fitted onto Bonikowski's belt. He withdrew a packet of Wrigley's Spearmint gum, took out a stick, and offered the pack to me.

"No, thanks."

He tossed the pack on the table, unwrapped the stick, and folded it into his mouth. Something about his features had been vaguely distracting, and as I watched him work on the gum, it came to me. His skin was exceptionally pale, not unexpected for someone who probably spent the majority of his time behind a desk, but his lips were what had drawn my attention. They were as colorless as his skin. I wondered if his wardrobe selection, right down to his glasses, was a deliberate attempt to appear less formidable than he surely must be to have advanced to Homicide. Certainly his passive demeanor had been non-threatening.

"You know, Steve? This story you've given us....Well, it's all very improbable."

I said nothing.

"So, I think you're going to need to do a couple of things to clear yourself."

"Like what?"

"Before we wrap up, I'd like you to provide a DNA sample and fingernail scrapings for elimination purposes."

"I don't know. You may very well find one of my hairs in her car since I leaned inside to put the keys on the floorboard. That doesn't mean I killed her." I cleared my throat. "When was she killed?"

Ashcroft considered my question before answering. "Sometime Friday."

I pictured her as I'd seen her last and tried to remember everything about the encounter. Everything I'd done. "I saw her Friday morning. I stood next to her in the barn. I didn't touch her, but what if one of my hairs got caught on her clothing?"

"Okay. So your statement so far explains all that. We would need more before we could charge you."

"I guess."

"Good. We'll give you a ride back to the hotel, and I'd like you to consent to a search."

"Of what?"

"Your belongings."

"What are you looking for? Specifically?"

"I can't answer that in detail, but whoever murdered Nicole Austin will have an unusual type of soil caked on his shoes."

"Not related to a horse barn, I hope?"

"No. Not at all."

The door clicked open. Detective Bonikowski returned to her seat and sat there for a moment before speaking. "You know, it's occurred to me that you've referred to Ms. Austin as Nicole throughout this entire interview. Referring to her on a first-name basis indicates more than a superficial five-minute encounter."

I didn't say anything.

Bonikowski leaned forward. She rested her elbows on the table, clasped her hands together in front of her. "Why did you call Ms. Austin on the night of April the 22nd at ten-thirty?"

"I refer to her as Nicole because I've done a lot of research on her, and I've talked about her to friends, and that builds a certain level of familiarity even when it's not earned through mutual contact. When I called her Friday evening, I had no intention of speaking with her. That would have been unsettling since I was, and am, a virtual stranger. But finding her keys in the street was troubling. I had hoped she would pick up, then I could have hung up knowing she was okay, and that would have been the end of it. Hell, I still wouldn't have given her much thought if I hadn't been jumped in the restroom at Sully's."

"She didn't answer?"

"No. Her machine picked up."

"Did you leave a message?"

"No."

"Why not?"

I blew out a breath. "She doesn't know me. What was I going to say, 'I've been researching you'?"

"So, you stand by your story that, except for a five-minute, unplanned interaction in Barn…" she glanced at her notes, "in Barn 4 at Churchill Downs, you have not met her before or since. You do not, in fact, know her at all and have had no further communication with her."

"That's right. I couldn't have said it better myself."

"Do you know anyone she works for or with?"

"You mean someone in Marketing?"

"Yes."

"No. I don't know any of her coworkers."

"Then, tell me, Mr. Cline. Why did someone use her work phone Monday, April the 25th, at 4:27 in the afternoon to call you?"

"What?"

"It's right there in her phone records. April 25th, a call to..." She read my cell number.

"Oh." I cleared my throat. "I used the phone on her desk to call my cell so I could get her work phone number."

"And why would you do that, Mr. Cline?"

I glanced at Ashcroft. "I figured the more I learned, the more likely I'd be able to figure out what was going on."

"So, you wanted to be the *hero*?" she said sarcastically. "Find out what happened to this young woman?"

"No. I wanted to figure out what the hell was going on so I could avoid getting jumped again, or having my room tossed."

"You said you never went into her apartment. Is that correct?"

"Yes."

"Monday morning, you called her work number at 11:15 and her home number at 11:19. Why?"

"I wanted to find out if she was still missing."

"Did you leave a message on her answering machine Friday night or Monday morning?"

"No. I hung up when the machine picked up."

"Maybe you didn't bother leaving a message because you knew the incoming message cassette wasn't in the machine."

An eerie buzz filled my head.

"Maybe you took it because what's on the tape is incriminating, and you didn't want anyone listening to it. Maybe the story that some guys roughed you up and demanded a tape is just a load of crap."

I sat back in my chair, stunned.

Ashcroft leaned forward and propped his elbows on his knees. "Why don't we do those things I suggested and move toward clearing you as a suspect."

I had a sinking feeling I was about to do exactly what Detective Bonikowski had planned all along. "Check away," I said, "because nothing related to Nicole's death is going to come back to me."

Chapter Eighteen

The sunlight warmed my back as I leaned against the windowsill in my hotel room and watched Ashcroft and Bonikowski go through my belongings. If I ended up being convicted, it would be for stupidity, plain and simple. I must have been crazy to have consented to a search. Then again, my refusal would have prompted them to get a search warrant. Either way, they would have gotten what they wanted, and I had no idea whether one or the other was more ominous from a legal standpoint.

Although I couldn't see him, I heard Bonikowski's partner sifting through my things in the bathroom while she stood at the foot of the bed and snapped on a pair of latex gloves. She emptied my duffel on the bedspread. When she lifted a pair of briefs by the waistband and held them at eye level, I felt my face getting warm. Why hadn't Ashcroft taken the duffel? But he had gone straight to the closet and was presently sealing my loafers in an evidence bag.

Bonikowski's partner stepped out of the bathroom and addressed Ashcroft. "Nothing in here. What do you want me to do next?"

"Check with security. See what they have to say about the break-in, and see if they bothered to look at video. Either way, we'll want the tapes covering the time frame, at least an hour before and after the break-in, and any parking lot video they've got."

The detective pulled off his gloves as he left the room.

Video. Why hadn't I thought of that? Why hadn't Fortman?

I rolled my head, and as I reached up to rub the back of my neck, I caught sight of my keys lying on the desk. Noticed the brass key from Kessler's room at the bed-and-breakfast and its little round disc with the number four scrawled in black ink.

Shit. Nicole's composition notebook was in Kessler's room. I hadn't told them that I had it, and I wasn't going to now.

"Something wrong?"

I looked at Bonikowski and lowered my arm. "Just sore."

She nodded and went back to work on the duffel, unzipping side pockets and checking beneath the support flap that spanned the interior's base. I glanced at the keys. I'd clipped the bed-and-breakfast key onto my keychain, which, thanks to my regular job, happened to be crammed with an odd assortment of keys tagged with strips of bright fluorescent tape.

Even if Bonikowski picked them up, I doubted she'd question the one key that, in my mind, stood out.

Ashcroft had finished with the closet. He brought his clipboard and evidence bag over to the bed closest to the window. "Do you have any belongings at the track?"

"No."

"Anything in the hotel's baggage storage?"

I shook my head.

"Safe?"

"No."

"Does laundry services currently have any of your clothes?"

"No. Everything that I brought with me is right here in this room."

He nodded. "I need to take a look at your boots."

I bent to unlace them, and a searing pain shot across my lower back. I sucked in a breath and braced my palm on the edge of the window unit. I tried again, planted my hand on my shin and worked the denim through my fingers so I could get at the laces.

Ashcroft cleared his throat. "Why don't you just sit on the bed, and I'll look at them."

I glanced at the digital clock. Two-thirty, which meant I still had a couple more hours to go before I could take another pain pill.

Well, shit.

The box springs creaked as I sat down and leaned backward, pressed my palms against the mattress. I draped my leg across the bed. Ashcroft referenced his clipboard as he studied the tread, and I suspected he had a photograph, possibly of a footprint casting.

The temptation of collapsing on the quilted bedspread and closing my eyes was a strong one. Go to sleep for a month.

Bonikowski had finished her work and was standing quietly by the bureau with her arms folded. I shifted my gaze and caught her staring. She quickly averted her eyes, and I realized she had allowed herself to slip out of cop mode, at least for a second.

Ashcroft stood, and I lowered my foot to the carpet and sat up with difficulty.

"How long will you be in town?"

"Until after the Derby."

"Don't alter your plans without telling me."

I nodded, signed for the shoes and my notepad, the only items they removed from my room, and closed the door behind them.

I took a shower and changed, and a half hour later, I was heading downstairs to the hotel's café when my phone rang. "Cline."

"Where are you?"

"At the hotel," I said and frowned at Kessler's tone of voice. "Are the horses okay?"

"Oh…yeah. They're fine. Foiley thought you might have been arrested."

I grinned as I scanned the café. "He was jumping the gun," I said. "It's not sundown, yet."

"What?"

"Nothing."

"I'm coming over. Stay put."

"Okay. Hey, wait. I was going to eat in the hotel's café, but they're not open. Meet me in the Cardinal Hall of Fame. It's right in front of the hotel."

Kessler disconnected.

Although it wasn't quite four in the afternoon, the restaurant was pulling in a modest crowd. I had been seated at a table by the window and was looking at the menu when Kessler walked past the hostess' podium and paused in the doorway. He spotted me almost immediately, crossed over, and pulled out the chair opposite.

He took a good long look at my face before he sat down. "If you could walk over here, I guess you're not too banged up, but Jesus....What the hell's going on?"

I told him about the accident.

"You hit a concrete divider and walked away from it?"

"Mercedes builds a nice car," I said, and it wasn't the first time since last night that I'd thought of my father dying in one. Almost a year ago, now.

"Tell me about the police. Jay said you made...'an appointment'?"

"Yeah," I said, and Kessler began to sigh. "That, or they would have picked me up for sure," I added.

He narrowed his eyes. "You think this is funny, don't you?"

I chuckled. "No." I held up my hands. "Sorry. I'm just so goddamn relieved I wasn't hauled in and charged for murder, I—"

Our server stepped up to the table right smack in the middle of my comment, and she looked at me now with wide eyes. I picked up the menu and held it in front of my face as I ordered, afraid to look at either one of them for fear that I'd start laughing. Guess I'd been more strung up than I realized.

When I relinquished the menu, Kessler looked like he was going to jump over the table and strangle me. I rubbed my face

and shifted my gaze out the window at the never-ending traffic
streaming down Crittenden. A slick-looking Brook Ledge semi
carrying a load of horses turned onto Central.

Kessler had ordered coffee, and I'd asked for another soda, so
we filled the time until our server returned with small talk.

Once our drinks arrived, he took a sip of coffee and looked
at me pensively. "Okay. What gives?"

I described the assignment, which he knew about vaguely;
then I told him the rest.

"You should go back home. I'll get someone else to come
out."

"I can't. The cops may very well find a reason to lock me up
if I tell them I'm leaving."

"They can't just do that. This isn't the Wild West."

I set my Coke on the table and nodded slowly. "They'd find
a way."

"Jesus Christ. Why do you always get involved in this crap?"

I looked up from my drink. "One of those times, if I remember correctly, I was helping you."

Kessler stared at me for a moment, then said softly, "You're
right. I'm sorry." He fiddled with his coffee mug. "I guess I had
better get used to it, hadn't I? This propensity of yours..." he
waved his hand, "it's your nature—your curiosity and a need
to take risks. Isn't it?"

I shrugged.

"Yeah. You know it is. That's why you're thinking about a
career change."

I almost laughed. Like my current situation *was* a career.
Managing a bunch of guys whose only ambition was to rack
up the hours working a menial job, killing time between one
six-pack and the next.

"If they try to question you again," Kessler said, "for God's
sake, don't talk to them without a lawyer. I know someone here in
Louisville. Someone good. I think I'll get him onboard now."

I shook my head. "I don't want you doing that. Not now.
It's not necessary."

"You don't think so?" Kessler said with a heavy dose of annoyance vibrating in his voice.

"I don't know what evidence they've got, but I'm pretty sure it's taking them in another direction."

Voices and the sound of a wailing child spilled into the breezeway as the Hilton's automatic doors slid open. A disorganized line had formed at the front desk and snaked into the foyer where a number of tourists and a great deal of luggage choked the available thruway.

I squeezed between a pillar and potted plant in order to cut through the lounge. An inviting space and one I'd had no reason to use during my stay. The cool grays of the carpet and plush furniture were offset by warm honey-colored molding and a see-through fireplace. The gas flames weren't lit, and the television above the mantel played to an empty room. The footage behind the news anchor featured a pan of the Twin Spires. Not surprising considering the fact that we only had nine days to go before the Derby. As I continued past an overstuffed chair, I glanced back at the screen and froze.

Nicole's picture was framed in the upper right-hand corner.

"...worked in the Marketing Department at Churchill Downs. Her body was found in a wooded area on the southern edge of Riverfields Reserve Wednesday afternoon. If you have any information about this brutal slaying, call...."

The unexpected mention of her death sucked the breath from my lungs. As I stood stock-still, the jumbled voices and the sound of a ringing phone, even the kid's screeching, faded like someone had clamped a pillow over my head. The room swirled around me. The colors fused into bands of light and dark and began a slow rotation around my head. I clamped my hand on the chair's armrest and knocked against an end table as I crumpled into the seat and put my head between my knees. Felt the jacked up cadence of my heartbeat pulsing along my spine.

Jesus.

Must be the Vicodin. Or maybe the fact that I hadn't slept in thirty-seven goddamn hours. Well shit, I could hide behind whatever excuse I damn well chose. Maybe facing the raw truth that someone had snuffed out a young life had finally caught up with me because I'd been trying damn hard to keep that fact from sinking anywhere beyond the most superficial level of conscious thought.

Past atrocities that I'd witnessed whirled in my mind, a grotesque kaleidoscope of disturbing images. Blood dripping from my nose; a muzzle flash hissing from a gun aimed at my chest; a young woman lying dead in a horse's stall with her panties bunched around her thighs; flesh sloughing off a man's fingers as he reached out to me while flames rode up his chest like something alive.

I sat up and allowed my weight to sink into the cushions, closed my eyes, and swallowed hard. A soft current of air feathered down from the ceiling register and chilled my skin while footsteps echoed on the tile as some of the new arrivals headed toward the elevator bay.

Greed and a lust for power drove men to commit horrible acts, and the repercussions rippled outward with unspeakable damning consequences. Corey had been affected, and so had I. So had a little girl in Virginia whose life had been irrevocably shattered on a cold winter's night.

I swallowed again and rubbed my face. When I opened my eyes, the anchorwoman had moved on.

"...Dow ends down nine while Nasdaq finished down eleven as inflation worries persist. In other news..." she was saying, and I almost tuned her out until I noticed a still shot of an oil derrick displayed on the screen behind her.

"...bucked the trend as stock skyrocketed. Company officials announced yesterday that Matthew Sturgill the third will take over as President and CEO this June."

Skyrocketed because of Paige, I thought.

Chapter Nineteen

The chain shank clinked against Ruskie's halter as the big chestnut horse strode down the shedrow in Barn 41. We were on our fourth lap, and it wasn't the first time that I had marveled at the ability of such a large animal to move so silently across the ground. The colt probably topped the scales at twelve hundred pounds, yet that soft clink was the only sound he made.

Of course, the footing consisted of a powdery loam and sawdust mix, and his sinewy legs were marvelously adapted for speed and efficiency and the ability to propel his mass across the ground with minimal exertion. Next to him, I felt like a graceless lug. Stiff as hell and still hurting, but well rested. I had gone to bed before seven, and between the Vicodin and exhaustion, I had slipped into a dead, dreamless sleep.

Ruskie watched me from the corner of his eye, canting his head ever so slightly, and I was convinced he was wondering why I was slowing him down when I usually matched his pace with ease. He took up the slack in the lead for the third time, and I tweaked the leather, generating a subtle vibration that nudged the chain against the sensitive flesh covering the bridge of his nose, a silent, private communication. He slowed again, and when he worked his mouth, I half expected him to sigh in annoyance.

I was smiling as we approached the short aisle farthest from his stall, but the lighthearted moment evaporated as I caught sight of the two Hispanics who'd been standing in the doorway for the past ten minutes. Ten minutes spent with their hands jammed in their jean pockets and their hard eyes tracking our progress around the shedrow.

During the morning's work, no one stood around for long on the backside, not eight days before the Derby. Not unless they owned the damn horses. The younger of the two spat, and a sticky amber-colored wad of chewing tobacco shot through the air and landed in my path. He sneered and said "*maldito chota*" in a voice loud enough to ensure that I heard his words. Although the exact translation was lost on me, his manner and expression more than made up for the language barrier.

Apparently, a couple of detectives had been in the barn yesterday afternoon, rousting grooms who were catching up on their sleep or their drinking in Barn 41's tack rooms. Jay said the cops had been here for an hour, interviewing anyone who might have known Nicole or seen something suspicious Friday, a week ago today.

One week, seven days, 168 hours, give or take, since Nicole stood outside Gone Wild's stall with a piece of paper clamped between her fingers. One week since she tried to conceal her interest in Rudi's Derby runner by drifting farther down the shedrow to admire Storm and engage me in conversation. At least that's how it seemed now—that she had been covering up. Although I had to admit, my recollection may very well have become colored by everything that had happened since. Knowing about the page torn from her composition notebook certainly cast that encounter in a different light. One thing I knew for certain, the only time she had seemed truly relaxed was when she'd spent that moment embracing Storm.

Thinking about her interest in Gone Wild, I realized I had foolishly avoided giving Rudi a good hard look because I liked him. Bill Gannon and Edward Utley had been more appealing suspects. I thought about the thugs who'd jumped me in the restroom. Although I'd had no way of knowing it then, one of them could have been coming down from an adrenaline buzz after murdering her the day before. New York, for instance.

Two guys the cops weren't interested in because they'd rather look at me.

Then again, the person responsible for Nicole's death could easily be someone whose path I had yet to cross.

It was six-forty, minutes before sunrise, and the backside was hopping.

Ruskie and I stepped into the short aisle. The guard had left his post and was standing outside, talking to a track official and Detectives Ashcroft and Bonikowski.

Shit.

Kessler stood in the aisle, listening to some guy I'd never seen before, and he hadn't noticed the cops. Behind him, Jay stepped out of Ruskie's stall with a pitchfork and rake in his hand and bailing twine wound round his fingers. He focused on Ruskie's legs.

"Jay," I whispered and jerked my head when he looked up.

His gaze shifted to the entrance as Ruskie and I continued down the shedrow.

Maybe the cops were here to conduct more interviews. They would certainly catch a larger subset of people this time of day compared to yesterday afternoon's sweep. But if Ashcroft had changed his mind and was here to pick me up, I didn't want it happening on the backside in full view of the media.

We circled around again, and as we emerged from the short aisle, Ruskie eyed the growing crowd. Both of us had grown accustomed to the never-ending presence of the media and the constant stream of foot traffic, but this was getting out of hand.

A Hispanic exercise rider reined his colt into the alley and launched into a string of rapid-fire Spanish at the sight of the throng. He quickly dismounted, slipped the reins over the bay's head, and passed directly behind Detective Bonikowski.

She had been watching a female groom slop water over a horse's back but started when the bay colt passed by within a couple of feet. As she pivoted around, our eyes met. She watched me lead Ruskie into the turn; then the chestnut's rangy body blocked her view.

Great. Now she knew exactly where to find me, though I doubted we'd be doing much talking as long as I held Ruskie's lead.

I glanced in Storm and Ruskie's stalls as I passed and didn't see Jay or Kessler.

Goddamnit.

Jay was waiting for me midway down the shedrow on the Longfield Avenue side, away from the prying eyes of the media circus taking place between Barns 41 and 43. I stopped, and Jay stepped in front of me and took control of the horse.

"Get outta here. I'll call you when they're gone, and you can fucking bring me back something to eat."

I grinned. "Does Kessler know?"

"His idea. Don't want you snatched up with the press watching." Jay turned, and Ruskie followed as if changing humans in mid walk was an everyday occurrence.

I cut between the spruce bushes and the barn's foundation and resisted the urge to look for Bonikowski. I picked up my pace as I followed the lane that took me past the next three barns whose southern walls faced Longfield. When I cut around Barn 26, I had a clear sightline all the way to the Derby barns. The crowd had grown, and I was certain Ashcroft's frustration was mounting. How he would interview anyone in that environment was beyond me.

I followed the lane as it curved along the backside's outermost boundary, hemmed in by barns on my left and the ten-foot-high chain-link fence on my right. The morning had grown brighter, and as I looked toward the east, I was surprised by the sight of hot air balloons dotting the sky. They hovered above the trees, slow-moving, gelatinous spheres backlit by a sun that had just crested the horizon.

Oh, yeah. Yet another Derby event.

I smiled. Good thing Gallant Storm had put in his morning work early, when only a hint of light had seeped across the sky. Horses usually don't look up, but knowing him, he would have spotted those balloons, either when he was cooling out or, worse, when he was on the track with all that open space and the freedom it invited boiling in his blood.

I left Churchill by Gate 6, and as I approached Wagner's Pharmacy near the corner of Fourth and Central, the balloons blossomed with color as the sun rode higher in the sky.

Wagner's Pharmacy was a misnomer, really, because it was part café, part sundries, part liquor store, and one-hundred percent unique. The glass door eased shut behind me, efficiently dampening the street noise while jumbled voices and the sounds and aromas of sizzling food flooded my senses. I'd been inside once before, and I swear, the place was straight out of a Forties movie. I looked for an empty seat. Booths lined the wall on my left. Tables and chairs filled the center of the room. A Formica counter stretched down the right-hand wall where customers sat on barstools upholstered with pumpkin-colored vinyl and watched the cook fry up their eggs. I stepped down the sloped floor and slid onto an empty stool at the end of the counter, planted my boots on the runner.

Wooden plaques hung above the grill and featured seriously dated paintings of eggs and bacon, coffee and toast. The damn things had to have been tacked up there before my mother was born.

First impressions are often flawed by preconceived, erroneous notions, and my initial look inside Wagner's had taken me by surprise. The establishment that so many people talked about and patronized, backsiders and the wealthy alike, was a dump. But it had an irresistible charm, mainly because it could not have existed anywhere else in the world. Everywhere you looked, on every square inch of wall space, hung period photographs of horses and jockeys and the men and women who owned and trained them. Directly across from where I sat hung an eight-by-ten glossy of Secretariat after he won the Kentucky Derby in unbelievable fashion on May 5th, 1973, and I had no doubt it was an original that had been carried across the street and had decorated that space for thirty years.

Pure and simple, Wagner's was a walk backward through time. And the food was damn good, too.

I ordered bacon and eggs and biscuits and gravy and was halfway through my meal when my cell rang. I wiped my fingers on a napkin and flipped the phone open. "Cline."

"Coast is clear."

I smiled. "Who'd they talk to?"

"Mr. K," Jay said, referring to Kessler. "Bill Gannon and his employees, couple Hispanic stable hands, me, the guy Kessler was talking to."

"Know who he is?"

"From what I heard, guy's an owner. Maybe a potential client."

"Did the cops interview with the press around?"

"Used an office. Even so, the reporters were buzzin' round like flies on shit."

"Apt description, there, Jay."

He grunted. "Get your ass back here, and bring me something to eat."

I closed my phone and was scraping the last bit of egg and biscuits and gravy into the center of my plate when someone stepped alongside my shoulder and placed a hand on the countertop. A small, feminine hand. I turned my head.

Detective Bonikowski stood at my side in her fashionable suit—this morning's choice, a charcoal gray herringbone— paired with a pink silk blouse with the buttons left undone at her throat.

"Detective."

"Mr. Cline." She swept the room with a practiced glance before her gaze returned to my face. "What are you doing here?"

"Taking a break." I gestured toward my plate. "Eating."

"You take breaks in the middle of walking a horse?"

I smiled. "Not usually."

"Did you think we were coming to hook you up?"

"It crossed my mind."

"And now?"

I glanced at her and sighed. "No. Your shoulders are relaxed. Your hands are nowhere near your weapon or cuffs, you're unbalanced with most of your weight on your left foot…and you're alone."

Her mouth twitched. "I wouldn't need backup to handle you."

I swiveled around on my stool and squinted at her, wondering if the implied meaning was simply a case of wishful thinking on my part. "How'd you find me?"

"Driving past. Looked in the window…you know? Advanced police work."

I grinned.

"Anyway," she said. "I have some good news for you."

"You do?"

"The preliminary test results are back, and your DNA sample does not match the killer's."

I bowed my head and drew in a deep breath. "That was fast."

"The PCR test is a kind of filter. It doesn't run through the full process necessary for a conviction, but it's a useful guidepost for elimination purposes. Of course, you're not totally in the clear. Just because you didn't physically kill her doesn't mean you didn't have a hand in her death."

I said nothing for a moment but watched the cook expertly wield a pair of metal spatulas as he scrambled eggs right on the grill. "You realize the barn you went to this morning is not the barn where I saw Nicole Friday, right?"

"Correct. We're tracking her movements, a job which includes talking to everyone who was in Barn 4."

"You'll have a tough time locating everyone she spoke with Friday morning if she was on the backside any length of time. People move around, and you're talking a week, now. I gotta tell you, doing that kind of job, especially while the track's dark, it's hard to tell one day from the next. Lots of people aren't going to be too clear about what they did or didn't do a week ago."

"By dark, you mean no racing?"

"Yes. The spring meet doesn't start until tomorrow. The races make it easier to remember what you did on any given day."

She nodded slowly. "Have you thought of anything else that might help us?"

Now that she wasn't so quick to believe I was the killer, I said, "Those two guys who jumped me in Sully's. You need to figure out who they are."

"Would you be willing to come downtown and talk to our forensics artist?"

"Sure. As soon as I can get away."

She glanced at my plate. "Looks like you're almost done."

I smiled. "I need to clear it with my boss."

She nodded and handed me her card. "If you need a ride, call me, and I'll send someone to pick you up." She slung her purse strap over her shoulder. "Anything else come to mind?"

I described the two Hispanics who resented the fact that I had talked to the cops. Told her I didn't know their names, but she had an idea who they were.

"And Eduardo Sanchez didn't come in this morning. He works for Bill Gannon, and he knows Nicole," I said and realized I'd gotten the tense wrong. I cleared my throat. "My asking questions about her irritated him."

"Any idea why?"

I shook my head. "What about the hotel's video?"

"They've already recycled the tapes."

"Shit."

"Anything else?"

I set my fork on the plate and stared at Secretariat's picture without really seeing it. "I've been discounting Rudi Sturgill because I like him, but...."

"Go on."

"When Ashcroft took my shoes, he mentioned that whoever killed Nicole would have a specific type of soil on his shoes. If the killer used a car as his means of transportation, which I figure is a given, I assume he would have left traces of the same soil in his vehicle."

She shifted her weight and crossed her slender arms. "Probably."

"The interior of one of Rudi's cars was recently gone over with a strong-smelling cleaner, and according to Rudi's driver, the carpet was shampooed."

"The car involved in the crash?"

"No. A light-colored Lincoln Town Car with luminescent paint. Reminded me of a pearl."

After Detective Bonikowski left, I downed two Vicodin with the last of my orange juice and ordered Jay's breakfast to go.

I spent the rest of Friday afternoon working with the Louisville Metro PD's forensics artist and now had a glossy printout of side-by-side shots of New York and his partner folded in my pocket. On my way back to the hotel, I purchased a *Louisville Street Guide & Directory* at a gas station on Central Avenue. Once I got back to the hotel and showered, I pulled on a pair of jeans and switched on the desk light.

I flipped through the pages until I located River Road where it parallels Waterfront Park. To the west, it terminates almost immediately at 9th Street. Next, I traced it east, past River Road Country Club, past Zorn Avenue. Past Cox's Park and…Indian Hills.

Detective Bonikowski asked me if I had ever been on Indian Hills Trail. From its northernmost point at River Road, it headed south and almost immediately passed beneath I-71, eventually terminating at Old Brownsboro Road. My eye was drawn back to the quarter-mile stretch between River Road and I-71. A dark green rectangle represented an area of parkland on the east side of the road.

Riverfields Natural Reserve.

According to the news anchor, Nicole's body had been found on its southern border.

Chapter Twenty

I wanted a better look at the area where Nicole's body was found, something more informative than lines on paper and inch-and-a-half grids. Driving was out, so an aerial shot was my next best bet, and that meant getting on the Internet. I pulled on a pair of freshly laundered socks and a long-sleeved Henley that smelled like fabric softener; then I laced up my boots—slowly. I had been holding off taking the Vicodin until dinner, but my muscles were cramped after an afternoon spent at the police department working on composites of New York and his buddy. I hadn't seen either detective, which had been disappointing in an odd sort of way.

I stuffed my notes in the street guide, snatched my denim jacket off the bed, and headed downstairs. Not unexpectedly, the Business Center was full. I wandered into the hotel's restaurant and ordered dinner: a hamburger, fries, chocolate shake. While I waited, I unfolded the backup notes I'd made in the shedrow and copied them into a brand-new notepad.

When the meal came, I shoved them aside and relaxed into my chair. I had chosen a seat by the window. Traffic streamed off Crittenden onto the fairgrounds' access road. When I had walked over to the track in the predawn dark, the balloonists were already arriving in their SUVs and Suburbans and pickups. Besides the sunrise race, the Derby program included a balloon glow tonight and a repeat tomorrow.

I poured ketchup on my fries and screwed on the lid. As I set the bottle next to the napkin dispenser, I glanced at my notes and noticed the Dry Ridge Road address for Bill Gannon Racing Stables. I flipped open the street index and located Dry Ridge on page 215. Edward Utley kept his horses on Dry Ridge, but it was impossible to tell where either farm was located by looking at the map. I found Nicole's street, but nothing about the location stood out. Nothing I didn't already know from being there. I thumbed through my notes until I found her landlords' address. They lived on the next street over. On Cherokee Road. Except for Snoopy Sanchez, who lived at the track, everyone else lived out of town. Everyone except Kessler's client, Edward J. Utley.

I looked up his address—512 Poplar Hill Woods—then flipped to the index. As I drew my finger across the fine print, my breath caught in my lungs. Poplar Hill Woods was located in the Indian Hills subdivision. I opened the book to page 130 then flipped back to 129. Utley lived on a short cul-de-sac less than a mile from Riverfields Natural Reserve.

As I stepped off the bus an hour before dusk, the majestic churches on West Catherine Street glowed in the warm light. I turned north at Third and noticed Kessler's rental in the church lot but didn't see the red Buick parked in front of the bed-and-breakfast until I was halfway down the block. Utley's car.

Damn.

I glanced at my watch. When the Hilton's Business Center still hadn't been an option after dinner, I had called Kessler to see if I could use his laptop. As it turned out, he was going to some swank restaurant with Utley and his wife, so I wouldn't be interfering with his plans or computer time. I frowned as I climbed a flight of steps rising from the sidewalk and passed between decorative wrought iron gates. From the way Kessler had talked, I hadn't expected to run into them.

The sharp odor of fresh mulch and damp soil hung in the air as I stepped onto the front porch. I fished out my keys and was sorting through them when the door opened. Ricardo, one of the owners, greeted me while Kessler and Utley and a woman I assumed to be his wife entered the foyer. Utley was talking. Something to do with architecture.

"Evening, Ricardo," I said.

"Steve." He glanced at my jeans and said, "Are you here to use the room?"

I smiled, realizing his assumption had been a logical one. Both Kessler and Utley were exquisitely turned out, wearing elegant pinstripe suits and silk ties. A diamond cufflink flashed at Utley's wrist when he rubbed his chin. His face looked moist and smooth and as hairless as a baby's butt, and if I wasn't mistaken, clear varnish coated his manicured fingernails.

God help me if I ever did *that*.

"Yep," I said, answering Ricardo's question. "For a couple hours."

Mrs. Utley stood beside her husband, a woman of ample proportions and short stature with wavy brown hair and professionally applied makeup. An amused smile played across her lips as she turned away from the men to examine a stained-glass window set above the staircase.

She possessed a classy poise that had me liking her immediately.

My gaze shifted to Utley.

"...a symmetrical façade with decorative floral patterns and, of course, exaggerated stonework joints. Now this," Utley said as he pivoted slowly on his heel, "is a fine example of the Richardsonian Romanesque style with its heavily rounded arches above the doors and windows, and as you surely must know, Louisville is home to the second largest collection of cast iron architecture. I'll have to show—"

Utley's voice faltered as he caught sight of me standing by the door. He narrowed his eyes, and both Mrs. Utley and Kessler turned to see what he was looking at.

"What is *he* doing here?" Utley said. His eyes widened as he looked at Kessler. "Is something wrong with the horse?"

"Oh, no. Steve's here to use my laptop."

"Laptop? What on Earth for?"

"Research," I said quickly.

Utley stepped toward me. "Aren't the authorities looking for him in relation to a murder investigation?"

"No, sir," I said, ignoring the fact that he hadn't addressed me. "They aren't."

"But I heard—"

"What you heard was erroneous—" Kessler said, and I interrupted him.

"Everyone who saw her last Friday is being interviewed. Weren't you?" Because you should have been, I thought.

"Of course not."

"Did you know her?"

"That's none of your business." Utley grasped his wife's hand and pulled her toward the door.

I moved out of his way. "Do you know where her body was found, Mr. Utley?"

He glared at me as he brushed past Kessler. "This is obscene, talking about that poor woman."

Utley yanked the front door open, and a current of air laden with his heavy cologne swirled around my head and closed my throat.

Mrs. Utley craned her neck and stared as her husband hustled her across the threshold. Kessler hung back, thanked Ricardo for his help securing their reservation, and gave me a pointed look as he clicked the door shut.

Sighing, I turned toward Ricardo. "Well, that went well," I said, and he chuckled.

◇◇◇

It occurred to me as I switched on Kessler's television and plugged in his laptop that my father was an extremely neat man. He'd left very few of his belongings lying on the desktop or coffee table. His car keys and cell phone charger sat on the night stand closest to the door. I used the restroom and noted the row of toiletries lined up on the windowsill: his shaving kit, a comb, styling foam, a nail file, an open package of Halls Mentho-Lyptus cough drops. The cellophane crinkled when I picked up the packet and turned it in my fingers. I was reminded of a time when, as a child, I had been fascinated by my father's belongings. Stepfather, I guess you could say, though at the time, mercifully, the truth had eluded us both.

On more than one occasion, I had snuck into my parents' bedroom to examine the contents of his bureau, pulling open what drawers I could reach, feeling the wood glide on silken tracks, fingering the piles of handkerchiefs, the leather belts rolled into neat coils, the billowy Turkish cotton pajamas. And occasionally, when I'd opened the drawer that held his undershirts, I would catch of whiff of his scent amid the sweet smell of soap. Even today, every now and then, some combination of odors triggered a vivid memory of him that knocked me into the past like a sledgehammer to the brain.

God, I missed him.

I replaced the cough drops and walked back into the bedroom. The evening was growing dark. As I switched on the bedside lamp, Kessler's keys caught my eye. The rental key was there, too. The idea of borrowing his car was attractive, but to what point? I wouldn't be able to see anything, and since my wallet had been stolen, I had no license, not to mention permission. Instead, I brought up Google and ran a search for "Louisville" + "aerial" and came up with something that looked promising on a website titled *Louisville/Jefferson County Information Consortium*. It featured an interactive aerial map of both city and county.

I keyed in Edward Utley's address at 512 Poplar Hill Woods and was rewarded with an up-close-and-personal view of his mansion's complicated roofline. Nice house, circular drive in front, in-ground pool in the back, lots of woods to the north that formed a buffer between his property and I-71. The current view displayed a scale of one inch equaling 126 feet, but I saw that I could manipulate it all the way down to twenty-five feet or less, when the image degraded into blurred digital blocks. Or

I could pull out to seven hundred feet. Between the aerial views and the Louisville street map, I was able to locate the area where Nicole's body had been found. And when I compared that site to the red dot that sat squarely on Utley's property, it told me a hell of a lot.

The news anchor had announced that Nicole's body was discovered on the southern edge of Riverfields Natural Reserve which appeared to be a densely wooded area cut with winding trails. Plenty of secluded places to hide a body, not to mention the appeal of a lake located near the southern boundary.

She'd been within earshot of I-71 but miles away from help.

A lonely place to die.

The reserve was bordered on the west by Indian Hills Trail and on the south by the I-71 easement, but what I found particularly interesting was a dirt road that left Indian Hills Trail and ran parallel to I-71. It took me five minutes, readjusting the image as needed, to follow the road to a spot where the surface changed from dirt to blacktop and became Riviera Drive.

Riviera Drive emptied onto Blakenbaker Lane. Make a right on Blakenbaker, pass under I-71, turn left at the second paved drive on the left, and a minute later, Edward J. Utley would be keying his garage door opener.

Fuck yeah.

I leaned back against the wicker chair. So…why the hell hadn't the cops talked to *him*?

Even though Detective Ashcroft was the lead investigator, I called Bonikowski.

She picked up on the second ring. "Bonikowski."

"This is Steve Cline," I said. "I have a question."

Metal clanged in the background amid the noise of running water. "Wait a sec," she said. Her voice was muffled, as if the phone were tucked against her shoulder. The sound of someone cranking a squeaky faucet shrilled in the earpiece. "What can I do for you, Mr. Cline?"

"Are you looking at Edward J. Utley?" I said, and knowing she likely wouldn't tell me word one about an ongoing investigation, I continued. "If you aren't, you should be."

"And why's that?"

"Well, I touched on it during the interview," I said and reminded her of the fact that he boarded his horses next to Gannon's farm where Nicole had once worked. "So there's a possibility they know...knew each other. And it's conceivable that she may have dealt with him in the course of her job with Churchill's Marketing Department. Utley has an aggressive, hands-on personality. He wouldn't hesitate approaching her department if something displeased him. And he's a man who is easily displeased."

A breath of air buffeted her phone's mike.

"So," I said, "have you interviewed him?"

"He's on our list, but we haven't talked to him yet."

"Have you tried?"

"What's your point, Mr. Cline?"

"You don't know where he lives, do you?"

She was quiet for a moment. "What's that supposed to mean?"

"He lives less than a mile from Riverfields Reserve. I've been looking at an aerial map. Very interesting. Lots of detail. Details that wouldn't necessarily be obvious from the ground. And what I saw on this aerial map was a dirt track that heads east off Indian Hills Trail just before the road passes beneath I-71. It parallels the interstate's easement, and there's a lake to the north, practically touches the dirt road by the looks of it." I told her where the track ended and how simple it was to get to Utley's house from there. "Maybe you should be checking out his car."

"You thought the same thing about Mr. Sturgill, if I recall."

"True." I smiled. "I'm keeping an open mind."

"So are we, Mr. Cline. So are we," she said, and I had an overwhelming impression that I was still firmly lodged in her suspects' column.

"Have you tried to contact him?"

"He was in Lexington today. So, no. We've been following other leads."

"He's downtown right now," I said.

"How do you know that?"

"He's one of my father's clients. They went out to dinner together."

"Do you know where they are?"

"No, but I think I can find out."

I found Ricardo and John in the kitchen, chopping vegetables and running a blender—mixed drinks judging by the bottle of Maker's Mark. Well, Ricardo was actually sitting on a stool, swinging his leg while the blender whirred. John paused in the middle of slicing onions and green peppers while something delicious-smelling sizzled under the broiler.

Ricardo slid off the stool and switched off the blender. "What can we do for you, Steve?"

"Where did my father go, do you know?"

"Vincenzo's," Ricardo said reverently, which prompted a sardonic chuckle from John. "On Fifth between Market and Main."

"Thanks." I turned to leave.

"Join us for dinner," Ricardo said and raised his eyebrows, "because surely you aren't planning to go there?"

I paused in the doorway and smiled. I could almost hear him thinking *dressed like that?* "No, I just wondered where he went, and thanks for the invite, but I've already eaten."

I started up the steps two at a time, a maneuver which I aborted before I reached the first landing. Vicodin could only do so much.

Before I reached the sitting room on the third floor, I realized I couldn't give out Utley's location. Embarrassing him in front of Kessler would be disastrous, especially when the timing of a police visit would so obviously point to me. I flipped open my phone and hit REDIAL.

When Bonikowski answered, I said, "I couldn't find out where they went, but they left here at eight-fifteen, so I expect Utley won't be home until close to eleven."

"And where is here?"

"Rocking Horse Manor on—"

"South Third?" she said.

"Yeah."

"What are *you* doing there?"

I didn't particularly want her to know I was using Kessler's laptop. "I stopped by to visit my father."

"Kind of hard to do when he's not there, Mr. Cline," she said.

"I'm just hanging out. Watching T.V."

"There's 'T.V.' at the Hilton, you know?"

"It gets boring there."

She chuckled. "Good night, Mr. Cline."

"Good night, Detective Bonikowski."

By nine-thirty, I had painstakingly gone through Nicole's composition notebook, looking for proper names that I could run searches on, all for naught. I had no doubt that her first entries on a new job would have been complete and copious, with full names written down for each and every coworker.

I set her notebook aside, flipped open mine. I had collected data on everyone except Eduardo "Snoopy" Sanchez. He was an unknown, and I didn't like it.

I picked up a pencil and jotted down my top suspects: Utley, Bill Gannon, Rudi Sturgill. I scrawled Sanchez's name below Gannon's.

Rudi Sturgill. He looked good, if only for the fact that he'd befriended me and had been handy when I was attacked in the men's room. But, he'd had plenty of subsequent opportunities to do me harm and had helped me instead. I drew a question mark above his name.

Yaseen Haddad, Senior Software Engineer. He was out of the picture now, since the missing tape was undoubtedly the cassette from Nicole's answering machine, not a data storage tape.

I turned Nicole's notebook over and examined the faded binding and black-and-white marble pattern, discolored and dirty with a few reddish-brown stains. I sniffed them and was not surprised when I detected a faint odor of iodine. She'd worked foal watch as I had, and most nights I would get off work with iodine blotches discoloring my fingers and the sleeves of my sweatshirt if I'd been careless. Occupational hazard. I flipped through the pages, and when I found the spot where she'd torn out the page, I smoothed my fingers down the tear.

What did you see, Nicole? What did you see that was so damning, it cost you your life? And why now, three years later?

Chapter Twenty-one

Saturday, a week before the Derby, when the announcement came over the loudspeakers, instructing horsemen to ready their horses for the first race, the air practically hummed with excitement and a heightened sense of purpose as a soft murmur rolled through the barns like distant artillery. This, after all, was what we were here for.

Straw rustled as Ruskie stepped into his doorway and pricked his ears.

I smiled. "You know what that means, don't you, boy?"

He focused his attention on the road, and his gaze didn't waver as I levered my ass out of a folding chair whose nylon straps sagged like a hammock. I picked up my soda, smoothed my hand down Ruskie's handsome neck, and checked Storm as I strolled out of the barn. I stood where I could see what was happening at the gap and still keep an eye on the horses.

A small crowd had gathered to watch the runners file onto the track. Jay stood among them, arms folded, watching crews from barns scattered throughout the backside converge and line up before starting off toward the grandstand. As we had planned, he was going to shadow one of the crews taking their runner over for the race. I'd be doing the same thing later in the day. If Churchill's protocol varied from what we were accustomed to, we wanted to know about it. Neither one of us could risk making a mistake come the first Saturday in May.

One week to go and counting.

A benign sun shone down on the procession, sleek brown horses and splashes of color beneath a wide blue sky. I leaned against Barn 38's concrete wall and watched until all I could see was a vague impression of the horses' heads nodding above the rail. And that's when I heard a noise that gave me chills—the unexpected sound of cheering that swelled from the stands and drifted across the infield.

I supposed I was an idealist to be moved by that sound because the truth of the matter was that many racing days at tracks across the country unfolded with a great deal less fanfare. I sometimes wondered how the jocks felt, performing in front of a nearly empty grandstand in the bitter cold or stifling heat or stinging rain, risking their necks while the patrons stayed home to watch their T.V.s. But I'd wager many of the jocks didn't give a flying fuck who was watching or even whether they were paid because nothing could compare to sitting astride a thousand-pound eager thoroughbred galloping at forty-some miles per hour.

I drained the last of my Pepsi and started back when the platinum Cadillac eased around the corner and moved silently toward the barn. I glanced at the vehicle, recognized Bill Gannon behind the wheel, and was already dismissing him when I noticed one of the passengers in the back seat. Rudi Sturgill peered out the window. I shifted my gaze to his companion. Not his wife, as I guessed, but Paige. Gannon pulled the car behind a blue Ford Explorer and switched off the engine.

Rudi unbuckled his seatbelt with difficulty. I opened the door for him while Paige strode around the back bumper with a bounce in her stride. She looked absolutely terrific.

A peach-colored skirt layered with lace and crinkly fabric and ruffles swirled around her calves, and her white spaghetti-strap blouse was decorated with all kinds of pearls and beads and embroidered…stuff. She'd completed her look with a frilly hat, eye-catching earrings, and strappy high heels with silk ties laced around her ankles. Kind of reminded me of a gypsy.

Grit crunched under Rudi's heel, and I tore my gaze away from Paige as he latched onto the doorframe and struggled to hoist himself out of the car. I gave him a hand and helped him catch his balance as he pivoted to face me.

A sling supported his left arm, and the dark circles under his blue eyes spoke to the stress he'd been under.

He blew out a breath. His natural good humor lit up his face before an emotion I couldn't identify shifted in his eyes, and his expression grew somber. Gannon, on the other hand, was a cinch to read. He cut around the hood and looked prepared to run a pitchfork through my hide for getting anywhere near his client. He grunted, scowled at his wife, who had remained in the car, and practically stomped into the barn.

Rudi watched him with speculation before he turned to me. "God, look at you. How in the hell can you be working so soon? I could hardly stand the ride down here to see my horse."

"He's back to work," Paige said, "because he's not old like you."

Ignoring her comment, Rudi rolled his neck and eased some weight off the sling by supporting his elbow with his right hand. "I gotta tell you, Paige, I'm not looking forward to sitting through an afternoon's race card."

"Oh, Rudi." Paige sauntered over and tweaked his collar before smoothing her hand across his shoulder. He looked the part of a Southern plantation owner, dressed in a cream-colored linen blazer and navy slacks. "A couple of Mint Juleps will fix you right up."

"Mint Julep, my ass. Bourbon straight up, maybe."

She rolled her eyes. "Oh, you're so sad. What do you think, Steve? My little brother here needs a driver and someone to watch over him, wouldn't you say?"

"I don't know. I think he needs more time in bed."

Paige grinned. "Smart ass."

Paige contented herself by standing in the alley with her arms folded and her face lifted to the sun. I continued down the shed-row and noticed Gannon squatting in his horse's stall, palpating the colt's fetlock. I moved past Ruskie's doorway, slid onto the tack trunk, and rested my back against the wall. Planting my boot on the lid, I draped my arm over my knee and watched a group of men stroll around the corner of Barn 43. Journalists. One of them lifted his camera, and the shutter whirred when he focused on Paige and clicked off a string of shots as she stood in the alley with the sunlight warming her shoulders.

Rudi paused outside Gone Wild's stall and spoke to Gannon. I leaned my head against the stall front and closed my eyes, listened to the soft murmur of their voices while a jet roared overhead and the faint call of the race drifted from the grandstand.

The Derby barns were located in an isolated area tucked away in the southwest corner of the backside. Good for security and intelligent as far as avoiding the inevitable equine pathogens that cropped up from time to time. Since most of the horses in the Derby barns wouldn't run until next weekend, activity in our area stalled in the afternoons. Guards observed the goings-on 24/7. An attendant who had arrived with an uninspired-looking colt stabled on the Longfield side seemed to have settled in for the long haul. He had brought a cooler, lawn chair, and boombox. To be honest, I was surprised more trainers didn't keep an employee in the barn throughout the day. Of course, the tackrooms were crowded at night, and Derby grooms on the whole were a special breed.

When I opened my eyes and lifted my head, I caught Paige staring at me. She turned away, but there had been something in her unguarded expression and stance that had triggered a brief subliminal response that I didn't quite understand. An impression of danger, which made no sense at all. Well, maybe it did. Paige was unlike any woman I had ever known. Aggressively intelligent, dominant. Wild.

I'm sure Brent had his hands full.

Saturday afternoon, I gave Jay a much needed break and didn't leave the track until sometime after seven in the evening. At the hotel, I showered and changed, ate a quick dinner, and arrived at the bus stop before nine with the intention of retrieving Nicole's notebook. I had left it in the bed-and-breakfast. Safe from the cops. Safe from anyone who might gain access to my room.

The sun had set a half hour earlier, and the sky had that translucent quality it gets just before twilight when the color deepens from sapphire to indigo. I waited. Kicked some loose gravel into the gutter. Watched the traffic.

In the past week, I had been lucky with the buses, but thanks to the balloon glow at the fairgrounds, traffic was shot to hell. After standing at the stop on Crittenden for twenty minutes without seeing one TARC bus, I decided to walk to Central and pick up the number four bus.

I caught a break in traffic and cut diagonally across Crittenden. As I walked between the rows of cars parked in the Super 8's corner lot, tires squealed. A red Caprice swerved in front of a van heading west on Central. The Caprice blasted into the motel's parking lot and fishtailed as it cut between the rows of parked cars. The bumper dipped as the driver slammed on the brakes, but I didn't realize the activity had anything to do with me until both front doors swung open.

New York and his buddy straightened behind the car's open doors.

As I spun around, I had an impression of the Hispanic pulling something from beneath his jacket. Something small. Small enough to conceal in his closed hand. Not a gun. I hoped.

My boots felt like they were mired in quicksand as I sprinted back the way I'd come.

Two strides took me across the grass verge bordering the lot. I came to a screeching halt on the sidewalk. Traffic streamed north and south on a green light. Six lanes of traffic blocking my route to the hotel and safety.

I glanced over my shoulder. They had fanned out. The Hispanic was closing in fast. New York had angled toward the Super 8's portico and would easily cut me off if I headed that way. Between the traffic at my back and their positions, they would soon box me in.

I looked past New York and glanced down the street. A south-bound TARC bus lumbered toward us in the right-hand lane.

TARC buses were not unlike those in any mass transit system—ugly, boxy, unimaginative—but that goddamn bus was going to save my ass. I stepped to the curb, stood right under the TARC sign and waved my arms like a fucking lunatic. The bus began to slow.

New York was yelling then, but my eyes were fixed on his partner.

He grew indecisive, hesitant as the bus rolled in behind me with a high-pitched squeal of brakes and hiss of air. It was one thing to attack someone in a deserted parking lot, but coming after me with a captive audience right over my shoulder would have been crazy. The doors slid open with a soft pneumatic whoosh. The Hispanic jammed whatever he was holding in his pocket as I turned.

I vaulted the steps, watched the doors close, listened to the diesel rumble. Felt the drive shaft spinning beneath the floor as the bus pulled away from the curb.

New York jumped behind the wheel. The Caprice lurched forward, then stopped just as quickly so the Hispanic could get in. As the bus continued through the intersection, New York gunned the little red car out of the lot and onto Crittenden.

The light turned yellow.

He muscled the Caprice into the right-turn lane and barreled through the intersection.

The bus driver said something.

I turned toward her. "What?"

"Your fare," she said curtly.

I fished some coins out of my pocket and dropped them into the box.

The driver flipped a wad of chewing gum between her teeth and cracked off tiny air pockets caught in the gum. "This bus detours into the fairgrounds before going to the airport, you know?"

"Oh. Okay."

"Special Events Schedule." She blew a bubble and sucked it back into her mouth.

"Sure." I sat heavily on the bench seat behind her, glanced at the riders: families with kids, solo passengers, teenagers. "What's the stop like at the airport?"

She cracked off half-a-dozen mini bubbles. "What you mean?"

"Where do you stop?"

"Right at the terminal," she said and glanced in the auxiliary mirror above her head. Narrowed her eyes and looked at me like I was an idiot. She blew a huge bubble and popped it.

As long as New York and his partner didn't board the bus before we arrived at the airport, I'd be okay. There would be security at the curb. And a cab ride back to the Hilton.

When the driver pulled into the left-turn lane and waited for a break in traffic, I moved toward the back. New York hadn't been able to pull completely into the turn lane, and I could see the Caprice's roof. Another step took me within range of the car's windshield. The windows were rolled down, and the Hispanic nervously drummed his fingers on the doorframe while New York white-knuckled the steering wheel. He must have caught movement in the bus window, or maybe the Hispanic saw me and said something. Either way, New York snapped his head around, and our eyes met.

He smiled an evil smile, raised his hand, and pointed at my face. Squeezed off an imaginary round.

I backed down the aisle. If he had a gun, what had stopped him from using it in the motel's lot?

I flopped into a seat and sweated. Pulled out my cell and flipped it open. The bus rocked as we swung into the turn and motored toward the fairgrounds. Hopefully New York's crude attempt at mime had been for intimidation purposes only and wasn't something he could back up with the real thing. Conscious of the stares I was catching from the other passengers, I swiveled in my seat and watched the Caprice follow us.

Across the aisle, a young blond man sat sideways with his legs sprawled across the neighboring seats. He balanced a brown paper bag on his stomach. The paper crinkled as he shoved it down the bottle accordion-style and took a swig. Four Roses bourbon. He had the sleepy, heavy-lidded look of someone who was either morosely apathetic or stoned out of his mind, or both.

I scanned my recent calls list, found Detective Bonikowski's number, and pressed it. A faint outline of Kentucky Kingdom's steel coasters slipped silently past my window as I listened to her voicemail switch on. I left my name and number. Told her it was urgent.

When we slowed and turned left at Gate 1, the kids fidgeted with growing excitement now that they were getting a good look at the hot air balloons. They billowed above the field to our right—a riot of color and light that dwarfed the people and vehicles beneath them.

The Caprice followed us.

I returned to the empty seat behind the driver and ignored her annoyed glance in the mirror. She cracked off another string of bubbles.

Up ahead, three lanes fed directly into a tollbooth, but we detoured onto a spur that bypassed the booths. Two event workers stood on the grassy median directing traffic, a fact New York took note of because he moved into line, which put him behind two cars, a jeep, and a Volkswagen Beetle.

The bus driver popped her gum and wriggled in her seat, checking mirrors, slowing the bus to a crawl, and I realized she was preparing to cut across all three turn lanes. She pulled straight ahead. I wheeled around and watched the workers force everyone else into a right turn. New York and Co. wouldn't be able to follow.

We rolled past parking lots and a large building on our right before we pulled into a circular drive in front of Freedom Hall. The driver coasted to a stop, and the doors opened with a whoosh. Everyone began to file out.

I considered what I knew about the fairgrounds' complex. I could see a sizeable portion of the northwest end from my hotel window, and I'd had all week to look at it.

The way I figured it, I had three choices: ride to the airport, disappear in the crowd, or wait for the next bus to the hotel.

What would I do if I were him?

That answer depended on his ultimate goal. Had he planned on killing or kidnapping me? With trepidation, I watched the last of my bus mates push through the doors to the South Wing.

Killing me meant he only needed to get me alone. I slowly turned my head and looked at the driver as she dipped her chin and tweaked an earphone into her ear. Killing me here meant killing her.

I listened to her smacking her gum as she spoke softly into a microphone. "Yeah, babe. That's what I said."

If I were New York, and my endgame was making sure I didn't live to see another day, I would get my ass over here to see if I was still on this bus. Sitting on this bus like a goddamn sitting duck.

I moved alongside the driver.

She looked up. Stopped talking. Stopped smacking her gum.

"How long are we going to be here?"

She glanced at the digital readout on the dash, blew a bubble, sucked it back into her mouth. "Five minutes. We're ahead of schedule."

"Can we leave now?"

"Gotta stick to the schedule," she said, and I had a feeling she'd enjoyed saying it.

"I need to catch a flight," I said, hoping to get her moving.

"Schedule." She blew a bubble and popped it.

Right.

I stood on the bottom step, checked the brightly lit lobby and the road leading back the way we'd come. Right now, New York didn't know where I was, and I wanted to keep it that way.

I stumbled out of the bus and breathed in the cool night air as I crossed the sidewalk and pushed through the doors, knowing I could come face to face with him at any second. No security. No cops.

Great.

I asked the ticket takers where I could find security, and a blond girl who was probably still in high school told me they were around somewhere.

"Call them."

She frowned. "Is something wrong?"

How 'bout I jump over this fucking counter, and you'll see if something's wrong? "Just call them, okay?"

She picked up a clunky two-way radio that resembled a police scanner and fiddled with the dial. We heard voices, but none responded to her request. When her second attempt went unanswered, I started across the lobby.

"Hey…" she said when I didn't pay the admission fee.

"Call security," I said over my shoulder.

I threaded through a noisy hall filled with parents and squealing kids wearing pink foam bunny ears and jumping on inflatable games.

No fucking cops. No New York, either. I kept my pace close to a jog and was approaching the food stands when I caught sight of two men in uniform crossing the lawn beyond the open doors. Cops or security. Either one worked for me.

The cool evening air chilled my skin as I exited the building on the east side. I spun to my right and realized I had already lost them in the crowd. There must have been five thousand people milling beneath the balloons that towered sixty feet in the air. Dozens of them.

Standing under the lights with the hall lit up behind me was akin to slapping a target on my forehead, so I moved away from the door. Four quick strides put me in the crowd, walking among the balloon crews with their pickups and vans and gear. A gas jet switched on with a roar and blast of hot air. I flinched. The checkered balloon above my head rocked slightly, like a sluggish giant come to life. I continued deeper into the maze of balloons, splashes of color against a black sky.

Okay. Think. The main entrance hadn't panned out, but there were bound to be other entrances where I could find someone on duty. Someone who knew how to operate his fucking radio. One problem: I didn't know where they were, and just as I had risked running into New York in the hall, I risked running into him coming through one of the entrances.

I moved farther into the field. The night was punctuated with random blasts of propane. A vender walked past carrying a bouquet of metallic helium balloons. A handful of glow sticks that he'd stuck in an apron pocket rose and fell with each step he took.

When my cell rang, I paused next to a white crew-cab pickup that belonged to the guys manning the Meijer balloon.

"Cline."

"Detective Bonikowski returning your call."

"I just saw those two guys, the ones I worked on the composites for."

"Where?"

"They were waiting for me across the street from my hotel, and they followed me when I caught a bus, not the bus I'd intended, as it happened."

Bonikowski said something as a gas jet blasted a mini inferno into the US Bank balloon that loomed directly in front of me.

I pressed the phone against my ear. "What?"

"Where are you?"

"At the fairgrounds, somewhere in the middle of a grassy field, standing between a black Meijer balloon and a patriotic red-white-and-blue US Bank balloon."

"Are you safe?"

I pivoted 360 degrees. "For the moment."

"They followed you onto the grounds?"

"They sure the hell did. I lost track of them, but it's conceivable they're still looking for me," I said. "Are you going to send someone?"

"Yes. What were they driving?"

"A red Caprice. I didn't catch the plate number."

"Can you find a cop?"

"I'm working on it."

"Keep a low profile. Stay where you are as long as you think it's safe, and call me back if you see those guys. Otherwise, I'll call you when I get there."

"Are you leaving now?"

She blew out a breath. "Patrol should be there soon."

"Good."

I disconnected. Taking her advice literally, I sat on the ground and leaned against the crew-cab's back tire. Except for pockets of light when the balloons fired up, the field was dark, and if New York was still here, he'd be sweeping his gaze across the shifting crowd, not looking at the ground.

A skinny young man with a ponytail, one of the Meijer crew, walked around the truck's hood, nodded at me, and proceeded to lower the tailgate. The shocks dipped slightly as he climbed inside, and a few seconds later, I heard him shifting and dragging stuff across the bed's ribbed metal. I thought about asking him if I could hide in his truck as I glanced at my watch. Nine-forty.

The flame beneath the US Bank balloon flared against the black sky. A crowd had gathered around the basket, and the sudden, brilliant light shone on their faces and cast shimmering halos in their hair. A man edged around the crowd. A man who wasn't paying attention to the show. A red-headed man.

Rudi.

I jumped to my feet and followed him as he headed north. He moved purposefully through the tangle of balloons and people and vehicles, sweeping his gaze left and right. He turned and stopped abruptly and didn't notice my approach. When he waved his arm above his head, I realized I'd been mistaken.

What a fucking idiot.

The guy wasn't even wearing a sling. A woman and two little girls wearing pink bunny ears hurried toward him. The mother released the girls, and they bounded across the grass, waving their arms and pointing. I looked past them as they set off toward what had to have been the largest balloon on the grounds. A giant, pink Energizer Bunny.

Okay...bunny ears. I got it. I rolled my eyes and turned back the way I'd come.

The Meijer balloon hovered in the distance. As I closed in on the Suburban belonging to the US Bank crew, and had the white crew-cab pickup that I'd been leaning against in sight, a man I did know peered into the truck's bed as he walked past. He raised a walky-talky to his lips.

New York.

Chapter Twenty-two

"Fuck." I wheeled away.

My back stung as someone knocked against my shoulder.

A man clutched my denim jacket as he caught his balance, and in the brief millisecond before I shook him off, I realized he wasn't just some drunk fairgoer, but New York's partner—the Hispanic guy who'd held me down in the men's room.

He straightened and brought his arm around. Light glinted off a vicious-looking knife gripped in his right hand.

He didn't take time to correct his balance but swung the knife in an awkward roundhouse.

I jumped back, and the blade sliced harmlessly through the air.

I tracked its trajectory and moved in. Grabbed his wrist with my right hand and latched onto his triceps with my left. Levered his arm into a hold similar to the one they'd used on me in the restroom and braced his locked elbow against my stomach. Forcing him to bend at the waist, I rammed the top of his head into the Suburban's grille.

He groaned, and some of the fight drained out of him.

I slammed his wrist on the bumper. The knife bounced out of his hand as I latched my fingers in his hair. I yanked his head back, fully intending to slam his face into whatever Suburban real estate was handy, when two men pulled me off.

One of them screamed at me, something about his truck, but my focus was on the Hispanic. He braced his forearm on the bumper and straightened.

He turned toward me and assumed a fighting stance. Blood streamed down his face.

"Get the fuck off!" I yelled.

As I wrenched my right arm free, New York's partner pivoted and slammed his boot into my gut. Air shot out of my lungs as I dropped to my knees. The two guys scattered, wanting no part of this.

I hunched forward and tried to drag some oxygen into my lungs.

I couldn't get up. Didn't have enough breath to do anything but cover my head and watch him through the gap between my arms as he lined up for another go.

He let swing. Aimed the next kick directly at my face.

I dove beneath it, felt his boot graze my ear. I knocked my shoulder into his anchor leg and latched onto his calf. Jerked sideways. Felt the heel of his cowboy boot scrape my back as he stumbled and tried to catch his balance. He landed on his side.

I scrambled to my feet. Smacked into the bumper on the way up. Felt dizzy from having the wind knocked out of my lungs. New York had zeroed in on us. He was striding down the grassy aisle, slipping the walky-talky into his jacket pocket.

I backed around the Suburban's front fender. Backed right into the side mirror. Didn't have the breath to run.

The Hispanic was already on his feet. Wiping the blood off his forehead with the back of his hand. Moving in on me with determination and anger blazing in his eyes.

I watched him come. Kept my arms loose at my sides and let him get close.

He was a sloppy fighter. Without a weapon, he was in big trouble.

New York was a different story.

The Hispanic swung like I thought he would, an unimaginative straight punch aimed at my solar plexus. I blocked the strike, stepped in quickly, and snapped my arm around. Slammed my elbow into his ear hard enough to rupture his eardrum, maybe even crack a bone. He yelped and staggered sideways. I grabbed his wrist, twisted the joint until his arm locked up, and brought my foot down. Heard the elbow pop.

I jumped away from him as New York strode around the Suburban's hood. His expression was calm as he withdrew his hand from his jeans pocket and clicked the switchblade he carried. The blade sprang from his fist. He wielded the knife, moving it slowly back and forth as he hunched his shoulders and stepped toward me.

Backing up, I shook my right arm out of my jacket and wrapped the denim around my left forearm, remembered how proficient he'd been when they'd caught me in the restroom. He licked his lips and advanced with his weight on the balls of his feet.

New York's partner rocked to his knees and groaned. Looked like he was going to puke.

In the instant when I glanced at the Hispanic, New York lunged. He brought the knife upward in a short jab. A tough move to guard against. I blocked the hit but felt the blade tear through the denim. I stumbled backward. Caught my balance. Waited for his next move.

He tried again. Same move. Same result. Then he totally caught me off guard by following the strike with a sweeping kick that hooked behind my calf and knocked my feet out from under me.

I hit the ground hard, rolled once toward the back tire. He moved in. Waited for me to try to get up. I'd be at my most vulnerable then, so I rolled back toward him, scissored my legs around his, and took him down.

He was quick. We both regained our footing at the same time. My jacket dangled from my arm and slipped to the grass as a propane jet flared with a sudden blast that drowned out the sound of my panting and someone yelling. New York took his eyes off me briefly as orange light spotlighted his face and lit up the inside of the Suburban like a midday sun.

I backed up another step.

Something metallic glinted amid a jumble of gear laid out beneath the Suburban's liftgate. A long steel pipe. The metal coiled into a wide loop at the center, but the ends were straight, easy to grip.

I wrapped my fingers around the cold steel as New York moved in for another strike. I lifted the pipe.

It was lighter than I'd anticipated but better than nothing. I swung it downward. The metal caught New York's hand in a stinging blow.

He pulled back in surprise.

I gripped the pipe with both hands and pivoted. Stepped forward and swung the loop of metal up hard and fast, like I was hitting a backhand lob with a tennis racquet. Put all my weight behind it.

The metal cracked into his jaw with a vicious shudder. He stumbled backward. Fell on his ass.

The flame behind me died. In the sudden quiet, a woman screamed.

New York rolled onto his stomach and scrambled to his feet. Spun to face me.

I waited with my legs spread, weight on the balls of my feet, the loop of metal held at the ready. Never would have guessed the fucking tennis we'd been forced to practice in Phys. Ed. would have done me any good.

Thanks to the pipe, my reach far exceeded anything he could muster, and he knew it. He glanced at the growing audience, latched onto his partner, and hauled him to his feet. They took off and disappeared into the crowd.

The two men who had pulled me off a moment earlier stepped in front of me as I stared at the length of steel in my hand. Polished stainless steel. That's why it wasn't as heavy as I'd expected. I tilted it upright and examined the end that had connected with New York's jaw. The impact had crimped the metal.

If New York was responsible for Nicole's death, the cops would get a DNA match for sure.

One of the men rubbed his face and pushed a mop of curly hair off his forehead. "That guy...he had a knife."

"He sure the hell did."

I flipped open my cell left-handed and glanced at the readout as I walked toward the front of the Suburban. Nine-forty-seven. Only seven short minutes since I'd talked to Bonikowski. I pressed the detective's number and tightened my grip on the phone to keep my hand from shaking.

"What was their problem?"

I glanced at the man with the curly hair. He had a subtle accent. European...German. "They wanted to kill me," I said, and both men exchanged glances.

"Bonikowski." Her voice came through the earpiece clear and calm. Businesslike.

"This is Steve Cline," I said as I crouched in front of the bumper and scanned the grass, looking for the Hispanic's knife. "Those guys," I said and realized I was still panting, "they're on their way out of the fairgrounds right now."

"You see them?"

"This second? No. They just took off." I drew in a deep breath. "The Hispanic's got blood on his face, and his arm's messed up. The other guy's got some damage, too."

"What happened?"

I straightened and stepped backward, searched a larger area. "They found me."

"And...."

"They lost their nerve." I glanced around. Those who'd seen the whole thing were still riveted to the spot. The rest of the crowd milled past, unaware that anything out of the ordinary had taken place.

"Hold on," Bonikowski said before covering the mouthpiece.

I asked the guy with the curly hair, "You got a flashlight?"

"Sure."

"Get it, would you?"

The detective came back on the line. "Where are you exactly?"

"Uh..." I looked around. "Standing directly north of the Meijer balloon, east of the US Bank balloon, in front of a red Chevy Suburban."

"Stay there."

"Yes, ma'am."

Her breath buffeted the phone as she disconnected.

Half past midnight Sunday morning, we were heading south on Louisville's surface streets after a brief stop at University Hospital. I powered my window down an inch, and the cool night air swirled into the Crown Vic's cabin as I eased against the backrest: government issue, economy vinyl. I glanced at Detective Jeanne Bonikowski, noticed the numerous gold rings on her right hand as she readjusted her grip on the steering wheel. Couldn't see her left hand or recall a wedding band. A faint floral scent clung to the car's interior.

She had arrived at the fairgrounds wearing a pair of low-rise jeans and a heavy black leather belt with metal studs. Kind of reminded me of biker or S&M garb or a Rottweiler's collar. She'd softened the look with a ribbed jersey tucked in beneath a baggy acid-washed denim jacket. I wondered if she had taken the night off now that they were a little over seventy-two hours out from the discovery of Nicole's body. Maybe, maybe not. She wasn't in Homicide, but I had the distinct impression that a position in its ranks was within her grasp.

New York and Co. had successfully eluded the responding patrol units, but the techs had bagged and tagged the metal pipe I'd used in my defense—something called a Squeeze EZ that balloonist use to *squeeze* the air out of those monsters so they can pack 'em up and go home. The US Bank crew had been forced to borrow another one. The techs had also swabbed a promising smudge on the Suburban's grille.

They had collected the Hispanic's knife, which I'd found earlier with the help of the German's flashlight. Surprisingly, it had come to rest in a groove between the bumper and grille.

Bonikowski hoped they would be able to recover some viable prints since the sheath had a section of inlaid bronze.

If those two had had anything to do with Nicole's death, they were toast.

The cops had interviewed plenty of witnesses, and they'd taken their customary photographs, which included several shots of a longish but superficial cut below my right shoulder blade. I hadn't noticed the injury until the German balloonist pointed it out.

I noticed it now.

"What's changed?" Bonikowski said, breaking the silence.

"You mean, why have those guys switched from wanting the tape to wanting me dead?"

She nodded as she slowed for a light.

"I've been wondering that myself."

"So…what's different? Think about it in terms of cause and effect. And timing."

"Well, a week ago, when those two went after me in Sully's, no one knew I was interested in Nicole's whereabouts."

"And now?"

"Hmm." I shifted in my seat. "Monday afternoon, I asked Snoopy Sanchez some questions—"

"Snoopy?"

"Uh, sorry. Eduardo Sanchez. He rubs horses for Bill Gannon." I glanced at her, noted her frown. "Grooms horses," I added and she nodded. "I asked Sanchez what he thought about his boss and his relationship with Nicole. That was Monday afternoon. Tuesday, Gannon was on my case, telling me to stay the hell out of his affairs." I smiled. "He didn't actually use that word, but it fits. The guy's got a hands-on policy when it comes to his female help, and he's got marital problems. Several domestics that resulted in disorderly conduct and criminal damage charges, and one DUI."

"How do you know this?"

"Court records."

She squinted at me like maybe she was reevaluating her previous assessment. A marginal upgrade from hotwalker to file clerk. She turned forward and stared through the windshield. "He didn't hide his annoyance."

"Right. That kind of drops his name farther down the list, doesn't it?"

She shrugged.

"Then there's Rudi Sturgill. He wanted to know what was going on when he saw the tail end of Gannon's outburst. I didn't tell him. I actually thought Gannon might, but apparently he didn't. So Rudi didn't learn that I was looking into Nicole's disappearance until Wednesday evening," I said, remembering that I had also told him about Nicole's note-taking. "His sister, Paige Sturgill, might know. They're close. Then, Edward Utley found out yesterday."

"Utley," she said slowly, giving both syllables equal weight.

"Yeah. Edward J. Utley, who just so happens to live a mile from the dump site."

"The time between his learning about your involvement and the attack tonight was the most immediate." She slowed as she drove under the I-65 overpass and approached Oak. The drone and thump of tires overhead filtered through the window. "Of course, those two punks could be working for themselves, but I don't think so."

"Neither do I."

Bonikowski turned left at Central and a couple of minutes later she was pulling into the Hilton's lot. She coasted past two patrol cars and an unmarked detective's ride, gave them a good hard look before she swung the Crown Vic under the portico's bright lights.

"I don't see how anything I've said or done could be construed as threatening. Not enough to trigger a reaction as desperate as attempted murder." I stared through the window. "I'm no closer to knowing who killed Nicole than I was eight days ago."

"You've touched a nerve somewhere." She rammed the gearshift into park and turned to face me. "How?" She looked tiny sitting there in her two-sizes-too-big denim jacket.

I shrugged. "I don't know."

I powered up the window as she reached to switch off the ignition. She opened her door and slid out, strode around the Vic's hood. I got out and followed her into the lobby with a great deal less energy.

Cortney, the night clerk, eyed her approach with a mix of admiration and caution. He tore his gaze from her and lifted his eyebrows as if to ask what in the hell had I gotten myself into this time?

I smiled.

Bonikowski's partner stood beyond the sundries section, in a cramped hallway that linked the front desk to the manager's office and security. He had been speaking to a tired-looking man dressed in shirtsleeves and a crooked tie, but as soon as he saw Bonikowski, he cut through the hall and intercepted her.

He glanced at me before speaking. "We've cleared the perimeter, hallways, stairwells. Nobody's here that shouldn't be. Access to the building's wide open though." He described the entries. "But I figure two guys can cover it."

Bonikowski nodded. "Any chance you can get some of those doors locked down for the night?"

"Not a chance," he said. "I asked."

"You gave them the pictures of our boys?"

"Sure did."

"Yo, man," Cortney said as I drifted over to the desk. "You keeping the LMPD busy?"

I ignored his comment. "Anybody been in my room?"

Cortney jerked his head toward the office. "Cops had Frank check your lock's data. Ain't nobody been in or out since you left."

"Good."

His gaze slid over to Bonikowski. "You getting some private protection tonight?"

I smiled. "Hardly."

"Hmm, hmm, hmm. That's too damn bad."

Chapter Twenty-three

I didn't tell Kessler about the body armor that I'd squirreled away in his tack trunk as soon as I stepped into the barn these past two mornings or the fact that a couple of unmarked police cars arrived at the Hilton at the ungodly hour of 3:45 so they could set up a loose tail as I walked from the hotel to Gate 5. One-point-one miles of wide-open boulevard that arched above the railway tracks. Zero egress, unless you were talking straight down.

I didn't tell him that I was essentially acting as a lure, trying to catch two guys who might have committed one murder and were planning their second.

But in the past two days, they hadn't put in an appearance. Either they had given up, or they'd noticed the tail. Somehow, I couldn't stop thinking that their absence was more ominous than if I'd seen them.

And I never did tell Kessler about my unplanned detour into the fairgrounds.

Gallant Storm planted his left hoof in front of his nose as he bent to the grass. I glanced at my watch as I took up the slack in the lead. Eleven-thirty Tuesday morning. Kessler had flown back to Washington Park once he was satisfied that both horses had sufficiently recovered from Sunday's breeze—the last demanding workout they would have before race day. Another reason not to tell him.

A black Crown Vic cruised down Longfield Avenue. Bonikowski.

I smiled when my cell rang. "Cline."

"You're wearing your vest, aren't you?"

"You like me, don't you, Detective?" I said.

"I'm a good cop, Mr. Cline. Having my witness killed wouldn't look good on my record, now would it?"

"Gee. Don't get all emotional—"

Ignoring me, she said, "So, you have the vest on or not?"

"I'm not wearing a long-sleeved denim shirt because I need to sweat off a couple pounds."

"When do you expect to leave the track?"

"I'll be on the grounds all day," I lied. Jay cut through the short aisle and stood in the doorway until I acknowledged him with a nod. "Detective Bonikowski?"

"Yes."

"Would you consider sharing Nicole's work history?"

"Why?"

"It might be instructive viewed from an insider's perspective."

"Inside, as in racing?"

"Yes."

"I'm not prepared to share that with you at this time."

"Okay. Thought I'd give it a try. Talk to you later, Detective?"

"Later." She disconnected.

A lazy breeze rustled the trees near the perimeter fence. "Time to go, boy."

Realizing the gig was up, Storm snatched a mouthful of grass before lifting his head and allowing me to guide him toward the barn. We approached the turn into the long aisle as a Caddy pulled between barns.

Gannon. And he had company.

Rudi stepped around the front passenger door as I led Storm toward his stall. The colt flicked his ears and focused on Jay as he opened a hefty paper bag from Wagner's. Jay's second meal of the day, if I wasn't mistaken. We had fallen into the habit of buying each other breakfast on alternating days, though I had avoided explaining why I was suddenly reluctant to walk across.

Car doors clicked shut followed by Gannon's voice and the sound of the tack room door swinging open on squeaky hinges. I turned Storm loose in his stall and latched the guard, then propped my ass on the tack trunk while Jay sorted through the bag. He'd switched out his BLAME THE DOG Ttee with a black cotton mesh muscle shirt with the single word DON'T stenciled across the front. A shirt better suited to the warm day than the denim one I was wearing.

"They was out of biscuits and gravy, so I got you hash-browns instead."

"Thanks."

He lifted a Styrofoam cup out of the bag and extended his arm vaguely in my direction as he tracked Rudi and Paige's entrance into the barn. And I'm pretty damn sure he wasn't looking at Rudi. Paige walked down the exact center of the aisle, placing her high heels in the powdery footing with concentration. She wore a frilly hat and simple sundress that showed off a lot of bare leg.

I reached for my iced tea as Jay shifted. His hand swung out of my reach. "Yo," I said and snatched the drink.

Suppressing a nearly overwhelming desire to snap my fingers in front of his face, I slipped off the trunk and fished my egg sandwich out of the bag.

Gannon emerged from the tack room carrying a bridle and Irish martingale. He joined Rudi outside Gone Wild's stall while Paige stayed well away from the horse. Maybe she didn't care for them, or maybe she didn't want to risk dirtying that white sundress she was wearing. She folded her arms and drummed her fingers. When she canted her head and swung her gaze in our direction, I felt my heart rate spike. She strolled toward us and paused next to Jay.

"Morning, boys."

I smiled. "Paige."

Jay kept his mouth shut. That in and of itself wasn't surprising. He had little use for small talk, but judging from his flat expression and overall stillness, I figured Paige could have knocked him over with a flutter of those long eyelashes of hers.

"Mr. Gannon has a runner today?" I asked, though I already knew the answer. He had a colt entered in the second race, a favorite if the morning-line odds were any indication. Based on the day's race card, I had made plans that necessitated Gannon being at Churchill and was pleased to see he was already on the grounds.

"Oh, yes. He's got a runner," she said with a sarcastic edge to her voice. "A class horse, or so we've been told. Rudi's thinking of buying the damn thing, like he needs another."

"You know how it is," I said. "Horses get in your blood."

She blew out a breath. "Something's in his blood all right."

On that note, we both turned and looked at her brother. The bruising along his cheekbone had darkened to black with a lighter streak of greenish-yellow feathered beneath his eye. He wasn't as pale as he'd been the last time I'd seen him, and he looked a good deal more comfortable with the sling. He leaned against the doorframe and spoke softly to Gannon.

I unwrapped my sandwich and took a bite, glanced at Jay, and smiled. The Wagner's bag sat open on the tack trunk, forgotten, while his meaty fist still gripped his breakfast sandwich wrapped in a double layer of greasy waxed paper.

"Food's gonna get cold," I said, and he tore his eyes off Paige and glared at me.

Sunlight flashed in the alley as the Caddy's rear passenger door opened. Yaseen Haddad, Senior Software Engineer, slid off the backseat and stretched.

I raised an eyebrow. "Yaseen…?"

Paige turned toward the alley and called to him, "We won't be long."

"He isn't afraid of horses, is he?"

She rolled her eyes. "With him, it's impossible to tell. He spends much of his time puzzling over our cultural differences. Maybe racing's taboo in his country."

"Not in Syria. At least I don't think so," I said, imagining that Yaseen spent a good deal of time puzzling over *her*.

Paige raised her eyes slowly to my face. "How'd you know that?"

Shit.

"Racing's popular over there," I said casually. "The United Arab Emirates hosts the richest flat race in the world."

"No. I mean, how'd you know Yaseen's from Syria?"

I shrugged. "I didn't. His name sounds Syrian."

Paige lowered her cool blue eyes. Her gaze seemed to settle on my throat; then she turned her attention to Jay. She took her time appraising his bulky shoulders and thick bare arms before her eyes fell to the mesh stretched tightly across his chest. "What's *don't* mean?"

Jay's expression remained impenetrable. "Don't mean nothin'," he said, "to you."

Paige lifted an eyebrow, and her devilish smile made me think of her boyfriend, among other things.

When Rudi called to his sister, I glanced beyond the roof overhang. Gannon tossed the tack in the Caddy's trunk and waited impatiently alongside the car. Rudi inclined his head in my direction before turning to leave.

"Look at that, would you?" Paige said under her breath. "Bill's annoyed that Rudi hangs out with you so much, conniving with the enemy, and all. And it looks like he's had an impact." She twisted around and swept her gaze over both of us. "Ciao."

While Gannon slipped behind the wheel, Paige swiveled onto the backseat next to Yaseen. Before the door swung shut, I caught a brief flash of skin as she crossed her tanned legs. I smiled as I imagined Yaseen squirming in his seat.

I left the track Tuesday at noon and, for the second day in a row, unlocked a dusty red pickup parked in a lot reserved for track employees. I had leased it from a foreman who worked in Barn 39 for fifty bucks a day. Yesterday, I'd spent the afternoon in Versailles, searching Woodford County's criminal records database for information on the Sturgills, ironic considering I'd used Rudi's money to do it.

Though unexpected in some ways, what I had uncovered confirmed my long-held belief that wealth came with a heavy price.

I cranked over the engine and pulled out of the lot, reflexively scanned the street and checked the rearview mirror, looking for cops. I hadn't expected to see them, and I didn't. They were leaving my safety in Churchill's hands while I was on the grounds, a decision that was fine by me.

On the surface, the Sturgill family lived a fairytale existence that most of us aspired to. Yet, in the brief time since I had accepted Rudi's invitation to the Thunder party, I had seen cracks in the veneer that were supported by yesterday's findings.

After a brief stop at the Voter Registration Office, where I had collected everyone's birthdates—an ID qualifier necessary for obtaining criminal records—I started with the patriarch, Matthew Sturgill, Jr. He had no criminal history. Not even a parking ticket, something none of his children had been able to duplicate. Matt the III came the closest with one DUI. Not bad considering the fact that he undoubtedly attended numerous social events.

According to Paige, Rudi had lacked discipline when it came to his job in the family's business, a trait that apparently carried over to his personal life. He had accumulated four DUIs. I suspected he'd added a fifth last Wednesday when he'd plowed his Mercedes into the median. As for Rudi's other transgressions—four counts of check fraud—I assumed his father had intervened financially in order to bail him out.

Corey was right. He hadn't grown up.

But if the father had been busy with Rudi, he'd had his hands full with Paige. She had been arrested twice. Once for DUI and once for lewd and lascivious acts.

I spent a minute or two contemplating what lewd and lascivious acts Paige might have committed in public and missed my turn onto the Henry Watterson Expressway. I turned around on the airport's grounds, near the end of one of the runways, and picked up the ramp.

The media would have latched onto that kind of story and run with it, but I had surfed the Internet thoroughly enough to know that Dad had managed to keep his family's exploits out of the papers.

I pushed the Dodge up to sixty and enjoyed the physical act of driving and the freedom that came with it. I took the Bardstown Road exit and twenty-five minutes later, after zigzagging cross-country, I turned onto Dry Ridge Road. When I found Gannon Racing Stables and turned between the gates, I pulled onto the grass verge and stopped.

Either I was becoming paranoid or just plain cautious, or maybe Bonikowski was wearing me down, but I'd left the vest on when I exited the track. I didn't need it here. As I reached up to unbutton the denim work shirt, my fingers brushed the slick material. Several of the shirt's buttons had come undone, and I wondered if anyone had realized what it was.

I tossed the shirt and vest on the front passenger seat, leaned forward, and tucked in my T-shirt before coasting down the lane. Not unexpectedly, the property wasn't in the same league as Rudi's Wellspring Farm. The drive was rutted and in need of grading and a fresh layer of gravel, and the white board fence had dulled to a yellowish gray. Grass obscured the lower planks, but the fields were in good shape, and the horses pastured in them looked healthy and content. I idled past the main house, Gannon's I assumed, and parked in a dusty lot fronting the first barn I came to.

Country music drifted into the cab when I switched off the engine. I stepped out of the truck and considered the approach I wanted to take as I crossed the lot and paused at the barn's entrance. The air was laced with the pungent smell of barley straw and the sweet scent of alfalfa.

A nice-looking open-cab John Deere 5325 sat midway down the aisle, hitched to an empty manure wagon. The usual clutter of rakes and pitchforks and brooms had been left propped against a stall front.

Footsteps sounded in a walled-off room to my right, a stall converted into a tack or feed room. A shoe scraped across a wooden floor as the door swung open. A young woman had her hand on the doorknob as she tucked a crinkly brown bag and can of Sprite against her waist. She was looking over her shoulder at another woman who crouched in front of a mini refrigerator with her long honey-brown hair slipping forward off her shoulder like a curtain.

"Hey, get that bag of chips, will you?" the woman at the door said. She turned and flinched. "Oh."

"Sorry. I didn't mean to startle you."

She lowered her hand from her mouth and caught the door as it bumped against her hip. "Can I help you?"

"I hope so," I said. She had frizzy red hair that hung in a plait down the center of her back. The other woman stepped behind her as I moved out of their way. "Did either one of you know Nicole Austin?"

They nodded, and the redhead spoke first. "We both did."

"I work for the *Courier-Journal,* and I'm following up on her employment history for a story my boss is working on."

"You're a reporter?"

"No. I do all kinds of research for the Editorial Department, though." As I withdrew my notepad and pencil from my jeans pocket, I mentioned a reporter whose name they would recognize if they paid attention to that sort of thing.

The redhead lifted her chin and gestured toward the straw bales stacked farther down the aisle. "Let's sit down. We're on our lunch break."

They parked their lunches on a central bale and sat opposite each other.

Neither one of them had been close to Nicole or knew much about her life outside work, so we ended up talking about the operation, the horses, the season's new foals. Shelly had balled up her lunch bag and was draining the last of her Sprite when I finally worked the conversation around to Gannon.

"Did Nicole have problems with anyone she worked with? Other employees or management?"

They exchanged looks.

"The rumor is, your boss has an eye for the ladies."

Shelly's partner, Roseann Gruley, checked to make sure we were alone as she leaned forward and looked up at me from beneath a sweep of sexy bangs. "He's got more than an eye for us."

Shelly frowned. "Roseann."

"It's true. He's a touchy-feely kind of guy, if you get my drift. He takes a liking to you, the next thing you know, he's trying to talk you into working foal watch. The pay's better, but I wouldn't be caught dead working here at night. Not by myself."

Shelly crossed her legs and planted her elbow on her knee. She squeezed her Sprite can until it creaked. "It's true. He's like that, but don't mention our names to anyone, okay?"

"I won't. And you might not want to tell anyone that I was here asking questions. I wouldn't want him angry at the two of you."

Shelly nodded.

"Nicole worked foal watch," I said. "Did she ever complain about Mr. Gannon?"

They shook their heads. Both of them were around my age, maybe a little older. Nicole's contemporaries for sure, and I thought it unusual that they hadn't known her better.

"When she quit, do you know what job she took?"

Roseann paused with a potato chip halfway to her mouth. "Uh-uh. I thought she went straight to Churchill, but I don't know for sure."

I looked at Shelly and she shrugged. "What about Mrs. Gannon? What's she like?"

"We hardly ever see her," Shelly said. "She's away a lot."

The potato chip bag crinkled as Roseann searched for any chips left in the bottom of the bag. "She works for Humana. But the rumor is, they don't get along."

"Anyone in particular come between them?"

Roseann lifted her shoulders.

I showed them the sketches of New York and Co., but neither girl had seen them before. I tucked the drawing in my back pocket and propped my ass on the tractor's front tire.

"Are they the ones?" Shelly's eyes looked huge.

"There's no evidence of that, but they may know something."

"Tough-looking guys," Roseann said, and I couldn't agree more.

"Did Nicole have boyfriend troubles that you know of?"

Shelly balanced the Sprite can on her knee. "The guy she was dating back then broke up with her."

"You know his name?"

"Brian Gilstrap."

I wrote down his name. "Do you remember when this happened?" I said, and Roseann shrugged. I glanced at Shelly, and she shook her head.

"Oh, I remember, now. They broke up right before Christmas." Roseann leaned against the stall front and flicked her hair behind her ear. "Remember, Shelly? They were having that huge Christmas party next door. Brian was their stud manager, so of course, he was invited. Anyway, he took Nicole, and right after that, or maybe even that night, he told her he was moving to Florida, and he wasn't inviting her to go with him."

"Next door?"

"Yeah. Millcroft Farm." She sighed. "A real class operation."

Millcroft Farm. Why wasn't I surprised? "So, Nicole went to a party at Millcroft. Did she go over there for any other reason?"

"Oh, sure. She'd wait for Brian to get off work sometimes."

"Have either of you heard of a man named Edward Utley?" When they shook their heads, I said, "He boards horses at Millcroft. Would he have been invited to this party?"

"Oh, sure," Roseann said. "That was the whole point, to thank the clients and management."

Chapter Twenty-four

Ricardo stepped into the hallway at the far end of the foyer as I crossed the carpet and headed toward the Rocking Horse Manor's elegant mahogany staircase.

"Afternoon, Steve."

I lifted my hand in greeting. "I'll be upstairs for a while."

He nodded. "Help yourself to ice and drinks in the fridge."

"Thanks."

"There's an extra glass in your father's room."

"Okay." I paused. "Is he back yet?"

"No. I believe he's due in any time now."

When I reached the lounge on the third floor, I grabbed a Coke out of the mini fridge and glanced at my watch as I let myself into Kessler's room.

Two-fifty Tuesday afternoon. I'd driven straight back from Gannon's farm and still had plenty of time to get something accomplished. I eased the door closed and started around the foot of the bed. A dark shape in the bathroom caught my eye. I spun around. Kessler had left a tuxedo encased in plastic hanging from the shower curtain rod, ready for this evening's dinner at the Hyatt. A Kentucky Thoroughbred Owners and Breeders event ticketed at $150 per person.

I stood in front of the desk and rolled my neck, surprised by the tension that fizzed in my muscles. I pictured Edward Utley and Bill Gannon surrounded by their peers, drinking cocktails and dining, schmoozing with the press. I wondered if either would think of Nicole tonight. Wondered if one of them had washed her blood from his hands.

And what about Rudi? As much as I would have liked to, I had yet to remove his name from the mix.

I plugged in Kessler's laptop. While I waited for it to power up, I flipped open my cell phone and keyed in *67 followed by Rachel's work number. She'd been avoiding my calls all week, and I wanted to know why.

"Claims, Rachel Forrest. How may I help you?"

I tightened my grip on the phone.

"Hello?"

"I have to mask my number so you'll answer the phone?" I said, conscious of the raspy edge to my voice. "What the hell's going on?"

"Jesus, Steve," she said. "I can't believe you."

"Me? You're the—"

"I saw you."

"What?"

"On T.V."

Fuck. Had the media discovered that I'd been interviewed as a suspect in Nicole's murder? They hadn't approached me, but a crew had filmed me hand-grazing Storm just before lunch, and I had paid them little attention. Like most backsiders, I'd grown immune to their presence.

I glanced at the television, felt my face burning. Any of the news stations would have accumulated more than enough footage to broadcast while the announcer explained that I was a *person of interest* in a murder investigation. And they would have undoubtedly dragged Kessler's name into it. I closed my eyes. "It's not what you think," I said. Empty words that I didn't believe.

"Sure."

"Really. I'm no longer a suspect, in fact, I'm working with the police. You know that assignment—"

"What?" Her voice rose in alarm. "What are you talking about?"

I paused and realized we had been talking about two different things. "What exactly did you see?"

"Oh, no you don't. You're in trouble again, aren't you?" she said. "Oh, God. Don't tell me you're somehow involved in that investigation...that woman who worked for Churchill."

"It's on national news?"

"Of course it is. How can you be involved in this? Oh, God. Tell me you're not involved."

"I was interviewed by the police because she was in the receiving barn while our horses were still in temporary stalls. They're interviewing everyone she came in contact with that morning. Her coworkers. Everyone." The laptop's screen flickered as the icons scrolled down the left margin. "I don't get it. If that's not what you're upset about, why haven't you been taking my calls?"

After a pause, she said, "You didn't tell me Corey was going to be there."

"What?"

"Derby coverage, Steve. I saw the two of you on *11 News at 5.* Horses on the track, trainer interviews, backside shots. You were in one of them, just like you said you'd be, and so was Corey. The cameraman seemed quite taken by the two of you working together. A good-looking couple." Her voice broke off. "How the hell did you think I'd feel when I saw her?"

Jesus. She still didn't trust me, and I supposed she was wise not to. I hadn't exactly been forthcoming during the course of our relationship, and I had been attracted to Corey. In Louisville and earlier, when I'd helped her find her brother. "I didn't know she was coming."

"Oh, sure."

"Come on, Rache. Kessler flew her out Monday afternoon, and she was gone by Wednesday morning. Jay was sick, and we needed someone to fill in."

"I thought....I'm sorry, Steve. I assumed she'd been there all along—"

"And you figured I wouldn't tell you."

"I don't know. Maybe...."

After an uncomfortably long silence, I cleared my throat. "This isn't going to work if you can't trust me. Whether I tell you who I'm working with or not shouldn't even be an issue."

"Turn it around, Steve. How would you feel if I was hanging out with some guy?"

"I don't know."

She blew out a breath. "Yeah, right."

"I'm sorry it threw you," I said, and after a moment's silence, I cleared my throat. "Rache, come on. Talk to me."

When she didn't respond, I closed the phone.

Fucking great.

I tossed the phone on the wicker desk and slouched against the chair. Just fucking great.

I clicked on the Internet Explorer icon, then cracked open the Coke. Swallowed half of it. Couldn't help wondering if I was subconsciously looking for an excuse to end our relationship. I loved Rachel, but during the last couple of months, she'd been dropping hints that she wanted more. A deeper commitment on my part, maybe even a marriage proposal. I suspected that her idea of our future included visions of a safe job, a three-bedroom home in suburbia, matching cars in the garage...and two kids. And that scared the hell out of me. But it was not something we could settle or even discuss on the phone.

I pushed back the chair.

Nicole's composition notebook was still tucked among the magazines piled on the coffee table where I'd left it for safekeeping. The binding creaked as I bent back the cover and flattened it on the desktop. I flipped open the spiral notepad I kept in my jeans pocket and turned it sideways, divided the page into three columns. Although the events of the past week had distracted me from Nicole's compulsive note-taking, I was determined to find out where she had been working and what information she may have held in her hand that morning in Barn 4.

I had to admit, I had been disappointed when I realized that she hadn't been working for Gannon. He had seemed the perfect suspect, but Edward Utley was quietly taking over that role.

I scrawled *6/02 – 7/03 Gannon Racing Stables* across the top of the page; then I scanned Nicole's notes. Her entries began on September 5, 2003, and ended February 20th of the following year.

I jotted down those dates as well.

Nicole had worked for Gannon a little over a year, and it wouldn't have surprised me in the least to learn that she had held six or seven different jobs in a similar fashion.

Before I leafed through the foaling records that she'd compiled beginning in January, I considered what I knew about the thoroughbred breeding industry. Today's equine population was an amazingly mobile one, with horses being trailered and flown all over the country and, in fact, the world. They were as transient as the people who worked with them, nomadic to the extreme, and that fact could make pinpointing the farm more difficult than it might have been.

On the plus side, stallions remained on the farm unless they were sold. A good stallion had the potential of earning millions in the breeding shed. Risking injury by shipping him off the farm would be foolish. So, the mares went to the stallion, not the other way around. And savvy breeders often avoided moving newborn foals whenever possible. Instead, they shipped pregnant mares to whichever farm was home to the stallion the mare was scheduled to be bred to next. At least that's how it was done in Virginia and Maryland. In Kentucky, with a huge selection of stallions within a half-hour drive, I had to consider the fact that the mares likely moved around more than I'd anticipated.

In any case, I focused on the stallions. With luck, they would help me determine the farm where Nicole had been working. I flipped toward the back of her notebook, where the foaling entries began in mid-January. The first one was dated January 12, 2004, and described the beginning of a normal delivery that degraded into a difficult birth:

...but the foal's leading hoof wasn't visible. I called Mike, and he told me to call him back if I didn't see a hoof in ten minutes. When the hoof did appear, it was sideways. I was ready to call him again, but the mare scrambled to her feet, and the foal slipped backward in the birth canal. When she laid down again, and the hoof slipped back into view, it was in the correct position.

Soon afterward, the foal's hips had locked against the mare's pelvis, and Nicole had called for reinforcements. It took them half an hour of straining and sweating and slopping on buckets full of KY Jelly before the foal slipped onto the straw. She ended the entry with the following: *The way things have worked out so far this season, I'm looking forward to a nice peaceful delivery. Note: Storm Squall will be bred back to Spy Kat if she hasn't suffered significant damage to her birth canal.*

"Bred back" was a misnomer. It sounded like the mare would be bred back to the exact same stallion, but the term simply meant that she would be bred instead of being left open for an entire season. I read the rest of Nicole's notes. The last entry was dated February 20th, when she switched to a fresh book.

During that time, she had delivered five foals, more than I expected that early in the season. I flipped back through the pages and listed the newborn foal's pedigree as well as the stallion the mare would be bred to next. Afterward, I ran a search on each stallion and jotted down the farm where he stood. The results were interesting if not conclusive:

bay colt:

Pleasant City (sire)	Meadow Crest Stud, KY
Storm Squall (dam)	
bred back to Spy Kat	Meadow Crest Stud, KY

bay filly:

Good as Gone (sire)	Wellspring Farm, KY
Myalibi (dam)	
bred back to Good as Gone	Wellspring Farm, KY

ch. filly:

Pleasant City (sire)	Meadow Crest Stud, KY
Silence Thief (dam)	
bred back to Pleasant City	Meadow Crest Stud, KY

bay filly:

Gulf Point (sire)	Diamond K Farm, KY
Attagirl (dam)	
bred back to Thunder Gulch	Ashford Stud, KY

bay filly:

Game Set 'n Match (sire)	Gulf Breeze Stud, FL
Dianna's Girl (dam)	
bred back to Good as Gone	Wellspring Farm, KY

Okay…so maybe Nicole was a magician because it sure as hell looked like she had worked on two farms simultaneously—Rudi Sturgill's Wellspring Farm and Meadow Crest Stud in Paris, Kentucky. But my instincts told me she had been working for Rudi three years ago when she had written whatever was on that ripped-out page that she had taken to the barn eleven days ago. Notes she'd referenced as she looked in on Gone Wild, Rudi's Derby runner.

Gone Wild whose sire was Good as Gone.

Out of curiosity, I looked up Meadow Crest Stud's owners and management. The names meant nothing to me. I scrolled down their stallion list and found Pleasant City, clicked on his name, and was linked to a conformation photograph of a rangy-looking colt with a devilish expression.

The floorboards in the hallway creaked. I turned as the door swung inward, and Kessler stepped into the room.

He raised his eyebrows. "Didn't think I'd find you here. You're still researching?"

"Yeah."

"I thought you weren't a suspect anymore," he said as he tossed his duffel on the bed and moved alongside me.

"I expect my name's considerably lower on their list since none of the evidence from the crime scene implicates me, but I'm well aware of the fact that I'm still on it."

Kessler stepped into the narrow space between the bed and desk and looked over my shoulder. He looked from the laptop's screen, which still displayed Meadow Crest Stud's webpage, to the chart I'd just finished. He gestured toward it with a casual wave of his hand. "What's this?"

I glanced at my watch. Four-ten. "I don't want to make you late."

"I've got time." He sat on the bed as if to emphasize the point.

Without preamble, I handed him Nicole's notebook. "This belonged to Nicole Austin," I said.

I told him how I had come to have the notebook in my possession, why I thought it was significant, and why I couldn't give it to the police at this point without getting into a whole lot of trouble.

A pair of windows fronted the street. Except for the faint whoosh of traffic sounds that rose from the pavement three stories below and hummed across the glass at sporadic intervals, the house was as quiet as a tomb. Thick limestone walls did that. I could hear Kessler's breathing and my own. On the nightstand, the alarm clock's minute hand advanced with a soft click.

Conflicting emotions of anger and concern, and undoubtedly frustration, tightened his jaw and simmered in his eyes. "I can't believe this," he whispered.

"When I took the notebook," I said, "I had no idea Nicole was dead. And if you remember, I was attacked and...uh, I didn't have an opportunity to tell you, but my hotel room was broken into."

Kessler's frown deepened. "When?"

"When you were away the first time," I lied because, in fact, it had happened right before he left. "I needed to figure out what was going on." I licked my lips. "I still do."

"Jesus." He sat up straighter and rolled his left shoulder as if easing a cramp.

"I'm trying to confirm where she was working when she delivered these foals." I handed him the chart. "The police have her complete work history but are reluctant to share it with me."

"I can't imagine why," Kessler said as he smoothed his thumb down the edge of my notepad. He jerked his head toward Nicole's composition notebook. "All the writing she must have done in that thing and she didn't mention where she was working?"

"No. She was precise about all kinds of mundane details, but she never named the farm or referenced her coworkers by their last names. Come to think of it, I suppose that's natural. If I were taking notes at work for some reason, I wouldn't be using last names unless I thought of the person in that manner." I hooked my arm over the back of the chair. "On the rare occasion when she talked about someone in a manner that indicated he was her boss, she simply referred to him as Mike."

"Helluva lot of Mikes in the industry." Kessler indicated the laptop with a nod. "Any of the managers at Meadow Crest or Wellspring listed with that first name?"

"Not on Meadow Crest's page." I swiveled around in my seat and brought up Wellspring Farm's website. "Nope."

Kessler leaned forward. "Click on the stallion list."

I did, and the names scrolled down the left side of the page.

"You've been there in person, right?" Kessler said.

"Yes."

"And you got a tour?"

"Yep. I saw all of the stallions."

"Good as Gone and…" he glanced at my chart, "Spy Kat were there?"

"They sure were."

"Click back to Meadow Crest Stud."

I did, and we both stared at Pleasant City's photograph.

Kessler rubbed his face and yawned. "When did she take these notes?"

"End of 2003, beginning of 2004. What are you thinking?"

"My guess is that Pleasant City used to stand at Wellspring Farm when Nicole worked there, but he was purchased by Meadow Crest since then."

I nodded slowly. "Makes sense. What about this entry?" I pointed to the fourth foal on the list.

"Looks like the mare, Attagirl, is being boarded at the farm you're trying to identify but is taken off the property to be bred. Diamond K Farm and Ashford Stud are local, you know?"

"I hadn't checked."

Kessler folded his arms and jerked his head toward the screen. "Key in Brisnet.com." When I brought up the page, he said, "Let's switch places, and would you mind getting me a Coke?"

"Sure."

I went on the errand, and when I returned with a Kentucky Derby glass filled with ice and a cold can of Coke, Kessler had brought up a page titled BREEDER ANALYSIS—HORSES BY YEAR FOALED. The listing was for Meadow Crest Stud.

"Pleasant City's got a few unnamed foals listed for 2005 and nothing earlier than that while he was at Meadow Crest."

Kessler began another search, typed in Wellspring Farm, and hit enter. We scanned the page together, and there was Pleasant City's name listed through 2004.

Kessler picked up the Coke can and cracked it open. "Looks like it's a lock. Pleasant City used to stand at Wellspring."

I nodded and said softly, "Nicole was working for Rudi Sturgill."

Chapter Twenty-five

I left the bed-and-breakfast and made it to Churchill before the last race. If Rudi had stayed for the entire race card, there was a good chance I'd catch him on his way out. I squeezed the Dodge between a Honda Accord and mid-sized pickup in Lot 9 and slammed the gearshift into park.

Gate 1 reminded me of a Roman coliseum. That impression was bolstered by the sound of cheering that swelled like a bubble ready to burst before rolling over the grandstand roof as the announcer called the finish of the second to last race. I wondered if the architect who had designed the curved and columned entrance had had this effect in mind.

Moving against a steady stream of patrons heading for the exit, I passed through the gate without paying or being processed by security.

If at all possible, I intended to find Rudi, and I had twenty-five minutes before the next race in which to do it. By omission, he had lied to me all along, and I wanted to know why.

And had he set me up?

I wanted to know that, too.

I ran a quick sweep of Churchill's ground floor, then detoured through Gate 17's magnificent rotunda with its iridescent glass sculpture suspended overhead. The late afternoon sunlight hit the curved glass and fractured into rainbows of swirling colors. Despite the fact that only one race remained, the place was still packed.

Finding Rudi on the ground floor had been a crap shoot, anyway. Unless he wanted to view the horses in the paddock, I assumed he hung out in Millionaire's Row or the Turf Club or a dozen other high-end suites off limits to most race-goers.

My phone rang as I stepped from beneath the grandstand roof. "Cline."

"Steve. Kenneth here. I got that information you wanted."

I smiled at the sound of his voice. Kenneth Newlin, ex high school Physics partner and current NSA spook. He'd returned my call two days ago and had been amused by the imaginative way in which I'd gotten myself into trouble this time.

"Great. Hold on a sec while I get something to write on." I crossed the expanse of cement, threading my way between the crowd and stepping over trash and sticky-looking puddles. I paused alongside a vender's supply trailer that had been parked near a circular garden surrounding a life-sized statue of Aristides, the first Derby winner. After fishing my notepad and pencil out of my back pocket, I perched on the frame above the hitch. "Got it."

"Interesting group of people you had me check," Kenneth said.

"How so?"

"You'll see. I'll start with your victim as she's the most normal of the bunch."

I spent the next five minutes wearing down the lead in my pencil while Kenneth proceeded to unload Nicole's life history, starting with time and place of birth and proceeding to past residences, school records, family.

"Father's deceased," he continued. "No siblings. Mother's in a nursing home. Assisted living. Prolonged physical therapy resulting from a near-fatal car accident."

He ran through Nicole's work history, which confirmed what I already knew. Nicole had left Gannon Racing Stables in July of 2003 and had gone straight to Wellspring Farm, where she worked until March of 2004. From there, she had taken the job at Churchill. Her earlier jobs consisted of part-time work at

Kroger's food store and a fast-food joint before she transitioned into the horse industry.

"No criminal history, unlike some of your other persons of interest," Kenneth said, stringing me along.

"Okay, give."

"We'll get to that. Nicole's credit was nearing critical mass. Besides the usual rent and car payments, she'd effectively wiped out her savings with monthly withdrawals earmarked for something called Christian Church Homes. They manage the nursing home where her mother lives. With her salary, it didn't take long. She'd maxed out two credit cards and had begun on a third. At the rate she was going, she never would have recovered without help."

I glanced up as the horses for the last race were led down the runway and into the paddock. "Good. Thanks." A crowd had gathered along the paddock rail, but Rudi was not among them.

"Anyway," he said as I focused my attention back on the conversation, "if you think her situation sounds dire, she was doing a whole hell of a lot better than Rudolph Sturgill. His farm...what's it called?" Papers rustled in the background.

"Wellspring Farm."

"Yeah, yeah. Right. The farm's essentially bankrupt. Sturgill, Sr. should have kept it under his thumb because the financials have been in a downward spiral ever since junior took over seven years ago. Excessive spending, poor investments, piggybacking loans, and rotten management practices. I figure the banks will begin foreclosures within the next six months."

I shifted my position to take advantage of a wedge of shade cast by the trailer's thin metal shell. The sun glinted off the bronze statue and shimmered among the silvery leaves of a nearby hedge. A sea of crimson tulips cupped the sunlight and glowed as if lit from within. "You'd never guess it to look at the place."

"Well, believe it. There are gaping cracks in the foundation that won't easily be remedied."

"Unless Dad steps in and smoothes things over."

Kenneth grunted, then recounted the Sturgill family's numerous brushes with the law and seemed particularly amused by Paige's antics. "Rich girl's wild side. Jesus, the media loves that crap."

"Yeah, but Daddy took care of that, too."

"Apparently."

I switched my line of enquiry to the track personnel. "You get anything on Eduardo Sanchez? His DOB's printed on his Churchill license, but he often doesn't wear it, and on the rare occasions when he does, I can never get close enough to read the damn thing."

"Yeah, I got him," Kenneth said. "He's a piece of work." More papers rustled in the background. "Endangerment of a minor, invasion of privacy—read peeping-Tom, public intoxication, drunk and disorderly."

"You know what the endangerment charge was for?"

"Supplying Ecstasy to a seventeen-year-old in exchange for sexual favors."

"Shit. What about his boss, Bill Gannon?"

He told me what I already knew, except for a few specifics. "That last domestic, he took a baseball bat to his wife's Lexus. You need the dates?"

"I have them, thanks. What about his business?"

"Uh, just a sec." Something buffeted the phone. "Oh, one more thing on the wife. She filed for divorce April 25th."

"Not a surprise," I said.

"William Gannon might have relationship problems, but his business instincts are solid. The stable's got a healthy cash flow. Last year's income after expenses and taxes topped $600,000."

"You find out anything about the Sturgills' oil company, ACS Industries? They've been in the news lately."

"You know about the change in management, right?"

"Yep."

"Well, I don't believe their new CEO has a thing to do with the stocks going up like they are." He paused and cleared his throat. "Think about it. Sturgill's son has considerably less experience. Now, if the father had been slipping, suffering from lapses in judgment, I might buy it, but he appears as shrewd and capable as ever. This is just speculation on my part, but I suspect the management change was designed to mask the true reason for all the stock activity."

"A revolutionary development in the company's oil exploration division. Something that will catapult them to the top," I said, remembering Rudi's assessment of his sister's work.

"Excellent inference."

I pictured Paige at the Thunder party, strolling down the conference room with the city's lights sparkling behind her. Remembered her words. "Something that will make atmospheric washing of little consequence."

"Huh?"

"Nothing. Something I overheard." I looked up when the PA switched on and realized that the horses were out on the track. The announcement rumbled across the plaza.

"Where the hell are you?"

"At the track. So, what else did you find on ACS Industries?"

"Money, and lots of it. As with so many things, following the money is the most telling, expedient means of assessing motive and priority, whether we're talking a huge conglomerate like ACS Industries or an individual. Who does a man spend his money on? His wife? His mistress? Himself? Financially speaking, the company has always been rock solid. Recently, however, they sustained a gross expenditure in the 400-million-dollar range."

I gasped. "What?"

"And that comes on the heels of a 120-million-dollar purchase in March. Roughly fifty percent of the funds were sunk directly into their Exploration Department and toward improving their CAEX."

"Computer-assisted exploration," I said.

"Hmm, you've been busy, I see."

I thumbed my notepad. "This development, it must be something else."

"Judging by the money they've invested, I'd say it's ground-breaking, no pun intended."

I chuckled. "I suppose the oil industry has risk management down to an art form. They wouldn't have pursued it unless they were certain of at least moderate success."

"I believe you're right, but what does this have to do with your dead girl?"

I stood and headed toward Gate 17 and the exit. "I'd always assumed that whatever got her into trouble was horse-related, but now that Rudi Sturgill has rocketed to the top of my suspect list, that opens up the possibility of her having done or seen something detrimental to the Sturgill family."

"Possible."

I glanced at the escalators as I stepped into the rotunda. "Do me a favor, will you? Keep looking into ACS Industries. The Exploration Technologies Department and Paige Sturgill in particular. She's the department head and a genius according to her brother…uh, Rudi. Not Matt."

"I didn't find much on Rudi," Kenneth said. "Very little, in fact."

"You mean in the company?"

"Correct."

"That's because he's no longer involved."

Kenneth didn't say anything for a moment. "How do you mean?"

"He used to work for his father but never had much ambition or interest. The way he talks, I assume he hasn't worked there in years." I paused near the turnstiles. "Why?"

"Okay. Well, that fits. Then again, it doesn't. His ACS e-mail account has been dormant. Until a couple of months ago."

"What?"

"It went active on January 29th."

"His being online again doesn't make sense, but he lied to me about knowing Nicole, he could be lying about everything." I turned and leaned against one of the turnstiles. "See what you can find out about Rudi's renewed involvement then. What he's doing. Who he's talking to. And see what you can dig up on a guy named Yaseen Haddad, both work-related and personal. I think he's from Syria. All this talk about ACS Industries' computer upgrades being part of the new technology they're introducing brings him into the spotlight. He works for Paige Sturgill."

"You owe me, you know?"

"Believe me," I rubbed my forehead, "I know."

"We'll discuss my fee later, but I gotta tell you, your timing couldn't have been better. The project I was working on got scrapped," he said with disgust deepening his voice, "which means enduring all the bureaucratic bullshit while the bosses figure out who's doing what. Real work has essentially ground to a halt, so your puzzle's a nice little diversion."

"Lucky me." I cleared my throat. "You're sure you won't get caught."

His amused laugh buffeted the phone. "I can't get through this company's backdoor, I might as well throw in the towel, go sit on a beach somewhere, and drink margaritas 'cause I sure as hell wouldn't be any use to the agency or this country."

"Just out of curiosity, how do you do it?"

"Intercept the early stage of a certificate exchange. Fool both—"

"A what?"

"Certificate exchange? It's an authentication process. Verifies identities. So, I fool the computers into thinking they're directly connected to each other while all their communications are routed through *my* computer. Basically a man-in-the-middle attack. Ah, and speaking of computers, I haven't summarized your Edward Utley and his Computer Management Services."

"Oh, yeah. Him."

"Sounds like you don't like the guy?"

"I don't, but that's beside the point. What do you have?"

"Not much of interest. No criminal record." He paused. "The company's revenue last year topped seven billion."

"Fuck."

"Aptly put."

I thanked Kenneth, closed the phone, and was turning toward the glass doors fronting the taxi lane and parking lot when my eye was drawn to the second level. The last race had been run, and the track's patrons were streaming toward the exit—a shifting collage of bright colors and frilly hats. Casual, elegant. Varied. Except for a knot of men who converged at the top of the elevator. Their dark suits and demeanor immediately reminded me of Henrik, although he was not among them.

Security? Bodyguards? Two of them stepped onto the escalator while a third jogged down the parallel flight of steps, drawing ahead of the rest. I looked for their employer and inhaled sharply when I caught sight of Paige.

What the hell? Although Rudi seemed amenable to the idea of being shadowed by someone like Henrik, I had never seen any indication, nor could I imagine, that Paige would submit to that kind of restriction.

I looked more closely and suspected the men were employed by an older gentleman who stood beside Paige. Dressed in an exquisitely tailored suit that managed to appear expensive and casual at the same time, he smoothed a broad, deeply tanned hand over graying hair that swept across the top of his head from a low part. Paige said something, and he bent toward her. Voices and footsteps echoed off the lobby's hard surfaces, and the sound of idling vehicles drifted through the open doors at my back.

I wondered who he was and what he did for a living that necessitated having three bodyguards in attendance while he spent a leisurely afternoon at the races.

He nodded in response to Paige's statement, and as he straightened, he glanced at the glass sculpture overhead. His gaze fell on me briefly before he checked the location of his point man, who had preceded them to the first level. He stood to my right, hands loose at his sides as he scanned the crowd.

Paige turned and faced forward as they neared the bottom of the escalator, and I noticed Yaseen standing close behind her. He tried to look nonchalant and unaffected, but his eyes repeatedly returned to the small of her back or drifted lower as he admired her ass.

I couldn't fault him.

More people filed onto the escalator or took the stairs. I watched for Rudi, hoping that he was straggling after them, but he didn't show.

When Paige and her escort stepped off the escalator and headed for the exit, I realized I wasn't the only one watching them. A man who had been leaning against an intricately paneled column to my left quickly raised a cell phone to his ear and said something. He tracked the group's progress across the lobby, then moved past me. A thin coiled wire trailed from an earpiece and disappeared beneath his jacket's collar.

Track security? I didn't think so. A cop? Maybe.

I glanced down the wide corridor that accessed the bulk of the grandstand, scanned the balcony overhead and the steps that descended to the rotunda's tiled floor; then I swept my gaze around the lobby and glanced outside toward the paddock and horseman's lounge. No one else had taken an interest in Paige and her escort, so I strolled toward the exit.

Stretch limos and taxis and a few Lincoln Town Cars lined the sidewalk. Paige and her entourage had already changed course and were headed toward a cream-colored limo.

The guy who'd been tailing them strode farther down the sidewalk, and when he cut between a tomato-red Cardinal Cab and the back of a limo, a Chevy Impala that looked a whole lot like an unmarked cop car moved alongside him. Another man joined him, and they piled into the vehicle. The driver eased the Impala into the far lane. A respectable strategy. He wouldn't get bogged down in traffic, and he wasn't right on their ass, either.

I considered following the limo, but when I shifted my gaze to Lot 9 and the traffic bottleneck waiting to get off the lot, I realized the attempt would be futile. Instead, I pushed through the doors and crossed the taxi lanes. I walked around the back of the cop car and took note of all three men as I came up alongside them. White, mid-thirties, clean-shaven, short hair, conservative dress. Cops? I now had my doubts. The Louisville PD was considerably more diverse.

Their attention was focused on the limo, but the driver shifted his gaze to the side-view mirror as I passed. Resisting an urge to look over my shoulder, I continued down the fence line and stood where I could watch Gates 1 and 17.

Eventually, both vehicles moved toward Central Avenue. The limo cruised past; then the Impala's driver took his eyes off the road and stared at me with a bullying arrogance. My reflection and the pattern of the chain-link fence that stood behind me slid like liquid across the glass. I should have looked away but didn't.

I never did see Rudi. When the men and women arriving to clean up the grandstand and grounds outnumbered the stragglers leaving the track, I reclaimed the Dodge and returned it to the lot on Fourth Street.

Chapter Twenty-six

Jay slung his backpack onto the tack trunk and propped his backside on the lid. When I didn't look up from the page I was reading in Nicole's notebook, he cleared his throat. "I'm set."

I nodded.

He shifted, and in my peripheral vision, I noticed him cross his arms over his chest. "What's up with you?"

I closed the book. Lifted my head. "What's that supposed to mean?"

"You barely said ten words all day."

The lawn chair's nylon straps creaked as I sat forward and rested my elbows on my knees. Jay's comment was ironic coming from a guy who frowned on small talk, but he was right. "Sorry. I've been distracted."

"Ain't like you," he said. "You worried about this weekend? The horses?"

This weekend. Wednesday was drawing to a close. Hard to believe the Derby was almost here. I glanced in Storm's stall, then looked over my shoulder at Ruskie. He had moved into the doorway when he heard Jay's footsteps, curious but not overly interested. Horses have excellent internal clocks, and he knew his evening meal was still some ways off. I squinted at my watch. Half an hour in fact.

The last of the day's sunlight angled across the waist-high wall, spotlighting the shedrow in an orange glow and shimmering like gold on straw that had spilled into the aisle.

I stood and crossed over to the exterior wall, where multicolored leg wraps and bandages shifted on a lazy breeze. I had waited all day for a chance to confront Rudi, but at eight-thirty, it wasn't going to happen. Even now, the residual tension I'd dealt with felt like a suit of armor weighing my limbs. I turned to face Jay.

"The horses are fine," I said, answering his question. "I'm fine. Their races are going to unfold the way they're meant to, whether I allow myself to get nervous or not, so no…I'm not worried."

He grunted.

"I'll be focused when I need to be." I indicated Nicole's notebook and told him what I had uncovered. His face remained unreadable throughout.

Jay glanced at the guard and lowered his voice. "You think Gone Wild ain't who he's made out to be?"

"Yes." I eased farther down the aisle and looked in on the colt before returning to our section of the shedrow. "Whenever Nicole delivered a foal, she took meticulous notes, including observations of the foal's markings. Not the thorough description required by the Jockey Club but good enough to determine if the horse standing in that stall," I jerked my head toward Gone Wild, "matches the physical description she documented when he was born."

"She was blackmailing Sturgill," Jay said.

"Probably. It makes sense, doesn't it? What better time to hit him than right before the Derby when he'd be desperate to keep what he'd done quiet."

"Too desperate," Jay said.

"As it turned out…." I set her notebook on the tack trunk and folded my arms. "Think about it. She watched all the Derby coverage and media attention unfolding around the horse, and she ends up pulling out her notebook to see if he was one of the colts she delivered, and somewhere down the line, she realizes the physical descriptions don't match. So she calls Rudi, and that's where the infamous tape comes into play, the one those punks are looking for. She must have used her answering machine to record the conversation when she called Sturgill and told him

what she knew. Then she rips the page out of her notebook and
brings it to the shedrow just to make sure, or maybe she was
supposed to hand it over in exchange for the money. I don't
know. Either way—"

"Her plan backfired."

"Fatally, in fact."

I rubbed the back of my neck and admired Gallant Storm's
beautifully chiseled head, steel gray with a discernable white
blaze that widened between his nostrils. He was an intelligent,
hugely talented horse, but Ruskie remained my favorite in
Kessler's barn. I suspected that my contempt for Utley was the
reason that I'd never gotten one hundred percent behind Storm.
Irrational, but there it was.

I pivoted and watched Ruskie watching me. He'd come a long
way since Kessler claimed him from a trainer who'd botched the
colt's introduction to racing. I shuddered to think what he might
have become if he'd started out under Kessler. With his talent,
he would have been a formidable Derby contender in his third
year, but luck and timing had been against him.

Timing.

I flipped open Nicole's notebook.

"You gonna tell the cops?" Jay said.

"Just a sec." I checked the dates for each foaling entry, then
paged back to the gap where the torn edge of notepaper was
visible in the crease. "Jay, when was Gone Wild born?" When
he didn't answer, I looked up. "You got a *Form* 'round here?"

Jay opened the tack trunk and pulled out the latest *Daily
Racing Form*, flipped through the pages, and grunted. "Says
here, the colt was born January 3rd."

Timing.

"Close," Jay said.

"That's the risk, isn't it? Everybody wants their foals on the
ground as early as possible so they'll have that extra growth and
coordination behind them, but every now and then, a mare will
drop her foal weeks before the due date," I mumbled as I reread
the entries surrounding the missing page.

On December 29th, Nicole wrote about the difference between working foal watch as opposed to day shift. She wasn't required to clean stalls, so she was catching up on her reading. The next entry that had anything to do with foaling was dated January 12th. At 10:45 p.m., Nicole had delivered a huge bay colt by Pleasant City out of Storm Squall. She'd ended her entry with: *The way things have worked out so far this season, I'm looking forward to a nice peaceful delivery.* That line seemed to indicate that an earlier difficulty had occurred.

I leaned against the stall front and closed the book. "What would you do if your mare delivered a valuable foal a day or two before New Year's?" I said as I turned to look at Rudi's Derby contender. "Maybe Gone Wild *is* who he's supposed to be. Maybe he was just born too early."

"Hard to prove unless someone talks."

"Exactly. Like the person who delivered him."

"Other people would know," Jay said.

"Maybe...probably. But not everyone would resort to blackmail, and not every farm employee keeps track of facts like Nicole did. Say Gone Wild was born in December. Let's just say December 31st for argument's sake. Because of the archaic manner in which the industry defines a horse's age, he'd technically become a yearling at the stroke of midnight when one year slides into the next. His racing career would be over before it began."

"His bid for the Derby, anyway," Jay said and I agreed.

"What would you do in Rudi's position?" I indicated Nicole's notebook. "I have a feeling Rudi told the staff that something happened to Gone Wild. Something that would cause them to lose track of the horse...forget he was ever born."

"How'd he do that?"

"I don't know, but it's gotta be one of those scenarios. Either Gone Wild isn't Gone Wild, or he's a four-year-old."

"You gonna tell the cops what you know?"

I nodded. "After I talk to him." Jay frowned and shook his head, and I had an uncomfortable feeling he was remembering the last time I hadn't taken the proper precautions and had ended up with three pieces of shot embedded in my shoulder. "He's involved. He's got to be, but I can't believe he killed her."

Jay shrugged. "He had someone do it."

"I don't know. It just doesn't feel right."

The sun was on a slow slide toward the horizon, and as it dipped behind Barn 47, the bulky shadow cast from the roofline crept up the side of our barn, plunging the shedrow into cool shade as smoothly as if a blind had been drawn.

"When her death was announced on the radio, he was shocked, Jay, truly shocked." I slipped my cell phone out of my pocket and called Bonikowski, made arrangements for police coverage while I walked back to the Hilton. When I hung up, Jay pointed his finger at me.

"You screw up and aren't here to help when you're supposed to, I'm gonna find your ass and kill you myself."

As per instructions, I gave Bonikowski the necessary time to put several cars in place before I left the track. Before the attack at the fairgrounds, I had fallen into the habit of taking a shortcut to the Central Avenue overpass, but that route included numerous choke points that New York and Co. could use to advantage. Choke points the cops were ill-prepared to cover. So, I kept to the main drag where I was more accessible but supposedly more easily protected. A catch 22, I'd decided.

Up ahead, an unmarked unit had pulled across the entrance to the gravel lot adjacent to Wagner's Pharmacy. The driver had me in his side-view mirror and was in an excellent position to follow once I turned the corner. Four guys walked by in the opposite direction. I glanced over my shoulder. Two men were following me, both Hispanic. Backsiders. A man and woman stood at the curb as the woman unfolded a pamphlet. Tourists.

Wagner's doors were shut tight, and thick metal cables had been strung around the gravel lot. They hadn't been there in the morning. I inclined my head, acknowledging the cop as I passed; then I turned east at Central. In the distance, the light towers rising above Cardinal Stadium caught the last rays of sunlight and sparkled like tinsel against a cloudless sky.

I paused at the intersection of Central and Second. Both the gas station and shopping center were packed. In fact, the entire area was buzzing with activity.

Last night, when I'd returned from the track, a crowd had been waiting to get through the Cardinal Hall of Fame's front door, and the Hilton was certainly filled to capacity. Churchill was enjoying record crowds as well. Horses were being trailered onto the grounds day and night, and the mounting excitement was infectious. For the first time that day, I felt my spirits lift. Screw Rudi and his deceptions. I was lucky to be here, taking part in one of the industry's most celebrated events, an event that apparently transformed Louisville into Party Central.

A stretch limo cruised west toward the grandstand while a cop car headed in the opposite direction. I was still waiting for a break in traffic when I noticed a security guard standing in the gas station's lot. Additional security was positioned along the shopping center's perimeter.

I nodded in greeting. "What's going on?"

"Security to keep the squatters out."

"Squatters?"

"Yeah. People come from all over looking for a place to camp. They'll pull their cars and vans in here if we let 'em, and before you know it, they're setting up barbeque grills and sleeping bags and whatnot."

"Wow."

"Every year, we get folks we gotta run off."

"Interesting." I wished him a good night, then drifted over to the curb.

The police car that had cruised toward the Hilton earlier zipped past in the opposite direction. I crossed to the sidewalk on the north side.

The new overpass, with its wide lanes and grassy median, arched gracefully above the train tracks. A long line of white-roofed boxcars swayed gently as a CSX locomotive rounded a stretch of track that curved past the stadium. The wheels' hypnotic clacking competed with the Doppler effect of cars zipping past on my right and the blast of an air horn from another train approaching from the south. Beyond the stadium, Louisville's skyscrapers were visible on the horizon.

My cell phone rang as an unmarked unit cruised past and disappeared over the rise. From experience, I knew he'd turn around in the Super 8's parking lot.

I glanced over my shoulder and checked the traffic as I slipped the phone out of my pocket. No red Caprice. No cop car, either. When I turned back around, a black Jeep crested the rise and picked up speed.

My adrenaline spiked when I noticed two occupants behind the glare of the windshield, but the passenger's window was rolled up tight. He wasn't getting ready to sight down the barrel of a gun. It's nothing, I told myself. Just some asshole driving too fast.

I thumbed the side of the cell, began to lift the cover.

Tires squealed as sidewall scraped the curb, then both right wheels thumped onto the sidewalk.

I froze.

In the next instant, the Jeep lurched onto the sidewalk and accelerated. The mirror snapped, then spun off, tumbled through the air like a black bird. Metal screamed on concrete, creating a fountain of sparks as the Jeep bore down on me.

Traffic streamed over the rise. No way I'd get to the median without being hit. Only one option.

I'd had two weeks to notice the bridge's intricacies: the flimsy decorative rail that topped the barrier, the heavy pipe sculptures spaced every forty feet.

Spinning on my heel, I lunged toward the bulky sculpture I'd just passed. The cell phone flew out of my hand as I gripped the cold steel. Don't look down…don't fucking look down. Just do it.

I looked over the rail.

Forty feet of empty space, maybe fifty, between the bridge's underpinnings and the gravel roadbed. The CSX engine thudded under the bridge. Heat blasted upward and rolled from beneath the girders. I yanked my head around, watched the Jeep's grille mushroom before me, close enough now that I could make out the pattern etched in the glass covering the fog lamps. Gritting my teeth, I tightened my hold on the pipe and swung over the rail. Felt myself swing out into space like a pendulum.

My boots bumped against the concrete as the Jeep screeched past in a blur of color and noise. Vibrations shuddered through the metal pipe beneath my palms and pulsed through my chest as traffic whizzed across the span.

I looked under my arm, and a surge of fear snatched the breath from my lungs.

Fuck, fuck…fuck.

Auto racks rocked along the track ten feet below my boots, and the combination of noise and vibrations…and my own fear threatened to loosen my hold.

A ledge skirted the bridge. I concentrated on relaxing my arms, allowing my weight to sink downward until the tread on my boots skimmed the gritty surface. I straightened and found I could actually stand on the balls of my feet.

A siren wailed in the distance.

Clammy sweat coated my skin and spread across my palms. My left hand slipped. I tightened my fingers and sucked in a breath. The very act of breathing rocked me away from the wall with each inhalation, an admittedly minute shift, but it scared the shit out of me.

I pressed hard against the wall, felt an echo of the day's heat seep into my shirt. Tried to ignore the vibrations that pulsed through the bridge and rattled around in my lungs. Tremors flooded my muscles in cold waves, chilling me to the bone while sweat trickled down my face. When I readjusted my grip on the pipe, the blended odors of enamel paint and rust mixed with the tangy smell of diesel exhaust.

I flinched when the northbound train exploded from beneath the overpass in a shuddering wall of noise and heat and wondered how I was going to get off the goddamn ledge.

And where were the cops?

I swallowed, then forced my head back, blinked sweat out of my eyes. The black pipes and curved metal sculpture and railing came into focus. I would need to change my grip in order to climb back up. Changing my grip required me to actually let go.

Beneath me, the trains continued their lumbering slide past each other, cars rocking, metal creaking, the soft whine of steel against steel, quieter now that both locomotives were some distance off.

I pictured each step I would make to get back over the wall. Rehearsed it in my mind and tried to imagine that I was standing on the ground, not clinging to a foot-wide ledge ten feet above the crushing weight of railcars traveling fifteen miles per hour.

I wasn't entirely successful.

After of minute's hesitation, I tightened my right hand until the fingers cramped, held my breath, and let go with the left. Lunged upward, felt my fingertips brush the smooth steel. I gripped the rail and let the momentum swing me toward the next handhold.

A man peered over the railing the next section down, and I nearly lost my grip.

Navy uniform. Peaked hat. A cop.

"Hey. Hold on," he yelled. He signaled to someone as he spun out of my line of sight, and a half a minute later, he and his partner dragged me up and over the rail.

I flopped onto the sidewalk like a landed fish. One of them keyed his mike while I levered myself into a sitting position with my back slumped against the concrete barrier.

An unmarked car sat on the sidewalk to my left with its grille strobes and high beams flashing while a gray LMPD cruiser faced oncoming traffic with its bumper nosed toward the curb.

Reflections rode down the blue and gold stripes as vehicles streamed around his car.

The cop who'd first spotted me listened to a broadcast, then announced, "They got 'em."

Chapter Twenty-seven

The bedspread slipped to my waist when I bolted upright, out of breath and disoriented by a jumble of disturbing images that had jerked me awake. I threw the covers off and lowered my feet to the carpet, gripped the edge of the mattress, and hung my head.

Like most dreams, this one had made no sense, but that didn't diminish its impact. I had reached for my father as the dream intensified, grabbed his shoulder, wanting to save him from a danger I could not comprehend or, in fact, see. But his head swiveled around, and the person…no, the thing that had looked back at me was not my father at all.

I swallowed.

The room was cold, and the rumpled sheets were damp with sweat. I glanced at the alarm clock. Two-thirty.

Thursday.

Two days and counting.

Two days before a staggering 150,000 people partook in the town's annual rite of spring, compliments of Churchill Downs. I had looked forward to my time in Louisville, but after all that had come to pass, I would be happy when the job was over and done.

I showered, strapped the body armor over my T-shirt, and took an alternate route to work, cutting through dark neighborhoods and squeezing between a gap in the fence that bordered the train tracks.

Avoiding the damn bridge.

Gravel crunched under my boots as I stepped over the rails. In the south, a lone headlamp hovered over the tracks, so distant, the thrumming of her engines blended into the fabric of the night.

I should have called Bonikowski to tell her I was leaving, but I was tired of that, too.

I had identified New York and his partner in a lineup, but they weren't talking and wouldn't give up who they were working for despite the serious charges lodged against them. It saddened me to think that Rudi might be responsible.

An hour later, when the morning work got underway, I set aside Nicole's notebook and, with it, the memories it brought to mind: her slender hands balled into fists when Bill Gannon stepped beneath the barn's shadowy eaves and the sound of rustling paper as she tucked her notes out of sight; diffuse light shimmering on keys left lying in the street and Yaseen Haddad's conflicted emotions of contempt and lust that shone in his dark eyes; a grimy restroom floor and a lingering echo of pain; my belongings scattered across the carpet and brightly colored balloons tethered like malevolent creatures against a nightmare sky while a gas jet's light flashed orange on lethal steel.

I remembered the unexpected memory of my father that had caught me by surprise and the coolness of paper, the ruffled edge beneath my fingertips as I traced the rip in Nicole's notebook. I pictured Paige's beauty and the fleeting ugliness glimpsed beneath the mask, a byproduct of seething hatred for her father.

And I pictured precise lines and a dark green rectangle plotted on a map, coordinates within a grid. A sterile reminder of Nicole's last moments on this Earth.

As I tucked Nicole's notebook into the tack trunk, I closed my mind to the icy fear that had clawed its way through my chest when the Jeep crested the rise. Blocked out the fear that still lingered like a bad taste in my mouth, an echo of the physical assault of sound and heat as the train rumbled past ten feet beneath my shoes.

Unimaginable tonnage slipping over the rails. Mindless and unforgiving.

I didn't think again of New York or his partner or even Nicole until Detective Bonikowski flashed her badge at a guard stationed near the mouth of the alley. She strode toward me. Strode right past two Hispanics and seemed unaware of the apprehension rippling in her wake. Both men stopped in their tracks before conveniently discovering they were needed elsewhere.

My attention ratcheted back to Storm when he pinned his ears. He jerked his head upward in annoyed little jabs as Jay slopped a sponge full of sudsy water down his black mane. I glanced beyond the horse's rump and noted the ever-present media, the cameramen and photographers with cargo vests and pants loaded with gear and the reporters scavenging the backside like ants.

Ever since Nicole's death, ever since the cops had shown an interest in Barn 41's personnel, they'd been extra vigilant.

As Bonikowski stepped to my side, I checked the shedrow. Kessler was within earshot on the other side of the waist-high wall, thumbing through the *Daily Racing Form*.

Detective Bonikowski folded her arms under her breasts. "Why the hell didn't you call me when you left the hotel?"

"I left early."

She narrowed her eyes. "Big deal. Someone wants to get at you, all he's gotta do is stake out the parking lot. The Hilton's, the Cardinal Hall of Fame's, Arby's. Any one of those would work, or have you forgotten how easy it is to pick up a tail?"

"No." I cleared my throat. "I'm sorry."

"And what's wrong with your phone?"

"I lost it on the bridge."

Keeping her eye on Gallant Storm, Bonikowski reached across and tweaked my collar. "At least you wore the vest."

Water curtained off the colt's belly and squelched under his hooves as he stepped sideways. The scrape of his aluminum shoes sounded hollow, belying the weight and power behind those slender legs. He shook his head, and when a high-pitched wheeze escaped his throat, I automatically turned my head. He sneezed, and a glittering spray of water droplets arced through the air and coated my chest and arms.

"Shit." Bonikowski pressed the back of her hand over her nose and mouth and stepped backward.

I clamped down on a smile. "Any progress with those two?"

She glared at me. "No, and if their DNA doesn't match the killer's, it's entirely possible they'll make bail, so you need to be doubly vigilant."

"Who's going to—"

"Vigilant about what?" Kessler said as he stepped alongside her.

"Your boy here," Bonikowski looked from Kessler to me and stated matter-of-factly, "has been offered police protection but isn't sticking with the program."

"Protection?" Fuck. I shook my head. "Interesting terminology, Detective."

Kessler narrowed his eyes. "What the hell are you talking about? I thought they were arrested?"

Bonikowski raised an eyebrow. "They were, but it's doubtful they were acting alone."

Kessler looked at both of us in turn. "So, you're using my son as bait?" he said slowly.

Bonikowski's eyelids flickered in response to the harshness in his voice. She shot me a glance. "Offering him protection."

"Tell me, Detective. Can he go home?"

I jerked my head around.

"At this point? Yes. I'd say he's free to go."

"Well, that's something, anyway," I mumbled. Freedom to leave meant I had dropped way down the suspect list. I looked at Kessler. "But I want to stay. Just two more days."

I glanced at Jay. At the fat sponge resting against the horse's stifle as Jay's attention focused on the conversation. A pencil-thin stream of water trickled down the colt's muscled gaskin, looping across a lacy network of veins that were still distended beneath the thoroughbred's fine coat.

Kessler planted his hands on his hips. "I don't know…"

"Just two days. I should be fine."

"I don't know if it's possible for you to be fine anywhere," Kessler said, and Bonikowski's lips twitched. He fished a key from his jeans pocket and held it out to me. "No more walking. Use my rental from this point on."

"Agreed."

Bill Gannon walked past as Jay flipped a sweat scraper out of his back pocket. Gannon glanced at us as Kessler emphasized his point. "Two days, then you're out of here."

I nodded.

Kessler scrubbed his face with his hands and looked disgusted as he turned and headed back to the shedrow.

Bonikowski watched Jay flick the sweat scraper. "How are you going to contact me?"

"Pay phone."

"Won't help if I need to get in touch with you."

I told her I'd buy a phone once I got off work; then I gave her Jay's number for the time being, and that seemed to satisfy her.

Without warning, Jay tossed me a Hershey's chocolate bar. I fumbled the catch but latched onto it before it slipped off my lap. I slid my spine deeper into the lawn chair, propped my shoes on the edge of the tack trunk, and rested my neck against the tubular frame. I wagged the chocolate bar at him. "Thanks."

Jay lifted his chin in acknowledgment as he scooted across the trunk's lid until his shoulders rested against the stall front. He settled his backpack across his thigh.

It was one o'clock Thursday afternoon, and the call for horsemen to ready their runners for the second race had just come across the loudspeakers. I peeled the wrapper off my chocolate bar while Jay scoured the inside of his backpack for God knew what.

He lifted a CD player and stack of CDs out of his pack. "Glad you didn't have to leave."

I paused with the chocolate bar halfway to my mouth. "Thanks."

Jay shrugged. "You know the routine."

I smiled.

"And you know how to handle yourself. Don't gotta worry about you keeping up your end of the job."

Damn high praise coming from Jay. My gaze shifted to Gallant Storm. He'd been dozing in his doorway, but his ears twitched at the sound of Jay unzipping one of his backpack's many compartments. I finished off the candy bar and was crumpling the wrapper when Jay's perplexed expression caught my attention. He reached into the backpack and withdrew a packet of chewing gum and a tape. He turned the cassette over.

I leaned forward. "What's wrong?"

"This ain't mine."

I sprang from my chair and snatched the tape out of his hand, turned it over, and read: *Panasonic, side 2, INCOMING MESSAGE TAPE*. "Holy shit."

"What?" Jay said.

"This is it." I held it up. "The missing tape. It's got to be." I looked down at Jay. "That morning when Nicole was in the receiving barn, your backpack fell over. I picked it up and jammed your CDs back inside. Nicole must have thought it was mine, and when she saw Rudi...I don't know. Maybe she was afraid he'd get the tape, so when I left to get the hot water, and everyone else had turned to see who was coming in the barn, she must have zipped it into the compartment with the intention of retrieving it later."

"When she came back," Jay said, "it were you she was looking for."

I tapped my fingernail on the cassette, listened to music drifting from the Longfield side of the barn. "No wonder everyone thought I had it."

I spun around and cut through the short aisle. A kick-ass song by Linkin Park played softly in deference to the horses.

The groom who had arrived a couple of days earlier closed his copy of *Men's Fitness* and watched my approach with a mixture of curiosity and alarm playing across his face. I paused and looked over his shoulder, located the source of the music. A Sony CFD CD/radio/cassette recorder with dual cassette decks.

I slipped my knife out of my pocket, sliced the bailing twine that he'd used to attach the handle to the electric conduit, and yanked the plug out of the outlet.

"Hey."

"Mind if I borrow this?" I didn't wait for an answer but spun around and carried the boombox into an unoccupied office at the end of the aisle.

The doorknob felt cool under my fingertips as I turned to close the door. Jay had stepped into the short aisle. I swung the door toward the jamb, blocking out my view of the groom as he stood beside his chair with his mouth open and the magazine dangling from his hand with the pages curling apart one by one.

I locked the door.

A slight tremor shook my fingers as I switched out the tapes. I hit PLAY. Nothing. I rewound Nicole's tape and began again.

The tape caught the sound of a ringing phone. On the third ring, a voice I knew well came through the speaker.

Rudi Sturgill saying hello.

"I know what you did," a feminine voice said. Shaky, nervous.

"What? Who is this?" Rudi said, and I could hear the first stirring of alarm creeping into his voice.

"Nicole Austin. Remember me?"

He didn't say anything for a moment, and I could imagine what was going through his mind, the desperation he must have felt as he put it together.

"Yes." His voice was a raspy whisper.

Nicole cleared her throat. "You forged Gone Wild's foal papers, changed his date of birth." She drew in a shaky breath. "And I can prove it."

"I don't know what you're talking about."

"Yes you do." Her voice sounded strained. "I kept excellent notes about the horses I foaled, and Littlemiss delivered her foal December 30th at 11:55 p.m., which was about 24 hours too early. Do you remember what you told me when I came to work the next day?"

Rudi said nothing.

"You told me her broad artery ruptured, that she had collapsed instantly and landed on her foal, killing him too. It happens, I know that. In fact, I thought that whatever caused her to foal prematurely had caused the rupture. Although looking back, I remember thinking it was strange that you weren't upset when she delivered her colt before the New Year." She swallowed. "But you'd already decided to make them disappear."

"This is ludicrous. No one could get away with that." Rudi's voice was clamped down tight with mounting panic.

"You did, or at least you tried. And I can prove it. I wrote down every detail of the birth, including the colt's description, his tail tag number. Everything. Gone Wild is that colt, and my notes and testimony would prove it." After a pause, when neither spoke, she sighed. "I guess you should have changed the dam's name, too, then I might not have caught on."

"I couldn't because of the DNA requirements," he said slowly. Sadly, if I wasn't mistaken. "What do you want?"

"One million dollars."

"Jesus…I can't pay you that."

"If the colt wins, you'll get twice that, not to mention the millions you'll get from stud fees."

"I don't have that kind of money lying around."

"You'll come up with it," Nicole said with a bit more confidence. "Otherwise, people are going to find out, and your reputation will be ruined."

"Wait…. All right. I'll get the money, but I need time."

"Friday afternoon. Five o'clock."

"I can't come up with it that fast."

"Sure you can."

After a pause, Rudi said, "Where?"

"Gate 5."

"What guarantee do I have that you won't try this again?"

"I'll give you my notes."

"You could make a copy."

"I could, but I won't. Look, Mr. Sturgill, I don't like doing this, but I've got to. Friday at five o'clock. Be there, or I go to the authorities."

Static filled the line when she hung up. I pressed STOP, then ejected Nicole's tape.

The groom pounded on the door. "What the hell you doing in there?"

"Just a sec."

His boombox had the ability to record and play back…and copy. I checked the other deck. He had been listening to a CD, but he'd left a Sony hi-fidelity audio cassette in the deck. I slipped Nicole's tape back into the slot and copied it onto his tape, verified that I'd captured the entire conversation, then removed both tapes.

I pocketed them, swung the door open, and came face to face with the groom, Jay, and the security guard.

I handed over the guy's property, minus the tape, hoping he wouldn't notice. "Sorry for the misunderstanding," I mumbled as I brushed past them. Jay followed me back to Kessler's side of the barn.

I slapped the original tape in his palm. "Keep this safe."

"What are you doing?"

"Going to see Rudi."

Chapter Twenty-eight

I eased Kessler's rental down St. Michael Street, past duplexes and track housing in a modest neighborhood, and was surprised when the road dead-ended at the cemetery's border. Apparently, I'd chosen the wrong way in.

The door alarm chimed as I lowered my feet to the pavement. I withdrew the keys and climbed out, clicked the door shut. The day was heating up. If the trend continued through Saturday, the change in temperature would be a factor during the race.

Sticking my hands in my pockets, I strolled toward the cemetery fence. In the distance, sunlight glinted off metal poles supporting a canopy near one of the many lanes that crisscrossed the grounds. The sight of the striped canvas standing out against the sky was an unwelcome reminder of my father's death.

In contrast to his graveside service, Nicole's seemed lightly attended.

To be honest, I had no idea whether I would find Rudi, but a slim chance was better than none. I drifted along the perimeter, changing my perspective, spotting a woman I assumed was Nicole's mother. Frail-looking, seated in a wheelchair in the front row. No one else looked remotely familiar.

I was thinking I had wasted my time, had unnecessarily put myself at risk, when I glanced beyond the gathering and noticed a black Crown Vic parked in a lot attached to commercial buildings along the cemetery's southwestern border. Bonikowski and her partner. They were in a perfect position to observe who came and went.

I wondered if Bonikowski had spotted me and figured I'd hear about it soon enough.

As I turned to leave, a silver Dodge Ram caught my eye. The pickup was parked beside a turnaround near the cemetery's entrance and was somewhat obscured by an overgrown hedge. Its nose was angled so that the driver would have an unobstructed view of the service. I squinted at a familiar pair of gold and navy stripes that tapered off above the front wheel well. I took a step or two forward, caught a portion of an elegant logo, and confirmed that the truck was one of the fleet belonging to Wellspring Farm.

He was here.

I backtracked to St. Michael Street and peered down the property line separating the cemetery from a group of residential lots. A ragged hedge of untidy shrubs and trees had grown up alongside the fence and formed a loose boundary. At the far end, the pickup's back quarter panel protruded past lilac bushes swollen with blossoms.

Keeping behind the thicket and out of the cop's sight, I reached the Dodge and yanked open the passenger's door.

Rudi whipped his head around and opened his mouth in surprise as I slipped onto the seat and closed the door.

"Goddamn you," I said through clenched teeth. "You killed her, didn't you? That's why you're here. Out of guilt."

A click sounded at my back. The door flew open. Before I could turn, something cold and hard pressed against the base of my skull.

Rudi's bloodshot gaze slid past my face. "It's okay." He licked his lips. "Wait by the car."

I eased around on the seat in time to see Henrik slot an automatic into a holster under his arm. He thumbed the snap. "Give me cause to regret my acquiescence," Henrik said to me in a soft, measured tone, "and I'll tear you apart."

A sickening sweet smell of lilacs drifted into the cab as he closed the door. Henrik stared through the glass with cool emotionless eyes as the sunlight bore down on his short yellow hair. A film of perspiration gleamed on his scalp. He smoothed the flaps of his sport coat, and after a brief moment, he glanced at Rudi before turning and walking calmly toward a Lincoln Town Car parked farther down the street.

I pivoted to face Rudi, unclenched my jaw. "I know what you did."

He began to shake his head slowly, as if trying to get through to a child. "N—"

"You killed her."

"No." His voice came out in a throaty whisper. "I would never—"

I leaned closer, splayed my hand on the console. "Cut the bullshit, Rudi," I yelled. "I know what happened. When Nicole realized your Derby horse was none other than the bay colt she delivered on December 30th, she tried to blackmail you."

The color drained from his face.

Conscious of the fact that Henrik was nearby, I continued. "Gone Wild, sired by Good as Gone, out of Littlemiss. Hard to accept missing out on all those lucrative races for two and three-year-olds, wasn't it?" I said bitterly. "He sure as shit wouldn't be running in the Derby, but what the hell? You figure there's no harm in changing the date by a couple of days, and you know what? I don't begrudge you that, but Jesus, Rudi. Killing her...."

"I didn't—"

"I've been a goddamn fool," my throat felt clogged, "trusting you...."

Rudi shook his head. "You've got it wrong."

"Damn right I did, but not anymore. Whenever the evidence pointed in your direction, I gave you the benefit of the doubt. Second-guessed myself while, all along, you were fucking setting me up."

"No."

"Inviting me to the Thunder party so your goddamn goons could jump me," I said and was aware of my heart pounding in my chest. "Making sure I was on the backside when they searched my hotel room. You even asked about Jay, remember?" I swallowed. "All that bullshit about us being so alike." I looked at him in disgust. "I'm nothing like you."

"I swear, I had nothing to do with her death. You've got to believe me." A tremor jerked his hand on the steering wheel.

His fingers were puffy and tinged with residual bruising beneath the cast's soft edging. Streaks of yellow and green still feathered across his face as they did mine, compliments of the air bags that had saved our lives. He licked his chapped lips, and as he searched my face, I was once again reminded of the shock he'd experienced when Nicole's death had been announced on the radio.

"Tell me this, Rudi. Did you send them to stick a knife in my gut?"

His eyes widened. "What?"

"And the Jeep? Was that your idea too? Running me over?"

"I don't know what you're talking about, I swear to God I don't. You've got to believe me." His voice cracked.

"But she was blackmailing you."

Rudi bowed his head. "Yes."

"Who did you go to for help?" I said.

Rudi slowly lifted his head. He looked like he hadn't slept since the accident. Since they'd announced the discovery of Nicole's body.

"Who, Rudi?"

He shook his head.

"Your father?" I said. "Paige?"

His eyes tracked slowly toward the gravesite. Cars were starting up, pulling away, sunlight flashing on chrome, winking off glass. He swallowed. "I never wanted this." He turned and looked at me with his eyes full of unshed tears. "You've got to believe that."

I withdrew a copy of the tape, tossed it in his lap.

"What's this?"

"A recording of your conversation with Nicole. The original's on its way to the authorities. You should have twenty-four hours. I suggest you tell the police everything you know."

He closed his eyes and swallowed. "You don't know what you've done."

"Maybe I do."

Rudi opened his eyes and looked at me. Red splotches had risen to his cheeks.

"Your old e-mail account at ACS Industries has been reactivated. I think you better find out why."

"What?" He opened his mouth and stared at me as I got out and walked away.

Friday afternoon, Oaks Day, extra security covered the backside while the mouth-watering aroma of mesquite barbeque drifted down the alley between barns. Grills and pig-roasts and banquet tables had been set up at various barns throughout the backside, and we'd had to endure the tantalizing smells all morning.

Jay and I sat side by side on the tack trunk—our one and only chair had gone missing—and watched the shifting crowd. I dragged a french fry through ketchup at the bottom of my to-go box and popped it in my mouth, watched the Derby Festival Queen and her court of four lovely ladies walk past. Flawless makeup and silky skin. Bare shoulders and stiletto heels. Red roses in their hair and satin the color of vanilla ice cream.

Jay paused in mid-bite when he caught sight of them. He bit into his cheeseburger and swallowed. Dragged the back of his hand across his mouth. "Damn."

"Exactly." I broke my stare and scanned the slice of backside visible from Barn 41. Five National Guardsmen walked past. The LMPD were here, too, and I'd even seen a couple of MPs mired in the foot traffic by the gap as they struggled to create a path for the horses.

Jay and I would have a quiet day, though, because the majority of the day's race card belonged to the fillies.

Jay's cell phone rang. He glanced at the readout and handed it to me without comment.

"Cline."

"Steve. Kenneth here. I've been monitoring Rudi Sturgill's reactivated e-mail account at ACS Industries."

"And?"

"Whoever's using it has been communicating with Terrence Lectron. You know him?"

"Nope. Uh…wait a minute. I've heard the name. Paige mentioned him. Who is he?"

"A senior partner at Lectron Oil in Houston," Kenneth said. "The guy's dirty. FBI's had him under surveillance for months."

"What for?"

"Embezzlement. They were getting ready to bust him when he made a last-minute reservation to go to Louisville. So the Bureau reexamined all his Kentucky connections and picked up on e-mail activity that they'd overlooked between Lectron and our person in ACS Industries." Kenneth sighed. "Not surprising that they missed it the first time around. Lectron's bound to be in contact with all kinds of industry professionals. Anyway, the FBI wants to figure out what's going on before they close him down."

"What do you think's going on?"

"If this was aboveboard, I'd say they were preparing to enter into a partnership, but this is definitely under-the-covers clandestine, so my gut says corporate espionage. I'd guess someone at ACS Industries is preparing to sell those vital schematics you talked about. Someone with no qualms about sinking the company."

"Someone with an axe to grind."

"Greed's a more likely motivator."

"You said he's here," I said. "What's this guy Lectron look like?"

The distinctive sound of a keyboard came through the earpiece.

"Okay. I got it. Mid to late sixties, large build but not fat. A head full of graying hair. Tanned, weathered skin. Wire-rimmed glasses. Bushy eyebrows. And the guy's got huge ears. An old man's ears. You know, they never stop growing?"

I chuckled. "A bit of trivia I could do without." I drew up my left leg and braced my boot on the trunk's lid while I tried to remember any unique qualifiers regarding the man I'd seen Tuesday afternoon, riding down the escalator with Paige and a significant protective detail. "Is his hair parted unusually low on the left side of his head?"

Kenneth paused. "You've seen him, then."

"Yes." I expelled a breath. "Do me a favor, fi—"

"You're gonna owe me for the rest of your natural life, you know that don't you?"

I smiled. "Yes, and I'm grateful." As a man strolled down the alley with an ESPN camera hoisted on his shoulder, I thought of the times Kenneth had helped me in the past. "Why are you doing this?" I said softly. "I appreciate it and everything, but why?"

"I owe you."

I frowned. "I don't—"

"I was having a rough time in school. Always the outsider. The geek. I was miserable. Suicidal, even."

"But you were—"

"Smart? Yeah, right. But when you're sixteen, being a genius isn't all it's cracked up to be. I was getting picked on so much, my mother transferred me to B.L.," he said, referring to the Boys' Latin School. "Then I get partnered with you in Physics. A jock. Popular. You were the first cool kid who ever treated me like I belonged." He didn't say anything for a moment, and I didn't know what to say to that. "It meant a lot. Made me see I had value and would be okay."

"So...I don't owe you?"

He laughed. "What else do you need to know?"

I pictured Paige Sturgill—brilliant, charismatic, unpredictable—and I considered the animosity she felt toward her father, a hatred so volatile, she was incapable of concealing it in public. Had she finally decided to strike back where it would hurt most? Crippling the company. Sell the very thing that was meant to propel them forward. Her lewd behavior, and even the men she latched onto, was her way of getting back at her father. Consciously or not.

But how did any of this connect to Nicole's murder?

Finances.

Rudi couldn't afford to pay off Nicole, but I doubted he would have gone to his father. He would have asked Paige.

The timing must have thrown her for a loop. Any scandal that involved the family would have been cataclysmic as far as her plans were concerned. She needed Rudi uninvolved in his own disaster, especially if she intended to set him up, and that's sure how it looked from here. Using Rudi's e-mail account virtually assured the authorities coming down on him. But after all I'd seen, I would have sworn that she genuinely cared for him. Maybe she realized the e-mail activity alone wouldn't be enough to prosecute him without other evidence of wrongdoing.

But something had gone wrong. Nicole had been killed, presumably without Rudi's knowledge.

Snapshot images of what I'd seen over the past two weeks scrolled through my mind. The bracelets on Paige's wrist catching the light as she argued with Rudi at the Thunder party. Both of them turning to look at me when I had naively assumed they were watching the fireworks. Scratches on Brent's hand as he'd tossed one back under the marquee. The icy expression I had caught on Paige's face when she'd stood in the shedrow on opening day.

I pictured her gaze lingering on my throat before she slowly lifted her eyes to my face, her expression impenetrable. Had she noticed the vest and recognized it for what it was, and had that knowledge prompted her to change her plans? Use a vehicle instead of a knife or gun?

"Yo, Steve?"

"Sorry." I cleared my throat. "Look into Paige Sturgill's activities, will you? See if you can connect her in any way with Lectron and that e-mail account."

"Paige Sturgill, huh?"

"Yeah, her." I gave Kenneth my new cell phone number, then disconnected.

I dialed Detective Bonikowski and left a message on her voicemail. It was time I told her everything I knew.

Chapter Twenty-nine

Something was wrong with Bill Gannon.

I had been vaguely aware of his stilted gait when he walked into the shedrow minutes earlier but had paid little attention.

I was aware of him now. And so were a growing number of people milling round the barn, despite the distraction of the day's powerhouse racing.

He stood rooted to the spot outside Gone Wild's stall, unmoving, staring at his horse. The colt had stepped to the doorway and extended his neck in greeting, and that's when my attention had first been drawn to the trainer. He had neither acknowledged the horse or stroked his face.

Gone Wild snuffled, and after nudging Gannon's chest for the third time, the colt lowered his ears and flung his head up and sideways in an instinctively defensive posture as he backed away from the trainer.

I took further note of Gannon's demeanor. His arms were clamped to his side, shoulders hunched forward, weight on the balls of his feet as if he were leaning into the wind. He had clenched his hands into knotty fists that blanched his knuckles. The color had drained from his face, as well, and perspiration coated his forehead despite the fact that the temperature was pleasant in the shade with a westerly breeze curling under the eaves.

I looked past Gannon and noticed Snoopy Sanchez hovering by the barn entrance, shifting his weight as he watched his boss with apprehension knitting his brow.

He didn't know what to do with his hands.

A curious sound drew my gaze back to Bill Gannon. Repetitive grunts as his chest heaved in ragged, accelerating breaths.

I slipped off the tack trunk and heard Jay stir behind me. He had been dozing on a straw bale wedged against the stall front.

Color returned to Gannon's face in crimson blotches.

Sanchez took a step forward as Bill Gannon lurched sideways. A guttural, inhuman sound rose in the trainer's throat as he latched onto the corner of their tack trunk and heaved it over. It came to rest with the lid propped open a couple of inches and the gear inside jarred against the lid. A can of hoof oil toppled in slow motion and rolled across the dirt.

Gannon lifted his head and stared directly into my face. He suddenly lunged toward the exit in an uncoordinated move, as if the nerve impulses traveling between brain and muscle were misfiring. His shoulder smacked into Sanchez as he rushed from the barn, knocking the smaller man off balance.

I walked to the doorway and paused alongside Sanchez. "What's going on?"

"The horse," Sanchez said. "I think he got pulled. Mr. Sturgill's going to the secretary's office right now."

My phone rang as the PA system crackled with an announcement for horsemen to ready their horses for the sixth race. "Cline.

"It's beginning," Kenneth said.

I cupped the phone closer to my ear. "What?"

"I intercepted an e-mail. Seems a malicious code is cascading through ACS Industries' computer network as we speak."

"But…" I stuttered. "I thought our guy was going to steal the schematics to sell."

"She probably has. It'll—"

"Paige? You have evidence?"

"Ms. Sturgill opened a dry account via a shelf entity in the Republic of Panama last week. She can wire funds from anywhere in the world with the click of a mouse, total privacy, and no governmental intervention."

I glanced at Jay, who was staring at me with a "what-in-the-hell-are-you-doing-now?" expression on his face. I raised my hand to indicate that I'd be back; then I turned and exited the barn.

"What the hell's a shelf entity?"

"An anonymous, generically named account already set up and waiting for a client to take it over. Think Swiss bank account, Panama style."

I wanted to catch Rudi before he left the racing secretary's office and decided to take the peripheral route that I'd taken the morning I tried avoiding the cops. I followed the perimeter fence behind Barns 40 and 39 and rounded the corner at 26. "Did she copy the schematics?"

"Hard to tell now that the system's crashing, but I assume she did, and the chaos is likely designed to cover her tracks." Kenneth paused, then said with a touch of professional admiration, "Smart woman."

"And vindictive. How will she hand over the data? What equipment will she need?"

"There are several ways, really. I expect she'll have a laptop with her to verify that she's received the funds from the buyer, so she may have the data stored on the hard drive. She could demonstrate the validity and scope of the schematics, and once she's satisfied the buyer, and he's transferred the funds, she could electronically dump the information into the buyer's computer. Or, she could have pre-stored the material on DVDs and simply hand them over. There are lots of ways for her to proceed."

Up ahead, a party was in full swing outside the main dormitory. Food, mariachi music playing on the radio, guys sitting on the steps and perched on the rooftops of a couple of pickups, kicking back a few. "Seems risky. She could be ripped off," I said as the music grew louder.

"So could the buyer if she faked the data, but it's interesting that you should say that."

I shifted the phone from one ear to the other wondering what else could possibly happen. "What?"

"She wasn't the only one to open an account."

"What do you mean?"

"You asked me to delve deeper into Yaseen Haddad, and to be honest, he slipped off my radar."

"Mine, too."

"He shouldn't have," Kenneth said ominously. "He's been communicating with Lectron. That was odd since Paige has been Lectron's contact so far, but I thought, maybe they had to get some technical points squared away in prep for the transfer. In any case, I dug deeper, and you'll never guess what I found." He paused for emphasis. "Haddad opened an account in the same offshore institution as Ms. Sturgill the same day he purchased a one-way ticket to Damascus. Either Paige is paying him a hell of a lot for the job—"

"Or he's going to rip her off."

"Honor among thieves, and all."

"How will he do it?" I asked as I approached the dorm. "Build a fake webpage?"

"That would certainly work. I don't know if he helped set up her account, but he obviously found out what institution she was using. Mimicking the transfer process would be brain-dead simple. All he's got to do is gain access to her laptop shortly before the meet, replace her Favorites bookmark with a bogus link that will direct her to the webpage he pre-designed, and with Lectron's help, he's got her."

It sounded like a lot was riding on his gaining access to her laptop, but then, he was motivated. "You suppose he approached Lectron with a sweeter deal?"

"Sure," Kenneth said. "He'll accept less money for the same goods. They just cut Paige out. She won't realize what they've done until it's too late."

"Right. He'll make it seem like the money went to her account," I said, "when it actually went to his."

"Dead easy."

As I approached Gate 6, someone whooped in the Churchill lot across Fourth Street. A group of men were horsing around near the red Dodge that I'd driven. Fresh mud coated the under-carriage and wheel wells. Mud? There was something....

A Lincoln Town Car caught my eye. Henrik was behind the wheel, but his attention was focused on the backside.

I followed his gaze.

A low-slung foreign import sat in front of the track office. The engine turned over as I broke into a jog.

"Gotta go," I said into the phone. "Thanks." I hung up without waiting for an answer and picked up my pace.

I reached the raised lane divider that channels traffic past the office as the Audi slipped into gear and cornered the turn. Rudi stared straight ahead as he pointed the sleek little car toward Gate 6. He didn't glance in my direction. Didn't notice me standing on the pavement waving at him. Didn't seem aware of much of anything. I stepped into his path.

The tires squealed, and the nose dipped slightly as the car came to a stop.

I jumped around to the driver's side and bent forward as Rudi powered down the window. He looked at me without expression. Said nothing.

I leaned closer. "Rudi," I said softly. "Call ASC Industries, and you'll find it's coming apart. Your sister's selling her depart-ment's breakthrough to a competitor, some guy named Terrence Lectron, and she's corrupting the company's schematics and data in the process."

His face had been blank, as if I had been speaking a foreign language, but life flickered in his eyes at the mention of Lectron's name. He licked his lips.

"Call them, and you'll see."

"He's at the track," Rudi said quietly, and I was no longer certain he was mentally competent. His world was crumbling and taking him with it.

"Who's at the track?"

"Lectron. Paige is entertaining him in our suite…said not to come. Not today," he mumbled.

"Rudi?" When he didn't respond, I said, "I'm sorry, Rudi. She may have compromised you because she used your e-mail account to communicate with Lectron."

He turned his head slowly, took his foot off the brake. I grabbed his shoulder, but the car lurched forward.

I ran after him. "Wait!"

I watched helplessly as he powered the car through Gate 6, ignoring the guard pointing at him and ordering him to stop. Henrik must have noticed me approaching Rudi's car, because he'd moved the Lincoln to the exit but hadn't been able to cross.

Rudi caught a break in traffic and blasted north on Fourth Street.

Jesus. What would Lectron do if Rudi crashed the meeting? I considered his efficient guards and didn't like Rudi's chances.

It took me fifteen minutes to get frontside, during which time I spoke to Bonikowski. Gave her a thumbnail sketch of what was going down. Told her Paige Sturgill and her boyfriend could be responsible for Nicole's death.

My Churchill badge got me through the main gate, but I would need a little ingenuity and a great deal of luck to talk my way past the attendants guarding the grandstand's upper echelon of elite suites and plush banquet rooms. Rudi had said Paige was using a suite—their suite. As far as I knew, Churchill's suites consisted of the Jockey Club and Finish Line Suites. Which would his father have chosen?

Simple. The Finish Line Suites. Private restrooms, bar service, a suite attendant, and as the name implies, the best seats in the house.

I considered my appearance as I approached the escalators. The attire worn to the racetrack during Derby week varied wildly, but anyone planning to spend their day upstairs arrived well dressed. My jeans were grubby, my boots more so. I was wearing a black T-shirt that was relatively clean but wrinkled from being jammed into my duffel, and though I was not aware of it, I expected I smelled like a horse barn. All facts I could use to advantage as I concocted a story that I hoped would get me past the attendants.

As I straightened my badge, the crowd shifted, and I saw Henrik.

I changed course and paused at his shoulder. "Why aren't you with Rudi?"

"He cut me loose for the afternoon. Why?"

"He's in trouble."

His gaze sharpened on my face. "What kind of trouble?"

I started toward the escalator. "I'll tell you on the way up."

Henrik grabbed my arm and pulled me in the opposite direction. "Elevator's faster." He flashed a pass, and the attendant let us proceed. The doors slid shut. "Okay. What's going on?"

What to tell him? "I think Rudi's sister is in the process of selling vital information to—"

A chime sounded, and the elevator doors opened on the second floor. A man and woman and three little girls wearing swirly dresses and wide-brimmed hats stepped into the car. The father reached toward the control panel but lowered his hand when he saw that the 5th-floor indicator was lit.

We rode up in silence.

The smallest girl twisted her arms like a human pretzel, latched her fingers together, and crossed her legs. She wriggled from side to side as she peered at me from beneath her hat's brim. She turned her gaze on Henrik and studied him until the doors opened.

"Paige," Henrik urged as we stepped into a crowded hallway buzzing with voices and a blur of activity.

"She's sabotaged the computers at ACS Industries," I said as we hurried past the open doors to a banquet room and a concierge's station. "I'm pretty sure some guy named Yaseen Haddad helped her do it, but he may be planning to rip her off."

People streamed onto the balcony to watch the ninth race as we turned into an adjacent corridor that accessed the suites.

"Paige has arranged to sell data for a new gas-sieve and some interconnected technology that's too complicated to get into right now, and if Rudi's gone in there and seen what he shouldn't have," I said, "he's in danger."

Henrik paused at a set of double doors accessing one of the suites and said quietly, "What makes you think it's going down now?"

"Because the buyer's here," I half whispered. "A guy named Terrence Lectron."

Henrik latched onto my arm and spun me around. Pulled me away from the doors. "He's here? Now?"

I nodded.

"You're positive?"

"That's what Rudi said. Paige is entertaining Lectron in their suite and told him to stay away."

"Fuck." Henrik flipped open his cell and pressed a softkey, repeated what I'd just told him.

I listened to his precise language and calm tone and decided he must be a cop. A plant. I turned my head as something heavy thudded to the floor on the other side of the wall. Henrik heard it, too. He closed the phone, slipped it in the holder on his belt, and in that moment it occurred to me how quiet the room was otherwise. No boisterous laughter, no race commentary. No excited voices.

We were standing face to face alongside the wall just before the entry to the Sturgill suite. I looked past Henrik as a man approached him from behind. A man I recognized.

I looked directly into Henrik's hazel eyes. Lowered my voice. "Are you armed?"

He seemed to stop breathing as his shoulders tensed under the sport coat.

"One of Lectron's bodyguards," I whispered. "Coming up behind you."

Lectron's man stepped in behind Henrik. His shoes hadn't even settled into the carpet when Henrik spun around and landed a blow to the guy's solar plexus that knocked the air out of his lungs. His eyes widened as he staggered backward with his mouth gaping open, totally incapable of making a sound. In a maneuver I couldn't see, Henrik came up with the bodyguard's weapon. He slotted it in his waistband at the small of his back with practiced ease. I doubted anyone else had seen the move. Then he astounded me by taking out his wallet and slipping it into the bodyguard's pant pocket.

Before the guy could draw in a breath, Henrik wrenched his arm in a severe-looking pain compliance hold and marched him around the corner. He summoned a big black guy working the concierge's desk. "Get some help and take this guy down to security." Henrik pulled his wallet out of the bodyguard's pocket and tossed it to the attendant. "That's mine. This guy's a pickpocket."

The attendant opened Henrik's wallet and glanced at the blond man's driver's license.

Henrik jerked his head toward the VIP elevators. "Use the elevators. I'll follow shortly. I need to attend to my wife. She's rather distraught."

The attendant flagged down some help, handed Henrik his wallet, and took control of the bodyguard, who'd finally caught his breath enough to protest as we headed back.

Henrik paused at the corner and glanced down the hallway. The doors to the suite were still closed.

"We need to get in there," I said.

"You're not."

"Why weren't you armed?"

"I am now."

"But, I mean—"

"I know what you mean. You can't bring a weapon through security." He noted my expression. "Obviously, there are ways, but working as Rudi's supposed bodyguard, I would not normally bring a weapon in here."

"But, you're not a bodyguard."

He shook his head. "FBI." He glanced at my face. "And I'm feeling pretty stupid right now. The detail assigned to Lectron didn't pick up on the fact that he'd left the Galt House, and I'd like to know why." He scanned the crowded corridor and the people milling round the balcony. "Good place for a transfer. Privacy in the middle of a hundred and fifty thousand people. A logistical nightmare for us."

"Get security involved," I said. "The cops."

"It's being coordinated."

I looked around. "Can't you just grab someone?"

"A potential hostage situation like this needs to be coordinated, and I've got nothing on me to prove I'm FBI. Better to wait."

"You don't have ID?"

"Undercover, it can get you killed in a hurry."

"I thought you guys always had backup."

"Depends. Not on low-risk assignments, and not today." He gestured toward the crowds. "Logistics. Law enforcement's maxed out. Wait by the elevators and tell them where I am, okay?"

"Okay."

Henrik stepped over to the suite's doors and listened. He glanced in my direction but was distracted by something on the other side of the door. He canted his head and listened for a moment, then dipped his hand beneath his jacket at the small of his back. When he tugged his pant leg up, I realized he was hiding the gun in his boot.

He smoothed out his pant leg, then calmly opened the door and went inside.

I stepped closer, stared at the elegant double doors. Warm honey-maple finish, beautifully crafted. The muffled sound of glass shattering and a grunt seeped through the wood.

My hands clenched.

I strode to the end of the corridor and checked the elevators. Nothing.

A young man with frizzy hair and a ruddy complexion pushed a stainless steel serving cart past me.

I followed him around the corner and touched his shoulder. "Hey. Hold up."

He stopped and straightened his back, looked at me inquiringly. He was younger than I'd thought. A teenager with bad skin. He wore a black long-sleeved server coat with a notched standup collar that looked uncomfortable and a matching ball cap bearing the caterer's logo.

I shoved my hand in my pocket and dug out the last of Rudi's cash. Unfolded a bill. "A hundred dollars if you let me borrow your cart for a minute or two." I gestured toward his chest. "I'll need your jacket and hat, too."

"Uh." He stared at the money and licked his lips. "I don't know, man."

"Two hundred. What's it gonna hurt? No one will know," I said, thinking he was temporary labor. Probably wouldn't make much more than two hundred the entire day.

"What the hell." He unbuttoned his jacket and tossed it to me.

I gave him the cash. Felt my fingers shaking over the jacket's buttons. I drew the ball cap low on my forehead, then peered into one of the chafers. Steam billowed toward my face, heavy with the rich aroma of pasta and tomato sauce and sausage. I searched the cart for anything that could be used as a weapon. Not a damned thing. I hunched over the trays, slipped out my pocketknife, and opened the blade. I tucked it alongside the cart's lip and draped a cloth napkin over it.

Drawing in a shaky breath, I wheeled the cart up to the double doors, pushed one open, and stepped into the suite.

Chapter Thirty

After a brief glance to check the room's layout and note where everyone was positioned, I kept my head lowered as if I were concentrating on maneuvering the cart across the tiled entry.

"Hey, we don't want that in here." Problem number one. Just my luck. A big fucking asshole. Six-three, three hundred pounds.

He had been leaning on the kitchen's breakfast bar, but he'd straightened and turned around when he heard the door open.

I kept my head down.

The room's layout was similar to a hotel efficiency, minus the beds.

The serving tray glided over the smooth tiles as I passed a bathroom on my left. Door open. No one inside. Several Comcast uniforms stacked on the floor alongside two grimy metal toolboxes. The point man had been armed, and I guessed that was how they'd gotten the weapon past security. Weapons. Sure as shit, the others would be armed, too.

Next up was the kitchen. Also empty. Beyond the breakfast bar that served the room, the space was furnished with a sofa and comfortable chairs arranged in an intimate fashion. Nothing intimate about this gathering though.

Rudi lay stretched out on the floor at the base of the sofa with his nose pressed to the carpet. Could have been drunk passed out if I hadn't known better.

A sideboard spanned the wall on the right. Henrik sat cross-legged on the floor at the far end with his back against the wall. The second guard stood over him with his right hand tucked under his coat flap.

Problem number two.

When the time came, Henrik would have to deal with him.

"I told you, we don't want no food." Guard number one shifted his weight off the counter, spread his legs, and clasped his hands in front of his crotch. He wasn't worried...yet.

Beyond the sitting area, three round dining tables took up the remaining space fronting a glass wall that opened to the balcony. Blinds drawn.

Paige, Yaseen and Terrence Lectron sat at the table farthest from my position with laptops open on the polished surface. Paige had her back to the wall. Her hands were balled into fists in her lap as she glanced at Rudi. Brent stood behind her with his hands on her shoulders.

Brent. He was the wildcard.

Problem number three.

I removed the lid to the lasagna, tucked it in the slot at the back of the cart. With Henrik's back against the wall and the sideboard between us, he couldn't see me.

Problem number four.

I needed to forewarn him. Say something to clue him in.

"Yo," guard number one said. "You fucking deaf, or what?"

I glanced at Henrik's guard, caught a glimpse of his gun's grip against the base of his palm. His focus was on us.

Good.

I slipped my fingers around the chafing tray's smooth handles. "Guy at the door said to bring it in," I said and was amazed that my voice sounded calm. "Said it was time."

Guard number one stepped toward me with his lips drawn back in a sneer.

I yelled Henrik's name as I hoisted the chafer off the cart and flung the contents into the guard's face. Caught a glimpse of

Henrik's man toppling as I drew back. Swung again. Struck the edge of the steel hard into my guy's face. He blinked.

The asshole was a goddamn freak.

When I drew back for another swing, he bellowed and came at me full force, slammed me against the wall with all three hundred pounds. The chafer spun in the air and hit the wall.

I lost my footing and landed on my side on the ceramic tile. He was lifting his coat flap away from his waist when I hooked my legs behind his calves and swept his feet out from under him. The concussion shuddered through the floor as I scrambled to my knees. I reached for the cart. Yanked the napkin out of the way. Probed for my knife.

For a big guy, he was fast. He got to his knees a second after I did. His hand slipped beneath his armpit as we faced each other, both of us on our knees, both of us out of breath.

His coat flap fell away, and as the gun tracked toward me, I slashed his arm.

The blade caught in the fabric, and the knife went flying. I grabbed his wrist with both hands. Shoved his hand above my head and twisted.

We crashed to the tile and rolled, locked together, arms stretched above our heads, both of us fighting for control. The sonofabitch was big and strong, but with all the fat he had to lug around, he was becoming winded. We rolled toward the wall. My knife had come to rest against the baseboard, almost under the gun.

I had a good strong hold on his wrist. The button on his cuff had popped off, and his sleeve was jammed up his arm. Tendons bulged under his skin.

I snatched my knife off the tiles and sank the blade straight into the flesh and tendons and veins transecting his wrist. Buried the blade deep into the meaty flesh of his forearm and yanked toward his elbow.

The gun slipped off his palm and clattered on the tile as a scream erupted from his lungs.

I snatched the revolver and pushed to my feet with my back dragging up the wall. Drew in a shaky breath.

I lifted my head. Henrik stepped into the foyer and paused as our eyes met. I don't know what he saw in mine, relief probably, but I read in his gratitude as well as embarrassment. I handed him the revolver. He tucked it in his waistband, kept the big automatic he'd snatched in his right hand. He yanked bodyguard number one to his feet and shoved him into a sitting position next to the others. Paige, Brent, who looked a little worse for wear, Yaseen. Lectron and his men, both of them subdued and bloodied, although my guy had the added tomato sauce and unidentifiable vegetable chips peppering his hair and smeared on his face and clothing.

"I'm bleeding, man," he wailed. "I need an ambulance."

Henrik tossed him a napkin off the cart and flipped open his cell. "Press it over the wound."

Henrik got back on the phone while I slipped off the server's coat. I lifted a napkin off the stack and wiped the sauce off my hands and face and jeans, peeled a strip of lasagna off my shoe.

Henrik had forced everyone on the floor with their backs against the empty wall space beyond the sideboard. He shoved a table and chairs out of the way. "Steve, watch Rudi for me. Don't let him get up."

I walked over to Rudi and squatted in front of him.

His eyes were open, and he had rolled onto his side.

He focused on my face. "Is Paige okay?"

"Yeah," I said softly. "She's fine."

Rudi swallowed. "She didn't kill Nicole, you know? She gave me the money so I could pay her off, but she never showed."

He reached around and braced his hand on the edge of the leather sofa. I helped him into a sitting position. Blood matted the hair above his right ear and trailed across his cheek. I grabbed a dishtowel off the counter and handed it to him as he leaned against the sofa and drew up his legs.

"Maybe Paige changed her mind."

Rudi absentmindedly kneaded the towel and seemed unaware that he was bleeding. He rolled his head and let his gaze drift across the laptops' glowing screens. "Why?" He indicated them by lifting his chin. "Look at what she had planned." He choked on a sob. "A million dollars is nothing compared to that."

"How much was she going to sell the schematics for, do you know?"

Rudi shrugged. "It's a moot point anyway."

"Because she got caught?"

"And the deal was going sideways when I came in." He rubbed his face. "Lectron balked at paying. Decided he'd get it for free. Claimed Yaseen was doing something screwy with the transfer. But, I swear. She had nothing to do with Nicole."

The guard I'd slashed was complaining about blood loss.

Rudi blinked back tears. "At first, I did think she killed Nicole, knowing she'd get her money back. It wasn't until after the funeral that I thought to check her alibi myself. The night Nicole was killed, Paige pulled an all-nighter because of a problem with one of the linkups to the chromatographer." He licked his lips, and when he looked at his sister, his eyes filled with tears. "Office surveillance tapes prove it," he said slowly, and I wondered if he was thinking the same thing that had crossed my mind. Nothing was going to save her from the corporate espionage charges she was bound to face.

"What about her boyfriend?"

Rudi narrowed his eyes. "That piece of shit? He's nothing but window dressing."

"Someone else, then?"

"No."

"That puts you right back on top of the list."

Rudi tilted his head back and laughed, rekindling my doubts about his mental state. A tear trickled down his cheek. He cupped his hands over his face and rubbed his eyes. After a moment, he drew in a shaky breath, looked at me, and swallowed.

"I'm guilty of many things, Steve. But murder's not one of them." He gestured toward Henrik. "And I have an iron-clad alibi to prove it. A goddamn FBI tail."

Detective Bonikowski gave me a lift back to the track.

Within minutes of Henrik's second phone call, the suite had filled with law enforcement and medical personnel. Guard number one and Rudi were carted off to the hospital. The rest of us had been processed at the federal building. Interrogated or debriefed depending on your perspective.

We hit a light at Breckinridge.

A tricked-out pickup with 35-inch mud tires and fog lamps pulled alongside the cruiser. A spray of mud coated the vehicle and pocked the windshield except for the swath left by the wipers. The truck's cab was bathed in red from the brake lights in front of us, and as we waited, the driver slipped his arm around the woman sitting next to him and drew her close. As he bent to kiss her, I thought of Rachel and felt sick to my stomach. Rubbed my face and sighed.

The light changed.

God. I shifted my arm on the doorframe and watched the pickup as we coasted down Third Street. Traffic was shit.

Mud.

The red Dodge truck that I had borrowed—rented—had picked up a lot of mud after I'd used it. But there was something....

"Hey," I said. "Bill Gannon owns a Cadillac STS. A really slick looking car that rides low to the ground."

Bonikowski turned her head. Waited for me to continue.

"The morning after Nicole was killed, blackish gray mud coated the Caddy's fenders. I never gave it a thought because I didn't know the car belonged to Gannon." I looked at her. "Anything special about the mud you guys were checking for? Ashcroft said there was."

Bonikowski stared through the windshield, probably debating how much she wanted to share. "There's a deposit of heavy peat along the southern edge of the pond."

"Peat's black, isn't it?"

She nodded. "Not like the usual sandy and alluvial soils along the river."

"Alluvial?"

"We've got a good forensics geologist onboard."

"And you've been paying attention."

"I always pay attention," she said as she pulled alongside Kessler's rental and jammed the gearshift into park. Left the headlights on, engine running. Cops. They were hard on cars.

When she shifted in her seat to face me, the scent of her perfume drifted past my nose.

"There's something else." She glanced through the windshield. "Daniel Spring," she said, naming the guy I thought of as New York, "is Bill Gannon's second cousin."

"When the hell were you going to tell me that?"

"Anything I tell you, you might act on. Get in my way."

I grunted.

"Besides, we just put it together this afternoon. Lots of cousins in Kentucky," she said, and her comment made me realize something that had been bothering me about her. She didn't have an accent. Certainly not a Southern one.

"Where are you from?"

She lifted an eyebrow. "Chicago. Why?"

"You don't have an accent."

Her gaze lighted on my face. "Everyone has an accent." She unclipped her cell phone and turned it over in her palm. "What are you going to do next?"

I sighed. "The guy I work with is so pissed at me, I'm gonna go over to the hotel for a shower and change of clothes," I said as her eyes were drawn to the stains on my jeans, "and not step foot off the backside until the race is over tomorrow evening."

She smiled. "I meant, what are you going to do when you go home?"

"Get back to work. Write one hell of a paper for that class assignment." I relaxed against the seatback. "Except for Sturgill, Bill Gannon is the one person who's hurt most by Gone Wild's elimination." I described his bizarre behavior earlier in the day.

She nodded, started to say something, then changed her mind. Opened her cell. "You still wearing the vest?"

I yawned. "Yes."

"Good. Keep it until you head to the airport. As a matter of fact, let me know when your flight is, and I'll drive you there myself."

"I knew you liked me."

She smiled, pressed a softkey on her phone. "Go right to the hotel, okay?"

"That's the plan." I climbed out, rested my hand on the sedan's roof, and ducked so I could see her face. "Good night, Detective." In the glow from the dash, she looked damned sexy.

"Good night, Mr. Cline." She raised the phone to her ear as she pulled off.

I turned over the ignition in Kessler's rental and slipped the gear into drive, glanced at the digital readout. Nine-thirty. The cool night air drifted into the cabin as I powered down the window and drove off the backside. When I turned right on Central, Bonikowski headed uptown on Fourth.

Traffic was ridiculous, but then, it *was* Derby Eve in Louisville. They were going to have a tough job of it—finding Gannon.

I crossed the bridge and caught the light at Crittenden. Yawned again. Sleeping would not be a problem.

The light changed.

As I coasted into the Hilton's lot, headlights cut on in the first aisle. I bypassed the portico, doubled back, and nosed the rental into the vacated slot. The lot was filled to capacity.

I switched off the engine and flipped open my cell. Keyed in Bonikowski's number as I opened the door.

A vehicle moved down the aisle.

I stood and stretched.

"Bonikowski."

"Hey, it's me. I forgot to give you my new phone number."

The vehicle eased to a stop along the rental's back bumper as I depressed the lock. The rental chirped, and the taillights flashed on the car idling in the center of the aisle.

"You in your room, yet?"

A silver car.

"No. I'm still in the lot. Why?" I glanced at the vehicle again, wondering why the driver hadn't picked up on the fact that I was arriving, not leaving.

…a platinum Cadillac…

"Do me a favor," she said, but I was no longer listening.

The Caddy's door swung open, and the sodium vapor lamps shone down on the driver's head full of white hair as he exited the vehicle.

"He's here," I said. I took a step backward. "Bill Gannon. He's here in the lot."

Glass crinkled under Gannon's shoes as he centered himself in the gap between Kessler's rental and the car to my right.

"Shit. Hold on," I heard Bonikowski say as the sound of squealing tires and a siren cranking over shrilled from the earpiece.

"Hurry."

Gannon raised a snub-nose revolver. Light winked along the polished steel as he pointed it at my chest. "Get rid of the phone."

"I'm talking to Detective Bonikowski," I said as I turned the phone's keypad to face him, like he could identify the caller simply by looking at the screen. My fingers trembled. "She knows you're here."

He dragged his jacket sleeve across his forehead and grunted, and I was reminded of the sounds he'd made in the shedrow earlier in the day. "I told you to stay out of my fucking way."

I swallowed. "I did."

Sweat glistened on his face, and he seemed to be panting despite the fact that he was standing still. His throat moved convulsively. He licked his lips. "Everything's ruined."

A siren cut through the night. Some ways off.

"Why? Because you lost a Derby runner?"

He sneered. "You fucking know why."

A car rolled up behind the Caddy. The driver glanced in our direction, saw what must have looked like a robbery. She rammed the gearshift into reverse. Tires squealed as she backed down the aisle. Gannon didn't seem to notice.

"Because of Nicole?" I said. In my peripheral vision, I saw a flash on the road. Red and blue lights.

"That stupid bitch." Gannon's face contorted into a hideous mask. His mouth was a black hole amid flaccid skin glistening with sweat. "Rudi thought she wouldn't talk after he paid her off, but women can't keep their damn mouths shut. The word would have gotten out eventually."

I glanced at the gun.

"It always does."

Noticed that the muzzle had tracked off to my right.

"Anything can go wrong in an investigation," I said. "And later, in the trial. Especially with a jury. You might not be convicted, but if you kill me, there's no way in hell you'll get off. The cops know you're here talking to me, and they're coming."

Gannon seemed to notice the sirens for the first time. He jerked his head around as a cruiser pulled through the intersection and barreled toward the lot's entrance with its engine roaring. I took another step backward.

They'd be here in less than thirty seconds.

I was thinking that a lot could happen in thirty seconds when Gannon lifted the gun like he was going to surrender. He squeezed his eyes shut, touched the muzzle to his temple...

"No!"

...and pulled the trigger.

Chapter Thirty-one

A human chute begins to form at the gap an hour before the big race. Three hundred, four hundred people—backside workers, friends, family—line up to watch the Derby horses walk over. With the Twin Spires framed beyond them, and the noise of the crowd, it was an experience I should have found inspiring, but the aftereffects of last night pressed against my skull and weighted my limbs.

Jay glanced at me over the horse's crest and frowned as we walked past Barn 44.

"Don't worry," I whispered and heard him grunt.

Kessler and Mr. and Mrs. Utley led the way, and I was glad to see that both of Kessler's daughters had joined him, Abby and Cassandra, his eldest daughter from Michigan, whom I had never met. Corey had flown out, and so had Rachel. She had shocked the hell out of me earlier in the day when she'd stepped into the shedrow. Both of them had gone back to the hotel to change and were frontside, invited to watch the day's races from Kessler's box.

Abby looked over her shoulder and flashed a nervous smile that nonetheless lit up her face. She had forgone her usual work clothes of dirty jeans and grubby T-shirts for a stylish dress and wide-brimmed hat. And heels that were going to be hell on the track.

Something in the curve of her cheek, the way she had glanced over her shoulder, reminded me of Paige, and my thoughts were drawn back to yesterday afternoon. To the disturbing sight of such a beautiful, vibrant, intelligent woman collapsing in on herself, falling to pieces as she came to the realization that she would likely grow old in jail.

Despite knowing what she had done, it had been difficult to watch.

Fortunately for her father and ACS Industries, and Rudi, the transaction had been stopped in time. No one would have unauthorized access to the technological advancements Paige had labored over for so long. And now that the authorities had access to Yaseen's records, the company would likely overcome the malicious code that had sent the hard drives crashing.

The very fact that Lectron had ensured that his men attend the meeting armed indicated, as Rudi said, that he was prepared to rip off Paige, take the schematics, and run. Whether Yaseen had set up an account with the intention of doing the same would be something for the authorities to look into if they were so inclined. Honor among thieves and a nice little triple cross in the making.

Gallant Storm paused and eyed the crowd, and Jay, the horse-man that he is, gave him a moment to take in the sights. We started off again and slipped in among the other three-year-olds converging on the gap.

I was positioned on the colt's off side with a chain shank clipped to the halter he wore over his bridle. His shoulder brushed my arm as he strode out, confident, ready to go, and it seemed that after two weeks on the grounds, he had finally acclimated and understood that this was the job he'd come here to do.

For all of Edward Utley's bluster and arrogance, he fell silent as we stepped onto the track. Kessler appeared amazingly calm, but when he placed his hand on Utley's shoulder to guide him, he was white-knuckling the program clutched in his fist. We were all nervous. Everyone except maybe Storm.

Of all the potential consequences resulting from Paige's actions, I was most worried about Rudi. Her treachery had dealt him a devastating blow. I wondered what would happen to him now. Wondered if he'd ever be allowed to take part in racing again.

We circled inside the chute then proceeded single file toward the grandstand, past a long line of photographers positioned by the outside rail. The sound of whirring shutters followed us like a freakish wave and set Storm's ears twitching.

I smoothed my hand down his neck.

The noise of the crowd had intensified as soon as the first horse set foot on the track, but as we neared the grandstand, a cheer rose from the crowd and rippled through the stands. We walked through the tunnel bisecting the grandstand and stepped into a swirling onslaught of color and noise. A crush of people crowded the ground floor and tiered balconies that decorated the wings like icing on a cake.

Storm's eyes grew wide, and he balked. After a second's hesitation, we got him going. He chewed nervously on the bit and swiveled his head around, taking in the sights, but once we took him into a saddling enclosure, he seemed reassured by the confined space.

The saddling went without a hitch. Kessler flattened his hand on the saddle's pommel and smoothed his palm down the overgirth one last time. When he looked up, our eyes met. Behind the excitement, behind the nervousness that he surely felt, behind the pure, unadulterated exuberance of the day, there was a mischievous glint in his expression that had me wondering if he had devised a ruse two weeks ago that would bring me to Louisville. Had Gordi really injured his foot? I had to wonder.

After all, this was what he wanted. My father. Waiting for the day when I came to my senses and decided to work for him.

Standing there, I was reminded of a hot summer's day at Washington Park when, feeling the weight of my father's death— stepfather's—I had watched Kessler from across the paddock as he saddled Ruskie. Wishing I had grown up with him instead. Wishing for the very thing he longed for now.

Ruskie had won that day, as decisively as he won the fifth race earlier in the afternoon on this, the first Saturday of May. The horse was an enigma.

I smiled as I looked at Kessler over the horse's back.

"Glad you're here," he said.

"Me, too."

Jay and I set off, leading Storm out of the saddling enclosure, and when I glanced over my shoulder, Kessler winked. I smiled as I turned forward, drew in a deep breath, and decided I ought to make the most of this once-in-a-lifetime experience.

The call came for "Riders up," and after Garcia was legged onto the horse, we circled the paddock twice more.

Our walk back through the tunnel was the last duty we had to perform before Storm's fate was beyond our control. Jay unbuckled the colt's halter and handed him off to a pony girl; then we grabbed an open space along the rail.

He drew Storm's halter up his arm, hooked the noseband on his shoulder, and planted his big hands on the chain-link fence. Sweat glistened on his shaved head as he watched Storm and the others loop around in front of the grandstand before setting off to warm up.

I smiled. There'd be no talking to him now.

While the horses warmed up on the far side of the track, my thoughts returned to Paige. I wondered what had gone through her mind when she'd heard about Nicole's murder. She had certainly been tense at the hospital, a reaction I had incorrectly attributed to Rudi's accident. Looking back, I realized the fragmented conversation that I'd overheard between brother and sister in the ER had been each accusing the other of the crime.

But neither had been guilty.

The horses headed toward the gate.

Earlier in the day, I'd heard from Bonikowski that all kinds of forensics evidence had been recovered from Gannon's home and car, and now that New York was faced with the prospect of being a scapegoat in Nicole's murder investigation, the cops couldn't shut him up. He'd helped Gannon pick Nicole up in the street outside her home, but he swore up, down, and sideways that Gannon told him he just wanted to scare her.

In his mind, coming after me became an act of self-preservation.

I hadn't been nervous earlier, but my stomach suddenly felt like I'd just dropped over the edge of one of those steel coasters at Kentucky Kingdom. I pivoted around and scanned the sea of faces until I located Kessler's box up in the stands. Abby was intent on watching the horses, as was Kessler; though, his eldest daughter had leaned toward him and was speaking in his ear. Utley sat unmoving in his chair, looking tense while his wife chatted with a woman in a neighboring box. I leaned to the side until I caught sight of Rachel. She noticed me looking and smiled. I waved.

Jay glanced sideways at me, then shook his head and went back to watching the horses begin to load.

Rachel leaned forward and said something to Kessler. As he nodded, she stood and smiled broadly, placed a gloved hand atop the frilly hat she wore and started down the steps. Her dress was strapless and short with a shiny belt around her narrow waist. When she reached a landing and started down the next flight, she bit her lip and focused on the stairs. I glanced back at Kessler's box. Corey snapped her head around and gazed at the starting gate.

My smile faltered. Her hands were folded in her lap, and she seemed unusually subdued. I wondered what was going on as I looked away, watched Rachel continue down the apron and squeeze between some of the other backsiders.

She reached my side and slipped her arms around my waist, tilted her head. "Steve…." She licked her lips. "I'm sorry. I've been such a—"

"Rachel." I pulled her close, ducked beneath her hat's brim, and kissed her, almost lifted her off her feet. She exclaimed as she grabbed her hat to keep it from slipping to the ground, and when she broke the kiss and looked into my eyes, the bell rang, and the starting gate sprung open.

"Oh." Rachel grasped the fence with her white gloves and leaned forward as the horses surged out of the gate, heads lowered, digging in, beautiful sleek coats glistening under the warm sun. All strength and determination and courage. Running for the joy of it.

Nothing more complicated than that.

Rachel glanced at me. "Think he'll win?"

Cheers rose from the crowd as the field swept past.

"Impossible to tell....I hope."

It took me a moment to spot Gallant Storm. Garcia had him well in hand, easing over to the rail in the middle of the pack. Rachel was bouncing on the balls of her feet. Beside her, Jay looked like he was clenching his teeth hard enough to crack a molar.

I thought of Gone Wild back in his stall, and I thought of Rudi and Paige. And Bill Gannon....And Nicole. One life ruined. Two dead. All because a bay colt was born twenty-four hours too soon.

As the horses passed the finish line for the first time, I shoved the images from last night out of my mind and focused on the race. Two minutes. Two minutes around the oval, and it would all be over.

The horses charged around the first turn, and between the infield crowds and tents, we could no longer see them. A blimp moved languidly across the sky. I inhaled deeply, felt the nervous tension twitching under my skin. I glanced at Jay. He watched the board. The digital readout displayed the frontrunners. Storm's number was not among them.

I smoothed my hand across Rachel's back. Listened to the crowd behind us and the cheers rising from the infield. You could gauge the field's progress by listening to those cheers—an audio wave tracking the horses. When the cheering swung toward the final turn, I stared at that patch of empty dirt, and above the shouting, above the sound of my pulse thumping in my ears, a distant rumble preceded the horses.

A tidal wave of sound swelled behind us, curling under the grandstand's roof before crashing down on us. It pulsed across the track as the horses barreled around the turn.

Rachel wrapped her arms around my waist and bounced up and down. "Oh, God. Oh, God. This is too much."

Behind her, quiet Jay was screaming. I caught sight of Storm and his green and blue silks, lying fifth and driving. He passed one horse, then another.

They were three wide now, bunched together on their way to the wire, pulling away from the rest of the field. Seconds later, they flashed past the finish line. Impossible to tell who had won from our vantage point, but I had heard Storm's name.

As the lights flickered on the board, I glanced into the stands and had my answer. Kessler had lifted Abby off her feet in unrestrained joy.

To receive a free catalog of Poisoned Pen Press titles, please contact us in one of the following ways:

Phone: 1-800-421-3976
Facsimile: 1-480-949-1707
Email: info@poisonedpenpress.com
Website: www.poisonedpenpress.com

Poisoned Pen Press
6962 E. First Ave. Ste. 103
Scottsdale, AZ 85251